SNAKEWALK

SNAKEWALK

Charles Wheeler

HARMONY BOOKS / NEW YORK

Published by Harmony Books, a division of Crown Publishers, Inc., 225 Park Avenue South, New York, New York 10003

HARMONY and colophon are trademarks of Crown Publishers, Inc.

Manufactured in the United States of America

Design by Jennifer Harper

Library of Congress Cataloging-in-Publication Data

Wheeler, Charles
  Snakewalk / Charles Wheeler.
    p.   cm.
    I. Title.
  PS3573.H425S6   1989
  813'.54—dc19   89–1920
                            CIP

ISBN 0-517-57205-2

10 9 8 7 6 5 4 3 2 1

First Edition

*T*o all my fellow "Cappers"—
those who have arrived, those on their way,
and those who may have taken alternate routes.
You either do or you don't.

ACKNOWLEDGMENTS

The following people are all directly responsible for this book's success. I want to thank them all for being alive.

Jaimie Wheeler
Diane Johnson
Bonnie Nadell
Michael Pietsch

ONE

They didn't want me for Vietnam. I had a problem with authority, they said. By the time I turned eighteen my police file had already soaked up more ink than my academic record. So I phased out of required subjects and hired on at Babcock shipyard. In two years I had saved enough for the down payment on my own fishing boat and returned to my original schoolmarm, the sea. I could drift for hours outside the Golden Gate, sitting cross-legged on the sun-warmed deck, alone with the silence of harsh lessons.

To the east, the happy snatch of California usually lay hidden behind a fat belly roll of fog. Terra firma, with all its gregarious little land crabs clinging to the roots of security: white lines, paychecks, chrome, plastic, and sitcom humor. I kept a small two-room apartment there, Tenth Street, Bay City, just south of Cutting Boulevard. A '53 Studebaker pickup got me back and forth to the boat, the shipyard, and bars, which were about the limits of my social explorations. I was happier at sea, coloring my seclusion with gallons of dago red, hiding my loneliness in laughter, head tipped back, mouth open, howling obscenities—unheard. With proper formality I would raise the jug and toast my independence.

I thought I recognized a place of my own, there between the Pacific Ocean and the land crabs. But I was never happy in one place. I couldn't resist descending into the deranged heat of extreme hangovers, where I could assume full guilt for every minute of my pain. My reasoning always seemed so very clear in the worst of moments. I was a simple fracture, broken somewhere inside, a loose, torn edge that found it easier to turn back into itself rather than out. The same choice presented itself again and again, like a message chalked across the blackboard of an empty class-room: Keep fighting or surrender, trade the pain for atrophy, a house, steady pie, white lines, and adherence to the land crabs' common manual, *The Adipose People's Guide to Life.*

This manual was a therapeutic construct of my own, an imaginary epistle written within the confines of the Bay City Jail. I had arrived there at the invite of agents in blue, several of whom had approached me one evening for some alleged misbehavior—brawling, public drunkenness, possession of a controlled substance. I vaguely remembered bouncing one of them onto his cheeks before another autographed my face with his can of mace and showed me a Buddy Rich impersonation with his PR-24. After feeding me through their computer they tacked on a few more tails, outstanding warrants, parking tickets, a couple of ingrown toenails, breathing, and eventually parked me in one of their dead-air spaces with a self-proclaimed murderer and an obvious queer. While my face peeled and my body healed, the Adipose manual took shape, occupying some painful, disfigured hours of alcohol dehydration.

My favorite chapter, of course, came at the end, the section on independent thinking. It suggested that original mental applications moved contrary to the normal flow of traffic. Dubbed with different labels— fucked up, cracked up, those who had spun their onion once too often— independent thinkers were all considered candidates for the State Farm. They were nuts, man, *Sausalito'd*, according to the manual anyway.

I carried this cranial notebook with me when I left, and, in the months that followed, nothing pleased me more than driving, drinking, and reading from the manual like some ethereal graffiti. I would roar with laughter, turning heads at stoplights. I would thumb busily through those pages, writing obscenities along the margins, then rip them loose and release them out my open window along local thoroughfares and freeways, where they would lift and swirl, rising with the McDonald hamburger wrappers, vacant as paper pigeons.

Through the off-season, when my boat was berthed, the Studebaker could always be found parked near a bar. I would flop in my rank little apartment just long enough to scrape the mold from some bread and make a sandwich, change my underwear, pass out, or ponder the warm body lying next to me on those musty, never-washed sheets. Two or three days a week in the shipyard was about all I could handle. I could pick up an extra double sawbuck here and there shooting pool whenever I needed it, but each morning made it that much more obvious that the time to shed that skin was growing near. I could taste it like a change in the weather. Besides that, I had been eighty-sixed, at least once, from every bar in a twenty-mile stretch of East Bay, Oakland to Crockett. Not all in the same day, of course, but that's where independent thinking got me.

I advertised my fishing boat for sale on a Monday, sold it Wednesday, then tried to drink myself into a coma for an undetermined spasm of time. That failed too, so I quit and after healing for three days on fruit juices and roast beef sandwiches, I cleaned the apartment, scraped all the moldy remains out of the refrigerator, unplugged it, and married my girlfriend, Elaine Sullivan, in a quick, casual ceremony before a justice of the peace in Reno, Nevada.

"Till we don't dig it anymore, huh?" I said, as we walked down the courthouse steps.

Elaine laughed. She wore a soft, light blue, knee-length dress and white sandals. That was Friday, May 13, about 9:15 A.M., a bright spring sun swelling new color into everything. Elaine looked very clean and fresh and insane. We bought some beer, drove about five miles out of town on a gravel road, and in the middle of a sage flat, beside a five-strand barbed wire fence, balled for an hour, sweating, with the windows open. It didn't hurt that much, wanting to believe.

We returned to Bay City where I packed independent thinking into the back of my Studebaker and moved my life and bride fifty miles north of the bay to Flatfield, a hot, quiet piss stop on the road to Sacramento. We bought a three-bedroom, two-bath home out at the end of Orchard Avenue—yellow stucco, cedar shakes, redwood deck, low down payment, 7 percent interest. Elaine secured a position telling bank. I worked steady, commuting to the shipyard in Bay City, and on weekends I mowed the lawn, barbecued, listened to the neighbors, lost my taste for beer, and stayed up late sitting on that back deck in a patio chair, chewing tobacco.

Common fencing separated the units of that subdivision into neat little zones, like an egg carton. The cubicle behind ours contained a young couple, their two little tow-headed dirt eaters, and a young, black Labrador retriever. The wife began to stay up late too, standing in her kitchen window, no more than fifty feet from me. She would take an hour doing dishes, then find other things to wash, carrying them to the sink, constantly sipping from a water glass—white wine, I thought. Just stand there, sipping, insomnia maybe. Not a bad-looking gal either, blonde, a little heavy. I had seen her outside in white shorts.

When the aura from their TV went off in their living room, usually about 11:00 P.M., she would disappear too for a few minutes, then return in her robe to stand at the sink again, under dim fluorescent lighting. One night she opened her robe slowly to the waist and stood there for several minutes, staring back. When I didn't respond, she pulled it closed suddenly and picked up the water glass.

They kept their dog in a four-by-eight enclosure on the sunny side of the house. He took to escaping, so the husband nailed a sheet of plywood over the top, and the two kids poked sticks at him through the slats.

I tried. Jesus. For eighteen months I walked sideways, my nose to the white line. Then one particular October evening the night breeze carried

3

promises of action south off the slopes of Alaska. Elaine didn't have much to say when I told her.

"Oh. You don't dig it anymore. Is that it?"

We had always fared pretty well in the meat relationship, feeding on each other occasionally, but the house, the paper vows, all that had grown moldy. Most of our time together was spent avoiding each other, practicing strangleholds in the bathroom mirrors. Elaine had her bank buddies in polyesters. I had misgivings and I knew Alaska might not hold any answers, but it would take some time to get there and even longer to figure things out.

That was the first week in November 1980. The accumulation of my entire life was stacked on one side of the garage floor, ready to load into the pickup—one suitcase, three cardboard boxes, two rifles, a shotgun, and too much fishing gear. I signed over my share of the house, the new car, the bank account, and the lawn to my bride. Our do-it-yourself divorce papers lay on the kitchen table, open, my signature fresh on its designated line, waiting for Elaine's. On the breeze that night, I could hear the faint sound of laughter returning. I would burn rubber back onto the freeway, my head out the window, teeth bared, paper flying.

That same week, two of my shipyard buddies, Raymond Waugh and Bob Collingsworth, invited me out for a last fishing trip in Bob's offshore cruiser—a few beers, a few final laughs. A light drizzle was falling. I watched it come, the storm, the water darkening, the anchored boat beginning to pitch on growing swells. Waves slapped at her sides. Not fear, I thought, just guilt, unsettled matters. I knew storms.

"What the hell's the matter with you?" Collingsworth joked. "This is the bay, man. We ain't outside. No reason to get all funny actin'."

Under early darkness, we bumped our way back through the bowels of the new storm. Bow spray flashed over the canopy, salting the top of the beer can between my hands. I watched, remembering myself, the boy in the rain at the edge of an artichoke field just north of Half Moon Bay, where I stood on a bluff overlooking that flat, gray-skinned Pacific Ocean. Three days of walking had brought me south from San Francisco, following the ragged flank of California. My eyes were constant upon the sea, watching the breakers and great, dumb rocks for any sign of wreckage, a life preserver, a body. Mud from the fields caked my leather boots. The drizzle had matted my hair and clothing to my thin frame, and there on that bluff, fist raised to the uncaring, chameleon sea and dark, unanswering sky, I had promised never to believe again in either man or god.

I should have been with my old man the day he went down. I was his first mate. Rigged the baits, took charge of the fishbox, the fuel tanks. What the hell good was a first mate if he wasn't there.

The old man had laughed that morning, fourteen years past, tousling my hair.

"Don't sweat it," he said. "Go to school for a change if you think you have to do something," and then at the door, leaving, "and get your knives sharp too. I'll have both boxes full by noon. You watch."

A fever held me back that morning he drowned, the flu or some damned thing. School had never kept me home before. I knew too, long before I started walking that coastline. The Coast Guard had already been searching for two days, aircraft, two cutters. No sign. The storm had come on fast, its dark breakers reaching, mouths open, somewhere near the Farallons I figured.

I closed my eyes, listening to the sound of Collingsworth's Mercury outboard, and found myself back on that bluff, easily into the irrevocable, defiant guilt of fourteen, the cold, wet certainty of mud, and the old man still out there, reclining somewhere on a kelp bed, his bones clean and white enough for any science class.

When Collingsworth yelled, I had just enough time to turn and slam forward, sticking my ignorant skull through the front glass. Consciousness found me suspended above the waves, my neck cradled by a corner of the window frame, the overturned boat sinking slowly. Saltwater swatted at my face, jolting exposed nerve tissue into odd spasms, my skull emulsified with repetitive bursts of brilliant light. My dull brain assessed the situation in slow motion, and I finally struggled free of the boat, kicking out through a side portion of the canopy into open water, away from the sinking craft. Boots, jacket, I thought, keeping my back to the waves, hooking handfuls of water onto my face in an effort to clear the blood from my eyes. Collingsworth and Waugh didn't respond to my calls, just wind, water, and the great gastric sighs of the boat in front of me. Then fatigue came warm, fast, moving me back onto the boat. I crawled up, onto the hull, vomiting, then farther up onto the bow curve, where I could lie flat. My heart pounded against the hull, my mind dark, shocked, my weight causing another rush of precious air from the boat's bladder. Just a few minutes, I thought. Ride it till she goes under. Get the boots and jacket off, but first, rest. Just rest.

Sleep nudged at my remaining senses, wanting. It would have been so easy too, way back inside myself with the dark so comfortable, promising. Curious fingers moved slowly over my face. I laughed.

"You dumb sonofabitch," I said softly, out loud.

My nose dangled down onto the open flesh of my right cheek. My

5

upper lip had been cut away, exposing gums and their protruding teeth, bucked out like a skull. The fingers moved up then, tracing the exposed edge of eye sockets with their useless contents—still alive, still dark.

As I lay there, the boat stopped its sighing. Not sinking . . . Jesus, not sinking, and a rush of security swept my adrenal gland, pushing sleep back and settling my head to the hull. Time found a number of alleys through the odd warmth of shock. One took me back, leaving with the old man that morning. It was his boat I lay on. The fighting, the torment, all of it had been the dream. Then the wind again. Jesus, you talk about being ignored. I couldn't even be sure I was laughing. The sound stripped away so fast, leaving my mouth agape, my cranial worm oddly conscious with the realization I was nothing, not even the barest, most basic smidgen of a fart up the nostrils of the universe—not even a sound.

That wind moved across my prone body already accepting of death. Not because it was weak, but because it expected it. Death was not the problem. I just couldn't handle being ignored in the process. I had fought too hard, too long, to go without voicing my opinion of the whole god-damn thing, just in case there really was someone or something up there orchestrating. The laughing had long since drained away, and I rose then on an elbow, fist clenched, rising to the possibility. It came more like a bellow than a scream, I thought. Like an animal. I never even considered that someone might hear it.

TWO

When their searchlight found me, lying on the overturned boat, my head was a little too altered to fully appreciate the situation. I remembered shouting several times to Collingsworth and Waugh, and each time it was the wind that answered back. The sound of another boat, especially the voices, seemed so strange, faint at first, then growing louder, out of the wind itself.

"There he is," two voices rang simultaneously, then somebody had my left leg, pulling, trying to get me back into the water. I kicked at him.

"Did you find my buddies?" I said, the words awkward, blunt.

Those in the boat conversed in low tones. The one in the water tried for my leg again.

"There's two other guys," I said. "Did you find them?"

"C'mon," a voice from the boat shouted. "Your buddies are all right."

"They're all right?"

"Yes. They're all right. They already swam in. Now c'mon. We gotta get you in, buddy, or you ain't gonna make it."

Jesus, I thought, they left me, just like that.

Back inside the harbor, they laid me out on the dock, wrapped in blankets, and that little voice in the back of my skull kept reminding me—not yet, not yet. Don't sleep. Then some dickhead cop knelt beside me, interrupting, his voice filtering through my cocoon. He had my wallet.

"Yes," I said, listening to the odd, muffled sound of my voice. "I'm Patrick Todd."

His voice searched its way through again, into my skull. Echoing.

"Whooo was driving? . . . Whooo was driving?"

He couldn't hear me laughing.

"I was driving," I said through the blankets. "I've been driving all my life."

Pleasanton County Hospital bound my limbs and stuck tubes in my veins, running more through my nostrils and down my throat. Somebody else's fingers probed my face, picking, flesh twitching, my optic nerves alive again, exploding my brain over and over with brilliant, nauseating light shows. I struggled, found an exit and waited, free, just above my body, comfortable, no pain, nothing. Somebody laid a clipboard across my thighs, taking notes. Scissors cut through my clothing, one boot—something wrong with that left ankle—then fingers probed the eye sockets again, slamming me back into my body, the pain. Every time they got to poking like that, it brought me back, and each time they finished, I crawled out again, listening to them. Beyond the curtains, they pitched pennies to see who would make the pizza run later.

"Betcha ten to one he don't make it," somebody said.

About 2:00 A.M. their time, a deputy sheriff entered my space and chained my ankles to the gurney.

"You're under arrest," he said. "The charge is manslaughter in the deaths of Raymond Waugh and Robert Collingsworth."

The attendant pointed out my broken left ankle.

"It's all right," the deputy said. "I ain't got 'em that tight. Can he hear me?"

"I don't know," the attendant said.

"Well I won't bother with his rights then."

Each time I crawled out, it took longer, more effort. My bunged-up carcass waited below me with its pain, its breathing becoming forced, as if restricted by those straps about its wrists and legs. And each time, as I strained, I could sense the scream again, building in the back of my skull, moving forward, growing louder. I knew, without a doubt, that when it arrived it would be my last.

Dr. John Stewart, a surgeon specialist, arrived about 6:00 A.M. their time, and it was he who screamed. First, at the chains, then at the other doctors and pizza eaters.

Another ambulance sped me to Walnut Creek, John Muir Hospital, an operating room. I knew I had one, maybe two escapes left, then the dark, heavy hands of anesthesia were pushing me under.

"I can't wait for your vital signs to rise," Stewart said. "Can you hear me?"

I didn't say anything. I think I smiled though, welcoming the sleep, whatever it was.

I spent the next five weeks in intensive care, quite taken with morphine's downy embrace, tubes in every orifice. The first practical thing my brain could squeeze out of its rising consciousness was how to mow the god-damn lawn and avoid stepping in dogshit. Shows what a year and a half of crabwalking can do for the skull. Somewhere near the end of that tangent, the problem rectified itself. The lawn, I decided in a slow motion moment of unparalleled joy, could revert to its natural state. As far as the dogshit was concerned, I would have to wait until the moment presented itself, which would only be a matter of time.

Being blind didn't bother me. It was obvious to me that night on the boat that I would never see anything again, and during those first five weeks, while I recovered, I accepted it. So I had taken on nature for a few rounds and came out of the match tits up. I'd handle it. All I would have to do was heal up, get tough again. But beyond the skull, once-familiar sounds and people came on like a bad acid trip. I didn't even have time to reevaluate my asshole. They did it for me, assuming I was too weak to do it myself.

Elaine visited once a week, Friday night usually, her voice hanging there beside the bed like an overdue bill. Our conversation was formed from driftwood, pieces of the past scattered about us, until one evening in the fourth week she found her nuts and broached the obvious subject.

"But you'll need somebody. . . . Won't you?"

Maybe it was just the drugs, my lack of compassion, but she had packed her emotional display into some tissue and was gone, it seemed, before the sentence had even finished. And in her place, the spirited presence of Mary Reynolds warmed the air. Mary worked the night shift there in John Muir's intensive care unit—my sundial. I marked each day with the arrival of her voice, and when business permitted, she found room to sit beside me and talk, much more concerned about my welfare at the time than I. She took my hand that particular night, telling me about her radical mastectomy a year prior, twenty-eight years old. She talked about fear, crazy irrational cracks in the human facade where the demons could squeeze through. Fear of being alone, that her husband would leave her for being physically incomplete.

"And six months later," she said, "after I had found my own strength, the bum finally did leave and I laughed. I told him I didn't need his kind of love anyway."

I told her about the old man, and the boy. Our hands were still together. She cried, quietly. Not for me, my morphine whispered, but for the world, the human mind and what it can do to itself.

During Elaine's visit the following week, Mary interrupted our interlude in cold storage.

"Would you like to try to get up and use the bathroom?" she asked from the foot of my bed. "Your wife can help."

Being on my back for five weeks, using bedpans, had left something to be desired. So Mary removed the catheter and helped me into a sitting position on the side of the bed. Elaine's nerves began to show as she and Mary helped me down onto cold linoleum, my arms about their shoul-

9

ders, my body foreign, trembling. Mary finished the chore, thin and strong beside me, her arm about my waist. Elaine followed, wheeling the IV unit.

I spent half an hour on the can, shaky, sweating, nothing working right. Elaine and Mary waited outside the door, each voice, each woman. My interest balanced on Mary, how she would feel in bed, warm against me, and something began to work—struggling. Love came so easy, I thought, and laughed out loud.

"What's so funny in there?" Mary called back from outside.

They eventually moved me into a private room, and in the days that followed, with a drastic reduction in morphine, my brain roused its sense of structure, envisioning the details of everyday living. I spent hours occupied with the basics of cooking, cleaning, how to do things alone, blind. I had no time for love, or emotions, or where the hell I'd be fishing next. Candy stripers helped me eat, sitting up in bed, feeding me actually. My hands couldn't work the plastic utensils to my mouth.

A male nurse entered my room late one night, uncalled for, and casually began asking me questions about the accident, and if I had any other injuries. His hand, all the while, worked slowly under the covers onto my thigh.

"You lookin' for anything in particular there?" I said.

"I just want to help you," he said.

"Well you're flirtin' with disaster, buddy."

As he flipped the covers back, I made a grab for him and missed. He stepped back, chuckling. I struggled to get out of bed, pulling the IV loose, banging my face into the guard rail, and knocking the metal shield from my eyes. The intrusion angered the hell out of me, but more, I was enraged by my inability to function.

"I'll kill that fucking faggot," I told them, after finding the call button. They performed some quick needle work on me, then redid the IV and bandages. The cocksucker denied it, said he'd just come in to check my IV. I'll kill 'im, I thought, and all the while, I could hear him standing there in the dark at the end of my bed, laughing at me.

After eleven weeks in the hospital, I returned home to Flatfield and Elaine, my skull a dull, empty morphine capsule, turbaned in white bandages. A parade of well-wishers greeted me like a stranger, their eyes, their one big collective eye, watching, taking my hand between theirs, like a woman's. They spoke loudly, a patronizing touch to my shoulder, as if the eyes had something to do with hearing. One asked if I would play the piano, like Stevie Wonder and Ray Charles. Another placed a harmonica in my hand.

"There's another little blind fella," he said, "plays the guitar pretty good, but I can't think of his name right now. I think he's a Mexican."

"I've got to go light on the music," I said. "It fucks my cat up."

I overheard him in the kitchen later, asking Elaine where the cat was.

They disappeared in a couple of days, back to their manuals. Elaine kept them informed, lowering her voice on the telephone at night, giving her commentary. But seclusion was mine and for the next couple of weeks I lay in a beanbag chair, the television on.

Three weeks after I left the hospital, a registered letter arrived from the state, the Department of Motor Vehicles, demanding the surrender of my driver's license to their nearest office. I complied, mailing in my pickled card. They eventually sent me a facsimile, an official state identification card with a new picture. My name was misspelled, and along the bottom, in bold print, it said: NOT A VALID DRIVER'S LICENSE. Elaine read it to me. At the time, I was standing in the living room, trying to laugh, my hands searching for something to grab. She had to restrain me from tearing at my bandages.

In the hospital, it had always been injections, my body measled with punctures. At home, it was pills, four times a day, lying in that goddamn beanbag chair. My system crawled with antibiotics, my skull with Percodan, Valium, just enough to sweat. Behind them, my center had already begun to twist like a wet towel. So I dumped the pills, hundreds of them, right down the growler's porcelain throat. But that towel continued to tighten, twisting, and Elaine the martyr continued her commentary with the others, the voices on the other end.

"He's that way because he's lost his sight," they would say. "He's blind and angry. They have a very high rate of suicide, you know. It'll be hard for you. He's going to have to make some adjustments."

I would make some adjustments allright. I would adjust them all with right hooks. Christ, what did they know about anger. I came off the assembly line with my nuts too tight. I didn't even get along with other kids in the nursery and when they pushed me out into that goddamn Adipose world of theirs, I starved, fasting on the tough hide of solitude.

A few days later, a Saturday bright and warm, Mrs. Johnson from across the street knocked at the front door. The flower lady, that's what the kids called her. I had seen her over there, kneeling in her gardens, a thin, dark stem under the wide blossom of her straw hat, tending her rows of reds, whites, yellows, purples. Delicate, light colored butterflies rose from the daffodils, daisies, petunias, and snapdragons, dancing onto the air like puny paper puppets. She was somewhere in her eighties, I thought. She marched right in without saying a word to Elaine, just walked right by her and crossed the room to my beanbag. Then kneeling, she placed something in my lap.

"It's banana bread," she said. "I made it this morning."

My fingers moved over the foil wrapper, looking. Mrs. Johnson leaned down, close to my ear like an old friend, whispering.

"I know all about it," she said. "God saved you to do good things, you know."

When I did finally make it back onto the freeway, seven months later, I was headed south through a May morning, courtesy of the state, Elaine driving. My possessions, besides a suitcase, included a white cane, a braille pocket watch, and two braille books. A starter kit. My destination was a blind school, the California Institute for the Blind, 218 Butte Street, Brookings, California, no more than a mile from my birthplace, where I had made my first crooked little footprints in the sand. They weren't about to let me sneak off to Alaska with my eyeballs and a D-minus in social behavior. The whole fucking thing had been planned. I knew it. The accident, the twisting. It was all part of the wash. You got to fit, man. You got to crabwalk like everyone else. You got to eat, think, and breathe that make-believe. They were sending me back, wet and blind, hoping I'd get it right this time, be a good little boy, a harmless consumer of the public pie.

At least the California Institute for the Blind represented an escape from the confines of my own house, for six months anyway. The night before leaving I celebrated alone at the kitchen table, a little brandy, some beer. Relief kept its distance, watching me from across the room. Knowledgeable sorts, the big, collective eyeball that stripped me of my identity, had already assured me of waiting benefits, how great it would be, there with my own kind. My own kind, I thought, trying to laugh. Just who the hell was Patrick Todd.

Fear is the damndest thing, the manifestations of weakness that crawl your goddamn skin, in and out of your orifices at will. The following morning, as Elaine drove on, closer and closer to my new beginning, sweat started beading along my hairline, so I cracked the window open a bit for a little fresh air. It had rained that morning, thundershowers. The tires hissed through wet stretches of pavement, slinging spray up into the fender wells. I laid my head back against the seat, eyes closed, listening to the expansion joints in the freeway click by like film frames. Rewinding. The old, silent film—first car, first kiss, first piece. In the *Adipose People's Guide to Life*, the chapter on common sense suggests that if time travel were ever possible, anyone going back would always stop at that first dip of the wart, when you thought you'd surely die, because in that moment you knew that nothing else in the world could possibly feel better. But I was headed all the way back to my literal beginning, my home town with the blind school I had never seen, dragging there at the other end of my mind's umbilical cord. I learned to smile and hate and ride a bicycle there.

Elaine turned the radio on. Rock. I reached over and turned it down, then continued thumbing through the manual, looking for something on blindness. The appendix had it listed: Blindness—void. This is a visual book only. Fuck 'em, I thought. I had never been in their club, never would be, either. I didn't want anything in their goddamn visual world.

I didn't want the sweat either, but it was there. A blind school, a nuthouse. I had seen blind people around there before, on the avenue, groping along, head down, that goddamn cane switching back and forth in front of them. I would watch them for a moment, then turn away, like everyone else.

"What are you thinking about?" Elaine belted, shattering the still. My nerves grabbed each other and jumped, like I had pissed on an electric fence.

"Jesus," I said. "Throw a rock at me next time, will you? Let me know when you're comin'."

"I didn't mean to."

"Yeah. I know that, but you ought to get that amplifier of yours fixed. Get a goddamn operation on it, or somethin'."

She would catch me like that all the time, like Al Hirt running a quick scale in my ear. No wonder my damn nerves were shot.

"I'm sorry," she said. "I just didn't want to drive all the way there without talking. You haven't said anything all week."

I raised my eyebrows.

"I don't know if you still want the divorce, or if you're going to come back home? Those papers just sit there and you never say anything. What am I supposed to do? Do you want me to sign them?"

Following the freeway, remembering the curves, hills, landscape, occupied the slack in my skull.

"Where are we now," I said, "Cordelia?"

"Almost to Red Top Dairy," she said.

Half an hour to go, I thought. A goddamn blind school, full of blind people.

"Do me a favor, will you?" I said, "and don't get all spastic over it. I don't feel like talking now, either."

"But that's just it. You never say anything. You never feel like talking.

You think you can live in your own little world and forget about everybody else."

"You got that right."

"Well I need to know about us. I've got the rest of my life too, you know. Are we going to try again, or are you just going to disappear? Everybody says you'll be different when you come back."

"Christ," I said, "everybody, huh? Bless their little hearts. Piss on 'em too, while you're at it."

The tires splattered through another wet spot, always a reminder, boats, bow spray. I felt a lot for that trumpeter swan next to me, but I couldn't tell her. It just didn't have a place anymore. She was right too, about the world thing, my own little world, with my own little fucked-up skull. I just couldn't let my guard down any further. That swamp, the dark hole in my skull where fear waited, was just too close.

"Can't you just tell me how you feel about me?" Elaine said.

"Nothing's changed. I can guarantee you that."

"You probably can't wait to get there, so you can fuck your brains out."

Jesus, I thought. Fuck your brains out. I could see them, what was left anyway, lying bruised and swollen on an unwashed sheet. Nothing else, just the brains, the shades drawn, a little daylight squeaking in.

"There's girls there too, you know." Elaine said. "There's probably even some young ones. You could go for that, couldn't you?"

"You're a trip, you know that?" I said. "I've got enough trouble in my skull without you throwing gas on it, and I'll tell you something else too, Flower. I've seen plenty of blind people and never once got a hard-on."

"Well you've been saving it for something, that's for sure. You're probably going to call your old girlfriends."

"My, my, and I thought you were worried about the rest of your life."

"I am, and I can't take much more of this."

"You got the bank and all your tight buddies. You don't need me around to crack your nuts."

"At least I've got some friends."

"Yeah, I know. Half of them were trying to lay me behind your back."

Elaine chewed her sock for a while on that one.

We topped the ridge overlooking Vallejo. I erased all buildings, all other signs of man from my film, leaving just the bare hills, like assorted buttocks, cropped with their spring grasses, and the bay beyond, a lively blue.

"I love you," Elaine said. "I've always loved you."

San Francisco Bay, I thought. Jesus, that first sail must have really loosened some sphincters. All those brown eyes watching Frank Drake and his boys cruise in.

"I'm sorry you're blind," Elaine said.

"Jesus H. Fucking Christ," I said. "I should've taken the goddamn bus."

"Well why didn't you? I didn't ask for any of this either, you know."

"I'll tell you why, goddammit. I didn't take the bus because I'm fucked up in the head. I cross a street half a block from my own goddamn bathroom and start sweating, because I don't know if I'll hit the other side, and it's all so fucking senseless, but it happens. I could stand there in the middle of a thousand goddamn people, and still sweat, because I'm afraid of being lost—and I ain't talkin' lost like you on a goddamn one-way street either. That's just simple mental illness. With me, it's crazy, because I know I'm not lost. I got all those people around me, and I know I can ask any of 'em, and they'll take me by the arm and lead me, and that's just it. Can you understand that? I don't want anybody leading me, and inside my skull, everything comes apart, my spit tastes funny, my body feels like it belongs to somebody else, and I want to take my fingers and just rip my goddamn face open. . . . That's why."

"You don't have to shout," she said.

I sat there, listening to my breathing, wishing that leaden weight in my skull would take me, like the anesthesia did, quick and heavy, if that's how insanity came.

"What would you like to discuss, dear?" I whispered.

"Will you stop that. It's not funny. I know I haven't been much help, but I do love you."

"Maybe I should've invited you to go to Alaska with me."

"If you don't stop whispering, I'm going to scream."

The laughter felt good, like opening a window. I told myself it would all be over in a couple days. A new life. I wouldn't even remember her.

"You know," I said. "Even if the Indians had known what was about to happen, they couldn't have done anything about it."

"What?"

"I loved you too, you know," I said. "I know it don't mean much, but I just ain't got room for it now. I wrote you that poem, you know, trying to explain it."

"You should've read it to me then."

"Christ," I said, turning my face to the window. Terry's Waffle Shop, I thought, right about there. Moving. Almost to the bridge—fifteen minutes to go, and now she wants the poem. At the time, I thought that had been something. A counselor with the Department of Rehabilitation had brought me two braille books and a cane, and I'd rubbed my goddamn fingertip raw learning those dots, cab, bag, cat. . . . Man. It was great, the first damn thing I found to feed my brain. I had been lying in that beanbag chair for nearly four months, listening to game shows, "The Rifleman," "Leave It to Beaver," slowly going mad. Two years, they said.

That's how long it might take me to learn it. In two weeks, I was one braillin' mutha. I could read it, write it on a hand slate, and even understand it. The cane helped too. I would force myself to go one more block each day, sweating. But I could get into those dots. I was proud too. Elaine and I hadn't made love in all those months, so I wrote her that first poem, trying to explain the fear and love, so proud of my new language, the new me.

I wrote that poem, corrected it, and rewrote it, waiting for the sound of her car in the driveway and her big feet coming up the walk to the door. Christ, a hard-on hit me so fast, I nearly passed out, thinking we might even wind up in the sack. I would read her my poem, she would grab me by the pecker and lead me down the hall. The scent from our hot and hungry *funichingilario* would drift back out to settle atop that page of dots, my first poem.

When the car pulled in I was sitting at the kitchen table, waiting, following her feet up to the door. She jammed by me, in a whisk and rustle of polyester, set her thermos on the sink in the same goddamn place she always did. Not a word. Too long, I thought, too twisted, both of us. "I wrote you a poem today," I said. She ripped off a good laugh, standing there at the sink. I could see her head back, those big, front teeth hanging out, like she was eyeballing an apple on a limb. "You're a construction worker," she said. "What would you know about poetry."

We crossed the bridge then, Carquinez Strait. I remembered that easy, numbing grip of hypothermia.

"I'd like to hear your poem someday," Elaine said. "Maybe you could read it to me when you get back."

She just didn't understand. There was no going back.

"I stood in the rain today, while downspouts bantered of love, and laughter, and inside, my mind beat helpless, like a fly at its window, mouth open."

"What's that supposed to be?" Elaine said.

"That's the beginning of the poem."

"That didn't rhyme, did it?"

"Yeah, I know. Piss on it anyway, huh."

Silence seemed to increase our speed. Pinole, Dam Road, Beach Avenue, Cutting Boulevard, the old apartment, there on Tenth Street—the faces. I made love to Elaine there, the first time, the first hundred times, naked, young. Then Hamilton Boulevard, our turnoff, and as the car began to slow, I felt like a coyote, trapped, chewing at his leg, with the sound of a four-wheel-drive moaning up the near canyon.

At the stoplight, we waited. Across the street, 40 Flags Motel. I remembered the article in the *Tribune*, the junkie they found there, some young gal, chopped into pieces, drug culture, accused the Angels.

We turned left, passing under the freeway, our sound trapped, then out, sunlight through the glass, onto my face. Standard station on the right, Exxon to the left, some guy in two-tone blue leaning over a windshield, wiping, the black hose out the back like a tail. I could do that, pump gas, wash windows. And a block farther on the right, Bayview Elementary, kids playing, sounds like geese feeding. Bending at the knees to shoot their basketball, the hoop so high.

Bay windows watched me from between trees. "He's coming back you know. Christ, I thought we got rid of him. He's blind now. No shit?"

Elaine shot down a side street to the avenue, San Gabriel. Plastic banners above a used car lot rattled at me as I rolled the window down, the morning breeze stale with used time. We turned right and slid into line, light to light with the others, idling, gassing, braking—everybody in a hurry except me. Grass Hut, Bear Club, The Corral, Playtime Club, Rosie's, The Buckhorn, Blue Door, then stopping again. The last light.

"Do you know where we are?" Elaine said.

I didn't answer.

"You want a hint?"

"We're at the goddamn Plaza," I said. "You got a Shell station over there, and the candy joint to the right here."

"How do you know?"

"Sixth sense. Comes with the conversion."

The school had to be somewhere in the next block, I knew that.

"Are you nervous?"

"Yeah, I'm nervous. So what."

"You look like you're thinking about something again."

"You're right. I'm thinking about some blind kid I saved here one day."

"You saved him?"

"That's right, just like Jesus."

"What did you save him from?"

"From himself. He was losing his mind out there in the middle of the intersection, on a red light."

It was some young guy, wearing a Giants cap—dark hair, some of it stuck to his forehead with sweat, pale useless eyes, and the spittle slinging off his lips as he tried to thank me. He had bounced out there like a jackrabbit in the headlights, and every time someone honked, his nerves exploded. I damn near needed pliers to get his fingers off my arm, and later that evening, in Ducci's, I was the local hero. Boyd Lynch, the bartender, had seen the whole thing. "They oughta have somebody out there watching those poor bastards, you know?" Boyd had said, and I nodded, drinking the free beer, thinking about the guy's baseball cap and how he might be in some dark room, the radio blaring, a ball game.

"I could sure go for some morphine," I said.

Elaine punched it, moving again, past the Red Barn burger joint, the car wash, water hissing, then the long wall of Brookings Bowl, our sound bouncing back. We turned right, then right again, behind the bowling alley. She crept down the street, looking, then hung a U-turn and parked at the curb. I swallowed.

"So this is where they hid it, huh? What's it look like?"

"I guess this is it," she said. "I can't see an address . . . it doesn't really look like a school. There's a two-story building over there to the right. This one in front of us looks like it might be the office, or something, but I don't see anybody."

I had my head out the window, taking deep breaths, cool air—nothing but my sweat and what sounded like a couple sparrows doing their thing in a nearby tree. I remembered the cartoons—when somebody was out of their mind, they always heard birds singing.

"Are you all right?" Elaine said.

"I'm fine. I just have to get in there and get moving."

I checked my watch then, running a fingertip across the open face, 7:45, fifteen minutes to wait.

"Why don't you just go ahead and take off," I said. "I wouldn't want you to be late for work."

"Could we please talk about the divorce for a minute?"

"Jesus," I said. "Can't you get it through your skull, it's over? We screwed each other for four years. Wasn't that enough?"

"You'll need somebody when you get out of here."

"Oh yeah, just like I'll need another asshole."

"Would you want a blind girlfriend?"

"You just don't understand, do you, Flower? I'm so damn sick right now I can't see straight. I think I'm losing my mind and all you can think about is crotch."

Elaine let the tears flow. I stuck my head out the window again, breathing, thinking the time had come to get my butt out and move. It didn't matter where.

"I'm sorry," she sobbed. "I promised myself I wasn't going to cry."

I took out my handkerchief and handed it to her.

"Yes," I said, "I know. So let's just do our little good-bye number now and I'll give you a call in a couple weeks. After the lobotomy."

"You know what my father said last week?"

"I don't think I even care."

18

"He asked me about the divorce, if we were still getting it. I told him I didn't know."

She blew, coughed a couple times, and wiped at her nose to stifle another sob.

"And he said, well you don't want to spend the rest of your life with That anyway, do you?"

"*That?* He called me *that?* Christ, and I used to like that bastard. Hell, I used to love 'im."

Elaine blubbered. The birds fooled around in their tree. The school was quiet, waiting—too quiet. It seemed cold, spooky. Attendants in white coats, I thought, a nuthouse.

"To hell with it anyway, huh?" I said. "I never wanted to be in their club in the first place, and when I get out of here, I'll tell 'em. I'll tell 'em, Hey, looky here all you dumb bastards. I feel, and bleed, and speak the same goddamn language, just like the rest of you, but you know what? I just flat don't give a damn. Never did, and never will. You bastards can't even feed your kids and keep your dogs off the freeway."

I had it then. Ready. Getting out, I took my suitcase from behind the seat and started down the sidewalk. Elaine opened her door and stood there.

"I'm sorry," she said.

"Don't let it bother you."

"You don't hate me?"

"'Course I don't hate you. I don't hate anybody. I just don't know how to love at the moment. My teeth are too tight. My face aches and something's prying at the back of my skull with a claw hammer, but it ain't gonna last forever. You can tell 'em all I got Jesus, if you want. They'll believe that."

I took a couple steps, off balance with the suitcase, but moving. That seemed to be enough.

"Do you want me to help you?" she said from the car.

I stopped again, fighting, then softened. Everything was so quiet.

"Sure," I said. "You can show me where the damn place is."

She came around the car to the sidewalk, moving in front of me. I followed her footsteps.

"Better than that," I said, "tell 'em I fell in with the devil worshippers."

Elaine turned right. My cane hit grass then followed the edge around onto a walkway, the sound bouncing back from the building in front of me.

"I feel like a water balloon full of red paint heading for the side of a bus," I said.

She waited at the building. The sound off my cane shortened with each touch, sweat flooding my throat, and the old film, the old life, began spilling from its reels.

"Are you all right?" she said.

I was down on one knee, the pavement cool, steadying.

"This is crazy," I said. "I think I need a beer . . . I think I need about fifty beers."

"I could take you somewhere. To a bar, if you want?"

I shook my head, blowing.

"I'm never going to see again," I said, "but that ain't the problem. I don't even think that has anything to do with it, you know, Flower?"

She stood quietly, a couple feet away, watching me. I shook my head again and laughed.

"Jesus," I said. "It's all in the head, you know? The whole thing. None of it's real, not even love. We just made that up for something to do."

"I could get you some beer," she said. "We could sit in the car for a while."

"I ain't gonna wear no goddamn baseball cap either."

"What?"

"Nobody'll know who I am, and when I get it all figured out, I ain't gonna say a goddamn word. Nobody'd believe me anyway."

I knew then why I had screamed that night, lying on the bottom of the boat. It had to do with insignificance. Aside from getting a hard-on and propagating, the rest was all in the head. You either make it up yourself, or somebody makes it up for you. And once in a while some idiot has to fight it, because he thinks there's more.

I stood up then and reached out, looking for the door handle.

THREE

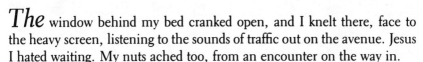

The window behind my bed cranked open, and I knelt there, face to the heavy screen, listening to the sounds of traffic out on the avenue. Jesus I hated waiting. My nuts ached too, from an encounter on the way in.

The room itself wasn't bad, for a two-man cell. My bed was a little short, with mattress and pillow both encased in plastic piss covers. Besides the bed I had a nightstand and a locking wardrobe with a coat rack and chest of drawers. A writing desk and chair separated my side from the other, where the stench of dirty socks hung like a dog blanket on a fence. That side belonged to Damond, my roommate, a side-show freak I had run into downstairs. Another door on my side led into the bathroom, a tiled chamber loud with disinfectant. Damond and I shared the can with Rusty and Reno, the act on the opposite side.

I had already put my clothes away, hung my jacket up, and checked the place out, a little squeamish about touching things in the tiled chamber. I had a lid tucked into one of my dress boots in the wardrobe and I considered a joint, then passed. Christ, I could do something right for once. What the worm needed was activity. Peace and quiet was giving me acid indigestion of the skull.

Opening the hall door, I listened. Quiet, too quiet, just that long tunnel, well waxed and douched with that same disinfectant. So I returned to the bed and lay there, my feet dangling over the end, both hands on the pillow, waiting for some unknown person to come and start my life for me.

When Elaine and I had entered the lobby half an hour earlier, I had set my bag down and straightened, an idiot smile pinching my face, my right hand ready to greet the whitecoats—nothing. Just a cold, empty room, stale with the smell of concrete and disinfectant. The smile palsied. I considered the door behind me, fresh air, freedom, a twelve-pack, maybe three, just to make the adjustment a little more casual. I had just reached for my bag when the sound of a woman's footsteps, from another room, straightened me again, smiling. She entered, crossed the room to our left, and pulled out a chair. A switchboard began to crackle and buzz where she had seated herself. I still held the smile.

"Excuse me," Elaine said. "This is Mr. Todd. He has an appointment this morning?"

"Fine. Just take a seat. Someone will be with you in just a moment."

Elaine nudged me across that dance floor to an armchair. I seated myself, a little soup beginning to bead along my hairline. My throat remembered the cold, wet sensation of beer and I damn near lost my tonsils in a fit of involuntary swallowing. Then the switchboard crackled again.

"Good morning, Zeke," she said. "Mr. Todd is here. . . . Yes, thank you."

Elaine leaned over toward me.

"I think she's blind too."

Her voice filled the room with all the subtlety of herring gulls announcing the arrival of a garbage truck. I nodded, wishing she would leave, just get the hell out of there. Long seconds groaned by in silence, and just as I started to turn, her hand lit on the back of mine, trembling, sending the lice of apprehension scampering through my body hairs.

"Will you be all right?" she said.

I nodded again, raising my eyebrows.

"I'm going to leave then."

She stood, leaning down to kiss me, her cheek wet.

"I'll give you a call in a couple weeks and let you know what's happening," I said.

Her feet moved quickly across the floor, out the door, and down the walk to the car. I listened to the motor start, pulling away, and then leaned forward, part of me racing to catch up. As her sound grew faint, pain and love flashed through my skull like dead rabbits alongside some country road, and in a mad flurry of inner wings, I ached, wanting to tell her I still loved her. Then she was gone, lost to the sound of a switchboard.

"Good morning. C.I.B. May I help you?"

My blind sister, I thought, sitting at her switchboard job, pleasant, happy. I could be that way. I wanted to be that way. Then another door opened somewhere in the building, and the clockwork tapping of a cane filled the hallway, coming for me, I thought. The sound grew louder, passed the open door, and continued on down the hall.

Someone else entered the lobby to my left, at the end of the room. No cane. A slice of morning snuck in around his feet like a dog.

"And you must be Mr. Todd," he said, stopping in front of me. "I'm Zeke Potter."

Black, I thought, then stood, smiling, as we exchanged hands—shorter than me, good hand though.

"He's a big one, Stephie," Zeke said. "I think I'm going to keep him on my side."

Pleasant Stephie had a very sweet laugh. My well-adjusted blind sister.

"Mr. Potter will show you to your room and help you get situated," she said.

"I've already got your bag," Zeke said. "Why don't you just take my elbow here."

I laughed a little, found the elbow, and latched on.

"Here we go," I said.

"You find something amusing, Mr. Todd?" Zeke said.

"Just me. I was laughing at myself for being so screwed up."

"Oh, I see. Are you really screwed up, Mr. Todd?"

"Yeah. Took a while, but I've been practicing on it."

"And you find that amusing?"

"Some of it. I was just thinking about you being black, and remembering a few things about eyeballs, and how they used to work."

"What makes you think I'm black?"

"Aren't you?"

"Well yes, my skin is black, but I thought you might be referring to something else I wasn't aware of."

"Nah. I was just thinking, that without the eyeballs, everybody's black—just seemed kind of funny, you know?"

"Oh, I see. Well I suppose everybody's entitled to their own opinion."

We exited the lobby, crossed an open, paved area, then entered the dormitory—another well-waxed floor, more disinfectant. I noticed footsteps then, somebody running down stairs. A small body bounced out a doorway to our left, hit the hall a couple times, and smashed into me head-on, scattering my nuts and sending my cane clattering off down the hall. Zeke dropped my bag and trotted after it.

"Damond," he shouted. "Where the hell is your cane?"

The small form in front of me put a hand to my belly and began feeling its way up. When it touched my beard, it jerked back like it had hit hot grease.

"Who is this, Zeke? One of the new students?" the voice croaked, high, raspy. An old lady or a midget, I thought, trying to ignore the pain in my nuts, laid out with little X's in their eyes. Zeke apparently recognized the expression as he handed my cane back.

"You're going to hurt somebody someday, Damond," he said. "If I ever catch you without your cane again, I'll damn sure report you."

"Sure Zeke. Whatever you say."

He slid around me, then banged out through the main door, running. Zeke nudged me with his elbow. I took hold, and followed him into the stairwell.

"That's your roommate, Mr. Todd."

On the second floor, I tapped my cane a couple times to let Zeke know I was out of shock.

"You'll be in room sixteen, Mr. Todd. If you count doors, it's the fourth one down on this left side."

Inside the room, Zeke set my bag in front of the wardrobe, then gave me a quick tour. In the bathroom, he pointed out two sinks just to the left of the door.

"You and Damond share the first one. There's a shelf above it for your shaving gear, if you ever decide to shave. To your right, there, is the shower. There's a bench and some hooks for your duds, and directly across the room is another door. That's Rusty and Reno's room, and just to the left of their door is the commode. It's a stall. The door locks."

I followed him back into my room, leaving the door open.

"Do you read braille, Mr. Todd? Good. The school rules are printed here, on the side of your wardrobe. I suggest you read them."

Zeke grabbed my hand, placing a key in the palm.

"This is your door key. It also fits your wardrobe. I suggest you keep them both locked whenever you leave the room. If you have any more questions, there's a house phone on the wall, by the stairwell. Pick it up and you'll get Stephie, down at the switchboard. Connie's the night counselor. She's in after five-thirty, downstairs. Don't leave any of your gear on the floor or under the bed. The janitors come in to mop every couple days. Someone else will be up shortly to show you around. It's been a pleasure, Mr. Todd."

I stuck my hand out. The door almost closed on it, so I moved it to my crotch, standing there alone between dirty socks and disinfectant. I moved to the window then, cranked it open, and pushed my face against the screen.

"That's right, you bastards," I said. "I'm back."

They ignored me. Chapter 2 of the Adipose manual. Always ignore anything you don't understand, and hope it goes away.

Traffic brings an odd sound to the observer, motion, the sound of time, people driving. Elaine driving north, somewhere on the freeway, the world moving by. Something I would never do again. I was starting over, but waiting first like some goddamn vegetable in a produce stand, waiting for someone to come and do something with me.

I lay down for a while, trying not to think, then got up, took a leak, checked the nuts out, both of them still there, then I remembered the rules on the side of my wardrobe. They pushed the usual kid stuff, keep your bed made, the floor clean, 11:00 P.M. curfew, keep the noise down, no stereos after 10:00 P.M., get your clean sheets and towels on Tuesday and Thursday mornings. Number six was a little more challenging. No alcohol, drugs, or persons of the opposite sex in the room with the door closed. Number ten explained the feeding schedule: 6:30 A.M., 11:30 A.M., 6:00 P.M. Two meals on weekends, 10:00 A.M. and 4:30 P.M. Just right for hangovers.

Out in the hall, the sound of a cane caught my attention. I followed it coming my way, tapping past my door, then stopping at the next, keys jingling, Rusty or Reno. He entered his room and rustled about, humming a pleasant but unfamiliar tune. The bathroom door was still open and that tiled chamber amplified everything. Before I could move to close the door, my blind brother entered the can, just humming away. The stall door banged. A belt buckle jangled. He sighed. I stood there like an idiot, my hand over my mouth, trying to think of something painful. Then the humming stopped and a couple farts cracked the still.

Christ, I thought he'd never finish, but he finally flushed and made his exit. I tiptoed to the bed, lay down, and pulled the pillow over my face.

Ten minutes later, he left his room and tapped back down the hall. I waited another few minutes, then grabbed my cane and tapped down the hall, running my hand along the wall. At the stairwell, I felt like a goddamn window washer feeling for the phone.

"This is Mr. Todd," I said when Stephie answered. "I'm ready to get started. I thought maybe you could tell me who to contact."

"Somebody will be with you shortly, Mr. Todd."

Counting back four doors, I tapped my cane along the way, using sonar, letting my bat sense get an idea of the hallway. I'd get that down quick, I thought. To hell with feeling walls and counting doors. I would get that cane technique down perfect—use the sound, the ears.

Back in my room, lying on the bed awaiting the sound of footsteps, I vacated my skull and took a little transcendental trip outside with the traffic. I used the cane, conscious of blind technique, but could still see clearly. This was similar to my dreams, which remained visual. They were always awkward too, twisted with an unnatural, double vision as I watched people react to my blindness.

All along the avenue familiar cars waited in bar parking lots, company trucks, pickups, junkers. I could see the faces inside those bars too, suspended in their dull, dark aura of smoke. They had been sitting there since I left town. Across six lanes of San Gabriel Avenue, Carson and

Klein Mortuary rose like a southern mansion, white wood, the red brick porch, circular drive, lush lawn, ivory curtains, and that black Caddy hearse in front, waiting. My old man had always said he would go at sea. No funeral, no expense, no smiling parasites, just a crab dinner.

As I moved along one store front, I caught a reflection in the glass—somebody following me, some guy in blue jeans and a T-shirt, sleeves rolled up to show off his guns, clean shaven, his hair dark, slicked back in a conk. Whenever I stopped, he would stop and lean against a pole, watching me, legs crossed, a toothpick in his mouth. When I moved, he moved. He seemed friendly enough, so I kept walking past the bars, their jukeboxes thumping, pool tables cracking, the dram dispensaries, mental cleansers. They had their own religion, all the essentials of the cocoon, without evolving. What the hell, everybody gets tired of fighting.

At the Bay City Limit sign, where the BART tracks cross, I made a U-turn and headed back. I was suddenly very tired and found myself esti-mating the distance back, questioning, but knowing I would make it. My buddy was waiting for me, leaning against a telephone pole, sucking at that toothpick, his hard blue eyes scrutinizing, following me close. As I passed, I smiled and nodded. He pulled the toothpick out.

"You really think there's more than that?" he said.

I didn't answer. A rush of guilt swept its hot breath across my face. Guilt for having never accomplished anything. Guilt for the double vision, for impersonating a blind man. I closed my eyes, but nothing changed.

It was nearly three hours before the knock finally arrived in the form of Stan DeLucca, head coordinator of school activities. I accepted his apol-ogy, forced a smile, and followed him downstairs. "I needed the nap any-way," I said.

We started with the east end of that first floor. He pointed out the TV room, coffee room, night counselor's quarters, and nurse's office. "How 'bout a shrink?" I said. "You got one of them hangin' around?" His laugh said a lot.

"We get a few cuts and bruises now and then, but nothing too big. The nurse is here mostly for the diabetics. Insulin shots, blood counts, that sort of thing, you know?"

"You go blind from diabetes?" I said.

"About half our students are diabetics. It usually affects more than just their eyes though, Pat. They lose a lot of sensitivity in their hands too. Makes it kind of rough on mobility and braille. Most of them wind up with guide dogs."

Christ, I thought. What the hell have you got to complain about, idiot.

"What I'd like you to do, Pat, is walk the length of the hall, down to the other end and back. See if you can stay in the middle. It'll give me some idea how far along you are with your mobility."

With a tunnel quiet like that, the sound bounces evenly. I just tuned in, like stereo, centering myself, and at the end, the sound pitches, like liquid leaving a bottle. Pretty damn easy. Going back, the hall widened at the main entrance, the sound giving way on the right side.

"Not bad, Pat. You look like a natural. Why don't you grab my elbow here, and we'll start on the other buildings."

Motion at last, I thought, brain food. But just outside the door, Stan stopped to check his watch.

"I tell you what, Pat. It's so close to lunch now, I think what I'll do is drop you off at the cafeteria, and we'll continue this later."

My slack snapped taut with the idea of waiting again in a strange place. I had no idea where the cafeteria was in relation to the dorm, but grabbed the elbow and followed. We made a couple turns, crossed an open area, and as Stan pulled the door open there was the disinfectant again. It smelled like they cooked with it. That was all I needed.

"You've got six tables along each side, Pat. They sit perpendicular to the windows. See here?"

Stan took hold of my cane, rapping table legs as we moved, the sound dissolving into the room's wide cavity.

"Straight ahead of you now are the silverware and trays. They don't like students getting in line until they're ready to serve, so I think I'll leave you here."

He put his hand to my shoulder, giving it a light squeeze.

"The other kids ought to be here in about five minutes, and I'll see you back at your room about one. Shouldn't have any trouble with that, huh, big guy?"

Sound swirled through the room as the door banged closed behind Stan. I stood there like a wooden Indian, lost. Yeah, sure, big guy, my saliva turning acidic. What's a matter, big guy, you're sweatin' again.

I began moving my cane around me like a second hand, looking for a table, or wall, a chair, anything. You're just crazy man, I thought. That's all, just sick. The sound of other canes and voices arriving outside helped, but not a hell of a lot. I had my back to the door, playing wooden Indian, when they entered, loud, crawling by me like some shod centipede, the room filling with their sound. Canes swatted my legs, nudging at my boots, as the length of its body moved past, grunting, laughing, the air beginning to vibrate, then adding the slap of trays and high tinsel tone of silverware.

27

I moved in the opposite direction, listening for the door, my own cane touching limbs, other canes.

"Hey, watch it, you creep."

"'Scuse me, 'scuse me."

"You're going the wrong way, you idiot."

Ten feet in front of me, I could hear the door swinging, fresh air. But as I moved toward it, a hand grasped my arm, pulling me into the line.

"I'll help you," she said, her face close, breath sweet with spearmint.

Speech mired itself in mud at the back of my tongue, choking that weak, idiot grin onto my face.

"You're Patrick, aren't you?" she said.

I nodded, turning to move with her.

"I'm Sally Andrews."

Eyeballs, I thought, counselor or something—she knew my name. Young. Saved for the moment. She looped her arm through mine and snuggled close, the soft, unmistakable curve of her breast against my forearm, no bra, and blood rushed to my crotch like dogs to wounded prey.

We continued through the line like that, arm in arm, quiet, Sally leading. Trays, silverware, mashed potatoes, peas and carrots, pork chop, slice of bread, and a carton of milk. She led me to a table next, and sat beside me, scooting up close so her leg touched mine. All about me, blind brothers and sisters hooked a healthy grease, gabbing as they fed—laughing, not sweating, their sound rising, swirling, then settling again, and Sally, the angel of darkness, beside me, touching, calling out names, introducing me.

"Are you a total, or a partial?" some guy asked from the other end of the table.

"I'm sorry," I said. "I don't think I know what you mean."

"Are you totally blind, or partially blind?"

"I guess I'm a total. I just never looked at it that way."

"You'll get used to it," the same voice said.

Blinks, I thought. That's what we all were, or what regulars fancied, according to the Adipose manual—close your eyes for a second and you'll miss it. I wasn't missing a damned thing.

Several others at the table squeezed giggles out through their mashed potatoes. My goddamn leg had even started to sweat where Sally's touched it, transferring heat.

"Who's your roommate?" a woman asked.

My answer ignited a common reaction—food spewed out from open mouths. Across the room I could hear Damond's voice flap to the top of its fence post, like a banty rooster crowing back.

28

As the others finished eating and vacated the table, my sweat subsided with the noise. I picked at my food a bit and drank some milk.

"This is the best table," Sally said. "I think they like you so far."

She continued talking while I ate, filling me in on who was cool, who wasn't. All the creeps sat across the room at their own tables. The battle for blood raged on inside my body. Lust screamed ragged invectives at reason, and Sally sat there, waiting patiently, as if we were going to fuck as soon as I finished the pork chop.

When I did finish, she showed me to the tray window, and once outside, wrapped herself about my arm again like we had something special. She didn't use a cane.

"I'm a partial," she said. "A month ago, I could see perfect."

Christ, I thought. If I had just a hint of eyesight, I would have been running, not walking arm in arm in the sun, my cranial worm on the critical list, heading for the rack with someone I didn't even know. . . . I just wasn't ready, and with each step the battle royal raged on inside, my nuts pummeling the brain, sensing victory, their spasm of orgasm building, preparatory to the warmth of contact, how she'd feel about me, tight, hot, moist. Christ, I thought I was going to pass out.

In the dorm, I stopped at the bottom of the stairs, facing her, one last feeble attempt.

"I'm in room sixteen," I said. "I can make it all right from here."

She moved up close, arms about my waist, looking up at me.

"I'm just a little out of sorts," I said. "I don't know what to tell you."

She pulled tight, face to my chest, hard against the pelvis.

"It's okay," she whispered.

I turned, taking her arm again up the stairs. On the second floor, stereos and voices pushed quietly through open doors. Somebody laughed behind us, or at us, I thought—some partial noticing my obvious physical condition. At the door Sally held close, rubbing her breasts against my arm while I fumbled for the key.

"You're the best-looking guy here," she cooed.

I was having one hell of a problem finding the keyhole, my brain a balloon again, racing for the side of the bus. Then, from inside the room, salvation croaked.

"It's ooopen."

My breath broke free, relieved. My crotch sank into its corner, disgusted, disappointed with the decision.

"Do you still want to come in?" I said.

"I don't think so. Classes are going to start in a few minutes anyway."

"It's ooopen," the room croaked again.

Sally tiptoed up, pecked me on the lips.

"I'll see you later this afternoon, okay?" she said, and trotted off down the hall.

I could still sense her body, warm, how it would have been, entering. How crazy the whole damn thing was, and I could see my slick-haired buddy, leaning against his pole, legs crossed, laughing his ass off.

FOUR

With sound, there are no white lines or right angles. Everything curves. The structural world I had learned through my eyes no longer applied where simple mobility was concerned. I knew it, but it was like the metric system, just taking a while to convert.

I stood in the open area between buildings with Stan drawing a diagram of the school on the palm of my hand. It looks a lot easier than it sounds.

"Okay," Stan said. "Now what you've got in front of you here is a *T*. See here? Like this? We're facing the entrance to the main hall, right now. That hallway is this part, here, and then you've got your top of the *T* up here, like this. Got it?"

I said, "Sure, no sweat." I didn't want to tell him the worm had lost the picture. Christ, as far as I could tell, in front of me was open air and beyond that the sound of traffic.

"All right. Now everything on the left side of the main hall here is administrative offices and the lobby. That's where you came in this morning. Was that your wife that brought you in? She's a good-looking gal."

They had checked us out. I should have known. The eyeballs didn't miss a thing, just like Sally scoping out my rounds in the cafeteria.

"Then on your right side here are classrooms. The last one up here by the top is the laundry room, and across the top here you've got two homerooms and the cooking and sewing classes. Pretty easy, huh?"

"Nothin' to it."

"We'll go in and check it out here in just a minute, but first, there's one more thing. On this right side here, the building extends a bit toward us. That's our only classroom with an outside entrance. It belongs to Ginelle Blase. She's one of our business instructors. Great gal too, Pat. Blind, got her masters in economics from U.C.L.A. I'd introduce you, but she's not in today. In fact, that's what took me so long getting around to you this morning. I had Lieutenant Farnsworth here, from the Brookings Police Department, and had to go over a few things with him."

"She got busted, huh?"

31

"Well? We don't have all the details yet, but apparently Ginelle was raped yesterday evening, in her home."

I don't know why I took it so personally, but I did. My skull narrowed down to the dark, angry radius of my arms. If I could just get my hands—

"She lives only about four blocks south of here. Same street. Walks it both ways every day. Everybody around here knows her."

That wasn't even animal, I thought, just man. Not weak, or young, or old, or predators, just man, some miserable useless joint. I could see that bastard, watching, waiting.

"Is she all right?" I said.

"Well, like I said, Pat, I don't have all the details yet, but I talked to her on the phone, and to listen to her, you'd never know anything happened. She's a strong gal, Pat. A beautiful black gal. . . . It's funny, you know? You never think much about it, till it happens to someone you know. I can't even imagine something like that happening to my wife."

"They get the guy?"

"I guess they're working on it. Nothing yet though. C'mon, grab hold. We'll go inside."

Outrage and injustice banged their washtubs against the walls of my skull, trampling some soft, heavy lump under their feet. Something male, some twisted, sexual, sickening . . . And that idea of the weak and the predator kept flashing through, but it wasn't natural. It wasn't caribou and wolves. It was a miserable, sickening violation, I thought, sickened even more by my own inability to function normally. Whatever the hell that was.

Inside the building, the first room, right side, Lou Abrams taught abacus and business skills—short man, small hand. I could tell he was blind by the way he stood and came around the table, talking, but watching his step too. He handed me his abacus. It was about the size of a postcard. I could hear other students, seated, quietly clicking their beads.

"The closest I've come to this," I said, "is keeping score over a pool table."

"Yes, yes," he said. "I can understand that. It doesn't make much sense to anybody until they become familiar with the process. But! By the time you leave here, I will have you adding, subtracting, multiplying, dividing, maybe even a few square roots, if you're up to it, and we'll do it all on a simple set of beads, like the one in your hand."

Thirteen rows of beads, five beads to the row, one upper case, four below, set in a flat plastic case. I returned them.

"What're we lookin' at in business skills?"

"Well to begin with, I usually spend some time with my students, so I have some idea of their capabilities, and, if I think they show some potential for the business world, we'll look into it further."

Something about his tone seemed insinuating, like he smelled gas on me. I could see myself, pushing beads, making change in a gas station—some asshole hands me a one and says it's a twenty.

Between rooms, a drinking fountain droned. I homed in on it—ice water.

"Didn't take you long to find that, did it, Pat?" Stan said.

I nodded, wiping a backhand at my mouth. Across the hall, through a doorway, the switchboard crackled—Stephie, my pleasant, happy, blink sister. How many times had she been raped.

"Next to the lobby here, Pat, is Dan Oakes's office. Dan's our chief administrator. Sharp guy, Pat, you'd like him. Blind too, blind from birth. He's been with the school since it opened in 1960. Before that he had a private law practice, and from what I hear, I guess he was pretty good at it. So, if you ever have any legal questions, he's the man to see. You can make an appointment through his secretary."

We started down the hall again. I tapped my cane, listening for the next opening, and when the little man, with his beads and business skills, had faded sufficiently behind us, Stan spoke low, confidentially.

"Lou Abrams used to be an attorney too."

The next classroom, right side, belonged to Ben Daly, the braille instructor. Ben and I had a good laugh, trying to get our hands together. He sounded taller. I couldn't remember the last time I'd laughed, clean like that. It was a large room, numerous tables and chairs, a braille library along the south wall and several small, individual workrooms along the opposite wall. As Ben continued with our tour of the room, typewriters, braillers, transcribers, I listened to the tone of his voice, pleasant, energetic, happy I thought, like Stephie. I hadn't expected blind instructors.

Next came the laundry room. Three washers, three dryers, free soap. At the top of the T, we turned right. Restrooms on the one side, the sewing and cooking class across, on the left, then we exited, out into fresh air.

"Just to your left now, Pat, is the woodshop. It's a metal door. Go ahead, tap it."

Concrete bordered the door on both sides.

"Now if you turn right, and follow this wall along the back side of the classrooms here, you're headed straight for the dorm. Why don't you go down and back, just to get the idea. See if you can tell where the building ends there."

The building ended where the sound off my cane broke free, where the sun touched my forearm and the side of my face. It ended at the corner of an empty classroom, Ginelle Blase's, open air, and beyond, the avenue, regulars with their white lines, their Donald Duck eyes jockeying for position, and at least one eyeball sonofabitch who preyed on blind women.

A rectangular courtyard separated the cafeteria from the main building. It was maybe 100 by 150 feet, patched with lawn, shrubs, and walkways. The dorm and woodshop formed its other boundaries. All the walkways and buildings were laid out in parallels and perpendiculars. You could find a line easily enough. Each building had its own sound too.

The gym extended south off the cafeteria, spacious, with a high, open ceiling. Stan showed me around—stationary bikes, parallel bars, wall pulleys, speed bag, weights, rowing machine, mats, and half a basketball court.

I laughed, a single note. "Get some real high-scoring games, I'll bet."

"Hey, you'd be surprised," he said. "Hang on a minute. I'll get the ball. You can take a couple of shots."

"That's all right. I think I'll pass on it, for now."

"Hey, it's good for you. C'mon. Take a crack at it."

Stan retrieved a basketball from an adjoining office and dribbled it back toward me, the sound spreading, rolling through the chamber like smoke.

"Here you go, Pat, comin' at you. One hop."

Every nerve in my body rushed to the front, extending like cilia, screaming in unison as they waved about, helpless. I held my hands just above my waist, palms out. My nuts filed a formal protest just after impact.

"Whoops, almost got you there, huh, Pat. Why don't you move right over here, like this. That's the free-throw line. See? You can feel that tape with your toes. Then I get under the bucket, like this, and clap my hands to give you a line of sight."

I took three shots, Stan clapping. No prizes. Shooting the ball was a trip. Releasing it like that into the void stirred the worm as much as anticipating its arrival on one bounce. The former was a quiet strangeness, though, free of the latter's shock potential.

"You guys don't really have games, do you?" I said.

"The partials will get in here and fool around once in a while, but you'd be surprised, Pat. We had a congenital here last year who made fifteen in a row. The partials haven't even beat that. I think my own best is only about eleven."

I checked the weights out, then the speed bag, taking a couple of raps before barking my knuckles on the frame. Stan was shooting free throws.

"That thing's adjustable, Pat," he called. "We might have to raise it a bit for you."

I flexed the humble hand, thinking of the rapist, hearing that queer again in the hospital, laughing at me. Weak. You just have to get your hands on 'em, I thought. Work close and fast.

We left the gym, headed back toward the woodshop. I walked beside Stan, without the elbow, concentrating on the echoes off my cane—eat good, sleep good, study hard to be a good blink, I thought, and whatever was left, blow that out on the weights.

"You're not going to have any trouble. I can see that," Stan said. "You can come out here in the evening, when it's quiet, and practice the buildings. In fact, you can get into just about anything you want here, Pat. Like the sewing and cooking classes. They're mandatory for the gals. The woodshop is mandatory for you guys, those that can handle it anyway. But if you're interested, I'll put you on the waiting list for sewing and cooking. They come in pretty handy, you know, if you're the independent type."

"I'll do it all," I said.

"That's the spirit. I'll work your schedule up this evening and get it to you by tomorrow morning."

Ramey Arreanas, the shop instructor, laughed a lot and talked fast with a slight Latin accent. I could tell by his voice that he kept eye contact when we talked. Not many regulars did that. Rubber mats coursed the interior of his shop between the tables and equipment, table saw, lathe, jointer, radial-arm saw, panel saw, cabinets of hand and power tools—and no disinfectant. Just that comforting odor of fresh-cut wood.

"You can make a house if you want," Ramey said. "I don't know how you'll get it out of here, but you can sure make it, kitchen cabinets, everything, but you'll have to show me you know what you're doing first. Right? Our number one rule in here is to keep all the blood inside the body."

Working wood, the idea of making something with my hands, caressed my twisted skull like cold beer—pleasant sensations forcing their way through the cramped, stagnant channels of my mind.

"The first thing you have to do is learn this place like the back of your hand. You'll have to pass a safety test and get checked out on every piece of equipment before you can use it. Then you'll draw me up a plan of your project, measurements, everything, what kind of wood, and why you want to use that particular wood."

Across the room, another voice rose, critical—somebody with Stan. "What the hell's she expect," he said. "She oughta have more sense than to be living alone like that."

"Yeah, what's the latest on that?" Ramey said. "They get that guy yet?"

35

"I don't know," Stan said. "I haven't heard anything more."

"When they git 'im, you tell 'em to bring 'im in here. I'll make sure he don't do it again."

"They're gonna have to catch 'im first," the other said.

"And they oughta castrate any attorney that defends a bastard like that, too," Ramey said. "You can bet there'd be a lot less of it going on. What'd that cop say, anyway? They must have some idea who did it."

"Ginelle says she knows who it is," Stan said. "She says it's some white guy that's been doing yardwork in the neighborhood for the past couple of weeks. Apparently he's come to her door a couple of times."

"Shoooot. They prob'ly got that dude behind bars right now," Ramey said.

"I guess they're trying to find an eyewitness," Stan said. "They're checking the neighbors, to see if any of them saw the guy around her place. Farnsworth says the D.A. won't touch it unless they can come up with an eyewitness."

"Hey, that's a bunch, man," Ramey said. "Ginelle's ears work better'n most people's eyes. You know that."

"I'm just repeating what Farnsworth told me."

Once Stan and I were outside again, I stopped just before entering the main building."

"That cop really said that?"

"That's what he said. I got a little ticked off at him myself. He started right off the bat, asking me questions about Ginelle—personal things, you know? Was she promiscuous? Did she have affairs here at the school? Did she ever display a preference for white males over black? So I got a little hot, I guess, but if you knew Ginelle, you'd know what I'm talking about. You can't find a better gal. I guess everybody's got their job to do."

"She's all right though, huh?"

"Some of the gals went down on their lunch break and saw her. I guess he knocked her around pretty good. She's got some bruises, and a little cut here on her neck, where he held a knife to her throat."

I could see the shadows, struggling, the dark shape kneeling, thrusting. I couldn't see the knife.

"And you know, Pat? The guy laughed at her. She said when he was leaving, he told her there was nothing she could do about it because she couldn't see him . . . and he laughed."

The main building seemed hot, overly hot, as we entered, laced with disinfectant. Bernice, a cooking instructor there, was blind. She liked her cologne too.

"We're baking cookies today," she said, grabbing my hand, towing me along the backs of seated students, introducing me. That goddamn tight,

36

unventilated room seemed stifling, as if all the heat in the building were generated there. The last voice in line belonged to Rusty, my can mate, a big hand, soft, like a full pup. The guy stuttered.

"It's a pleasure to be your neighbor, Patrick."

"You bet, Rusty."

Christ, I wanted to hug the guy. I wanted to hug them all, tell them we could fight it. We didn't need their club. We didn't need their shit, either. We were as good as anybody else, and I could see them all, sitting there giggling, making cookies, their baseball caps pulled down low over their eyes, and Bernice clucking about them like a goddamn mother hen. My guts started to rise, twisting the sweat out, as I passed Stan at the door. Bernice followed him out, squawking about some damned thing.

"I've got to go down to my office with Bernice for a minute," Stan said. "That's Gwenda's room next door, to your right there. She's your home-room teacher. Why don't you go ahead on in. Introduce yourself. You can knock off when you get done there. You know your way back to the dorm, huh?"

As their feet disappeared around the corner, I knelt for a moment on the cool linoleum, my head down, breathing slowly against the hot sweat of nausea. The rape, the blatant goddamn intrusion, the laughter of eye-balls, sitting in some goddamn nuthouse sauna playing with dough. That goddamn disinfectant. As my head cleared, I felt the distinct, skin-prickling sensation of eyeballs checking my act, someone nearby. My face reddened as I stood, and a couple of taps to my right I found the open door and walked in. The eyes were waiting, quiet, watching me—not a bad feeling, just intense.

"This is homeroom?" I said.

"You got it," she said. "It's nothing like next door, either."

"I guess I'll sleep better knowing that."

"We get into some practical arts occasionally," she said, "but not like that Sesame Street bunch over there. If you want to learn to cook, we'll get a braille cookbook and let you try some serious recipes."

"Anything else?"

"Anything your little heart desires. As long as it's within reason. Maybe some shopping, how to iron your clothes and do your laundry and pay your bills. We can set you up with a braille checking account. That's always a good place to start, and after that, who knows? Maybe some letters to your congressman, or some wine tasting."

She was very attractive, the voice, the way the eyes held on me, both strong, sexual maybe. That seemed to be the first connection my idiot skull usually produced. I wanted more though. I wanted to think she was sharp, caring, that she knew about blinks and how they could twist. I wanted to give in and open to her, like a breeze, or a saxophone. Trust it, move right up close and let it wrap around you.

"Who do I have to bribe to stay out of there?" I said, tilting my head toward the next room.

"Don't worry about that. It's already been taken care of. Believe me. You just wouldn't fit over there. They'd lose you."

I tossed my head, trying to smile, wondering what the hell she meant by that. She moved a chair then and came around the end of the table. She was a small woman, small hand, but strong like her voice, and the eyes again, still watching me close.

"So you're Gwenda."

"Yes, I know that," she said, "and you're Patrick Todd."

"How do you know that?"

"Oh, believe me, I probably know you better than you know yourself."

I tossed my head again, the laugh silent, defensive. "Well, at the moment," I said, "that's not saying a hell of a lot. There isn't much to know."

"Oh, I wouldn't say that."

"I'm curious then. What makes you think you know me?"

"I read your file. All I needed was the face."

My smile came slow, flat, covering tight teeth.

"It's quite an accomplishment," she said. "Where do you plan to do your graduate work, San Quentin?"

I excused myself, maneuvered the main hall easily enough, then lost it just outside the door. It should have been simple, but it wasn't. Echoes off my cane came faint, distorted, then gone, erased by a slight wind. I found bushes, the side of a building, a locked door. My goddamn skull throbbed, screaming obscenities at its own ignorance, my entire body aching, crawling through some twisted heat of madness, of prey and laughter and intrusion and so fucking dependent. Just to be able to move, to get in a car or on a bike and move away from it.

Then it eased. I had hold again, files and all, and moments later a car pulled up in front of the school and parked. I took a quick bearing, moved straight ahead, registered a familiar sound, and found the dorm entrance.

Upstairs in my room, someone had left sheets, towels, and one blanket stacked neatly at the foot of my bed, so I made it and lay there, tired, the tang of bitterness still sticky in my saliva. I could see them clearly through a dark place in the mind's eye, a thousand Adipose hands working my file like a K mart blue light special, their goddamn shallow eyeballs reading, nodding, studying through my past. Oh yes, note the fluctuation, the extremes of emotion, the abnormal highs and cold, silent depths. And let's not overlook the sexual inconsistency. Page after page of white paper rattling through their hands, then stacked again, neatly, into a shadow.

FIVE

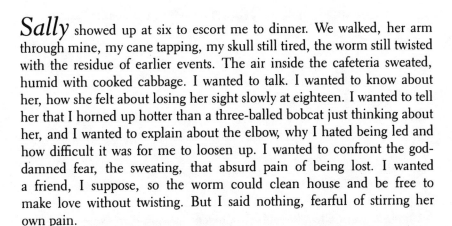

Sally showed up at six to escort me to dinner. We walked, her arm through mine, my cane tapping, my skull still tired, the worm still twisted with the residue of earlier events. The air inside the cafeteria sweated, humid with cooked cabbage. I wanted to talk. I wanted to know about her, how she felt about losing her sight slowly at eighteen. I wanted to tell her that I horned up hotter than a three-balled bobcat just thinking about her, and I wanted to explain about the elbow, why I hated being led and how difficult it was for me to loosen up. I wanted to confront the goddamned fear, the sweating, that absurd pain of being lost. I wanted a friend, I suppose, so the worm could clean house and be free to make love without twisting. But I said nothing, fearful of stirring her own pain.

So we ate quietly, then walked back upstairs, my mind screaming again about fucking or hiding. Damond wasn't in. I closed the door behind us and sat on the bed. Sally moved up in front of me, waiting—an eighteen-year-old partial, gradually losing her sight from retinitis pigmentosa. My hands unbuttoned her shirt and opened it, then touched lightly, running fingertips over her face and neck, the curve of her bare breasts. My face moved up to nuzzle stiff nipples. The hands continued down onto her warm belly, resting about her waist. I had to laugh then, pulling away, my head shaking slowly from side to side, craving the tranquility of some drug.

"Tell me, Sally," I said. "What's it like going blind slowly? Do you twist?"

"Ummm? I dunno."

"What about the classes then," I said, looking up at her. "You getting anything out of them? You got any idea what you're going to do when you leave?"

"Ummm?"

I held her close, my cheek to her breast. She placed both her hands on top of my head, touching almost absent-mindedly. That scream wavered back into view, its parched throat exposed, desperately in need of something.

"I'm really tired," I said.

Her fingers stopped moving through my hair.

"It's been a long day."

I backed away then and began buttoning her shirt.

"I just don't think I'd be any good for you right now."

She tucked her shirt in. I stood, and when I reached to open the door, she moved in front of me, hugging close, toeing up to kiss my mouth hard. A suggestive raincheck.

"I'll see you in the morning," she said. "It's okay. I'll come get you for breakfast."

I lay there on the bed for an hour after she left, imagining the fluid sensation of bodies touching—breasts, bellies, legs, the heat, and Jesus, that initial spasm of entry. My roommate, Damond, hopped in, hit a switch, and lit the room with country music, jabbing questions the whole time from his side. I tried to ignore him. It should have come easy too, the connection with Sally. I wanted her, or I wanted that part of it. I just didn't want to start over where I had left off. So I lay there, my hard-on like a sundial, registering the hour of my confusion. Elaine too, her voice, her sound was echoing—"You just can't wait to fuck your brains out. . . ."

Damond eventually altered his approach, providing an exaggerated disc jockey routine to balance his act.

"That's right," he said. "I'm heading for Nashville just as soon as I get out of here."

"I appreciate the performance," I said. "I'm just not in the mood right now. Maybe later, huh?"

I still had a hard time liking the little fucker. His first impression had left something to be desired, and very little in our subsequent encounters had done much to change that.

"C'mon," he croaked. "You mean to tell me you've never heard of Sonny James? He's the greatest. You must really be square, man."

"Look," I said. "I got nothin' against country music. I might even learn to like you too, but at the moment I'm just not interested in either. Savvy?"

"What a drag, man. A square for a roommate."

"Tell me something," I said. "What's with the fragrance? You homesick or something?"

"What's that supposed to mean?"

"That means it stinks in here, like someone's been jackin' off in their dirty socks. You ever take a shower, man? Or is that the way you ridge runners like it?"

"I don't touch anything in that slimy lavatory," he barked, then added a few jaded epithets in some queer tongue and donned headphones. Miniature guitars leaked out around his ears, and half an hour later, when the tape clicked off, he was sleeping, making little spitting, snarling noises, as if tearing raw flesh from the leg of something he had captured in Nashville.

I suppose everybody thinks about suicide at one time or another. Not actually making plans, but just thinking, wondering about others and how tight the stem has to twist to consider it up close. That was about 2:00 A.M., the rest of the dorm quiet and me lying on that strange, slippery bed plagued by the idea. The fact that I had even thought about it had a dogfight going between my ears. I finally opened the window, listening for sounds to concentrate on, envisioning the avenue at night, the parallel rows of amber lights, and behind them the black mystique of shadows, their faces gone, the day gone, and just as the circle seemed ready to turn back in on me, the cool, blind, mother of darkness slipped through the screen and laid her gentle hands to my face.

"C'mon, c'mon'," she said. "What's goin' on here? Why's my boy gettin' so screwed up?"

My buddy, the guy with the toothpick, leaned against his pole out there on the avenue, watching.

"The whole thing ain't even a piss in the ocean," I told them. "You don't start over. You don't even pick up where you left off, and the only thing you know for sure is that you want to live, because of some idiotic idea that it makes a difference somewhere down the line."

They listened, amused, my face between Mother Night's hands, toothpick nodding, his brow raised.

"I suppose," he said, "but if you don't straighten up, you're liable to wind up out here on the street again with a perpetual hard-on and your baseball cap pulled sideways."

We all laughed, nodding. Mother Night patted my cheek, then drew my face close to hers, touching.

"You got it made," she said. "Just take it easy."

Christ she was beautiful, and when I lay back down, she stayed, framed in the window, her chin resting between her palms. My schoolmarm, calmly explaining how to distinguish myself from the nervous energy of daylight, where everything moves too fast from one point to another, then off again, those hard skinny crablegs just clickity clacking along, missing

41

everything in between. That ignored area, she said, the space so readily passed by, was the dark side of things, the moon, the universe, the mind.

"Just take it slow," she said, "check it out. You won't find any faces, or fine bodies in red halter tops and white shorts with a little cheek exposed. It's all gone, sonny boy. No wet T-shirts, no makeup, no distant color, no airbrushed photographs. All you get now are voices, and in the dark you'll know immediately if they've got both their shoes tied."

Sleep finally teased me in and out of reruns, Sally's body, the file, the vague faces of blinks, laughter. Dawn approached in a whisper of eyelids, some closing, some opening. Unseen generators kicked on, flooding the air cells with megawatts. Birds cranked up their old Victrolas, and a couple of blocks away, some Adipose jerk started his car, flooring it over and over. Chapter 3, section 3, of the *Adipose People's Guide*. If it don't work right, floor it. It'll fix itself. If it don't sound floored, get your other foot over there and mash it real good with both feet.

To the east, behind the Sierra Nevadas, the sun sneaked closer, sliding on its belly to the incline, where it squatted like a Sumo wrestler, legs bunched. It paused there, face down in meditation. Then, arching its back, it stretched, catching its fingertips just barely over the ridge, and rose slowly, silently peering over to eyeball the good and bad alike. And seeing that nothing had changed in its absence, that everything remained as screwed up as ever, it stood, throwing its arms wide, half embracing, half warning, above the sound of time cards punching in.

A door slammed somewhere down the hall—first blink of the day. I grabbed my pocket watch off the nightstand, ran a fingertip across the open dial, 5:45, then put it to my ear to make sure it was still running. Out in the hall, a cane advanced. Not the usual cane technique either, this one had rhythm—tippity tap, tippity tap, tippity tap tap Wham. It smacked the wall on that base stroke and resumed its rhythm. The second stroke hit our door, Pow, like a rifle shot. Damond groaned and rolled up in his covers. I sat up laughing to myself, wanting to know who this blink was behind all that mischief. That's how I wanted to start the day, just bite the world right in the ass, let them know I was still around.

As I showered, my enthusiasm faded, and while I dressed, the taste of sweat returned. I made all sorts of excuses, standing there in front of the door, waiting, cane in hand. Just one more damn day, I thought. But what if Sally doesn't come for you? What if she's pissed because you're such a funny fucker.

Christ, I would rather have had ten hunched shadows winging razors at my belly, something I could fight back. When I finally hated myself enough to kick my butt out through the door, Sally was just topping the

42

stairs—bright, cheery, trotting up to me, her hair still wet. I took the offered elbow.

In the cafeteria, we ate quietly again, Sally beside me, all the other "right" blinks spaced evenly about the table, munching contentedly. I could see myself, an old man in a small, two-room apartment over a grocery store, with a bar next door. Just switch on the radio, pull my cap on, and wait for the ball games.

Sally and I made a date for that night, Friday night, both of us going through the motions of feigned concession, both of us knowing otherwise. I left her at the bottom of the stairs, thinking I had ten hours to settle the matter with my principles.

Stan delivered my schedule, and allowing for lost time and a possible seizure, I left my room early for Gwenda's homeroom. Downstairs, for once all the buildings and walks played back in place, verifying my map. The echoes came true, right through the main doors and down the hall, fresh with disinfectant, into Gwenda's room. Ten minutes passed before other blinks began to arrive, tapping along that well-waxed hall into other rooms. The last tap through came all the way down, a guy, I thought, by the way he walked. I was seated at the table, my back to the door. He entered the room and stopped behind my chair, his hand looking over the backrest, across my shoulder, touched my hair, then moving around to my face.

"Oh, sorry, man. I thought you was Gwenda."

"She got a beard too?"

"God, I hope not."

We exchanged names and hands and other pleasantries, street talk. Lance was from Vine Hill, a rough neighborhood in Pleasanton, just east of the Shell Oil refinery. I'd shot some pool out that way. He was short, strong, and had a nervous snicker, a three-note habit that followed damn near everything he said.

Out in the hall, another door opened on quick, light footsteps. Gwenda. The sound of her feet came very sexual, quick and light. It was obvious I hadn't changed a hell of a lot overnight. She entered the room, passed behind me, and came around the other side of the table, setting some things down. I sensed her eyes again, moving between us.

"Have you two met?"

Lance snickered.

"I guess that answers my question."

I smelled the element of a hot plate heating, then instant coffee as she spooned it into a cup.

"I apologize for being late," she said, "and for the mess too, whether

43

you can see it or not. We all have our bad habits, hmmm? And as soon as I have my morning fix here, we'll get busy. We'll just move right on into better things."

The smell of coffee expanded as she filled her cup with hot water, stirring.

"Coffee, Patrick? How 'bout a cup of tea? I've probably got a bag around here someplace."

"No thanks. I'll wait for the rest of the class."

"You are the rest of the class, Patrick, and it's nice to see you're still around. So tell me, what do you think of this nuthouse so far?"

"The food ain't bad. I haven't had time to look much further 'n that."

"You will, believe me. And what about you, Lance? Can I get you anything?"

"Sure. I could go for a little bit of the waitress."

"Yes, I'm sure you could."

She sipped at her coffee. I thought about her quick footsteps again, and her lips pursing over the edge of that cup.

"Lance got shot, Patrick. Did he tell you about that? Went in the right temple and came out the left—Boom, just like that. No more eyeballs. Isn't that right, Lance?"

"Yeah, heh heh heh."

"Oh, you think that's funny too, huh? Lance thinks everything's funny, Patrick, but he's learning how to be a good blink now. Aren't you?"

Lance snickered again.

"He's got a lot of girl problems too. Seems he falls in love too easy, then brings all his heartaches in here and expects Mother Gwenda to patch him up and make that little brain of his all right again."

"Yeah. I been tryin' to get in her pants for six weeks," he said. "I guess she's still in love with her husband."

"And Mr. Todd here was in a boating accident. Did he tell you about that, Lance? Cut his whole face off, but it looks like he had some pretty good doctors. They put most of it back in the right places. You're lucky to be alive. You know that, don't you, Patrick?"

I returned her eye contact, not overly joyed by the conversation.

"It's probably the best thing that ever happened to you. Going blind, that is. It probably saved your life."

"Geez, I'm glad you told me. Everything oughta be a hell of a lot better now."

"You never know."

She sipped her coffee again, watching, testing.

"Our boy Patrick here used to be a little bit wild, Lance."

"Maybe by some standards," I said. "By somebody else's goddamn file."

44

"C'mon now. You didn't know you had a file here? Born in Oakland, dropped out of high school, stole your first motorcycle at fifteen, and on and on. It would take us all day, wouldn't it. Not everybody accumulates that much paper, Patrick, and since you're a ward of the state now, they have to know everything about you, except for all the good things, of course. The state can't make mistakes, you know that, not with taxpayers' money. Why do you think it took four months to process your application. You didn't know that, Patrick? C'mon. I'm surprised at you."

"I returned that motorcycle."

"Right. A week later to the same coffee shop where the highway patrolman parked it."

Lance found it all very amusing, snickering away.

"Is this usual first-day procedure or am I just privileged?"

"Oh, it's not over yet either. Your file's still growing. Right, Lance? The night counselors have to make their reports so they can get paid. You're charted every day, by each of your instructors, so you might as well get used to it. There's going to be somebody watching every time you pick your nose. Not to mention people out there, on the street. You're a big blink, Patrick, a real curiosity. They're going to look to see if you pissed your pants or washed your hair, and when you get back home, your neighbors are going to watch everything you do through your windows. Everybody will know what Patrick's doing, and all Patrick will know is what's going on inside his head. Now how do you feel?"

"I'd just moon the bastards," Lance said.

Laughter broke the tension, Lance and me just carrying on, Gwenda waiting, our sound pushing out into the empty hallway.

"I take it that sort of thing doesn't bother you then," she said.

"Not really. Most of 'em don't have anything better to do anyway."

"Good. I guess we can go to work then."

Gwenda slid a raised-line writing board across the table to each of us, stiff cardboard with raised parallel ridges. Paper clips at the corners held a sheet of typing paper.

"Your left index finger marks the line you're on. Start your pen there, and as you write, think of the ridge as your line. Try and get the feel of bumping against it."

I worked the pen across in a series of loops, or large *e*'s, then dropped my finger down a ridge, found it with the pen and continued—more loops. My brain tried to function through its optic nerves, but the disconnect caused a heavy, dizzy sensation, like when you cross your eyes.

"You can feel your right margin with the edge of your palm when you get close. See? Feel the edge there? It'll take some getting used to, but it's important. You'll need it for your checking account, and besides that, I'd like to impress upon both of you the importance of remembering all your visual things. It'll make you a much better blink. Isn't that right, Lance?"

My brain kept plodding through learned technique, trying to follow the pen's action through the eyes. When I stopped, I lost all sense of the letter, or where the pen rested in relation to the next one. Printing went much easier, sort of a cursive print, envisioning each character and completing it.

"What should I write?" Lance said.

"Write your name, if you can remember it."

After a couple more lines of print, I moved down two spaces, and wrote:

Chrome and paint are only preservatives. There is no color.
The Adipose People's Guide now comes in braille.
Beauty is a sound inside my mind, changing.

I slid it back across the table to Gwenda. Such a simple thing too, writing, but it felt good. I'd worked the brain on something new, and nothing about sex.

Lou Abrams and his abacus came next, then braille with Ben Daly. After lunch, Stan directed two hours of mobility lessons, beginning with a couple of rounds of the buildings on my own, in and out. Everything fit. Echoes answered back into my abstract map. Sound is very much like the eyeballs in that sense, where a familiar object, a building, tree, the sidewalk, has no immediate substance of its own. They're just a code, an ignition of the memory and imagination. My cranial worm multiplied its blossoming confidence by six months and found its fighting weight. It was ready, out of the swamp and moving.

"You got that down pretty fast, Pat," Stan said. "I tell you what. Why don't you head on out to the curb in front of the school. We'll introduce you to some new ground."

I did so, and waited, facing the avenue a block away, my new-found confidence under sudden scrutiny. Stan pointed out a light standard, just to my left, a position object.

"Whichever way you're coming, Pat, you can turn when you sense that pole and you'll be on line right between the buildings."

The pole was about six feet away. I tapped it with my cane—aluminum.

"Now I'd like you to follow the sidewalk on around the cul de sac here. It ends at a fence on the other side of the parking area, but if you trail left, just before the fence, there's another walkway. See if you can find it."

The curb arched clockwise, then straightened. I sensed the obstruction in front of me and trailed left, following the lawn's edge. Just before the barrier, I hit pavement and turned.

"We call this the snakewalk, Pat. What you have here is a piece of property about fifty feet wide that extends from the school out to San Gabriel Avenue. It's like a little park, you know? You've got some spruce, a few pine. I think this one to our left is a mulberry, and this walkway sort of curves around through the trees. It's pretty nice. Some of the students come out here on warm days. There's a bench out at the end, on the right side. Why don't you go ahead and follow it out."

I trailed lawn, following the curves, the sound of traffic getting closer, louder, and with it, a clear distinction between the school behind me and that other world out there in front. About halfway, the sound of water stopped me. It came from my left, seventy feet away maybe.

"What do you have out there, Stan, a frog pond?"

"What's that, Pat?"

"The water."

We crossed the carpet of lawn to a split-rail fence, homing in on the sound.

"You got some pretty good ears there, Pat. I never even noticed that before. The creek comes under the avenue there, through a culvert, and drops off into a little pool, then runs on down past the fence here toward Brookings Hill. I'll have to ask the other students if they notice it."

I marked that sound on my map, crossed the lawn back to the snake-walk, and continued on toward the avenue. At the intersection, the snake-walk flared like a delta. The traffic seemed very close.

"Go ahead, Pat. You've got another fifteen feet of sidewalk there before you hit the curb."

So that was it. The Adipose River, or a tributary, both directions. Cars whipped by in the first lane, and with each step, I had a growing sensation of how it would feel to be struck and run over.

"Go ahead, Pat. You've still got another six feet or so."

My cane finally found the edge of the curb, cars and faces flashing by, right there. I could have reached out and touched them, and way behind me, a school full of blinks, my people, meals, a bed, my needs taken care of. Most of them anyway. That was security, being cared for. In six months I would take that same walk with nothing behind me. I would be leaving, and I knew then why Lance fell in love so easily, why any blink might. You could do anything, anywhere, if you had somebody. That would be your connection, your security, your elbow. You wouldn't be alone, so you wouldn't give a damn if it wasn't really love. You grabbed at any chance that came close enough, so you didn't have to go back alone. That's where I would be in six months. Alone.

My buffed-up confidence shriveled to its normal size as I walked back. Just a step, I thought, a simple step up. That first one always looked so high, through sweat, until you made it. After that, they all looked alike.

I worked some iron later that afternoon in the gym, fully aware then of my problem with Sally. My brain and balls still struggled for the deciding vote, though, regardless of the new awareness, and in the shower after exercising, with the help of a little soap and imagination, my balls won. I should have jacked off.

Sally parked next to me at dinner, her leg touching. All the arguing in my skull was over. Just that dull truth remained. The other blinks went about their ingestion quietly, as if everybody had considered love that day. I don't know why I had thought blinks would be any different than regulars. Because of the eyes, I guess, because it seemed that that alone would make the world so different, make it honest. It wasn't any different, just a parallel, a side street and a slower pace running alongside the main drag.

My pain of hours previous had become just a scratch. I no longer wanted to talk, not about whether I could love Sally, or if she could love me, or if she felt the same needs, or if that had been her reason for coming on so fast.

When we left the cafeteria, Sally walked beside me, but no more of the arm-in-arm bit. She remained so through the dorm and up the stairs, probably wondering if there would be a performance or if I would find another excuse. All I knew for sure was there would be no love in it for either of us, yet we would go through with it for the meat.

At the door, I put my ear close, listening, wasting time.

"He's always downstairs in the TV room till late," she said.

She closed the door behind me and then followed to the bed. My hands began with the buttons of her shirt, methodically. Anxiety struggled free and began to twist up inside me. Some goddamn lover, I thought.

"You know this is illegal, don't you?" I said.

"Ummm?"

"You know the only problem with the crotch taking control is that it never performs a complete coup. It just gags the brain, ties it up for a while and makes it watch."

"Hmmm?"

"Never mind. It doesn't matter anyway."

Sally sat on the side of the bed while I removed her sandals, then her jeans and panties. She had led all that way, then waited patiently to be taken. I dropped my own drawers, watching the entire world reduce to an area the size of our genitals—hot and throbbing and selfish, in the middle of a goddamn blind school. I wanted to open the window and laugh, straddling her, my cock in her mouth, draining both ends.

We rubbed bellies, necking, sharing the heat, legs moving like insects. She had a lovely body, a visual body. My tongue moved along the surface, with its sight memory, down across her belly and through her pubic hair, to the smooth, firm flesh of her inner thigh. I bit that tendon lightly, wanting to move into the apex, but the thought that someone else could have recently contributed to that pungent odor moved me back across her belly, to her breasts. She waited, not overly eager, just eighteen, watching as my left hand slid over her vagina, the middle finger searching, spreading, finding. She jerked slightly, pulling closer. I hit her button a couple more times, my own mind screaming, knowing exactly how long it would take me to come. As I entered, the warmth of her body drew me like a poultice, all my plumbing pumping, pulsing, frying another eleven million brain cells in a clumsy attempt to stop time. Sally lay there, waiting.

"Christ," I said, "what's the use."

I got off her and stood beside the bed, the sound of traffic faint behind the glass. Something that simple, I thought, and I had to twist the life out of it. It could have been a lot of things, especially enjoyable. No love for this blink.

Sally slid over to run a fingernail up the inside of my thigh.

"Christ, what can I say? I guess I just waited too long. I might just be screwed up too. I don't know."

She waited on the bed while I went to the bathroom, took a leak, and washed my wart off at the sink—almost an accusation, but what the hell. I was six months down the road, getting tough, alone.

When I returned, Sally had moved to a sitting position on the side of the bed.

"God," she said. "You sure came a lot."

Digging a handkerchief from my pants pocket, I handed it to her. She used it, then handed it back. I let it drop to the floor and stood there, silence beginning to throb in the room, the smell of semen heavy.

"I guess I better go," she said.

She dressed quickly, and as she pulled her jeans on, blood rushed to my crotch. I tried to ignore it, but Sally looked and stopped her dressing, running that fingernail up my thigh again, circling my brains. I remembered the woman, the neighbor behind my house in Flatfield, standing in her kitchen window.

"Well, I guess I better go."

She stood, zipping her jeans. My skull fought for something, amends I guess, or male pride, wanting it only because it was leaving, repossessed because of a bad performance. But I said nothing.

"See you tomorrow, Patrick."

"Yeah, see you."

She gave me a light peck on the mouth, then the door closed, and I listened to her trot down the hall. I was still standing there, beside the bed, hard, thinking how screwed it could really be sometimes.

I went to the bed then, kneeling, my face to the window screen, traffic cruising by in the distance, each cell complete with its own aches. My mouth opened for something, then closed again.

SIX

If nothing else, the affair with Sally gave me a bottom to bounce off, and true to form, the ascent took its own twisted course. Her odor lingered on the sheets, prodding my memory repeatedly with fits of anguish. I poked holes through that plastic piss cover all night long, and Saturday morning found me, hard-on in hand, begging for the sound of her footsteps trotting up the hall. Not for an elbow down to breakfast either. Christ, I was cured of that.

Remorse had finally burned through the veil of idiocy, manipulating my hormones into a rebellious mass, chanting to the logic of their primal drums. A touch of the ego lingered too, the humiliation of feeling the fool, but it was barely a trickle of cold water along the spine, and without classes to occupy my cranial cavity, my lusting for the *funichingilario* assumed all the proportions of any other simple obsession. Sensual Sally had been reduced to a vaginal fixation. All the boy wanted was another shot in the sack, a good, hearty overdose of yackey. Think of it as therapy, clean the tubes, man, and to hell with Love. I could figure that out when I got well, along with everything else.

In between hard-ons, I practiced mobility on the school grounds, out to the curb, down the snakewalk and back. As my circle of mobility expanded, so did my confidence. The urge to propagate was hanging in there too, craving something like complete immersion, balls and all, but as I tapped my way back to the dorm, a surge of purification convinced me there would be much more to life than the vaginal curse. I could classify that under basic consumption, surface rhythms of the eyeball kind.

This buoyant mood continued into the stairwell, but as I climbed, the worm squirmed. Something very peculiar. I stood on the top step, then walked back down, and then up again. I walked those goddamn stairs six times in a row. And each time, by all my calculations, the second floor sat perpendicular to the first. I knew they were parallel too, by external sounds, but something in that stairwell, the turn half way up, the way I

51

walked it, the way sound curled counterclockwise off the walls, definitely had the worm's number. It didn't matter, of course, as long as it worked, angles weren't for blinks, angles were for regulars. I still had my room and bed and bathroom facilities and a way to get there. But the damage had already been done. All practical applications would seem strange, functioning without angles, yet knowing, through my lingering sight memory, that the real world was different.

The gym provided some relief later that afternoon, quiet, peaceful, empty. I pushed iron, nothing too strenuous, just staying busy, lots of reps, force-feeding my skull a different rhythm. Then, after dinner, I rolled a joint and headed out the snakewalk to commune with the waterfall. It dabbled its invite. I crossed the lawn, fired the joint, leaned on the top rail of the fence and listened to the light slap of water falling from the culvert into the pool below. Thoughts of the sea moved in, with its unseen power. In comparison, the mountains seemed almost civilized, their secrets available. They held the infant waters, soft and babbling, and the winter's menstrual cycle, all those extremes of seasons, the visual things. Jesus, if you had never seen it, would it be there, or would it all be like the angles of the stairwell?

The answer was obvious enough. The worm would keep two sets of books. But how the hell did you replace something like the Sierras in June, the ground saturated with the thaw, and every color of the spectrum pushing free through it—or Caribou Lake and behind it, Caribou Peak, a conical white except where the dark, rough streaks of granite protruded through the snow. I had camped there one spring day, looking at its image mirrored, all of it so perfectly absorbed by the lake's surface, and marred only by the plunk of my sinker and fishing line. If I'd been born blind, would any of it matter?

I stayed out there for two hours, drifting, listening to the traffic. Night, I thought. I'm yours, uninvited, a little loaded, very much a part of the dark. As I crossed back to the snakewalk, a couple of trees got in my way and I had to work them over with the stick a bit before they would move. When my theatrics ended, I collected my scattered senses, took direction off the sound of traffic again, and headed back. In my room, Mother Night and my slick-haired buddy were waiting for me on the windowsill.

"You're just an amateur," they said. "You want to see some real twisting, just stick around."

Sundays can spin your onion all by themselves. They ain't even recess. They're an illusion, soaking in skim milk all day. In my past life, the eyeball stage, hangovers had always conveniently obliterated those weird time delays.

Just before 8:00, a van hauled off a few quiet, peaceful, god-fearing residents to their respective services. Traffic on the avenue crept quietly by in bonnets and bowed heads. By all means give them god, I thought. Tell them god takes care of everything. Chapter 6 of the Adipose manual, Faith. They had it right up there with High Fidelity and Baseball, Hotdogs, Apple Pie, and Hand Grenades.

I had just never noticed Sundays before, I guess. Like stepping out of the cave some morning to find everyone prancing about in tutus and pointed shoes. Fighting my own lucid demons had always, at least, offered some internal sense of reality. It was obvious to me that morning that Sundays were what made Milwaukee famous.

After breakfasting on cornflakes, I sat at the writing desk with the window open. The door was open behind me, waiting for some sound of activity, but blinkdom slept. In front of me, on the desk, I had Louis Braille's contribution to life. He had done a lot for blinks. Technology had done a lot, but Louis had done more with his braille cell. Six little dots, two vertical rows of three. Every letter in the alphabet came from one or more of those dots in different combinations—conjunctions, contractions, punctuation, numbers, shorthand, everything out of six small bumps. They made sense, too. The first ten characters, A to J, were constructed from the top four dots. K through T repeated the same sequence, with the addition of dot three in the first row. The final six characters followed the sequence adding dot six, with the exception of one letter, W. That was Louis's only fuckup, the only character out of place, the only one in his entire alphabet that strayed from the rhythm, and by itself, as a contraction, it stood for World.

So there was the world, at my fingertip, a mute world within arm's reach. To a regular it looks like sand scattered on a blank page. To the fingertip, it might be a love letter. And outside that radius, my ears moved. They could see around things, through things, beyond the traffic to whistles and wind and air buses—eyes looking down at eyes looking up. The sound of a quarter dropping to the floor rang different from that of a dime or penny. The sound of the mind hitting bottom is very quiet, personal.

I tapped on over to the gym again that afternoon, looking forward to a session with the weights. As I entered, three voices drifted across from the weight corner. Lance from homeroom was one. The others were new, a husky black with a cigarette rasp and the third gentle, another happy blink. I hung my cane on the rack by the door and started across.

"Hey man, what's hap'nin'?" the black voice called.

Max, the happy blink, answered him. We all laughed.

"Ain't that somethin'," Max said. "I thought he was talkin' to me."

"You're goofy," Lance said, adding his three-note snicker. "You've been standin' here for half an hour."

"Yeah, I know. Ain't that somethin'? I never know who's talkin' to who."

Following the cordials, I put 150 pounds on the bench press and worked it. Carter, the husky voice, did most of the bullshitting, trying to entertain.

"Yeah," he sighed. "I bin here almost two weeks now, takin' it easy though, if you know what I mean. I ain't found nothin' to soak my cock in yet, and I definitely got to take care of the man thing, before I get down to anything strenuous, like studyin'."

"Ain't that somethin'," Max said. "Ol' Carter's got to get some pussy before he can do anything else."

"Hey, that ain't no shit," Carter said. "I'd even settle for some stick pussy. Two years in the penitentiary makes a man hungry, if you hear where I'm comin' from."

"Shit," Lance said. "I got me some the first day I was here."

"Man, I don't wanna hear them lies."

Lance snickered.

"She's a fox too, man. Nice titties, real nice butt."

"What's her name, man?" Carter said.

"Got some head too, man, everything. She's nice."

"Well tell me her muthafuckin' name. What're you gonna do, keep it a secret?"

"I got that one nailed down, man," Lance said. "She's mine."

"If this ain't a bitch," Carter said, smacking the speedbag. "Not only is he stingy with his who'e, he's even afraid to tell us her name."

"Her name's Sally, man. But it ain't gonna do you no good. She's mine."

"Shiiiit, man. How you gonna act. What's this world comin' to, when a man won't even share his who'e."

I added another twenty pounds and pushed into it hard, just to keep from laughing, or crying. Carter batted at the speedbag, carrying on the whole time like he was pissed at Lance, then he decided it was time for a show of the testicles.

"You just fuckin' the dog over there, Patrick. Lemme put a couple quarters on there, see what you can do. You guys too. C'mon. Let's git in on this, see who's got it, and who don't."

"I think I'll pass," Max said.

"You're gonna have to pass. Shiiit. I didn't think we had any pussies in here."

"He ain't no pussy," Lance said. "We were in here a couple weeks ago, benchin', and he popped one of his eyeballs."

"Oh man, don't give me that shit."

"It's no shit. I was standin' right here. Scared the hell outa me, too."

"It hemorrhaged," Max said.

"Yeah, whatever," Lance snickered. "They had an ambulance here and everything."

"It don't look popped to me," Carter said.

"Ahh, it's no big deal," Max said. "It was just a hemorrhage. They gave me an alcohol block, kept me overnight, and I was back here the next day for classes. They're no good for anything anyway. I told 'em to go ahead and take it out, but the doc said I oughta wait till I'm done here, 'cause it might lay me up awhile."

Carter orchestrated the weights, adding ten pounds a clip. Lance was probably in the best shape, for his size, short, 145 pounds. He dropped out at 210. I got 250 pretty easy, but faked it, straining, and let Carter blow his asshole off, getting 255. He came off the bench, strutting, blowing, trying to get his breath.

"All right," he said. "The Kingpin."

Lance and Max snickered. Carter swatted the speedbag again.

"What'd you say that chick's name was?"

"It ain't gonna do you no good," Lance said.

"Goddamn. It's four o'clock already," Carter said. "That's time for cocktails, ain't it? I deserve one after that."

"What do you use," Max said, "a pocket watch or wristwatch?"

"Shit. I ain't got no watch, man. There's a clock on that wall, down at the other end. If I had a watch, I'd hock that muthafucker and have me a party with Sally baby."

The face of a clock, white with black hands and numbers, sat like a moon in my mind. Four o'clock, the hands said, black and white, like the old school clocks on the wall behind the teacher's desk.

Max stayed behind as the other two left. We listened to them exit, Carter still jabbering, Lance snickering.

"What do you think about that?" I said. "That fucker can see pretty good for a blink."

"Yeah, he must be a partial, like some of these other kids, you know? Losin' it a little at a time. Took me a year to lose it, 'fore it got bad enough anyway. I never thought it'd get that bad, you know? Not all the way."

"Yeah. I shouldn't get on 'im, I guess. Maybe it's just 'cause he's black and an ex-con. He's probably got his own head-trips."

"Yeah," Max said.

"So I'll give 'im an even blink's chance, anyway, huh?"

I worked out for another half hour, shootin' the breeze with Max between sets. He had just turned fifty, had nine kids, two still at home and three grandkids a loose daughter had dropped off. No insurance, no retirement. Said he had wholesaled cars for thirty years, too proud to accept aid.

"Ahh. It's no big deal. I'll figure somethin' out," he said. "I can always sell cars."

We left together, Max a step behind, on my left, his cane worrying my boot like a pup. His room was directly across from the stairwell.

"Cheesus, Pat. I don't know how you guys do it," he said. "And you're a total too, huh?"

"Black as night."

"Cheesus, ain't that somethin'? I've been here over a month and I still can't find my way around."

I dozed for a while and woke to the sound of blinks cheering down in the courtyard. I checked my watch, 5:40, and jumped. Christ, I had almost missed dinner. The cornflakes that morning hadn't been enough to generate a fart.

Downstairs, I found the alcove outside the dorm packed with blink bodies. Damond had his act out in front, crowing his negative bullshit about somebody. I sort of nudged my way through the crowd, excusing myself. Max was right in the middle.

"Hey, Patrick. What's happenin', buddy?"

"What the hell you guys got goin' out here, a fight?"

"No no no. Geri's out there roller skating. Wally and Willy are the ones making all the noise. I guess they're chasing her."

A set of skates made the corner in front of us, and headed toward the cafeteria. Wally and Willy weren't far behind, flapping along the back of the classrooms like a couple of geese in heat. They were just noise at the time, all three young, by their voices, early twenties I guessed. Wally and Willy were twins. In love with Geri, I suppose, or giving it a good shot anyway.

"Cheesus," Max said. "Listen to that. You hear her, Pat? Ain't that somethin'? I can't even walk around there by myself. Listen. Here she comes again. She's movin' too, ain't she? Never seen a day in her life, Wally and Willy neither. Ain't that somethin'?"

The skates were making about two laps to one of the runners, with some general squealing and grab-assing in between. Skating and running by ear, sounds and echoes.

When I entered, the cafeteria sounded empty except for some tinkering back in the kitchen. A warm body finally heard my call and emerged, a bit surly.

"You don't have to yell. I saw you."

56

"I'm sorry. I must've lost my mind for a minute there. I get that way when I have to wait."

She loaded me up with cold cuts, cheese, and bread, white or wheat. I grabbed a couple of cartons of milk and sat at the first table next to the silverware rack. Nobody used that table, so it suited me fine. Their affiliations were farther down on either side, the "creeps" and the "cools," most of them still strangers to me. We would all be leaving before long. They would rattle us loose onto the wind like dandelion seed, and we would blow off in different directions.

Outside, the sounds of the audience and performers had petered out. I made two dagwoods and bit in, wishing them all luck. Never saw a day in their life, I thought. Jesus, and all I had to do was make it through a Sunday. I could sleep through the rest of it. Those six months suddenly seemed so short, chunked into the weeks, studying, exercising, moving, and the quicksand Sundays.

Laughter on the other side of the glass interrupted my programming, a woman, almost familiar, then the cafeteria door swung open and I knew it belonged to Sally. My wart did a little flip-flop and smiled as she passed my perch, but she didn't respond. She got her tray and silverware and moved through the line, whispering to another warm body, some guy, the next in line, I thought. Both of them sounded gassed. A final pang of idiocy hit me dead center, then shattered and fell to the floor, a little hollow, but moving.

Sally paraded around the barricade with her tray and parked next to me, leaning over to smear a wet smooch across my cheek.

"I want you to meet my friend Michael," she said.

Jesus, her breath would have scared a dog.

"Hi, Patrick," Michael said.

He had parked opposite Sally, and took my hand like a partial. Good hand, good breath too. They got their feet going under the table then, both of them giggling. I hurried to finish my second sandwich so I could get the hell out of there. Christ, I thought I would get sick, Sally squirming next to me there like she had a couple of caterpillars in her shorts.

"Michael and I've been out finding bars all weekend, Patrick. Haven't we, Michael."

Michael managed a weak chuckle through his sandwich.

"Well, maybe not all weekend. Huh, Michael. We did some other things too."

They both hit the giggles again, their feet getting spastic. All I could think of was myself, standing there beside my bed with a hard-on.

"Michael's a real good bar finder, Patrick."

"That's great," I said. "I'm glad you guys had a good time."

They continued to coo and eye-screw each other, then Michael's toes got lost and started working up the front of my boot. I laughed and they jerked away.

It was gone then, everything, like I had wrapped it up in a paper sack and dropped it in a garbage can somewhere along the way and moved on. I could see the two of them, Sally and Michael, walking the avenue, arm in arm, with their partial sight. Cocktail signs flashed bright, their white glasses and red cherries and golden, electric bubbles. Then it began to fade and grow smoky. The two of them still arm in arm and all about, everything turned the color of granite, with those sterile neon advertisements gathering about them. I would rather lose it all at once, I thought. Loitering like that would damn sure spin my onion off its axis.

I bussed my tray, said good-bye to the new lovers as I passed, and outside, Sunday had packed its dogma back into the briefcase, loosened its tie, and headed for the office. A light breeze off the bay carried a touch of mudflats. I really did have it made, for the moment anyway. Not enough to laugh yet, but it was on its way. I could feel it, like Mother Night coming down the avenue, her black arms spread wide, herding the day's colors indoors to their electric lights. Time slows, everything slows, waiting. All that and never having seen a day in their lives. Jesus.

My slick-haired buddy leaned against a pole just outside the dorm entrance, grinning, fooling with that toothpick. What the hell, I thought. Grab another joint and meet Mother Night on the snakewalk. Let her take me on another trip through the sound of water. What the hell's the difference. It's all in the head. I thought of Sally and Michael again, out there on the avenue, arm in arm, sign to sign, as Mother Night overtook them, their granite-gray world growing dim, dusky, then dark. I wondered how high they would bounce when they hit bottom.

SEVEN

Blinks were no different than any flock of regulars out there on the avenue. We had quarterbacks and wide receivers dying for the flash and instant heroics. Others were down in the trenches, waiting for some regular to get the ball and call their slot. We had spectators and waterboys, commentators, cheerleaders, dissenters. Segregation was practiced in the dorm, just as it was in the cafeteria. Partials had declared the west half of our second floor upper class. They were all diabetics, all of them going bankrupt, watching their precious sight turn to smoke while they lounged under their private dark cloud, refusing to acknowledge their coming status as blinks.

My end, the east end, had a hell of a lot more going for it. We were mongrels—accident victims, congenitals, and a whole damn refrigerator full of diseases: glaucoma, retinitis pigmentosa, retrolental fibroplasia. Christ, you needed a medical dictionary to tell who you were talking to. To precious sight, we were living death, but like everything else in the animal world, we tried to sweat some essence of our own.

Just like sight, sound doesn't always carry clear. You have to pay attention to catch identifiers. My can-mate, Reno, sounded very similar to Maurice, a black guy in room seventeen across the hall. Maurice was losing it slowly through multiple sclerosis. Reno, only thirty years old, had suffered a stroke that rendered his whole left side paralyzed. Their vocal cords stretched in the same direction, dragging across a gravel bar, making them sound like good-natured drunks. When they laughed it looped out in slow motion, like some happy, fat-bellied butterfly you could chase down and catch in a jar.

I came in from the snakewalk one evening and damn near tripped over Maurice. He and Reno had planted themselves in the hall opposite each other, their backs to the wall, their legs stretched out in front. My worm was off in its own apple somewhere, and when my cane hit Maurice's leg, I skidded to a near stop, spun 'er to port, and hit Reno's leg. They both cracked up.

"What the hell're you guys drinkin'?" I said.

"I ain't drinkin' nothin'," Maurice said. "I'm just pretendin'."

They laughed again, like they'd just learned how.

"I wish I was drinkin'," Reno said. "I'd be out there doin' it too, if it wasn't such a pain in the ass. My left side loves to go, but after I feed it a couple drinks, it hates to come back."

"What do you do," I said, "stand there and spin in circles?"

They laughed again. I listened to it roll down the hall toward that dark cloud.

"I'll trade with you a couple nights a week, if you want," Maurice said.

"The only thing I'd trade for," Reno said, "is your pecker. Mine only gets hard on the one side."

The identical congenitals, Wally and Willy, could sneak up on you too. I had heard them around, but had never spoken with either, and one morning Lance and I wound up behind them in chowline. Acoustics in the cafeteria made it difficult to zero in anyway. My head ached too and I leaned close, trying to hear Lance carry on about some old girlfriend, some chick with a huge patch of pubic hair. He had to punctuate everything with his three-note snicker.

"It's no shit, man. It grew up all the way past 'er bellybutton, 'n' I was loaded one night, trippin' on it, 'n' told 'er it was gonna keep on growin' till it covered her whole body. I think she's Italian."

My right ear tried to follow, but the left strayed up ahead a few bodies, where the twins argued about a goddamn bottle of shampoo. It sounded like one guy getting ready for a new straitjacket.

"You hear that going on up there?" I said.

"Yeah, what about it?" he said, pissed that I had interrupted his story.

"The boy's a little strange, ain't he? Maybe it's the food."

"That's the twins, man."

Gwenda made an appointment for me to open a braille checking account that second week. I met her Tuesday afternoon at 3:00, grabbed an elbow, and headed out across the avenue to the Brookings Plaza. The old film ran as we walked through the complex, Ball's Drugs, Emerson's. Barbecued breath off the charbroiler in Chin's Hof Brau floated out across the sidewalk. Just beyond it, outside the bank's electric door, a woman stopped us.

"I'm sorry to bother you," she said to Gwenda, "but I've seen you out here so many times working with these people, I just wanted to tell you how much I admire you. I sit there at my desk and think how wonderful it must be, and how dull and boring my own job is. I bet you get a lot of gratification from this, don't you?"

"You bet," Gwenda said. "Every two weeks, when they lay that pay-check in my greedy little clutcher."

The woman paused, her wheels spinning, then she barked out a quick laugh.

"Oh," she said, "oh yes, well god bless you, both of you."

The appointment went fast. Security Pacific was the only bank offering braille accounts, and it was easy enough, a hundred bucks to open, a couple of signatures. I had my choice of checks from an assortment of background scenery, Muir Woods, early California missions, wildlife.

"How 'bout something in basic black," I said.

"Don't look at me," Gwenda said. "He's the one opening the account."

The bank officer cleared her throat, turning to look across at me.

"All right," I said. "How 'bout something white then, with a pair of shades in the background."

Gwenda's raucous laugh held the moment's hush as the bank personalities and their mumbling patrons turned to look. Then the machine rolled on again, the practiced banter, the titter of pens and shuffling feet. Gwenda picked up the book of sample checks and flipped through the pages.

"This one's nice," she said. "He'll take that."

Back outside, I voiced my complaint.

"It's got mountains on it," she said, "it's really you."

"Bullshit," I said. "Why's it have to have anything on it?"

"Because a nice-looking check will hold someone's attention, and whether you're visual or not, you've got to play the part. You've got to control the situation as much as possible, and visually oriented things help people relax. If you don't like it, fine. I was just trying to be helpful."

"God bless you."

"Yes, you got it, baby. That's it exactly, and there's a lot of them too. They think I'm out here training you guys, like dogs. They're the ones I should be teaching, them and the parents who hide their kids in closets for twenty years and expect us to change them in six months."

Chin's charbroiler hooked a finger up my nostril as we approached, squeezing my salivary glands. I could imagine dark shapes inside, bent over the counter, elbows planted, mouths wide to receive the big burg-ers—lettuce, tomato, red onion, cheese, and a mixture of juice, mayon-naise, and grease dripping off the bun.

"So they're a little screwed up," I said. "They'll make it. Everybody's a little screwed up."

"More than just a little in most cases, Patrick. Not everybody makes it to the Olympics, you know. The ones that come out of closets go right back into them when they finish here."

"Do you drink?" I said.

"That depends on what you have in mind."

"They got good cold beer here at Chin's."

"Yes, I'll bet they do," she said, "but if I'm going to drink, it's not going to be in a hamburger joint. C'mon, we'll go this way."

We hung a right and crossed the plaza, weaving through shade and sun, past shoppers and kids scampering by, testing their lungs and new sneakers. On the far side, we entered Petar's steakhouse. A carpeted hall took us past the dining room, toward the lounge.

"You're not eighty-sixed from here, are you? I hate surprises."

"Christ," I said. "I don't know. After a while they all look the same."

We sat at a small, tire-sized table against the back wall. The cocktail waitress was a little loud with her cologne, maybe because the place was empty. Mix her into a crowd, she would probably even out. Gwenda ordered a Beck's and a shot of Christian Brothers.

"What does he want?" the waitress said.

Gwenda ignored her and began whistling. I decided the cologne was probably in place of a shower.

"I'll have the same," I said, "thanks."

Dentist music parachuted down from overhead speakers. The bartender popped the tops on our Becks at the near end of the bar.

"You'll have to get used to that, you know," Gwenda said, "until people get used to you, until they know you."

The cologne returned with our drinks, leaning across to set my beer down. Quick light footsteps trotted out of memory and I raised my shot glass.

"To C.I.B.," I said. "It's done a lot for me already."

"Sure," Gwenda said. "To good ol' C.I.B. and staff, and don't forget, we're all getting paid to be nice."

"Let's not forget the files either."

"Whatever," she said, then slugged her shot down, sipped the Beck's and smacked her lips.

"I've already thought about leaving, too," I said.

"Oh really."

"I mean in six months, just so I don't get too attached to the place."

"And I think I'm going to be leaving about the same time. I'm just about blinked out."

"We oughta have another shot then, if it's that painful."

"We will, in a minute," she said, "and don't get me wrong. Some students are worth it, you know. The rest are just there on vacation."

The waitress brought my change in a small tray and set it down. Her cologne revived two other faces in the old film, one in Denver, one in Centralia, Washington. There were better jobs.

"You know," Gwenda said, "our good friend Bernice is doing her damndest to bring charges against me for playing favorites."

"Why? Because you teach cooking along with everything else?"

"Exactly. And I told Stan too, you're damn right I'm playing favorites. There's two or three students in the whole damn school who have a chance to make it. Which reminds me, have you met Geri yet?"

"Nope."

"I'm surprised."

"I heard her roller skating the other day."

"There's a little gal who's going places, and I don't mean on skates either. You'll meet her, but anyway, getting back to dear friend Bernice—"

"Who's the third?" I said.

"Lance. But I worry about him sometimes."

"So you saved us all from certain death, huh?"

"You're damn right I did. That woman's a closet case herself. She's right at home with those pants pissers, and I don't want to sound like I'm bragging, but there are things I can do for you guys that she can't, and Stan knows it."

Bodies had been filtering into the lounge, small groups, lobbing salutations about the room. The waitress hurried back and forth, stirring her cologne into the air, a sad smell, I thought. Maybe that's why I had never cared for it. I would rather taste their sweat. Across the table, Gwenda continued to clean her professional hamper out, politics, all the smiling faces drawing state paychecks, scraping blinks out of closets to fill the rooms because the Department of Rehabilitation was on their ass threatening to close the school. And me, always considering her in the buff. I just didn't know any better, never had a woman as a friend. I finished my beer then and checked my watch, 4:30.

"To hell with them," Gwenda said. "They don't have to know what kind of mobility lesson we're on."

"If it's up to me, I'll keep you here till two," I said. "I don't want you catching hell on my account. You've been a big help, you know. I mean it."

"Let's not start gushing, Patrick. They might pay me well, but besides that, I deserve it. Eight years is enough too, and if I stay, I'll just wind up like the rest of them."

Our waitress blew by, and I whistled to get her attention.

"Can we get another round here, when you get time? Did she hear me?" I said to Gwenda.

"I don't think she likes us. She heard you though. She waved."

As the room continued to fill with voices, the air tightened. Single sounds became one constant drone, cracked here and there by laughter. Gwenda bought the second round. The shot hit home, bullying its way back up into my face, pumped with alcohol honesty. I had to lean forward, closer to Gwenda, as I attempted to explain the sexual thing, the difference. She laughed.

"Maybe I'm just warped that way," I said, "but I've never sat in a bar with a woman before, drinking, without thinking something about the rest of the night."

"So what are you trying to tell me?"

"Just that I've never had a woman as a friend before. It ain't a pass, or anything like that. I just wanted you to know, 'cause it's important to me. It's a change."

She didn't respond, so I took a long swig off my beer, then leaned forward.

"Christ," I said, "just forget it then. Cheers. I was just trying to clean my skull up a bit. It's no big deal. I'll keep my mouth shut."

The air seemed strained between us then, the other sound crowding, pushing us up against the wall. I couldn't hear Gwenda, when she spoke, until I leaned forward and she repeated it, slow, articulate.

"I said, Do you know how to read a face."

"That's all right," I said. "I don't need to do that."

"C'mon, give me your hand."

She grasped my right wrist. I let her pull the hand toward her face and spread the fingers, like the branches of a tree.

"Okay," she said, "now just move it down slowly. See here, how your thumb and little finger ride across the cheekbones. They'll sense the general shape. Your ring and index fingers here sense the brow ridge, then the eyes, and your middle finger continues down the center, along the nose, then they all come together, closing across the mouth and chin. Go ahead, do it again by yourself."

Voices to our immediate left stopped to watch. My fingers moved down. Gwenda's eyes closed under them. Her face seemed small, heart shaped, the nose straight, small maybe, the eyes large, blue I thought. Her lower lip gave slightly as I touched her mouth, not full, but soft, bringing the cranial worm erect.

"Thanks," I said. "That was nice. I was a virgin."

When she laughed, I connected the sound to the face, her mouth open and the eyes almost a picture.

"You know," she said, "when I started this job it was different. I had such great ideals, all my wonderful goals of working with people. I was going to school, living in the Haight, and I'd dream about doing these things. I believed in them too, enough to spend six years there, just barely surviving. I did a lot of protesting. My only brother was killed in that fucking war. But you know, when I think about it now, the thing I remember most is this little Chinese restaurant. I'd go to the back door almost every day to buy a dish of peas from the cook. It was about the size of a cereal dish, maybe a little smaller. He'd charge me six or seven cents, sometimes a dime, but never any more than that. He didn't speak English, I didn't speak Chinese, but he knew there were a lot of days that dish of peas was the only thing I had to eat. So anyway, it all seemed connected, you know, the giving. I had to suffer first, before I could change the world. I'd attend my classes at San Francisco State, eat my dish of peas, do my protesting, and try to forget my brother was dead. I think that's why I remember the peas so much. It's funny too. I never remember the letter my mother sent, or the funeral, just those damn peas and how they taste without butter, or salt and pepper, and how much I loved my brother."

I sipped my beer, giddy with the exchange. I wondered about the other voices in the room, what they were talking about.

"He used to call me Weeds," she said. "He'd send me a letter every week or two. I told him I was a flower child and when he wrote back, he started addressing the letters to Weeds McCafferty. That's my maiden name."

I don't know why I laughed. Maybe because Gwenda sniffled loudly, and I was thinking about that damn room full of people, then Gwenda chimed in, both of us laughing, her really cracking it off like a mallard hen on eggs. Our foreheads almost touched, me trying to explain why I'd started laughing, her describing the faces, the heads around us, staring, then we both leaned back and let it go, let it blow itself out.

After the rush, we finished our beers and made our exit into warmer air, through the evening's shoppers and down the sloped parking lot toward the avenue. My cheeks still ached.

"That was fun," Gwenda said. "I'm glad we did it."

"It's good to get a little crazy once in a while," I said. "It's good for the brains."

"Yes, I know, and just in case somebody's watching, let's get back to business here. You see if you can remember your lesson for today, and I'll follow."

I laughed and tapped off in front of her. At the avenue I waited through the light sequence twice, listening to the moves, the regulars in front of me confined to their lights and lines. Booze dissolves fear, the skull relaxes, enough for sounds to distinguish themselves, a false confidence maybe, but it cuts the nerves and the twisting that blurs the image.

Cars panted at the line, and as I waded through their hot breath, I turned, smiling at the faces behind the knuckled wheels. Weeds joined me on the other side.

"Not bad for a blink," she said. "It doesn't appear you're going to have much trouble getting around. Just don't get back into your old habits, huh?"

"That's all lies anyway," I said. "I never did any of it."

I ate alone that evening at my antisocial table, still a little flushed but comfortable with the change. I had never set any goals in my own life other than living, but I liked the new action in my skull. I liked those quick, light feet and that heart-shaped face with the big eyes and soft mouth. It was close to seeing, touching like that. Enough to make you ache for some things, the personals, when the world shrunk soft about you. It seemed then that something I would really miss would be the face of a child, if I ever fathered one. To hold a kiddo there in your arms, to look down and hope that little skull didn't twist up ugly inside.

EIGHT

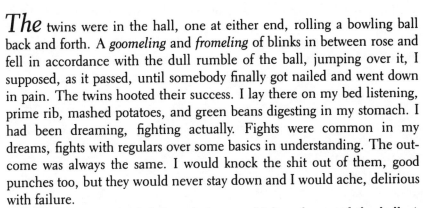

The twins were in the hall, one at either end, rolling a bowling ball back and forth. A *goomeling* and *fromeling* of blinks in between rose and fell in accordance with the dull rumble of the ball, jumping over it, I supposed, as it passed, until somebody finally got nailed and went down in pain. The twins hooted their success. I lay there on my bed listening, prime rib, mashed potatoes, and green beans digesting in my stomach. I had been dreaming, fighting actually. Fights were common in my dreams, fights with regulars over some basics in understanding. The outcome was always the same. I would knock the shit out of them, good punches too, but they would never stay down and I would ache, delirious with failure.

After the injury the kids lost their sugar high and vacated the hall. A hot Wednesday evening strutted by out on the avenue, hair combed, shoes polished, oblivious. I had to do something. Lying there alone, awake, made the worm squirm. So for lack of another remedy, I grabbed my cane and headed out, clean, no joint. Grass eased the headaches and the constant burning I felt in my right eye but it lingered too long, sometimes in the wrong places.

As the snakewalk curved under my boots, I got outside the pain with a flight through my past. Mile after mile of old highway rolled by on film. Mountain passes, LaVita, Rabbit Ears, Cedar Pass, Hatchett, and Donner. Black timber at dawn against the snow, aspen graveyards of the Colorado Rockies, Siskiyou high desert yawning south along Interstate 5 off Mt. Ashland, all the times, all the promises to stop someday and walk to that place over there, check it out, but miles had always been so crucial to the worm.

At the fence, I rested my arms on the top rail and concentrated on a hunting camp, Twelve Mile Creek, and its canyon cracking the high desert just north of Fort Bidwell. Thick, green scars of aspen coursed the creeks or huddled like vagrants around springheads on the slopes, their fresh, lively color contrasting sharply with that distant desolation of sage and mahogany. Where the canyon forked, a steep bluff rose like the crown of a Stetson, rimmed with a black line of ancient lava. Arrowheads and spent cavalry cartridges washed free each year on the flats along game trails. And along the creeks, wide gray flanks of old aspen sported knife-work names and dates that had grown gnarled, scabbed with age. Summer bled everything together like watercolors from a distance, but up close the twisted sage bore thin purple feathers, skunk cabbage toasted tan and brittle, and in higher thickets, where ruffed grouse burst from tangles of chokecherry to cock a dark eye from the sheltering limbs of nearby spruce, bead-sized berries dangled crimson, bitter.

The trail along Twelve Mile led up the canyon to Dismal Swamp. Beaver dams checked the stream, and in their calm waters, rainbow trout looked back, waiting. Bathing there left the body tight-skinned, with a walnut-shell scrotum, and at night, bedded beside that clear crisp chant of creek waters, the Indians returned, Modocs, and with them a longing, that lost smoke off dead ashes just before sleep.

Five golden eagles kept watch over the canyon the last time I walked it, a brood pair and three young, and in the early light of one dawn, while color still slept, I made my way up the north face, through thin black ribs of spruce and fir, then crawling through the tangle of white thorn and buckbrush that clung beneath the rimrock. I met the sun that morning on the eagle's ledge, beside their stick-pile nest. Three states touched in front of me, California, Oregon, and Nevada. On my left, below, Twelve Mile Creek ran silent, sectioned like a tapeworm by the beaver dams, and off the bluff, sage flats lay strewn about like patchwork quilts the dogs had dragged out. Beyond these lower slopes, to the southeast, an alkali flat, the arid eye socket of a dead lake, stretched south some ten miles toward Cedarville. That part of the valley floor was vacant, except at the extreme north end, where Twelve Mile protruded in a short tongue of greenery. There, beside that faint patch of life, a gaunt two-story ranch house stood like a grave mark.

All five eagles rode the walls of a thermal above the bluff, fly specks against the new day. Among other things, the ledge was strewn with the bones of small prey. I picked up the two-inch-long jawbone of a coyote pup and studied the tiny white pointed teeth, loosely fastened in dried tissue. I imagined the puppies snarling, rolling in soft, cool earth just outside the dark maw of their birthplace, the one I held lost to a rush of wings. Below the slopes, the ranch house came alive, a thin brown cattail of smoke arching up over its back.

So what the hell, I thought. I would take a bunch of blinks in there some day, follow the creek in, make camp. I could describe the whole damn thing, the canyon, the valley. They could touch things and skinny

68

dip, and around the campfire at night, with animal entertainment splashing in the background, I could tell them stories, bear stories, make them shit.

Ants, thousands of them, suddenly cut my trip short. That fence rail must have been the freeway to an ant orgy, and I had blocked it. Christ, I had them everywhere, my face, my neck, in my hair, and as I dusted their little bodies from mine, they cursed violently, vowing revenge.

"We're everywhere," they screamed, "and wherever you go, we'll be there."

The dispute settled, for the moment anyway, I stuck a chew of tobacco in my lip and decided it was time to move, find that bench out at the avenue and make it my ledge, take in the show.

The hardest part of finding something in the dark is the last few feet, when the immediate world narrows to the radius of your cane. I had expected to bump right into the damn bench, but found myself instead on open pavement, cars slashing by ten feet away, their sound curving south, taking my sonar with it. So I stood there bent, like a loaded old man, my cane reaching out, probing, my soft skull straining against the question of why sound curves in the first fucking place, and all those lucky bastards driving by with their eyeballs.

In the middle of this idiocy, I straightened and laughed.

"You dumb bastard," I said quietly. "They're gonna lock you up some day for being a visual nuisance."

An undercover ant made a break for it across my ear. I pinched him, then took a couple steps to my right, looking for an edge, lawn, anything.

"How's it going, man?"

This goddamn voice was no more than five feet from me, right there, hanging in the middle of sound. I jumped like I was snakebit, then attempted a laugh.

"Jesus," I said. "Not bad, I guess, considering I just shit down both legs. I was just lookin' for the damn bench. You sittin' on it?"

No answer. Goddamn pedestrian, I thought. Asshole. Watching me play clock. No footsteps though. Maybe the cars got them.

"You sittin' on the bench there?" I said.

My words soaked quickly into the sound, gone, unanswered.

"You dumb sonofabitch," I said again. "They will lock you up some day."

I faded right then, found the pavement edge, followed it left around a bush and hit the bench. I was only a couple feet away from it the whole time, and as I planted my cheeks, I could have sworn somebody was sitting at the other end. Nah, I thought, that's just your soft skull again, but seconds later a lull in the traffic made it very obvious. I could sense the body, and when I poked my cane in that direction, it hit something soft, a leg.

"Well kiss my ass," I said. "You're about a sociable sonofabitch, aren't you? What's a matter? You got something against blinks? Or maybe you just like to sit there and watch me make an ass out of myself, like I'm a goddamn act, or something. Christ."

I stood to leave, hot, then turned to him again.

"Piss on you," I said. "I wouldn't share a bench with a goddamn pervert anyway. I oughta . . ."

Taking a poke at him seemed the thing to do, but I noticed my slick-haired buddy leaning against a nearby pole.

"Ahh, you just ain't worth the trouble," I said.

And as I turned to leave, he started laughing, spinning me back around like some goddamn wind-up toy.

"You just ain't worth it, buddy. You know that?" I said. "None of you regulars are worth it. Go ahead. Laugh your fat ass off. I'd knock your goddamn teeth right out the back of your head, but you ain't worth it."

The guy was just blowing it by then. The more I said, the louder he laughed. Just clip him, with his mouth open, break his jaw . . . ah fuck it, I thought, turned, and started for the dorm, my teeth tight.

"Hey, don't take off, man," he said. "C'mon back. I don't mind sharin'. C'mon, grab a seat here. I apologize for stirrin' you up like that."

I stopped, my back to him, thinking about it, then turned and approached the bench, my hand extended.

"Yeah, me too," I said. "I shouldn't get hot like that. I'd explain it to you, but it's a long story. I'm Patrick Todd. I'm a student over here at this blind school. I've just been a little thin-skinned lately."

My hand hung there in midair, empty, my face reheating.

"Is that right," he said. "Well my name's Cole Saunders, and I go to the same damn school. Gimme your hand there, buddy."

He rose like a wall in front of me. The big meaty bastard.

"What the hell'd you do that for?" I said. "What kind of crap is that for one blink to do to a brother?"

"Goddamn that was funny," he said. "I think that's the funniest thing I . . ."

"Oh yeah. That was just fucking hilarious, wasn't it. You probably get a kick out of drowning puppies."

He laughed again, like a good ol' boy with a beer gut, long, heavy notes that took some time and effort to work free. Real though, I didn't doubt him.

"C'mon, Patrick. Sit down here and lemme explain it to you from my point of view. I ain't shittin' you one bit, ol' buddy. It was the closest thing to seein' again."

So this was Cole Saunders, who would never see again either, not with his eyes anyway. Just a big, meaty, slow-talking, ridge-running blink, who would try to teach me how to look at the world and myself through a patient eye, how to peel the skin back, just open that baby up for inspection, like some customs agent searching baggage for the lost tie to humanity. Regulars drove by, looking at the two of us sitting on that bench, turning their heads maybe. I leaned forward, spitting tobacco juice.

"Hey, you ain't pissed, are you?"

"I ain't pissed," I said.

"I was followin' you all the way out, damn near," he said. "I could hear you way back there, takin' your own sweet time. Then I lost you. No cane, no nothin', and I was right back to where I've been every night for the last month, sittin' here, thinkin' too much about too many things. Then here you come again. I bet it wasn't more'n five minutes, just tappin' and talkin' to yourself. I had to grab my face to keep from bustin' up, and you know, what was interesting about the whole thing was part of me wanted to say, Hi, Howdy, How you doin', 'n' part of me just wanted to bust up, but the majority just wanted to see what you'd do, how you'd handle it. I wouldn't shit you, ol' buddy. It did me good, 'n' you might think I'm a sick sonofabuck, but I got everything I wanted. So I suppose I oughta thank you for that."

"No need. I do it all the time anyway. I just thought you were some perverted regular, fuckin' me around, gettin' your kicks."

"A visual nuisance, huh?" he said, and laughed again. "Patrick, you're a card. Just don't ever let 'em catch you, man. They'll lock you up and steal your dreams."

We sat in silence for a while. The traffic seemed to do it, draw the doubt back, like we both knew it, dwarfing us.

"So other 'n that," Cole said, "what do you think about 'er, Patrick? You think there's anything good out there?"

"I don't know," I said, "but it'd go a hell of a lot better with a cold beer, wouldn't it?"

"Boy Howdy. I bin sittin' here every night, trying to get enough nerve up to go lookin' for a place. You know how it is."

"There's a beer bar just across the intersection up there. Used to be, anyway. The Wooden Indian. Used to be a biker joint."

"You think we could find that beer joint?"

"Unless they moved it."

"Goddamn," he said. "We're sittin' here wastin' good drinkin' time."

•　•　•

71

Two canes move a hell of a lot easier than one. You're never lost when you've got company. I would start on a new manual, I thought, a blink manual, tour the whole goddamn world and line it out nonvisually, for the expanding blink.

"They really got a wooden Indian in there?" Cole said.

He tapped along behind me, like Max.

"Yeah. It ain't a statue though. It's a motorcycle."

"I thought it mighta been a long-lost relative or something. I was all ready to check it out."

"Why? You part Indian?"

"You ain't much wrong. I couldn't tell you which part though. My mother was full-blood Karok."

"This one's an old eighty flathead, a scale model, about three feet long. They got it in a glass case behind the bar. Some guy in San Quentin made it—all painted, got fins on the cylinder heads, spokes, kick starter, everything moves too."

"San Quentin, huh? I heard of that place. They don't serve beer there either, do they."

Ahead, to our left, a car dinged the island bell in the Shell station. A semi braked to a stop at the intersection, then wheezed around the corner and geared on by. I waited through the lights twice again, setting my traffic fences, perpendicular and parallel. Some asshole honked at another asshole, his head out his window, yelling. Cole and I laughed.

"You sure you know what you're doin' here, huh?"

"Nothin' to it, man. Just listen to 'em," I said.

"They don't even have stop signs where I come from."

Traffic slowed, then stopped, panting on our left.

"Let's hit it," I said.

"Right behind you, ol' buddy."

I got off line, I guess, hit the center divider, and stepped over. Cole stumbled up behind me, and about three steps into the other side, a car—tires screeching, my own feet burning rubber in fast forward. The bumper just barely nudged my leg as I scrambled.

"What the hell do you think you're—"

"Kiss my ass," I shouted back to the guy driving. Cole was right behind me, his cane shredding my Levis, and on the far side, we both had some trouble laughing, but tried like hell.

"Touchdown," I said.

"Goddamn," he said. "What was that all about?"

"Left-turn lane, I guess. I forgot all about 'em."

"Goddamn, Patrick. That's livin' a little dangerous, ain't it?"

"You just have to keep notes," I said. "Once you get it down, there's nothin' to it."

The bar came easy after that. Sight memory filled in that stretch of buildings. Everything fit—the glass front of Pastime Hardware, my left hand running along the panes, then the rough wood siding of the bar, traffic quiet away from the intersection, then a thin slice of music protruding through a crack. I felt the wall, looking for the doorknob. Cole bumped by, his nose working like a hound's, and found it. Music spilled out onto its face as he opened the door.

"We got 'er, babe, right here. We got this mother freckle down now," he said.

And inside, an old acquaintance, a little ripe and in need of a change, wrapped her smoky arms about my face. That cellar atmosphere paused, checking us out, then moved on. We moved left, across the gritty floor to where the bar used to be. My cane hit the metal leg of a stool. My hand felt the seat, vacant. Cole crawled up beside me.

"Don't look like it changed much," I said.

"Be right with you guys," a woman's voice called.

I knew her, I thought. My brain strained with that small piece of information, sorting the stacks of faces, trying to match it up. I needed more.

"What'll it be, fellas?"

"Coors," Cole said. "Better make it two apiece. The first one ain't gonna last long."

She moved back to our right, opened a cooler, popped the beers.

"Goddamn, Patrick," Cole said. "If this ain't perfect, I don' know what is."

I recalled an old picture, the bar, the green and white motorcycle in its glass case, the pool table, a couple of support beams, and off the far end in the corner, the go-go stage, just past the jukebox, then a hallway past the restrooms, and out the back door—maybe half a dozen choppers parked there, shovelheads, sometimes a sport, or a knuckle, or a panhead, or even a Honda.

"And just keep 'em comin' there, will you, sweetheart," Cole said. "We got a lotta catchin' up to do."

She laughed, her attention directed at Cole, as he tipped a bottle and guzzled it.

"This just keeps gettin' better 'n' better," he said, taking a breath, "and I want you to know, I'm prepared to stay."

He drained the bottle, set it down, and picked up his second beer.

"He's serious, isn't he?" she said.

"Rena," I said.

"Patrick? Is that you behind all those whiskers?"

"I'll be goddamned," I said, stretching my body across the bar, hugging as best we could, Rena crying, my skull alive with the old joint, the old faces, and a younger Rena on the go-go stage, blonde, buxom, topless, a burgundy rose tattooed on her right hip, good legs, 1975, six goddamn years.

The room had gone quiet, watching. Rena seemed to notice, bit my cheek, cleared her throat, and pulled away.

"Maybe you're not Rena," I said. "Maybe you're just fuckin' with me."

"You're an asshole," she said.

"Oh, you remember."

"He is an asshole, isn't he?" she said to Cole.

Cole laughed.

"You just take off," she said. "Not a word to anybody—"

"I didn't think anybody ever cared," I said.

"Then somebody said you were dead, said they read it in the paper, some kind of accident, or something—"

"Just thought I'd try something different, you know."

"It wasn't that long ago either, was it?"

I sucked at my beer bottle, the cold, familiar feeling, the taste of old habits that never amounted to much, except for partial oblivion. Rena held my left hand on the bar, squeezing it.

"You're still an asshole," she said. "If you're gonna go off and die, or something, you oughta at least say good-bye to your friends. Who's this fur face sitting next to you?"

I introduced them, Cole very much the gentleman as he took her hand.

"We're both doing time down the street there, at the blind school," I said. "I don't need the eyeballs to see you're still lookin' good though."

"How the hell would you know?"

"You still got a forty-inch voice, stands right out there. What's ol' crazy Jack up to?"

"Don't ask. We've been split up for two years. In fact, when you guys walked in, I thought Cole here was C. J. He looks a lot like him in the dark."

"He's that ugly, huh?"

"Oh no. Now that I've got him up close, he's much better looking. Good riddance too, believe me."

"Why goddamn," Cole said, "thank you very much."

"You're still an O'Donnel then," I said.

"Still an O'Donnel."

"Rena here used to be Brookings's main attraction," I said. "Forty-inch chest, stood right out there too, get them tassels swingin' in both directions. Ain't that right, Rena."

"Goddamn," Cole said.

"All you momma's boys like them," she said, "'cause you don't have to pack them around."

"She's a pretty lady, Cole, inside and out. You oughta let 'im take a look at you, Rena, blink style."

She cracked up.

"I like his beard," she said. "It makes him look like a big teddy bear. I like that bump in your nose too."

"That's my Indian bump," Cole said.

"Well why don't you open your eyes then? I bet you've got nice, dark eyes."

The mood fell on the bar, like raw liver. Rena cleared her throat.

"They just ain't worth lookin' at," Cole said. "They just sorta stay closed like that by themselves."

"Let 'im take a look at you, Rena," I said. "He's harmless. How else is he gonna get your picture?"

"Jesus, Patrick."

"What's a matter, you embarrassed?"

"It's all right," Cole said. "I'm havin' a good time."

"Hell no, I'm not embarrassed. In fact," she said, "I kinda like the idea of this good-lookin' man touching me. Just give me a minute, will you? I want to make sure there's nobody in here that'll start wild rumors. It is my job, you know."

Cole roared, leaned back, and drained the last of his beer. Rena moved up to the bar, in front of him, setting the empties and ashtray aside.

"C'mon, big boy. Put that bottle down and give me your hands. C'mon, this is no time to get shy. I'm the one standing here with my tits on the bar."

"Oh goddamn," Cole said. "How'm I s'posed to go about this, Patrick?"

"Just start at the top," I said, "and work your way down."

"And stay on the outside of my halter," Rena said. "For now anyway."

The room went silent again, watching. Cole's breath came measured, like a child studying pilfered goods.

"Got mighty pretty hair," Cole said.

Rena's likeness flashed into my skull, blonde, dancing. I never enjoyed watching when I knew somebody, and the other guys sitting there, exposing their appetites, what they'd like to do.

"Mighty pretty face too," Cole said.

A woman farther down the bar laughed.

"I ain't ever done this before, either," Cole said, "so if I . . . GAAAWD-DAMN, would you looky there."

"Okay, big boy," Rena said. "That oughta do for now. I've got other customers to take care of. Drinks, that is. I don't do this for just anybody, you know, so go ahead and feel privileged till I get back."

Somebody squeezed the jukebox and Patsy Cline's "Crazy" made the rounds of the room, above the crack and thump of pool balls. I tapped my way down the hall for a piss call. Rena was talking to someone at the end of the bar, a woman, both of them giggling, and in the can, I heated the rock candy, sorting back through the pages of my ragged past, trying to get depressed, I guess. When I returned, there was another full beer sitting in front of me.

"Got another one for you there, ol' buddy," Cole said.

"About forty more oughta do it, huh," I said.

A small body had walked up behind us. I heard her footsteps, then a small hand settled against my back.

"Looks like all the fun's down at this end," she said.

Biker chick, I thought, a little country, little bit of the cocaine throat—nice voice though, sexy. I swung around on my stool to face her.

"I'm Tania," she said. "Rena says you guys are all right."

"She always did lie a lot," I said.

"She wouldn't lie about that," she said.

"Yeah, I know. She's an old friend. It was nice of her to do a couple blinks a favor like that, wasn't it."

"I know where she's comin' from too," Tania said. "I haven't met a woman yet that didn't like the boys lookin' at her. So go ahead."

I laughed. Cole was still facing the bar.

"Goddamn," he said. "I'll probably wake up any minute now."

I set my beer down and turned back to Tania. She moved up against my knees, her hands on my thighs.

"Should I close my eyes?" she said. "I'm kinda new at this too."

The room stopped again, as my right hand traced her face, gently down across the soft skin of her eyelids and lashes—large eyes, bigger than Weeds, I thought, the face heart shaped too, but the lips full, the nose a bit pugged. Then, looking closer, my fingers found a slight deviation.

"You broke your nose," I said.

"A couple times. Does it really show that much?"

Long, tight braids lay across the front of each shoulder, then the eyes again. I wanted them to be dark and the braids black, Indian black.

"What the hell's takin' you so long?" Cole said. "You're makin' me nervous."

My hands moved across her bare shoulders, the thin upper arms, then

76

back to her neck, following the tie of her halter top down to firm, well-nippled breasts.

"Well fuck me up the ass," some guy said at the pool table. "I think I'll go dig my fucking eyes out."

The clamor of laughter rose sharp, then trailed off. Tania's waist was thin, her belly flat. A spray of pubic fuzz rode up out of her hip huggers. I had to lean forward to reach her buttocks, tight, round, our faces almost touching, then moving my hand back to her face, I found her eyes still closed, and kissed her on the mouth. She kissed back.

"I liked that," she said.

"Thanks," I said. "I liked it too."

She gave Cole a nudge then.

"C'mon," she said. "Your turn."

"I don't know," Cole said. "This sorta thing could get addicting."

"C'mon," Tania said. "They're implants. I just got 'em a month ago. Could you tell, Patrick?"

"They're nice," I said. "I'd have liked whatever was there though."

"Really? I should've met you a couple months ago. You could've saved me some money."

Rena set a couple more beers in front of us.

"These are on me," she said.

I sipped the beer slow, my brain attempting to form Tania's likeness—not a picture, but the idea of a picture, black and white. A sense of shape formed, the female body, hips, the navel an inverted teardrop, the braids, breasts, buttocks, thin arms, then the smaller details, the nipples like pencil erasers, the broken nose, full mouth and long lashes, the pubic hair. Cole had thanked her then, and turned to the bar. Tania set the hand against my back again.

"I'll be back in a second," she said. "Let me go grab my beer."

"Goddamn," Cole said. "I don't know what to tell you, ol' buddy. I think I'm gettin' spoiled."

Tania returned with her beer. I scooted over and she slid a stool in between us, sitting close to me, legs touching. Rena rapped with Cole. Rueben, where the hell was Rueben—near Mt. Shasta, the closest big town was Ashland. Tania had her hand on my thigh.

"You know," she said, "I'd never known you guys were blind, if Rena hadn't said something."

"Oh yeah, why?" I said. "Because we never miss our mouth with the bottle?"

"You guys are different. You're not like some of the others I see walkin' around here. You act different. You act like you're having a good time. I like that."

I could see us running, pounding up Highway 44 on a chopper, Tania behind me on the pinion pad, braids trailing through moving timber and sun patches toward Lassen Park, maybe stop along Battle Creek. She'd sit on me in the cold water, a six-pack beside us, or a wine jug, her braids wet against me as my mouth moved up to hers. Christ, I thought.

"What's the matter," Tania said, moving her hand to the back of my neck.

"Nothin'. I just took a little cruise."

She pulled my head down toward her, kissing me on the mouth, my eyes closed.

"What were you thinking about?" she said. "You got so quiet all of a sudden."

"Just some old eyeball bullshit. It was nothin'."

A couple of bikes fired up in the parking lot, rattling the door with their sound. The jukebox bounced with Hank Jr.'s "Kaw-lija." Cole and Rena laughed about something.

We left at 2:00 A.M., the avenue cool, quiet beside us. My face and nuts were still warm from Tania's goodbye kiss and pelvic grind.

"You think we're too easy," I said.

Cole roared, swatting a backhand at my shoulder. We probably drank forty beers and the better part of a fifth, a little private stock Rena kept under the counter.

"When it's quiet like this, I can damn near see," I said.

"That's just the alcohol, babe."

"Don't you feel that? How everything stands out?"

"I feel somethin'," Cole said, "but it ain't standin' out."

"You got your buildings there, like a wall, and the street out here, and this light pole comin' up in front of us, see?"

I tapped the light standard and curved around it, Tania's naked black-and-white image centered in my mind's eye. At the intersection, I stepped off the curb and kept going.

"Isn't this the stretch with the stoplight?" Cole said.

"Fuck a bunch of stoplights. We ain't regulars. Why should we abide by their rules. Right?"

"What size shoe do you wear then?" he said.

"What's that got to do with it?"

"When you get your ass run over, I don't want to be wastin' my time goin' back for a pair that don't fit."

We were happy drunks, I suppose. We sounded happy under the wings of Mother Night, and then at the snakewalk, a fresh chew, light traffic, my skull light enough to feel like I was part of it.

"So what do you dream about out here?" I said.

"I don't dream. I think too much."

"You never dream?"

"Rarely. If I do, it's always about my mother."

"It's a gas, ain't it? The way the brain compensates for new things. I mean like Rena. I've seen her before, so the skull has her picture filed, but with Tania, or anything else for that matter, there's no visual file so the skull works around it. I get an image, shadows, maybe a shape from touching, but the face is always turned away slightly."

"Sounds logical."

"You get that? And the colors always fade? They ain't even black and white, just shades of dark. So what about your mom? You see her in color?"

"Sometimes."

"I wonder if it all goes eventually."

"I see 'er standin' in the river, pickin' blackberries. She's always wearin' the same old house dress. She had it forever, sort of light green and white checked. She's got it tied up around 'er waist, with a pair of the old man's wool pants on, tucked down into black rubber knee boots. She's got 'er hair up, pinned with a polished tine off a deer antler. And she's got purple berry juice on 'er fingers and a coffee can in 'er left hand."

"Yeah . . . I can almost see 'er."

"She's been dead twelve years."

We had to bang on the dormitory door to wake the night counselor, then laughing again in the stairwell, everything funny, then quiet, whispering in the hall, then laughing again at our idiocy. I could still feel Tania's mouth on mine.

"Let's take the whole damn school with us next time," I said. "Line 'em up like a wagon train."

"Why?" Cole said.

"Hell, why not. Might be fun."

"Think about it," he said.

"What're you pissed off about?"

"Nothin'. You're just forgettin' somethin,' that's all. See you in the mornin'."

"Sure," I said. "Pleasant dreams, pervert."

He continued down the hall—tippity tap, tippity tap, tippity tap tap Wham.

"So you're the musical cane," I said. "I should've known."

"Go to hell," he said.

I opened my door, then stood there for a second, the hallway still alive with the sound of his cane.

NINE

Stan DeLucca called it facial vision, the ability of blinks to sense stationary objects at a distance, poles, buildings, or anything else that might interfere with forward progress. The face is just lousy with nerve sensors. The mouth, sinus cavities, everything in the skull plays a part, but it's those skin lookouts that pick up the slightest difference in air pressure. Everybody has it to some degree. You just don't use it when you're following your eyeballs around. You don't use it when you've got a hangover either, because your entire body, even your hair, is on the critical list.

I had to use the handrail going downstairs that morning. Chicken soup squirted from every pore at the thought of eating, but I had to get something down. It should have been easy, a simple walk out the door, hang a right, then a left. But it wasn't easy. I have no idea what the worm had in mind, but it wasn't facial vision.

Trees should also be added to that list of stationary objects. They're easily recognized by the texture of their bark against the forehead. Christ, the worm didn't even register my feet trading pavement for bare ground until that tree trunk slapped the snot out of me, clacking my teeth together, whiplash. I couldn't even laugh. I just stood there, picking the bark from my thick skull, pain teasing my frenzied libido. Goddamn I was horny too. Hangovers just seemed to put the worm in extreme heat. It would have been impossible to do anything for more than five seconds, though, without vomiting.

A flock of quail tittered at me from a distance—west, I thought, Brookings Hill. I took my bearing, then wandered through bushes for another five minutes, spider webs wrapped about my face. I have no idea how I got there, only that I wound up at the split-rail fence behind the dorm, followed it out, cut across to the snakewalk, and headed for the cafeteria again, like I'd gone that way on purpose.

In quick succession, too quick to fully appreciate, I found that the cook had gone on strike, the eggs were steamed in the shell, and my only other choice was cornflakes. I took the eggs, a carton of milk, some toast, sat in my unsocial seat and pondered the prospects before me, hands shaking. I finally picked one up, attacked it with a knife, and dropped it so fast the sound reached my brain before the pain. Jesus H., I thought. How could they possibly get an egg that hot without cooking it? Runny eggwhites didn't help much either, screaming their cruel invitations to my already flimsy gut, so I drank half a carton of milk in one gulp, waited, took a bite of toast, tried the milk again, then hurried for the door. Cool, moving air saved me. It caressed my hot, sweating face as I took long, careful breaths.

Near the dorm entrance, I heard some blinks grab-assing, the twins and Geri. She shrieked as one of them scored some titty or something.

"Knock it off, you damn brats," she said. "You two are really retarded, you know that? I wish you would just stay away from me for one day."

European, I thought, the accent, maybe Italian—strong vowels. And by the time I reached them, I was smiling, easing around them in a quiet detour.

"Hey," Geri said. "Who's that trying to sneak by without saying good morning to me?"

"Good morning," I said.

"I know you," she said. "You're Patrick. I've seen you around. You sat at our table one day, then never came back. What are you, stuck-up?"

The twins landed on a nearby limb, waiting. Geri walked toward me, poking me in the stomach with her open hand.

"C'mon," she said, "shake."

I had to laugh as her small hand pumped mine. Short, I thought, maybe five foot, lots of energy. My crotch rose to the occasion.

"I want you to do me a favor, Patrick, and kill these two brats. I can't get a moment's peace with them around."

From my gutter, I watched a bedroom scene of their threesome flash by like a red sports car.

By lunch, my big guts had eaten half the little ones. The food cravings had expanded, swelling my salivary glands with the details of Chin's charbroiler. I could even taste the goddamn onions, and still no cook. Somebody said he left because he felt his talents were being wasted on a bunch of ingrates. I didn't trust my cane enough to attempt the avenue, so settled for bologna and cheese. It wasn't that bad—a little tomato, mustard, mayonnaise. As long as I didn't think about whiskey or eggwhites, I was fine.

The cold, slimy tendrils of the hangover began to dislodge in early afternoon. They had clung to my body, dragging along like wet, moldy pasta, all morning. Stan had me zigzagging along the avenue on mobility, scaring pedestrians, when in a patch of intense sunlight, I considered the possibility of living again. My first clear vision was of cold beer trickling down my decomposing throat. I then entertained thoughts of the Wooden Indian another evening, lying on the bar perhaps, with Tania sitting on my face.

Stan hustled me off the street and into the gym after the lesson. He had corraled most of the male students there and appealed to us for a favor. Bernice, obviously out of her mind and out of her kitchen, grasping for control of the dispute between her and Gwenda, was starting a dancing class that afternoon. He waited for the laughter to subside, then appealed to our sense of compassion. The response was the same. I could see a room full of blinks cruising like bumper cars.

"You'll be there, won't you, Pat?"

"Geez, I don't know, Stan. I've got a long history of bad ankles."

"Don't give me that. I'll bet you're another Gene Kelly."

"Seems like I always sprain one just before the dance starts."

"All right, if nothing else, you guys, do it as a favor to me, will you? It'll keep Bernice off my back for a while. So give it a shot, huh? You never know, you might enjoy yourselves. Right, Pat? You'll be there?"

The general mood seemed somewhat less than electrified, and after the other bodies filed out, I hit the weights, coaxing a little blood back into my brain. Max stayed too, sitting on a mat beside the bench shootin' the breeze. I told him about the previous night, Cole and the girls.

"Cheesus," he said. "Ain't that somethin'? Nice ones, huh?"

"Beautiful, man, but you've got to look at it in the sense of education. It ain't like you're really feelin' somebody up, 'cause when you run your hands over their face and body, you're introducing blind technique to the visual world."

"Cheesus, you guys. You probably tell 'em that too, huh. And cold beer. You know, I haven't had a beer since I got here."

"Check out the snakewalk later," I said. "If we're out there, maybe we'll take a run down."

"Hey, I'll be there. I wouldn't miss that for anything. What time?"

"Hell, I don't know. Eight o'clock?"

"You think the girls will be there?"

"The beer will. I don't know about the girls. They might've got enough education last night."

A dozen women and half as many guys showed up for the big dance. Damond was there, with a date, some pixie-voiced sweetie I'd heard in the cafeteria a couple times. I asked for an introduction. "This is Mr.

Todd, my very dull and culturally deprived roommate," he snarled and walked off.

Reno's girlfriend, Teresa, was there too, a lively Hawaiian partial with a voice like a macaw. I had heard her around. She probably didn't have any trouble getting that one side up.

Bernice dug into her stack of forty-fives, some older stuff, Jimmy Clanton's "Just a Dream," the Crests' "Sixteen Candles." Everybody was just standing around, picking at scabs, until Bernice started hooking bodies together. I danced with Teresa first, a fox trot. That's what Bernice called it anyway. I don't know what the hell Teresa and I did, but we had fun. She had a nice body. So did Camille, Geri's roommate, another partial. She liked to stay close, touching, moving easily, sensual—a little loud on the cologne, but the cranial worm got spastic anyway.

Bernice decided to use me to demonstrate a cha-cha next. I slid along the wall, headed for the door.

"Patrick? C'mon now, stop that. Where are you?"

The partials cracked up as Bernice felt her way through bodies looking for me. She finally gave up, settling on Lonny Charles, Carter's roommate, a tall voice, easygoing.

For partials, dance moves are important. It's style. Christ, it might even be art, but dance is their visual expression, in case someone's checking them out. Blinks just follow a natural motion, side to side, the Blink Rock. You just stand in one spot and shift feet like you're in a small boat. No hotshots or wallflowers. Geri and I rocked through one number, stiffly. I wondered if she had ever been to a goddamn school dance, if any of them had.

Then Bernice called a "Sadie Hawkins," and a lovely voice with very large hands moved shyly up in front of me. It was disaster. Nothing worked, not even the Blink Rock. We were feet on feet, she cut off the circulation in my left hand, and at one point somebody bumper car'd us, forcing our bodies together. It was like a damned judo match, so I suggested a move to the sidelines out of traffic.

Her name was Gretchen, big, not fat, just big boned, a nervous, awkward country girl with a voice like Lena Horne. We worked it slow then, easing into the side to side, our bodies about three feet apart. I was afraid to get any closer.

"This is the first time I've ever danced in my life," she said. "I'm sorry I'm so nervous."

"Yeah, me too," I said.

"Really?"

We both laughed. She seemed to relax a bit.

"I know you're just kidding," she said, and when the record ended, we just stood there, my right hand on her hip, her left about my shoulder, our clutched hands sweating, wondering who should let go first.

"Why don't we just wait for the next one?" I said. "It'll save some time getting back together."

We rocked and laughed with the next song, each of us aware of the other's nerves. The old film projector clicked on, all the homely girls that nobody ever asked to dance or out on dates because they weren't *Playboy* material. Eyeballs X 'em right off the sexy list, and you don't ever consider yourself in the rack with them because you never consider them period. And then there was Gretchen, the big beautiful voice in front of me, and I considered it. My crippled worm was still in heat and had to consider everything.

I thanked her when the song ended and gave her a hug. She went rigid, shaking, then tried to hug back.

"Next week," Bernice bawled, "same time, same place. All right?"

Gretchen and I funneled through the door about the same time, then walked back to the dorm together, a couple feet apart. She moved quietly, with easy strength, but silence hounded the sound of our canes, as if we'd bled our only topic. Afraid to be close, I thought, remembering the hug, the rigid body, shaking, both of us maybe.

"You know," she said, "this is the first place I've ever been where I felt accepted as a human being."

Cole didn't answer my knock that evening, so I headed out the snakewalk alone, nodded to my waterfall, and reaching the bench, sensed him sitting there at the other end. I didn't say anything, just sat, stuck a chew in, and leaned forward to spit. Some minutes passed before either of us spoke. Cole seemed to be wading in deep thought.

Then some leadfoot peeled out from the stoplight, banged through the gears, and jagged on by, windows down, stereo blasting Steppenwolf's "Born to Be Wild." Chapter 11 of the Adipose guide provides the proper technique for operating car stereos. First step, turn it up full blast and roll the windows down, so everyone within half a mile knows you're cool. Traffic seemed to be one continuous piece that night, the air warm with something besides exhaust. Fatigue maybe.

"You ever take a good look at yourself in the mirror," I said, "and not like what you saw?"

"Sure did. I can even remember taking the phone off the hook a few times."

"You stand there with your mouth open, checkin' out all the fillings you got from not taking care of your teeth, and way in the back you've got that dangler hangin' there, and you wonder what the hell it's there for, what any of it's for, then your breath fogs the mirror and you write FUCK YOU through it and leave."

"Goddamn, what wound you up? I was having a pretty good time till you came along."

"Christ, I don't know. I guess I'm still hung over. I used to get on everybody else's case 'cause I thought they could do better. I thought everybody could be better than they were and I'd twist that around in my skull till it got me into a fight and the next morning I'd be pissed at myself for being so damn stupid. I don't think I ever did anything right. Maybe that's one of the advantages of going blind. They ought to make it mandatory, take everybody's for six months, so they can get a good look at themselves."

"You thirsty tonight?" Cole said.

"Sure. I'm always thirsty. No whiskey though. That crap gets me too goofy, too goddamn horny. I'm already screwed up enough."

"Boy, you're just takin' yourself to the woodshed, ain't you?"

"There's just somethin' wrong if you've got to lose your eyeballs to get a good look at yourself."

"It's as easy as a walk in the woods, ol' buddy. Some people take it fast, some people take it slow. Depends on what you happen to be interested in that day. If you're just passin' through, you might as well go fast, but if you want to learn anything about it, you take your time, take a good look at everything around you, doodle bugs, lizards, what kind of tracks you got there on the trail. But there's more to walkin' quiet than just puttin' your feet down soft. You gotta be clean, or maybe that's your reason for bein' there, you're tryin' to get clean. . . ."

"Can you imagine having them back?" I said.

"You ain't much wrong."

"All the things you'd look at different," I said. "All the things you'd see that you passed up before."

"I s'pose that's the nature of things, ain't it?" he said. "How'd you lose 'em anyway?"

"Fishin' boat, a storm, comin' back in the dark. Hit somethin' and stuck my head through a window."

"It's the diabetes here."

"All right. You got to see it go in slow motion then."

"I s'pose. It didn't really take that long. Just eight weeks. I could see fine one day and two months later, nothin', not even light. My mother had it too. It never got 'er sight though."

"I've been watchin' some of the partials," I said. "You can see it jackin' them around."

"Yip. It's no toy, that's for sure. I can't think of anything short of dyin' that'd match it."

Carter's phony laugh broke the still to our left, then, on the snakewalk. Cocking an ear, I filtered out canes and voices through the traffic's sound fence.

"Sounds like we got company," Cole said.

Two canes, four voices, I thought, Max and Lance and Lonny Charles. Like Carter, Lonny didn't use a cane.

"Christ," I said. "Someday I'll learn to keep my big mouth shut."

Cole found it all very amusing, sitting back, roaring that goddamn laugh of his like it thrived on pain—mine.

"You fucker," I said. "I told Max, that was all."

"You was right, Max," Carter said. "They're both up here in front of us, sittin' on that bench."

And Max came on slow, like a true blink, the whisk whisk of his cane sliding along against the lawn's edge as if trimming it. The rest of the uninvited contingent mimicked his pace.

"You headed right for 'em there, Max," Carter said, "right on line, about ten feet."

"Hey Pat," Max called. "I made it, huh, buddy?"

I slid over, swatting the bench with my palm to show him a seat. Carter's hundred-proof breath moved up in front of us, replacing the night like an aerosol spray. Max polished the bench a bit with his hand, then squatted.

"Yeah," I said. "I see you made it."

"Cheesus, I don't know how you guys do it, you know? I'd a never made it out here by myself, so I was kinda tellin' the guys here, you know, about the beer and stuff? I didn't think you'd mind 'n' thought it'd be fun if we could all go down there."

"That's right," Carter said. "We got your number now, Patrick, you and your buddy Cole there. You ain't foolin' nobody."

Jesus I hated that laugh of his. It reminded me of a ripe breeze off the garbage pit, and he had to style it, always the same goddamn end, that long exasperated sigh, like the entire effort had been taxing, life was taxing, but he was handling it.

"That's right," Lonny Charles said. "We heard about the girls, and since I *am* the rooster 'round here, I got to be keepin' track of these things, y' understand."

"Ain't that somethin'," Max said. "Ol' Lonny there's the rooster."

"Yeah," I said. "I seen you doin' your rooster act out there on the dance floor this afternoon."

"Part of the job, Patrick, just part of the job. I seen you out there too, with that monster. What's a matter, you couldn't shake loose of that? I hope these girls at the bar ain't that ugly."

"That's personal, at the bar," I said. "They're friends of mine. I don't think they'd be too happy if I asked 'em to make a habit of it."

"Now ain't this a bitch," Carter said. "I don't know who's worse when it comes down to sharin' who'es, you, or Lance here."

Cole roared again. I dug into my pocket for a Rolaid.

The Wooden Indian had never been big on salt-and-pepper crowds. I doubted very much whether a few years had changed the format, but figured our arrival would be a good test. The shape of things wasted no time in establishing itself when we entered. Even the goddamn jukebox stopped, the six of us standing there, Carter and Lonny Charles in front. Beady little biker eyes glared through their rose-colored pimp shades in disbelief. I heard Carter swallow, and in that stagnant still it sounded like someone had flushed a toilet. I grinned and moved past them toward the bar.

"How do," I said. "Six drafts please."

"You guys are all together?" Rena said.

"All together," I said. "These are some of the fellas from the blink school."

"You haven't lost your mind then."

"Not all of it. Not yet anyway."

Rena served the beers, then touched Cole and had him move down a few stools. I figured he would explain the situation. He could've done it without laughing though.

"Hey, that's good beer, huh, fellas?" Max said.

He was on my left, then Lance. Carter and Lonny Charles were on the corner. Max's attempt at sincerity seemed to accent the quiet potential of the situation. It reminded me of narks and dealers, or algae and chlorine.

Rena finally kicked the jukebox and seconds later the pool game resumed behind us. My beer tasted like someone had washed a sock in it, but what the hell. It wasn't my idea. I could have said something, I guess, but figured blind would make some difference.

The r.p.m.'s began to pick up slowly then, not in concession but out of some modified tolerance. Carter apparently misread it as acceptance and challenged the pool table, setting his quarter on the rail.

"What the hell are you doin'?" I said.

"Oh hell, man, I don't know. I ain't done it in a long time, but I used to be able to shoot a little, catch the light on the top of the balls, you know? Get it just right 'n' you can play it off the spots like that."

What the hell, I thought, finish the beer and get the hell out of there.

Carter should have received an Oscar for his performance too—the blind pool lizard. When the game in progress ended, he approached the table, rappin' his shit about playing off the light, and plunked his quarter in. The balls spilled down into the basin and he racked them, sighing.

"Yeah," he told his audience, "I ain't done this in a while. It's gonna be kinda fun tryin' it again though. See if I can still do it. I used to be pretty good at it if the light's right, but like I said, it has been a while."

I heard him take a cue from the wall and stand there chalking it, waiting on the break.

"This gonna be for a beer, brutha?" he said.

Cole moved back beside me, amused.

"You keepin' an eye on this?" he said.

"I'm watchin'."

"You sure he's blind?" Rena said.

"He says he is."

"He ain't out there in the best company, you know."

"Who is it?"

"Floyd Pitt."

"Don't know 'im," I said.

"He's got a scar about a foot long down the right side of his face and neck he picked up in Oakland one night hasslin' with the Ravens."

"It's his quarter."

Carter ran six balls his first go, fast too, moving around the table, the chalk squeaking on his cue as he sighed, talking his game. Floyd Pitt didn't seem overly excited, thumping up to the table in heavy boots, sinking two balls, then missing.

Carter finished his side off, called the eight on a cross rail, and cracked it in.

"Cheesus, ain't that somethin'?" Max said. "Ol' Carter plays 'em off the light like that."

The stale hush had moved back into the room. My beer tasted more and more like someone had pissed in it. Carter was still standing at the table, waiting.

"Well goddamn," he sighed, "I guess I ain't lost it all, huh?"

Floyd and several others had moved from a floor table to the bar, leaving Carter alone with his game.

"That was for a drink, right, brutha?"

"Stick it up your blind ass, nigger," Floyd said.

Max cleared his throat and leaned toward me, whispering.

"Cheesus. It don't sound like Carter's gonna get his drink, does it?"

Cole nudged at me with his elbow, and some mental giant at the far

88

end of the bar bellowed, "Get 'im, Floyd. Teach that motherfucker a lesson."

Carter had moved back to his niche, conversing with Lonny Charles in low tones. Rena tapped the back of my hand and I leaned forward.

"You better get 'em out of here," she said. "Floyd says the only reason he ain't doin' anything is 'cause you brought 'em in an' you're a friend of mine. He might not feel the same way in five minutes."

"You want another beer, Carter?" I said. "I'll buy."

"I ain't even finished the first one, man. I think I need to find me some hard liquor. This beer don't get it, if you know what I mean."

With his departure, the Indian resumed its usual motion. Floyd Pitt and others, in very few words, discussed the future of Carter should he return, ever, then faded quickly into their one ups—this nigger and that, black-white confrontations.

Lance had gone with Carter and Lonny Charles on the liquor run. We had all chipped in for a case of stout malt and agreed to meet back on the snakewalk.

"Cheesus man," Max said. "I'm sorry 'bout that, huh? I didn't even think about it when I asked the guys. I just thought we'd all come down and have a couple beers, you know?"

"Don't worry about it," I said. "Your head was in the right place."

"I'll tell you," Rena said. "If that fucking nigger's blind, we're all blind."

Fog had rolled in while we indulged, shouldering its way up and over the Coast Range, then spilling out across the bay, sponging up twenty degrees of the land warmth. At the intersection, while we waited on the light, I could feel it against my face, cold, damp, pushing by like the collective ghost of old white-haired war veterans, shuffling to their chowline in sheepskin slippers. Carter's voice carried out to us from the trees as we neared the snakewalk. We crossed the lawn, homing in, and found them under a spruce. Lance passed the stout malt, half-quarts. Lonny Charles nudged my arm with a quart of gin. I hit it, passed it on to Cole, and it made a couple more rounds before the resident tension grew light enough to slip its moorings and rise like a dirigible. We could all laugh then, freely—our blind camaraderie.

Lonny Charles piped off the first joke. He got to stuttering, gassed up like that, pushing words faster than his tongue could flip them. He was a show all by himself, but the chain had started, our laughter rising like the heat off a campfire.

Each joke ignited the memory of two more, making the circle, holding that spark. When it passed my way again, I tried something with a little

more color. Maybe I was testing our strength, but common sense began to weigh out and I stopped midway. Cole cracked up. He was lying on the lawn to my left.

"I didn't get that one," Lonny Charles said.

"Yeah," Cole said, "what'd you do, forget the punch line?"

He started laughing again, and the fog's ghosts seemed to take notice, closing in about us, moisture slinging off their manes and heavy mustaches as they shook their heads in disbelief.

"Christ," I said, "what the hell. I stopped 'cause I didn't want anybody to get pushed out of shape."

"Ooooh, you mean one of them nigger jokes," Lonny Charles said. "Shit, a nigger joke's just as funny as a white joke."

I wanted to believe him. I wanted that camaraderie. I wanted blinkdom to be different, off the avenue with its eyeball crapola. The fog moved in closer, linking arms about us, waiting. I finished the joke, the two white slave owners bragging about who had the laziest black. A medley of weak snickers ensued, and in the following pause, prejudice entered the circle and stood there, hands on hips.

Lonny got it rolling again, a white joke. We all laughed. I came back with another and we swapped, black for white, back and forth, the laughter becoming real again, trampling that ghost there in the center of our circle, everyone except Carter. He made it very clear which jokes he would laugh at. Tops popped. Lonny finished off the gin bottle and pitched it over the fence into the creek. That pissed me off, but I kept my mouth shut, and when he opened a second bottle, a pint, and passed it, I took a hit, making some bubbles. I could feel it bully up into my face. And the others, I could see their teeth show when they laughed. I could feel it coming, like a boil to the surface. I wanted it to come then, feeling cheated out of the other, the camaraderie. Carter and I stood opposite each other, five feet apart. Lonny stood to his right. Max and Lance sat, their backs to the tree. Cole was still on my left, reclining. We hadn't really made it through anything, only postponed it. Some of us still had rocks left in our pockets and not enough sense to take them out and drop them on the ground in front of us.

"Fuck you, Patrick," Carter drawled. "Fuck you and all your buddies back there at the bar. You knew what was gonna happen when you took us in there."

Cole sat up. "Well goddamn," he said. "Looks like the party's over."

"Hey, fuck all you white muthafuckas," Carter said.

I angled off to him a bit, planting my right foot behind me.

"That's bullshit," I said, "and you know it. You wanted to go. Nobody had to twist your goddamn arm, and nobody made you get up and shoot

that goddamn pool game either. What the hell do you expect? You get out there and show everybody in the place you're a phony blink. You got no right gettin' the ass with me, or anybody else, either."

"Fuck you, Patrick."

I kept my attention there, between us, just cover, I thought, get inside, get a good hold on 'im. Cole didn't appear to be concerned, but Max and Lance had stiffened. I sensed a posture change, as if their nuts had dropped in ice water. Carter considered my dark form, our breathing becoming audible, our adrenaline rising to the occasion.

"C'mon," I said finally. "How the hell you gonna act?"

He didn't respond.

"Look," I said. "What say we forget it. I'll even make it up to you, if you want, buy you a goddamn watermelon or something."

Cole went into hysterics, flat out on his back, hands and feet pounding the ground. Max and Lance rose together, said something about bedtime, and drifted off into the fog. My attention was still crouched there, in that space between Carter and myself, waiting. Then Cole was on his feet, beside me.

"I wish you goddamn guys would make up your minds. If there ain't gonna be any action, I think I'll retire my own damned self."

Carter turned away and moved off to the fence. Lonny Charles followed.

"It's bullshit," I called after them, "and you know it too. There's no call for this."

Cole had dropped onto his hands and knees, rustling up empties, cans clinking as he dropped them in a sack. I waited a few seconds, then helped, crawling around the tree, looking with my hands.

"I think the rest made it over the fence," he said.

The fog deadened our cane echoes as we walked back, each of us carrying a sack of empties.

"I guess that ain't ever gonna change, is it?" I said.

Cole chuckled conservatively. "Oh, Patrick," he said, "a watermelon, huh?"

"Piss on 'em," I said. "That didn't have to happen. I might've started it, but it didn't have to end like that."

"I don't know what to tell you," he said. "I ain't ever been black."

"Yeah, but it's more than that, isn't it? We oughta be able to do better. We're out of that eyeball dump, or maybe we're not. Maybe it's just me, huh? Maybe I'm the dumb fucker."

We had rounded the cul de sac then. I took the lead to find our turn, tracing the whole damn evening back to my mouth, telling Max.

"I'll get smart one of these days," I said.

"I doubt it," Cole said. "You ain't no different 'n anybody else. When you was a baby you loved everything, then you grew up and learned how to hate."

We were in front of the dorm then, and I stopped, turning to face him.

"Maybe I oughta forget about the watermelon then, just save my money."

I figured Carter and Lonny Charles could hear us laugh.

Lance moseyed into Weeds's room first thing Friday morning, crashed into the back of my chair, snickered, then flopped down into a seat against the wall.

"Mr. Bright Eyes," I said. "I trust you got all your beauty sleep last night."

He snickered again.

"Maybe you've got a vitamin deficiency, or something."

"Why's that?"

"You seem to get tired awful easy."

"Hey man. You guys were startin' a race riot out there, 'n' both them dudes can see. They were probably packin' too."

Weeds had entered and moved around the table to her hot plate.

"You wouldn't be referring to our friend Carter by any chance, would you?" she said.

Lance snickered.

"Watch out for that guy," Weeds said.

"Why," I said, "'cause he's black and an ex-con?"

"Please don't make me laugh," she said. "He's nothing but a junkie. He beat up a seventy-two-year-old woman in the process of stealing her purse, then barricaded himself in his own mother's house, with the cops outside, and there's still some question as to whether or not he was holding her hostage."

"Bless his heart," I said.

"Oh he's a sweetheart, believe me, but anyway, he finally tried to blow his brains out and missed."

"Too bad," Lance said.

"And as far as his being an ex-con, he spent two months in the Alameda County J ward, then another couple on their farm out at Santa Rita, where he apparently put on a pretty good show about losing his sight, and that's how we got him. And yes, I agree, it's too fucking bad he's such a lousy shot."

"He don't like you either," Lance said. "He says you kicked him out of your class 'cause he's a nigger."

"Hmmm? Well I'll tell you, Lance boy, this is my classroom, and anybody who strolls in here his first day and puts his hand on my ass isn't going to stay very long. It wasn't by mistake either, believe me. He sees too well for that."

"What'd you do," Lance said, "hit 'im?"

"No, not at all. I told him very calmly, looking him straight in that one eye of his, that if he ever touched me again on any part of this body, I would cut his fucking throat from ear to ear, then I hustled our illustrious leader Stan in here and explained it to him in the very same words. If they want to put up with slime like that, it's their business. I refuse. He's no dummy though. I'll give him credit for that. You must've noticed he doesn't attend classes and he's still here."

"Yeah, why don't they kick his ass out?" Lance said.

"They'd love to, believe me, but all he had to do was mention the N.A.A.C.P. and dear old Stan walked the other way."

"That sucks," Lance said.

"He's just playing their game. He knows they don't want to draw any attention from Rehab, and I imagine he'll ride it out until they figure another way of getting him out of here."

"What's the story on Gretchen?" I said.

"This better not have anything to do with Gretchen."

"Nothing like that," I said, "different subject. I was talking to her yesterday in the ballroom. We had a couple dances together."

"Oh yes. Dear Bernice's ballroom. I'll bet that was a sight."

"It wasn't that bad. I had a nice talk with Gretchen too. She's got a beautiful voice."

"She should. She's a beautiful woman. Her only problem is she'd like to move in here permanently."

"So why's she have to leave, and they let an asshole like that hang around?"

"I really don't care to continue this any further. It's school policy, that's all I can tell you. Stan's already given Gretchen one extension. She asked for another this morning, but I doubt very much that she'll get it."

"She told me this was the first place she ever felt accepted as a human being."

"You can believe that," Weeds said. "She was adopted by a family of religious fanatics out in San Diego, where she's been doing the cooking and cleaning for god only knows how many relatives, not to mention her sweet stepfather who beat the hell out of her when she was nine and then made a regular habit of it for the next ten years, until a meter reader saw him doing it one day and called the cops."

"I'd kill that fuckin' stepfather," Lance said.

"You should hear the story she told her counselor. Talk about a horror story."

"So where does she go from here?" I said.

"Back. She doesn't have much choice in the matter. It's not that easy for an uneducated blind woman to get a job, and S.S.I. certainly isn't enough of an income to support someone living alone."

Weeds sipped at her coffee, twice.

"So," she continued, "let me take this opportunity to remind you both that everybody leaves, Carter included, and if I were you, I'd think about furthering my education rather than pickling what little brains you have left."

Lonny Charles passed me in the hall as I left Weeds's class. What remained of the previous night rushed to my face.

"Patrick, you crazy dude. What's happenin'?"

"Everybody's crazy." I said. "I've been watching."

"Just part of the job, brutha, just part of the job."

"How's your head doin'?"

"Oh man," he said. "You would have to remind me of that. I couldn't even get next to breakfast. You sure you didn't hit me with somethin' last night?"

Our laughs came weak, awkward.

"No hard feelings?" I said.

"Aw hell no, man. That was just drunk talk, you know that. I see that same shit happen every time people get drinkin'. Don't seem to matter who it is either. My family's the worst. They get to callin' each other nigger. They was just jokes anyway. A body got to be able to take a joke."

"You bet," I said. "That makes me feel better too. For a while there, I thought I was gonna have to quit drinkin'."

"I wish it made me feel better. Cain't be missin' no classes though. Umm umm, nossuh, cain't be missin' nooo classes. The boy's movin' on to better thangs, y'understand?"

Ginelle Blase happened to pick that same day to return to her business class, the only room with the outside entrance. Stan took me by on mobility. My guts knotted as we entered. The worm expected scars, I guess, bruises. But she was strong, very strong, and very much alive.

I stood at the bathroom window later that night massaging a headache with a little smoke—brain damage, I thought. I couldn't tell if I had bounced, or if I had just skittered along sideways. The grass worked though. Jesus that stuff was amazing.

Mother Night drew my face to the screen like she always did, touching.

"No love for blinks," I said, remembering the touch of certain hands, the faces softly illuminated like japanese lanterns, then gone, faded back. A few cars moved by out on the avenue, headed home, I thought, to warm sacks maybe, snuggle up to those buns, or maybe something cold and empty, unmade for weeks. They gave that impression of moving anyway, headed home. They could have been going backwards just as easy, looking up through their windshields at the stars, wondering themselves if they were going anywhere or just cruising along for the ride.

TEN

When stealing chickens, you just tuck their head under a wing. This keeps them quiet. The other chickens couldn't care less about the injustice if they don't hear any squawking.

We were expensive chickens too, nestled quietly out of the way in our little Adipose chicken coop. According to Weeds, the school received four thousand dollars a month for each student. They confiscate all your identification, then offer you a stint in the all-expense-paid coop, where they raise you and rehabilitate you. Christ, I was never habilitated to begin with. Besides that, they put a time limit on your stay, six months. If you didn't have your act together by then, you were down the road anyway, no more funds.

"It costs about the same to send somebody to prison," Weeds said.

"Yeah, I know. They ran that one by me in court. That was their reason for dropping the criminal charges against me in that manslaughter thing. Not because I was innocent, but because the asshole judge suggested it would be too much of a burden on the taxpayers to put me in prison and hire a full-time attendant to help me eat and shit and brush my teeth. That's if I was found guilty. It had already been dismissed once, but they appealed. This was the asshole appellate judge."

"You weren't even driving the boat, were you?"

"Hell no I wasn't driving. They knew it too, except I told that cop I was and as soon as he ran my name through his computer and found out I had a record, I was automatically guilty."

"Didn't you ever tell them different?"

"Fuck 'em, never said a word. Went to court thirteen times and never said a word. It wouldn't have made any difference anyway, you know that. They'd already gone that far with it, so they just twisted it around to make me look guilty, and then left me hangin' there. Oh yes, and besides having to hire this attendant to wipe my ass for me, the big-hearted bastard suggested I'd already received punishment enough by losing my sight."

"And now you're learning to be a good blink, with good brains."

Sure, I thought, and good brains, so I gave them a slight push toward the avenue. Stan had me working the lights at the intersection, a little social exposure. I made the rounds one way, then the other. Stan stayed on home plate, extending his congratulations for a clean trip each time I passed.

"You know, Pat," he said, "you surprise me. Most people have trouble with the left-turn lanes at first."

My headaches were doing a job on me. In addition to my ongoing fits with the regular world, somebody'd planted a hot charcoal behind my right eye. And walking circles out there in that goddamn, regular time zone wasn't my idea of further education—hot breath, everybody in a hurry. One guy crept over the line into the crosswalk, so I tapped his bumper. The spastic threw it into reverse and rammed the guy behind him. They exchanged greeting cards in a very adult, froth-flecked fashion while I smiled and waved. It had all been there in the manual—when in doubt, back up.

Stan shouted something at me from home plate, so I caned on across. Ernie Clappe, another mobility instructor, was there with him, having some sort of secret discussion. "I tell you what, Pat," Stan said. "I've got to go back to my office for a minute to take care of some business. Why don't you make another five or six laps, any direction you want, then call it quits."

I waited on the corner, giving them time to make the snakewalk, then crossed and headed up the avenue to the Indian. It was empty, except for the nerve behind the bar, a new voice.

"Why don't you let me buy you a beer," I said. "It might sweeten your disposition."

She grunted something in aardvark, then waddled off to the other end to count her herpes. I wasn't about to sit there with a headache and her both, so I finished the beer and left.

The school waited for me at the other end of the snakewalk, cool, quiet, like a home in its own time zone, all the other blinks in class. Aspirin and a nap headed my list of priorities, but as I turned into the stairwell, a scream exploded the air-conditioned hush of the hallway, scrambling my skull. I headed in that direction, and about halfway down the hall, it happened again, raising the small hairs on the back of my neck. I moved faster then, almost running, my skull trying to make the eyes work. In the confusion, voices pushed through an open door, ahead to the left, male voices and a woman pleading, sobbing. It was Gretchen.

Then Weeds had me, both hands clamped tight about my left bicep. Her feet had come hurrying down the hall behind me just as I reached the doorway.

97

"C'mon, big boy," she said. "You don't need to hear any more of this."

I let her pull me back a couple of steps, then stopped and pulled my arm free. She grabbed it again.

"C'mon," she said. "You're doing just fine. Let's just get it turned around here."

Gretchen bawled like a hurt calf, pleading, "No no no, please no."

"What the hell is going on in there?" I shouted.

"It's all right," Weeds said, "believe me. There's nothing in the world you can do here now, so let's just keep it moving."

Her hands were shaking as I followed her down the hall to the entrance.

"Now you've got it," she said. "You're doing just fine, Mr. Todd. My god, if I could just get in my car and leave and never come back to this place, I'd be such a happy woman."

By the time we got outside, she was crying. I dug the handkerchief from my left front pocket and handed it to her. She blew.

"I told her," she said, wiping at her nose. "I've been telling her every day for the past week, so she knew. She seemed fine too. I was talking to her just before lunch today and she seemed fine."

Weeds blew into the handkerchief again, then laughed.

"I trust this is clean," she said.

"Sure. I just washed it a couple weeks ago."

"Thank you," she said, and honked again.

"I take it she's leaving," I said.

"Ooooh, you noticed. Yes. I guess you could call it that anyway. Dear Stan handed her a bus ticket this morning, back to San Diego. She told me at lunch she had all her things packed and ready to go. Clappe was supposed to give her a drive to the Oakland depot at two, but at two o'clock, no Gretchen, nothing. Nobody'd seen her, nobody could find her, so I looked in her bathroom. She was standing on the toilet seat with the stall door locked. Stan and Clappe are in there right now trying to pry her fingers loose from the end of her bed. Jesus, Mother Mary, they could do something better than that, couldn't they? The nurse could sedate her, or something, anything but that. I was trying to find the nurse when I spotted you."

A light plane droned by overhead, filling that portion of the world with its sound. I thought of the pilot, looking down at so much and seeing so little.

"I don't want you going back in there, either," Weeds said. "In fact, I think this is one of those times when you can buy me a drink."

"I quit," I said.

"Well you sure picked a shitty time for that. C'mon, we'll go to my office then and have some coffee. I just want you where I can keep an eye on you for a while."

Cole's ideas on injustice were soaked in Crow. He had brought what was left of a half-gallon with him and sat there on the end of my bed, nipping. He had some ideas on my headaches too, proposing everything from tight shorts to a full moon as probable cause. I kept declining his offer of Crow.

"Well, I tell you, ol' buddy," he said, "if you really want to know the truth, it's clean livin' what fractures the peace of mind. If you'd keep a little antifreeze in your system, the bugs'd leave you alone. They can't live in it, you see. They get too relaxed 'n' get their ass washed out. So, I suggest you take a good, healthy bite of the bird here and get your butt in gear."

"Next weekend," I said. "If they ain't gone by then, I'll OD with you."

"Now you're talkin'," he said. "Here, let's drink to that."

Sleep had been shadowing the headaches for days, like wild dogs, ghosting about the perimeter of consciousness, waiting for fatigue to drop me, but the wait continued. I lay there a while after Cole left, then slipped my boots on, grabbed a handful of aspirin, washed them down at the sink, and headed out the door.

Mother Night found me later sharing a joint with the water gods. I had propped the upstairs exit open with a braille book. I finished the joint and flicked the butt toward the waterfall. Chewing tobacco came next, tucking that pinch down inside my lower lip. If I'd had anything else, I would have taken it too, and wondered just how many drugs I could stack, one on top of the next, until the whole thing toppled over.

"You care," Mother Night said. "Don't shit yourself."

We walked toward the avenue, hand in hand. At the bench, I reclined, resting my head against the back, my legs stretched out. Mother Night moved quietly over me, her cool hands behind my skull, pulling me into her.

"Of course you care," she said again.

Sure, I thought. It's all there in the manual too. The judge had his manual, the attorneys, the general public, the wives of my two drowned buddies brought theirs too, as did their friends and relatives and co-workers. Everybody had their manual open to Chapter 13, Perspective.

"You'll always care," she said, pulling me closer, fingers working gently through my hair. "Yes," she said, "care."

What we really needed, I thought, was a blink commune, a place for everyone to go after C.I.B. You couldn't have all those expensive blink chickens just hangin' out, scratchin' through the gravel along life's highway, collared with their expensive price tags, all those cars and semis whipping by, chickens spinning, feathers flying. We could raise our own fish in ponds, grow huge gardens, have real chickens and fresh eggs cooked to order.

I checked my watch then, almost 2:00 A.M., the avenue a long, silent tunnel, stretching for miles in both directions. I liked being nocturnal. I liked it a hell of a lot more than being a chicken, or partial. The good old kid-scaring, boogie-man night, that's what freaked regulars in the dark. It was too much like being blind, too much for their perspective.

"Last call for alcohol," I shouted. "It's time all you pie chasers made your move. Take it home to your electric lights."

Nothing, silence, not even a cricket acknowledged me out there in that burglar's workshop. Sure, I thought. It's all there in the manual, Chapter 13, Perspective—regardless of what the truth is, if you believe something contrary long enough, it becomes fact. And the wives, the two women with their lawsuits, each so painfully justified from her perspective of loss, and their attorneys, from that of gain. Without a guilty verdict against me for manslaughter, they had to drop their claims. And Collingsworth's mother, with tears in her eyes outside the courtroom—"Murderer," she said, "murderer. I wish I'd never heard your name." All for a simple sarcastic statement I'd made to a cop when the worm was tits up. I could put it all in perspective, if I really gave a damn.

The avenue waited beside me there, unused, walled with its buildings. I could run, I thought, no cane, just flat-out hit it and go, head back, mouth open, no sound other than that of my feet and lungs. Jesus, how you can run when you're a kid, and how the wind feels against your face. Especially downhill, down a grassy slope, with stickers in your socks and arms spread wide—just going for it. Doesn't matter where you stop either. It's all the same again, waiting for you. Freedom comes so easy, so inexpensive, when you're a child.

Three cars approached from the south then, ruining my run. Two passed fairly close together. The third trailed, a cop I thought, keeper of the night, herding a couple thick tongues across the city line, pissed too because his talents were being wasted on drunks and deviates.

This third car hung a U-turn at the intersection and headed back toward me, slowing, then stopping at the curb to my right, motor idling. As his door opened, the monotone of cop code garbled out from his radio against the night. His feet rounded the front fender, then onto the curb, keys jingling as he stepped up.

"Why good morning, officer," I said, smiling, still reclining. "Nice day, isn't it."

He seemed too busy scrutinizing the situation to respond immediately. Maybe he had never seen a blink chicken alive before.

"What're you doing here?" he said.

"Nothin' much. Just hangin' around takin' it easy, killin' a few ants."

"You got a reason for being here?"

"Yeah. I'm waitin' for Jesus to come and save my ass."

He smacked his empty palm several times, suggestively, with a heavy object, a flashlight, I thought, one of those three-foot-long chrome jobs. A portable squawk box on his belt applauded, blurting more cop code.

"You got some ID, buddy?"

"Not on me."

"Git up."

"No thanks. I like it fine right where I am. In fact, it was great till you showed up."

"I said, git up. I'm giving you a sobriety test."

"For what, drunk sitting?"

"You better git up," he growled, smacking his palm again with that dual-purpose flashlight.

"Why don't you go stroke your wart behind the elementary school," I said.

"You got a bad attitude, buddy."

He took a couple of cautious steps toward me then, and I had the strangest sensation I was about to become enlightened.

"I'm on private property," I said, sitting up.

His feet stopped.

"I'm a goddamned, full-fledged, card-carrying blink too, a fucking ward of the state, and a damned expensive one at that. I don't think they'd appreciate you making dents in me."

"You better have some identification then."

I could see the guy standing there in his dark blue uniform, legs spread in that classic stance, the belt, holstered gun, badge, shoulder patches, arm insignias, a little piss splattered on his polished black boots, and the eyes, those hard, omniscient eyes, like a couple identical deer turds on a buckwheat cake. I reached for my wallet.

"You guys must go to school to learn this act, huh," I said, "or do you just practice it in the mirror?"

Deputy Dog snatched my state card from my fingers and returned to his car. It took ten minutes to run my file through his radio, then he returned, stuffing the card into my open hand. I spat a trickle of tobacco juice at his retreating heels.

"Don't give up," I said. "You'll find someone to beat up yet tonight."

He opened his door and stopped.

"Don't press your luck, buddy," he said, then slammed it in gear and peeled rubber. I waved bye-bye with one finger and resumed my earlier position, listening to his sound fade south. Christ, I thought, and he gets paid for that.

A few minutes later he reappeared, made the U-turn, and cruised by, slow. When I waved, he punched it, hung a left a couple blocks down, then snuck up a side street and parked in the bank lot across the avenue from me, motor idling, that pleasant language from his radio scratching the night through an open window. Yeah, I thought, if I even cared.

My slick-haired buddy had watched the whole damn thing too, leaning against his pole, sucking that damned toothpick.

"What're you lookin' at," he said. "You think you've got the only perch in town?"

Fuck both of you, I thought, and got up, conceding the match. I nodded to my waterfall in passing, then snuck quietly back into my chicken coop.

At 5:00 A.M. I was up again, boots on, groping for the stall. My stream of urine searched the growler for a bull's-eye, that elusive, solid rattle of deep water. I was out of it. I had to be. I was standing in shit, numb to the situation, until it made a leap for my nostrils. Christ, I gagged so goddamn hard I thought I ripped the skin on the back of my neck. My urine, in the meantime out of hand, tacked casually about the stall while the rest of me struggled to retain consciousness. It just ain't that easy to gag, hold your breath, and piss straight at the same time.

After tiptoeing out like a ballerina, I stood in front of my wardrobe, my weak, sick mind searching for answers. It was definitely not the boots. Any thought of touching them brought on an instant seizure. Damond lay quiet, not a peep. I knew he wasn't sleep, because the little creep chewed things in his sleep, and besides that, he had been in the can an hour earlier.

"Missed the pot, didn't you?" I said. "I know you're not asleep, you little bastard. And I know you did that in there. It's got your goddamn name written all over it, and as soon as my sanity and coordination return, I'm going to introduce you to sky diving, pal, right through that goddamn window."

So I grabbed my cane, tiptoed downstairs and then outside onto a patch of lawn in front of the dormitory. My dance may have lacked something in style, but I was definitely involved, skittering about on that dewed surface, purging my nostrils and lungs with huge drafts of cold, clean morning air. I didn't even hear the door open, or footsteps.

"What're you doing out here dancing in your underwear, Patrick?"

Zeke Potter's voice hung there, twenty feet in front of me like a spotlight.

"Ah hell, you know how it is, Zeke. You got your fantasies, you gotta take care of 'em."

"I've always thought you were strange, Patrick, but this confirms my suspicions."

"Yeah? Well I'll tell you, Zeke, there's something a hell of lot stranger upstairs in our bathroom."

"Oh really? And what sort of strangeness might that be?"

"Somebody paved the floor in front of the can last night."

He turned, walked back to the door, and opened it.

"You gonna take care of it?" I said.

"In fifteen minutes I am officially off duty, Patrick. I haven't seen you this morning. We didn't have this conversation either. Is that understood?"

The door closed behind him. To my right, somebody else cleared his throat—Slick, leaning against the nearest support, always fucking with that toothpick.

"I'm gettin' there," I said.

He removed the toothpick, sucked at his teeth a bit, eyes averted, then put it back, shaking his head.

"Maybe," he said, looking at me. "If you can ever lighten up on the dark side."

ELEVEN

The cook returned on Tuesday. Somebody's god apparently explained to him that forty-five grand a year wasn't bad money for wasting your talent. He prepared salmon croquettes that evening, green beans, and some fancy French dessert with whipped cream. Most of blinkdom turned out for the occasion, not to welcome him back, but to resume their rightful place in the chowline. Geri was in front of me.

"Are you following me?" she said.

I had come down the stairs behind her and followed her across into the dining hall. She didn't use a cane. She be-bopped, sounded things by humming, whistling, snapping her fingers like she was grooving.

"Where'd you hide your twins?" I said.

"I beg your pardon. They don't belong to me, or anyone else for that matter, that I know of. I think they're from another planet. What are you laughing at?"

"Nothin'. I was just thinkin' that's a pretty good deal, two for the price of one. Always leaves you a spare."

"I see you brought your dirty mind with you tonight. You should watch that. You'll grow up to be a dirty old man. And for your information, I have very little to do with either of them. They're brats, and you're a brat for thinking such things."

I ate alone. My fancy French dessert had a hair in the whipped cream, and on my way back, just inside the dorm, Sally surprised me, hooking an arm through mine, her young breasts very apparent as she squeezed up to peck my cheek.

"My my," a black voice said. "Is this competition?"

A vivid contrast of black and white flashed through my skull. You dumb fucking eyeball racist, I thought.

"Patrick, I'd like you to meet my friend Sly."

I extended my right hand.

"How you doin' man? You a new student?"

"Not quite," he said, ignoring my hand.

Sally's right nipple grew hard against the back of my forearm.

"Sly works here," she said. "He's one of the night janitors. His real name's Sylvester, but I like Sly better."

"Yeah," Sly said, "and I like you better over here."

Sally left my arm abruptly, yanked away giggling.

"Whatever happened to Michael?" I said.

"Who?"

Upstairs, I pounded on Cole's door. Reno answered, cracking the door just enough to explain that he had just moved in and didn't know where Cole was, only that he'd left about an hour before. I could hear Teresa in the background humming, a quiet change from her usual raucous banter, and the radio low, classical music.

I checked the snakewalk next and found the bench empty. That black/white image had dogged my tap all the way out. I tried to pass it off, tucking a chew in—more of the Carter thing, I thought, or maybe just horny, jealous, but it was more. I knew that. Something had tightened in my chest, standing there with Sally and her new lover, something about the guy working there, fucking her on duty. I didn't have any trouble seeing myself with a black woman, but that situation stroked the bigot in me for some reason. What if he'd been white, I thought. Sure, what if in one hand and shit in the other.

Cole's cane entered the picture moments later, tracking toward me from the intersection. I moved out onto the sidewalk and as he neared, disguised my voice.

"Look out, you kids," I said. "Come over here out of the way. You don't want to get stepped on by the big dumb blind man."

Cole roared, his laugh very distinct against that wall of traffic. Beer bathed his breath.

"Yeah, some buddy you are," I said. "Soon as you know your way to the bar and liquor store, you forget about everybody else."

"I figured you was still on the wagon," he said, "'n' didn't want to feel responsible for corruptin' you again."

"You could've asked. It might've been time to jump off."

"To tell you the truth, ol' buddy, I wasn't thinkin' much about anything except gettin' out of that room in a hurry."

"Yeah, I seen you got a new roommate."

"Shit, I got two. He wasn't there ten minutes before Teresa showed up to christen the joint. Oh, yeah, it's funny all right. Your little ears weren't there. It was downright embarrassin'."

"He told me it only gets hard on one side."

"That might be true, but believe me, he makes do. Hey, I ain't shittin', I used to think I could take just about anything, but them two'd put pink in a whore's cheeks. If I'd stayed there any longer, I'd probably got a complex."

"You should've taped it. We could run some copies off and sell 'em."

"Which reminds me," he said, "now that you mention it. We got us a double date Friday night, with Rena and Tania. Hope you don't mind me answerin' for you like that."

Tania flashed through, another contrast of black and white, her body and braids. I could smell the leather.

"You ain't pissed, are you? I mean it ain't like I had it planned or anything. It was their idea. I just went down for a couple of beers to get out of the place. I didn't think you'd mind."

"Hell no, man, that's fine. I'm ready."

"I hope so, 'cause I'll tell you. I may not be an expert on the subject, but I believe that little gal's got some plans for your rounds. I just hope you can keep up with it."

"I hope they're drivin'."

By Friday, the cranial worm had grown another set of nuts. The same fantasy had been playing continuously for three days and nights, Tania and me on a 74, her in a flame-red bikini, driving, braids trailing, me in the sidecar with the ice chest and fishing poles. We would paint it black and silver and hit the interstates at 90 in one long extended frenzy of drugs and sex, laughing our way down the streets of little America. My slick-haired buddy just shook his head and averted his eyes. Mother Night threw her hands up, pissed.

"All that work," she said, "gone. He ain't got that many twists left 'fore his knot breaks off."

Christ, what could I say. I could already taste Tania on my mustache.

We arrived at the Indian about an hour early that night, tuning up for our 8 o'clock departure. Rena showed up a little after seven. Bikes continued to pull up out back, adding to the smoke and sound, that constant rattle of talk and pool balls, cracked here and there by hoots and laughter. Some friend of Rena's ushered Cole and me into the can and dusted our nostrils liberally. I was more than ready.

A stack of bottles had accumulated on the bar beside me by 8:30. The full ones drained down methodically, washing at something in my throat.

"She prob'ly just got hung up somewhere," Rena said. "She'll be here."

Rena and Cole hit it off pretty good. I could see them, faces close together. They had moved to a small table behind me. I elected to stay on my stool, listening to the jukebox kick its heavy boots. If nothing else, my

106

skull found genuine joy for those two. You didn't need eyes when you got that close together.

Tania finally called at 9:30, said she couldn't make it. Rena talked to her.

"What the hell," I said. "I need the sleep anyway. I ain't been gettin' much lately. She wore me out all week just thinkin' about it."

Rena and Cole suggested that the three of us go out, but I had already changed channels, and stepped out into that Friday night on the avenue. Seemed like every other car had a window down, stereo blasting. At the intersection, a snatch of Righteous Brothers licked my ear—"Soul and Inspiration"—then it was gone with the green, lost in that hue of genital pleasures.

And in the dorm—chaos. The blinks were out and doing it, stereos blasting on both floors, Beatles' "Hey Jude," Stones' "Wild Horses."

I would have given both nuts and a good dog to be at sea again, alone, embracing my depression like some goddamn tombstone. But Christ, I couldn't even hide. I no sooner closed the door in my room, two minutes maybe, not enough time to get a good headache, when someone knocked.

"C'mon, Pat, open up. We know you're in there. Teresa saw you."

Their Friday night pushed by like a drunk as I opened the door.

"They oughta make those goddamn partials wear their blindfolds all the time," I said. "How's a person s'posed to get any privacy?"

"We're having a hall dance," Max said.

"You'll have just as much fun without me."

"We're out of booze and Carter ain't around. They made Lance and me the booze committee and you know I can't find the liquor store."

We exited the store half an hour later, our arms heavy with loot—two gallons of Red Mountain burgundy, a couple of cases of beer, maybe a Coke or two by mistake.

"All right. Go for it, fellas," a happy male regular shouted as we crossed the intersection. I had a pint of brandy tucked in my hip pocket. It had a lot of air in it by the time we reached the dorm.

"C'mon," Max said. "We're having a good time, huh?"

I was sitting on the end of his bed then, and took the cup of wine he offered.

"Just one though," I said. "You guys are too wild for me. Makes me nervous."

I gagged it down, poured a second cup, and found Geri standing in front of me, so I filled hers too.

"This is great," she said. "Connie just chased everybody off the first floor. No more dancing down there."

"We could tie her up and gag her in her office," I suggested.

107

"So what are you doing, stuck-up?" she said. "Just sitting here?"

"Best seat in the house."

She bounced onto the bed beside me. It sagged with our weight, sliding our hips together, neither of us speaking for the moment, or moving. Then, out in the hall, the twins flashed by like they had hot grease on their ass.

"My god," Geri said. "Listen to those fools. They can't handle their liquor."

Somebody on the east end cranked up the Stones' "Gimme Shelter." A room on the west end responded with Barry Manilow full blast.

"That's like mixing beer and Pepsi," I said.

Geri bounced back onto her feet.

"C'mon. Let's dance," she said. "Let's get it started. This party needs some life."

"No thanks. Dancing makes me horny."

"Well come down to my room then. I want you to try one of my cookies."

"You smooth-tongued little devil," I said.

"C'mon," she said. "Get your dirty mind up. I made them special for the party."

I filled our cups again and followed her downstairs, the music funneling through behind us. We kept her door open, me on the end of her bed, cup in hand, cookie in mouth, while she looked through records. Connie padded up quietly to sneak a peek. I grinned in that direction and she left. Chocolate chips and wine left a little to be desired, but I munched the cookie, my mind on the short blind woman who'd made it. As a kid, she'd thought she was like every other Army brat in Italy, she told me. She could ride her bike, participate in games, run. Every time they gave her a cane she would drop it down a storm drain. I could see her, the shortcake in pigtails, be-bopping along with the other kids on their way to school.

She put a record on low, then sat beside me, close but cautious. I wondered if she had ever made love.

"This cookie ain't bad," I said. "You sure you didn't just go out and buy a pack?"

"Of course not. There's a half pound of chocolate chips in there and a cup of real butter."

I laughed, sensing her there, mind and wine reaching.

"You never answered my question last week," she said. "Why don't you sit at our table anymore?"

I sipped at the wine. Blind all her life, I thought.

"Silence is not sufficient," she said. "Nor is laughter."

She stood then, pushing at my shoulder. I wanted to lie back and pull her down on top of me.

"I want to know," she said.

"It has nothing to do with you guys," I said. "I'm just an angry blink. I'd like to take a bite at the world's ass someday."

"You're crazy."

"I'm serious too," I said.

"Why? Because you're blind?"

"That's part of it. I'd like to see some changes too."

"You can't do that. You've got to go on about your business and forget about changing things."

"Oh, I see. Just be a good blink and stay in my corner."

"I didn't say that. You're just beating your brains out, though, if you think you can change things. Everybody's got their own problems. They don't want to know about blindness and you can't be angry about it either. That's foolish."

I sipped wine, smoothing my feathers back into place. A set of hard-soled shoes hurried down the hall, then slowed, and Teresa's voice filled the doorway.

"C'mon you two. Connie's having a fit, so we're all going down to the bowling alley."

"That's a great idea," Geri said. "They've got a good jukebox there and good rum and Cokes."

She shut the record off. I waited at the door.

"Lock that, will you?" she said. "And remember, you're still wrong, but you can buy me a drink if you want."

At the stairs, I collided with Max and Lance and found myself maneuvered outside with them. The meditative chew found its way into my lip.

"Hey, right on," Max said. "Lemme try a little of that too. We're havin' fun. Right?"

Geri and Teresa were leading the main flock down the street, singing "Silent Night." I could see them passing through the aura of streetlamps, regulars moving to their windows to see who the hell was singing Christmas carols out there on the first of June.

We eventually followed at a safe distance. Halfway down the block, Max dropped to his hands and knees and emptied his guts on somebody's lawn.

"Oh cheesus," he moaned between heaves. "It's that goddamned tobacco. My head feels like it's on a spring."

Up ahead, the main group crossed at the corner, still singing.

"I'm sick, you guys," Max said. "Why don't you go on ahead, if you want. I'll be all right."

"You're right in front of a window, Max," I said. "Some guy and his wife are standing there watching you. He don't look too happy either."

"Awww cheesus. Tell 'em, will you, Pat? I ain't hurtin' nothin'. All I need's another minute or so."

Lance wrapped his body about a telephone pole, hysterical.

"Pat?" Max called. "Tell 'em, will you buddy? I ain't hurtin' nothin'."

Seconds later he was on his feet scratching his way down the sidewalk. And beyond the far wall, the splatter of bowling pins resounded with a dull, muffled thud. People rolling their balls, or maybe clubbing little white balls toward gopher holes, or swatting soft, fuzzy balls back and forth across a net—throwing, catching, hitting, Christ, half the goddamn world was ball crazy.

In the Brookings Bowl lounge, the jukebox played nonstop that first hour. Blinks danced, shouting back and forth, laughing. Regulars laughed too, across the floor at the bar, dice cups pounding their primitive drumbeat. The main group had parked in a large booth, a semicircle against the avenue wall. An energetic Irish accent had ushered Max, Lance, and my bones to a smaller booth beside them.

"The first one's on the house fellas," she said. "You folks look like you're having fun tonight. It makes me feel good to see you here."

"You oughta scheme on that, Max," Lance said. "She sounds about your style."

"Cheesus," Max moaned, "I just got here."

Teresa made the first assault on my introspection. She'd been standing at the jukebox, calling back over her shoulder for requests.

"C'mon Pat, you're next," Teresa said. "I already wore Reno out."

So we danced. I remembered the body and the transfer of heat from our dance class as she pushed against me—thirty-five, married to a Jewish attorney in Honolulu, separated, slowly losing everything except her X-rated laugh.

"What's a matter big boy, you shy tonight? C'mon, shake that booty."

Then Camille, another body, another sweet song, sensual rhythmic Camille with the professional tone, the manicured voice. Weeds said she was a real looker, a fox, my age, private secretary to some bigshot. Now she was transitional too, compensating with cologne.

A couple of regulars, checking out the pie, made their move on Camille and Teresa, dancing—old lines. Engelbert Humperdinck crooned in the background about *les bicyclettes*. Teresa cracked up, and behind me a small hand reached across the back of the booth to tousle my hair. It was Geri, half gassed but still sparky.

"Hey, stuck-up. You promised me a dance, didn't you? Or was it a drink? I can't remember."

We hit the floor, cheek to cheek—the Blink Rock. I had to bend some, my ass sticking out, and somebody swatted it, igniting laughter among the regulars at the bar.

"To hell with 'em," I said.

"Don't get mad," she said. "Okay? They don't know any better. If you're uncomfortable, we can just stop."

"I've got a better idea," I said. "Jump."

As I lifted, my hands under her arms, she jumped, wrapping her legs about my waist, just as natural as could be. I clasped my hands under her buns for support.

"I like this," she said. "You should have thought of it sooner."

She had her arms around my neck, face to face, and as the song ended, I kissed her on the mouth. Her little tongue flicked at mine, like she'd read about it, never done it. Hoots of approval came from both sides. Teresa dictated to the totals, drawing howls from that sector.

"Do you forgive me for calling you crazy?" Geri said.

"Nothing to forgive."

We were still on the dance floor rocking slowly without music. It's beautiful, that first glow.

"You're very hardheaded," she said. "You know? That's not good sometimes."

Willy, one of the twins, got a little spastic over the kiss and voiced his intention to kick my ass. We stayed for the next song, and a third, before returning to our seats. Willy was blubbering by then.

"Cheesus," Max said. "You ain't wastin' any time, are you."

Willy's lament rose behind us in the main booth.

"Why?" he pleaded. "Why? I love you. Don't you know that?"

I felt for the guy. Not a hell of a lot, but a little. Mostly because he was blind and drunk.

"Will you shut up," Geri shouted. "You're acting like a damned fool."

"Christ," I said.

"Hey. Fuck that chump," Lance said. "Go for it, man. I'm workin' on Camille. Maybe we can double up later."

Willy's dilemma continued, subduing the mood for a moment. In memory of all broken hearts, the room observed a few seconds of silence, except for the audible sob of the most recent.

"Don't let it bother you," Max said. "That's his problem. They ain't got nothin' goin'."

Somebody poked the piper and B. B. King broke the fast with his bluesy twang—"The Thrill Is Gone." Ghosts of the real world worked their way through the lounge, like janitors, from one end to the other. Wally finally coaxed his brother from the booth, still crying, and led him out, taking most of the laughter and a few regulars with them.

The evening wallowed for a while after losing a tooth like that, the dance floor empty. Conversation had thinned like the drinks, threatening to dissolve what remained of the cast, when the waitress delivered another round of stimulants.

"Paid for," she said.

A moment later, our benefactor made his way across to our side and asked Teresa to dance. She got up and joined him. I could hear them, no more than six feet from the tables. We could all hear her cussing him under her breath. When she ended the dance early, he followed, planted a knee on the seat beside me and sprawled across the back of the booth, whining, both of them growing loud.

"What's going on over there," the bartender called.

"Nothin' babe," Twinkle Toes called back. "Got 'er under control."

"He's a pig," Teresa shouted.

"Hey. I just wanted to finish the dance. That's all."

"Keep it down," the bartender said.

"Right," the guy said. "C'mon sweetness. Just one more. Huh? I'll be a gen'lman."

"One," Teresa said. "Just to shut you up, and that's it. I don't want you around me anymore."

They weren't on the floor ten seconds when she called him an asshole and slid in beside me.

"I swear," she said. "He won't keep his hands off me. He's all over me as fast as his fat little fingers can move. I mean everywhere too."

"We oughta kick his ass," Lance said.

"If he comes back," I said, "just tell 'im you're going to report him to your sergeant at arms."

She left and related the plan to Geri and the others, their small contingent of laughter rising.

"You really gonna get it on with 'im?" Max said.

"He's just a drunk," I said. "He ain't gonna do anything. If he does, you get down behind him on your hands and knees, I'll give 'im a little push, and we'll stick a chew in his lip while he's down."

"Oh cheesus," Max said. "That'd do it, too."

The drunk had recessed to the jukebox. We could hear him over there rapping on the sides, humming away like some jazzbo. Then he was back, sprawled across the booth again. For Geri this time.

"C'mon baby, you know. Just like you and the other guy done it. I played your song."

"No thank you," Geri said. "I don't dance with pigs."

Teresa's warning rose emphatically from their laughter.

"You better watch your step, buddy, we'll call our sergeant at arms."

The guy hesitated a moment, then backed off a couple steps and stood there.

"Your what?"

Adrenaline tightened my jaw. He's just drunk, I kept telling myself. Then he laughed.

"You can't shit me," he said. "You guys are all blind."

He was only a few feet away. I moved quickly, zeroing in on his laugh, my left hand finding his shirt front, bringing an abrupt end to his mirth. He moved easy, like a garbage can on wheels, and in the back of my skull, a faint voice ran toward me, arms waving.

"I told you," Teresa said.

The guy had both his hands on my wrist, trying to free himself.

"I hate that word," I told him, "especially when somebody uses it like you just did."

"Okay, okay," he said. "I believe you, man. Why don't you lighten up on the shirt?"

A knee to the nuts, I thought, hard, and when he bends, grab a couple hands of hair and bring the knee up into his face, and that voice in my skull grew closer and closer. I recognized it then and let go of the guy's shirt.

"You sure he's blind?" he said, staggering back.

Laughter rattled our side of the room again.

"You always act like this around women?" I said.

"Far as I know," he said. "Didn't think I was doin' anything wrong. Jus' havin' a little fun, that's all."

"And that's all we're tryin' to do," I said. "Just out for a little fun like everyone else. So take it easy on the girls, will you?"

"Hey, you bet, pal, you bet. No problem there."

He grabbed my hand and began pumping it between both of his. I stripped him off and returned to my beer, just as that voice arrived—my slick-haired buddy, standing there in the middle of my skull, breathing hard, alone in that empty room. "It's different now, you know," he said. "You know that, don't you? It's different and it can't ever be the same again, and the sooner you get that through your thick skull, the better off you'll be. None of it, man. Never again."

"Cheesus," Max said. "You showed him, Pat. You damn sure did. What'd you say to 'im?"

"I told 'im Teresa was your sister, and that you were packing a knife."

"Oh cheesus, you didn't?"

Geri and I danced once more that night, the new style. We didn't talk, just drifted. Most of the others had gone, leaving Teresa, Reno, Geri, and Camille in the main booth, so Max, Lance, and I joined them. I sat with Geri, our legs touching, holding her hand under the table. She leaned against me, quiet, her third rum and Coke, her head against my shoulder like we were teenagers following those Friday night pheromones into the first silken tangles of love.

Shortly after midnight, the others decided to leave. She wanted me to walk her back. When I declined, she seemed hurt for a moment, then patted my leg.

"It was fun, wasn't it?"

"Among other things," I said.

"You did have a good time?"

I kissed her again.

"I did," I said. "I had a very good time. I'd just like to have a couple more beers, that's all. Let it settle a bit."

Our waitress left too, leaving the three of us, Max, Lance, and myself, and two regulars at the bar. We carried our own beers.

"She's sure a neat little gal," Max said. "You guys'd make a good couple."

"Sure," I said, "as friends. I can't afford to get my brains all screwed up again."

"Bullshit," Lance said. "Friends? You ain't foolin' nobody, man, but I can tell you one thing. I bet'cha I get into Camille's pants. We oughta bet a six-pack on it. See who dips first."

"Cheesus, ain't that somethin'," Max said.

"Hey. It's no shit, man," Lance said. "Every time we danced, she was puttin' it on me. I even got a hard-on. She was goin' for it, man."

"Oh cheesus," Max said, "you know what that means."

"I was gettin' me some titty here in the booth too. You guys didn't even know that, huh? She's got some nice ones, man, nice and hard, nice nipples."

Two o'clock hurried our last beer down and pushed us out the door onto the street. I chewed. Max passed. At the corner, as we crossed, I turned down the middle of the street, walking without my cane. It was clear, narrow, no parked cars, no traffic, just the dead end up ahead at the school.

"You gonna get your ass run over out there," Lance shouted.

I tried it just a few steps the first time, jogging.

"What the hell you doin' out there?" Lance said. "You're crazy, man."

I laughed, my head back, letting it dissipate into the night about me.

114

That's how I wanted to run, face up, mouth open, the laugh trailing out behind me like smoke.

I tried it again, faster that time, maybe ten steps, my legs awkward, out of balance, and when I hit the rise of a manhole cover, it jarred me out of step. Pain replaced the flimsy fantasy pounding behind the eyes. What in Christ's name is the matter with you, I said to myself. Why do you always have to beat your damn head against everything that makes you feel. Why don't you just say it. She's blind, man. That's all there is to it. Just be honest with yourself and say it. You don't want to spend the rest of your life with a blind woman.

TWELVE

Saturday morning at Sambo's, five blocks north of the school on the avenue, two sticky kids screamed and yanked at each other in the booth behind me. Their father's cigarette smoke curled up and over, invading my lungs. Across the table from me, Elaine spewed an endless line of Adipose gab, gossip, friends, acquaintances, family, strangers, all of it well masticated and blown out between her big front teeth like so much exhaust. I lipped ice from my water glass and chewed it.

That was the real world and I was sick of it. I was sick of myself too. Eight hours earlier in the bowling alley lounge, I had considered love with a blind woman and backed away, and somewhere in that restaurant, Little Brown Sambo, secure and happy with his palm tree and tiger butter, smiled back at me. Everything was fish bait. He knew it and I knew it. That's what he was laughing at. You get the right color, something that flashes, catches the eye, and when you catch fish you stick with it until they quit biting. That was the real world, red booths, white tables and counters, cartoons on the walls.

The waitress slid my breakfast in front of me. I looked at it, poking around with the fork—two eggs, sunny side up, a wad of hash-browns lying there like somebody's Kotex, and a couple fake sausages on each side, like ears. A small tuft of green parsley and slice of orange made it look just like Sambo's picture. I chewed more ice.

"You're not hungry?" the voice across the table said.

A faint humming, something that had started on my short run the previous night, finally revealed itself. It was my onion spinning. Centrifugal force had just slung another layer off, splattering it along my cranial walls like a blown tire. As the r.p.m.'s increased another would go, then another, smaller and smaller, until the last one parted and the only thing left in the center was the scream.

"How come you're not eating?"

"Because I'm not well."

"I know you guys had a party last night."

"Oh really? Did you get wet thinking about it?"

"Why'd you order then, if you're not going to eat?"

"Look," I said. "I know you didn't drive down here today just to take me out to breakfast. You've got something hanging in the back of your throat there like a gob of phlegm, and I just wish to hell you'd spit it out and get it over with, so I can be sick in peace."

"I was just trying to be nice."

"Christ. I oughta have my goddamn head examined. I should've just screamed this morning the minute I heard you, just flopped right out onto the floor and quivered there like a dead fish."

She fell silent then, forking more food to her mouth, chewing, slurping coffee. The guy behind me swatted the ass of one of his kids. I put my fingers to my ears, squinting.

When Elaine knocked, earlier, I'd been lying there fingering my wart, thinking about Geri, how we had danced and how she would feel on top of me there without the denim between us—just reach around, part the labia, and work up into her, hot, wet, and Geri working down. Sure. I wanted her in bed, but I couldn't handle being with her—that perfect blind couple down the block, taking their vacation on a goddamn Greyhound, the neighbors smiling, waving goodbye, then turning, looking curiously at their hands. Chapter 17 of the Adipose guide—wave to everything, cows, trees, trains, Arabs, they'll understand.

I hated myself, but I still wanted her. Christ, I could feel her vagina slipping over me, pulsing—then the knock. Quick, light, female, I thought, coming to a sitting position. I could see Geri standing there in pajamas, wanting to straddle me. My hands found my jeans, pulling them on, thinking I had to hide the hard-on.

"I'll get it," I said, but the rodent had already hit the floor.

"It would appear that I already have it," he said.

Elaine's voice didn't penetrate my skull until her second volley filled the hall.

"I'm his wife," she said.

My wart snuck back, like a snail in salt. My hands left the jeans half buttoned, moving up to cradle my head.

"Who do you think you're kidding?" Damond said.

Elaine trumpeted again—laughter.

"Let her in for crissakes," I said.

Damond bounded back to his sack, leaving the door ajar. Elaine squeaked it open a little farther, then flowed in quietly, like a good dose of gonorrhea, closing the door behind her.

"I didn't know you had one of those," Damond said.

Elaine's laugh had a way of swiping back and forth across your belly like a straight razor. My onion began to revolve, slowly, whomp whomp whomp, like the rotary blade of a helicopter.

"You could say hello," she said.

"You'll have to excuse me for a minute," I said. "I'm having a terrible nightmare and can't seem to wake up."

"I was coming down to visit my family anyway, and thought I'd stop by and take you out for breakfast."

"Yeah, I'll bet. How's my car running?"

A momentary spasm of joy settled over me as my words choked her jaw.

"Fine," she said, sharpening the word to a tempered point.

"So you thought you'd just stop by and take me out to breakfast, huh. Is that on my money or yours?"

"I tried to call last night, but I couldn't get an answer."

"Yeah, I can imagine. They close at five, like any other store. If you want a blink, you've got to hit the hotline here in the dorm. The number's secret though. It's the only one we've got."

"Don't you want to go? I thought we could stop by Aunt Rosie's after. Everyone's been asking about you."

My fingertips rubbed small circular patterns on my temples.

"What the hell," I said, standing, "I've got to shower first, and you can forget about Rosie's after. I have absolutely no intention of socializing today."

She watched me strip the jeans off, then followed me to the bathroom door. I swung it wide.

"Go ahead, get your nose all the way in," I said. "This place is full of surprises. Maybe you'll catch some strange prong."

"No thanks."

"Well maybe Damond will entertain you while I'm gone. He's a disc jockey. How the hell'd you find my room anyway?"

"I asked some drunk black guy downstairs. He was just sitting there on the floor where I came in. You guys must've had a pretty good party last night."

Maurice, I thought, soaking his M.S. in a little morning sun. She couldn't tell a disease from a drunk.

The shower helped, soaking me warm, then cool, face up, eyes closed, wondering if you felt anything when you drowned, or if you just blacked out and missed it all. Nah, hell no. You would scream first—no sound though, just bubbles. All the sound would be inside your head. Then you'd black out and drift down, crab dinner, recycling, and the little fish would zip up and hit the brakes, staring at the shape of that scream twisted into your face.

Damond had maneuvered Elaine into his favorite game, the country quiz show. She talked to him, pretending to pay attention.

"When you come back," Damond said, "I'll pick out some favorites for you."

"You might not have the ones I like," she said.

"Trust me. I've got 'em all."

"He's sure weird," she said, following me down the hall.

A few blinks stirred, stereos low, and downstairs, Geri and Teresa stood near the entrance talking with Maurice.

"Good morning, sergeant at arms."

"Good morning," I said.

Pain exploded in all directions. I wanted to keep walking, out the door, out of the whole goddamn world, but I didn't. I stopped beside Geri. The shortcake started to move toward me.

"I'd like you all to meet my wife," I said. "Elaine, this is Teresa and Geri, and Maurice."

I was moving then, out the door, cool air, Elaine hurrying to catch up.

"Who was that?" she said.

"Who the hell you talking to, someone across the street?"

"You seem to know them pretty good."

"That's right. They're blinks. We all know each other. Why? You think they're weird too? Or just drunk?"

"You can sure tell that short one in pajamas likes you."

My cane hit the curb, turning right, trying to sense the car.

"I parked on the other side," she said. "Do you want my elbow?"

The car still smelled new, clean. I rolled the window down and rested my head in the opening. She drove to the stop sign before talking again.

"The short one looks blind," she said. "You know what I mean? How they keep their heads down? The other one and the black guy keep their heads up, like you do, like you can see. Don't they teach them how to look here?"

The rotation of my onion had increased to a light humming, then in Sambo's, I heard that first layer come loose, flopping off to the side, gone. Elaine, the screaming kids, the goddamn cartoon, all of it rendered down to soup, squirting from my pores.

"You know," I told her, "I've got to fight for every goddamn second I sit here with you. Can you understand that? I ought to have my goddamn head examined for even coming."

"You're getting loud. People are staring at you."

The waitress brought our check, setting it at the edge of the table in its plastic tray. I had heard the cash register earlier, to my left, and made a line for it. By the time I had paid, Elaine had moved up alongside me.

Then out in the car again, I had the window, my face hanging out, getting airbrushed on the avenue. It reminded me of being a kid, the back seat of the car, the smell and motion, the vibrations—how easy it was to sleep in the back seat of that '55 Packard.

Sweat began to ooze again at the stoplight, slack air, exhaust. I felt better moving, through the smell of Red Barn burgers, past the hiss and slap of the carwash, people with their shoes shined waiting for the black guys in blue coveralls to wipe their windows with blue rags—then the long resounding wall of Brookings Bowl and its lounge, where blinks danced.

"You just missed my turn," I said.

"I thought we could take a little drive if you're not in a hurry."

"Oh yes, the phlegm. I almost forgot."

"I just want to talk. Can't we do that?"

"I wish you'd just forget I'm alive, like I forgot about you."

Two blocks farther south, she turned right. I followed her trajectory, anticipating the stop signs, the curve, then the slope as we headed up Brookings Hill, an old parking place, the cul de sac on top surrounded by leggy eucalyptus. On the west side you had a view of the bay—Brooks Island, Angel Island, the Gate. We'd balled there a few times, and as we cruised the incline, I opened my mouth, letting the air billow my cheeks. My laugh sounded strange.

"You know," I said, "all this time I thought you were stupid. You're not though, are you? You're very clever. If I had any sense at all, I'd have guessed it a long time ago. You don't even fart, you know that? It just ain't normal."

"We've got a lot of apricots on the trees this year."

I laughed again, the air pushing it back into my throat.

"But that's the plan, isn't it? The insurance? You drive me out of my fucking skull and collect the prize money?"

She started the sniffle routine then.

"Jesus H.," I said. "Yes, anything. Let's talk and get it over with."

"Do you know where we are?" she said.

"Oh, I think I could probably guess, but why don't you save the suspense and just tell me."

"We used to park here."

I tranced, quickly placing what remained of my skull in safe deposit.

"Do you remember how nice it was?"

"I remember how different it was. I was driving then."

"It could be nice again."

"C'mon. Let's knock off the bullshit. Nobody parks here now except old people. They sit here and watch the sunset and forgive each other for being alive."

The freeway rushed by below us at sixty plus. Elaine picked at a fingernail.

"You know why they like the sunset?" I said.

"Because it's pretty."

"Because it reminds them of death. The end. They want theirs to be that way, quiet, 'n' full of color."

Elaine picked at that damned fingernail, squirreled with her own thoughts. In front of me, the bay spread its polluted body for the pimps of industry, and beyond the Gate, my old adversary waited. That was the closest we'd been in months. I could see it off Duxbury reef, headed in one evening dragging six lines, and up ahead the birds working, gulls, cormorants, the fragile terns, swirling, all black in the distance like a swarm of insects. As I neared, their shapes emerged, the herring gulls, plump, gray, circling, the black, angular cormorants folding and plunging into the feeding frenzy below, where the salmon and mackerel had trapped millions of anchovy against the surface.

By the time I arrived, everything was gone—birds, the sound, the fish. Just the flat, silent swells remained, spotted here and there with waiting gulls, or the gobs of off-white foam churned by that flash of panicked baitfish. I cut my engine and drifted through the calm, savage silence, cranking my lines in, watching the froth hued a dirty, angry orange in the setting sun. In the minutes to follow, night and day came together before me, their flesh exposed, bleeding, mixing, then healing into the scar colors, the purples, magenta. Light, then dark, over and over, day after day in that futile, surface display, until you finally closed your own eyes and accepted the drowning.

Elaine and I had always parked in the opposite direction, facing east, anesthetized against sunsets in our own feeding frenzy, our mouths open wide, as if screaming the word *more*, feeding until the struggle had ended and she spit me back out. We didn't know how to talk then either, or know there was a blind school at the base of the hill, where blinks walked through the manufactured glow of streetlamps, singing.

"You'd better get on with your talk," I said. "I'm just about ready to puke my face off."

She picked at that damned nail, that annoying little click, click filling the immediate space, everything the same too, the place, the bodies, everything but the mind. It came so clear, the other times, how her vagina felt, breasts and legs and belly and parting the thin, wet hairs and lips with my tongue. She had never wanted me to look at it in the light. She would grab my goddamn hair to keep me from looking at it—all her colors of the sunset, lightly frothed, pungent, moist from hiding.

"Do you remember my friend Jan at the bank?" she said.

I nodded. I remembered her—short, blonde, small waist, good breasts and figure. I had never tasted her, but I would have—openly.

"Some of the other people at the bank have been talking and Jan says they think I'm divorcing you because you're blind."

I tried to laugh. My mouth opened, trying. Maybe I was and just couldn't hear the sound. It isn't like the vagina. You can't taste it to make sure it isn't just your mind inverted.

I sat up then, resting my head against the back of the seat.

"It's funny, isn't it," I said, "how idiots always pick a high place when they think they're in love. They can stare down at the lights, or whatever the hell else is there, and pretend. Christ, what's it matter anyway. It just wouldn't be the same without you, they say, 'cause they've got it all right there with them. They get down on the seat, hide their face, and play the game—inchworm inchworm. If they could get their mouth open wide enough, they'd swallow each other."

"Is that what you always thought?"

"How the hell do I know what I used to think. That was another life. How 'bout starting this baby up. I think I've seen this picture before."

"But I don't want them thinking that about me."

I did laugh that time. I could hear it inside, mostly behind my nose and sinuses.

"It don't even faze me, Flower. You can tell 'em any goddamn thing you want, as far as I'm concerned. Tell 'em it's me that wants the divorce. Tell 'em the truth. Tell 'em I'm divorcing you 'cause you can see."

"I thought maybe by the time you finish here, things might be different."

I opened the door and got out.

"I mean between us," she said, "things could be better between us. I promise I won't bother you again until you finish. Everybody's telling me what an adjustment it must be for you, but what about me? It's an adjustment for me too, you know."

I leaned forward, looking through the window.

"The only thing I want at the moment is the distance to increase between us. I don't want to hate you. I don't want to hate anybody, especially myself, so we get a little distance, a little time, and pretty soon none of it ever happened. You'll find another bone, another game, and go your own way. It's that simple."

"I don't want anybody else. Couldn't we just try?"

I walked halfway down the hill, a chew in my lip. You would never know there was a city down there unless you had seen it before, or ran into it, or fell on it, splattering. Her tires crunched along slowly behind me, the motor idling, Elaine inside, sitting behind the wheel, her true colors hidden, her mouth crying. Just start over again tomorrow, I thought.

She delivered me onto the curb in front of the school.

"Will you call me sometime?"

"I don't know," I said. "I'll try."

"I mean just call. We don't have to talk about anything."

"I'll try."

I rolled the window up and closed the door. It didn't sound like my car and as I turned, the blind school wasn't singing anything special either. I felt blind, heavy headed, with the immediate world uncomfortably tight about me, like a wool sweater in a hot room. I had to make a conscious effort to keep my head up, like I could see, then my right shin engaged the concrete bench in front of the dorm and everything stopped, time, the onion, the sun, everything, while I relished that physical pain, so refreshing because I knew exactly where and why it hurt.

"What're you doin' there, ol' buddy, tryin' to rearrange the furniture?"

"What the hell're you doin' out here?"

"Waitin' for you. I hear you had a date this morning."

I sat next to Cole, rubbing at the dent in my shinbone.

"Who told you that?" I said.

"Teresa. I laughed too. Hope you don't mind."

"Not at all, man. You should've been there, it was great, very enlightening, lots of color too."

"To tell you the truth, I was a little surprised. I didn't think you'd have the mustard for it after all the excitement last night."

"What'd you hear about that?"

"Just goin' back to get some sleep, huh? Mr. Sergeant at Arms?"

"Be nice, man, I'm on the critical list."

"I hear you're a heartbreaker too, stealin' little girls' hearts without tellin' them you're a married man."

"Yeah, fuck it. Why not . . . gives me somethin' to think about when I can't sleep."

"You know what you need is about a dozen raw crawdads. That'd straighten your act up."

"What I need is a nice, cold mountain lake. I'd just lie there till I turned the same color as the water, then I'd get out, sit in the sun, drink a couple cases of beer, and listen to the rocks wear smooth."

"I know just the spot too. It's liable to be dark though, time we get there."

"I'll settle for the lobotomy then."

"We can handle that too, on the table saw."

"The shop's locked up till Monday."

"Suffer then."

Cole followed me inside to the stairwell.

"I'm gonna take a little nap," I said. "See you later, huh?"

"You better take some vitamins too, if you got 'em there, lover boy. You're gonna need 'em."

"What makes you think so?"

"'Cause you're havin' company this afternoon. Tania caught up with Rena and me last night 'n I guess she felt pretty bad about standin' you up, so they're comin' by later for the grand tour. Tania said somethin' about makin' it up to you, whatever that means."

His laugh filled the stairwell, sweet and genuine, and as my warped skull touched the pillow, I could see Tania, waist deep in my mountain lake—braids wet, draped over her bull's-eye breasts. Her legs looked short in the water, that black pie reflecting. I'd do her dog style, I thought, right there on the shore, knees in the gravel, just part them colors and pray for the coma.

Cole pounded on my door about five with a care package. We drank one there and carried the rest out to the snakewalk. The traffic sped by, indifferent, loud. The beer tasted good enough to chew.

"How's your colors these days?" I said.

"Fine, how's yours?"

"You know what I mean. Do you still see 'em?"

"Yeah. Seems I can still bring 'em around if I want."

"You remember what a pussy looks like?"

"Goddamn. Your ol' lady must've really put the spurs to you."

"I don't mean working it, just looking at it. I always thought they were beautiful. I mean the thing itself, not the bullshit that goes with it. Them assholes that did all the braggin' in school probably never took a good look at it."

It's funny sometimes how the faces come back when you're lonely. I could remember each vagina, too, as different as the faces and the personalities. All lovely, all connected to that sadness, the quiet moments when you thought about spending the rest of your lives together—the soft spots.

"They always reminded me of earth colors," Cole said. "There's always more there 'n what you see from a distance, like when a Caterpillar makes a fresh cut through an old hillside 'n' you've got earth exposed that ain't seen the sun in who knows how long. Seems too, the closer you get, the more it feels like it's pullin' at you, gettin' you up there close enough so you'll touch it, 'n' when you get there, seems you can pick out all these

124

tiny, little specks of color, every damn color you can imagine. Twenty feet away it don't look like anything but fresh dirt. Up close, it's all there, the beginning and end of everything."

"I don't know about that."

"Well drink your beer then. You got to perk up. Here, lemme open that for you. I don't want you wearin' yourself out, little fella."

"You're worse 'n Geri."

"Or as good. I don't think you've tried either of us, have you?"

"That ain't funny, and besides that, I was serious."

"What the hell's the matter with you? Ain't none of it worth gettin' down over. You gotta learn how to laugh more, take it easy. It was all here 'fore you got here and it'll be here when you're gone too."

"I agree. That's like Tania too, sayin' she's got to make it up to me. She don't."

"I was just repeatin' what I heard. I really have no idea what she had in mind."

"Yeah, well she don't. Makes it seem too much like a whore house."

"Boy, you are really outa the water, ain't you. You ain't thinkin' about passin' that up, are you?"

"Hell, I don't know what I think anymore."

"Maybe I oughta walk down to the bar and tell 'em to forget it then."

"I just don't want 'er crawlin' in the sack with me 'cause she thinks she hurt some blink's feelings and has to make it up to me."

"Here, lemme open that for you. I keep forgettin' how far gone you are."

"Fuck you. I'll give 'er the tour anyway. She might like it."

In a quiet stretch, between flocks of traffic, we heard Tania and Rena coming down the sidewalk, laughing, Tania's higher, the cocaine cracking, Rena's lower, a little heavier gauge, smooth. My balls were crawling before she even sat down, placing that small hand on my thigh. Spring had come to Buzzard's Roost.

"Hi," she said.

I tipped the beer can, emptying the remains into my throat.

"Look," I said, "I don't want to hear any goddamn sorry's, or any of that bullshit. I had a good time last night. It ain't like it was the last day of the season or something, right?"

"I just don't like doing that to people I care for."

"Yeah, I don't imagine anybody does, but it's over, all right? I mean I contemplated suicide a couple times, but I ain't quite ready to retire, so why don't we split this beer, then, and call it even."

The lake scene flashed through again, Tania, waist-deep, black and white. When she handed the can back, I leaned over and kissed her on the mouth.

"You don't have to make anything up to me either," I said. "I'd just as soon sit in the bar and have a few beers."

"Your ass. You're not getting out of it that easy. It has nothing to do with making something up, either. I've been so horny all day thinking about it, I can hear my ovaries screaming. See? Look for yourself."

She took my left hand and put it down against her crotch. She had shorts on. I believed her.

Damond was into his headphones when we entered the room.

"Is that you, Elaine?" he said.

"What the hell is that?" Tania said.

"My roommate. We're in the process of getting a divorce though."

"Who's Elaine?"

I untied her halter top and lifted it over her braids.

"My wife," I said. "She paid me a little visit this morning. Does that bother you?"

"No way. I kinda thought you'd have one of them around. You're a good catch."

"You too," I said.

Our belt and button race lasted only a few seconds. She'd just shaved her legs.

"I don't know what you two are up to," Damond said, "but I have no intentions of leaving."

Moments later, obvious sounds filled our small chamber.

"What are you doing?" Damond said.

He was obviously no partial. Either that or he did things different.

"You two are disgusting," he said a minute later, and left, slamming the door.

Tania and I hooked up with Cole and Rena a little after nine, back at the Indian. I checked my ears on the way in to make sure they'd quit wiggling.

"We were about to put you guys on the missing persons' list," Rena said.

We sat at the bar, had a couple of beers, our legs touching. My skull was on vacation—lots of thoughts, but none of them sticking. Tania eventually took a hike to the other end to talk with someone. She was still there when Cole and I left. I shouted good-bye to her. She shouted back, and out on the avenue, the world seemed soft again, open.

"You know," I said, "seems like every time I come out of there, I've got a different record playing in my skull."

"I've got to admit," Cole said, "you do sound a hell of a lot better. Maybe that's all you needed."

I stuck a chew in and spit the excess from my lip.

"So tell me," Cole said, "did you get a good look at your colors?"

"You ain't much wrong."

"Well?"

"Well what?"

"Well what the hell color was it?"

"About the same color as a week in Jamaica."

THIRTEEN

Mother Night kept dealing, a fresh deck, a new hand, whether I was ready or not. A population explosion turned them face up, filling the first floor, so they moved Geri and Camille upstairs. My genius, of course, quickly pointed out the potential of this situation, all that color just four doors down—like cutting a long, slow line in front of a recovering coke addict.

Tania's image had left me more than subdued for several days, especially where Geri was concerned. We would pass in the hall or cafeteria, both of us silent with things to say. We would stand there together for uncomfortable seconds, piddling at scraps of dead conversations, then move on. She always sounded like a question. I sounded like cold feet.

Upon my request, Stan had issued me a divorce from Damond and moved me across the hall into an empty room. Lance was supposed to be my new roommate. His clothes, bedding, and guitar case were piled on the end of his bed, but he'd taken a week's leave to deal with a family of crabs somebody had shared with him on a visit home. Carter and Lonny Charles were our can-mates. I kept that door locked.

The new blinks, a real flock of mavericks, were herded in by state cowboys. We had a hype, a pants pisser, a used-car salesman, and half a dozen wall crawlers. The hype, a diabetic partial named Alan, sniffed Carter out in ten minutes. They disappeared for a couple days, then returned, "right," very mellow.

Damond scored the pants pisser, a Neanderthal type who ate without utensils. Rusty got the car salesman, another fading partial, flashing the last of his cubes. This bald-headed shyster had said he sold Mercedeses to rich old ladies in the South Bay. I introduced myself, poking his gut a little as I offered my hand. He made it quite clear that blinks disgusted him.

My skull had done some rearranging of its own, taking on some new theatrics—lightshows. These were usually preceded by a strong, dull surge of pain behind the right eye. The following brilliant explosion would light my entire cavity, then drain away in distorted luminous shapes, like blobs in a lava lamp, swirling, elongating, separating, and finally disappearing somewhere behind my nose, taking my equilibrium with them. Weeds saw me drop one day on my way to the cafeteria, so I confessed about the headaches. She made an appointment with a specialist for me that same afternoon.

"You really amaze me," she said. "What if that had happened in the middle of a crosswalk?"

"That's right, huh. Somebody'd probably recognize me and treat me to some tire tracks."

We were in Weeds's Mazda, headed west along Cutting Boulevard toward Kaiser Hospital. She had named the car Morris. It had a hum in its skull just like mine, and through my open window, the indelible tincture of downtown Bay City painted my nostril hairs.

"How many times has that happened?" she said.

"I don't know, couple, I guess."

"Did you say anything to Clappe? You shouldn't have even been on mobility, you know."

"Nope."

"What do you think of him, anyway?"

Ernie Clappe, some burnt-out hippie, had replaced Stan as my mobility instructor. I had ditched him the first day and spent the afternoon at the Wooden Indian. The next lesson we had spent together down at the corner of Solano and San Gabriel in the Ivy Room, drinking beer for two hours.

"He's all right for a longhair—a little fat maybe, gets puffing a bit and his thighs rub."

"You haven't noticed anything strange?"

"Why? Is he queer?"

"Oh I don't think a big, strong guy like you would have any trouble with him."

"Don't bother me, as long as he doesn't get too personal with it."

"I just thought you might've noticed something. Some of the women have been complaining about him. Geri filed a formal complaint with Stan. She says she'll never go out on another lesson with him."

"What's he doin', tryin' to put the make on 'em?"

"He tries to engage them in deep, psychological discussions that usually lean toward sexuality."

"He'd probably sweat too much for me anyway."

"Geri says he carries a clipboard with him on lessons and taps it against his leg while he's walking. I saw it on the table in the coffee room. I'd give good odds he's never even written in the damned thing. He just uses it to draw attention. . . . You think it's funny, huh? Well laugh about it next time you're on a lesson and you hear something tapping."

Young children filled most of the seats in the waiting room, sitting quietly with their parents and eye disease. One little girl kept shuffling through magazines—"What's this one, Mom? No I don't like that. What's this one?"

In his office, Dr. Barry Decker positioned my skull in a slip lamp, a vertical vise with a chin rest. Weeds stood close, on my right, watching, exuding slight hints of pheromone. The doc noticed too, following his eyes in her direction—young guy, strong personality.

"What's your relationship to this man?" he said.

"He's just a friend."

"Oh?" Then to me, peering into my skull through his optics. "You say you've just started getting these headaches?"

"They've been around awhile," I said.

After examining the other eye, he explained to both of us about the degenerative process, how a piece of glass in the back of my right eye came under constant attack by white blood cells, but in a losing effort. This caused the inflammation, and the conflagration received full media attention along the optic nerve into the midbrain. My head was still clamped in the vise.

"So, Mr. Todd and friend," he said. "There are three ways of dealing with this. I can prescribe pain medication and anti-inflammatory drugs, I can give you an alcohol block, or I can remove the globe."

"Alcohol blocks are out," Weeds said. "They're no good."

"Oh? And how it is that you happen to know about these things?"

"Oh, I just know," she said, doing her Shirley Temple impersonation. I had to laugh to break it up.

"I'm sorry," the doc said, "did I miss something?"

"I don't mind the show," I said, "but this seat's giving me a headache."

"Is he always like this?" the doc said.

"Except when he's worse," Weeds said.

I decided to take my third option, the removal, an enucleation the doc called it. All the necessary papers were signed—hospital billing and a liability waiver in case I didn't wake up after the operation, which he scheduled for the following Tuesday. A silicone implant would replace the globe. Muscle tissue would be tied together in front of it. A perforated conformer would allow it to drain and heal and in a couple months I would be fitted with an acrylic prosthesis.

"You're sure this is what you want now," the doc said.

"Positive. I've got a lot of things to do," I said. "They'll go a hell of a lot easier without the headaches."

"Most people need a sedative just to consider it," he said.

Weeds had been eye-fucking him the whole time and as we crossed the parking lot to her car, I commented on it.

"Oh really. Is that supposed to imply something?"

"Oh hell no. I just thought I'd have to throw some cold water on you two, that's all."

"I happen to find him attractive," she said. "Is there something wrong with that? Especially his eyes. They're a very light blue, very expressive."

"Oh yeah, can't forget about the eyeballs, can we?"

"Like I always say, if you've got 'em, use 'em."

We left the parking lot in silence, returning east on Cutting Boulevard. Kaiser Hospital was on Fourteenth Street. My old apartment was just off Tenth—the marina, the boat, the old Studebaker, the eyes.

"You could always take the drugs, you know," Weeds said. "They won't solve your problem though. They'll just delay it for a while."

"I ain't worried about it."

"Why are you so testy then? I thought you might be having second thoughts."

"Hell, I don't know. Maybe I'm jealous. Not to mention your being married," I said.

"That's right, and very happily too, I might add."

"Glad to hear it. What say we change the subject then?"

"No thanks. As long as you've brought the subject up, I think we should continue it, and since you seem to be so interested in what I do, maybe I should mention the little visit your wife made last Saturday, or the dark-haired little number you took behind closed doors."

"You guys don't miss a thing, do you?"

"I told you before, your private life is over. These counselors get paid well for keeping notes, and lately you seem to be their favorite subject."

"I guess I'll have to give 'em something to write about then."

"You no doubt will, and while we're on this subject of spouses and infidelity, what's your status? Married? Separated? Getting divorced, or just planning to start a new relationship on top of the last one?"

"You're takin' notes too, huh?"

"I'm just curious."

"Well don't let it bother you. It's no different 'n you spreading your feathers for the doc back there."

"Oh, I think it's a lot different."

"Fine. Think whatever the hell you want."

"You read the rules," she said. "It's a state institution. They don't like to see students get into things they're not serious about, especially with other students of the opposite sex who might have a tendency to fall in love."

"Why didn't you just say that in the first place?"

"Because I wasn't mad enough in the first place."

"Well ease your mind, sister dear. I've already lost what was left of mine just thinking about her."

"You've also had a lot more experience, too, and people have this funny way of getting together at times."

"Yeah, it is funny, huh."

"And I'm not certain, of course, but from the talks we've had, I think she's probably still a virgin, and I just don't want to see her get hurt. She's a smart cookie, believe me. She's going places, and I don't think she needs to start it off with a broken heart."

I thanked her for her concern and rode the remaining distance in silence.

Sally and Max were in the alcove spreading a few feathers themselves as I approached the dorm. I laughed.

"We happen to be good friends," Sally said.

"Christ. Watch your wallet, Maxie," I said, and ducked Sally's insult.

A strange rapture tumbled into the stairwell from the second floor as I climbed. A chorus of blinks, one of them Geri, had surrounded something in the hall. The object of their affections was spouting gospel—another new voice, a nervous male.

"Shut up, you fool," Geri shouted. "You're not in church anymore."

Laughter rattled loose in the audience.

"Hell waits for all sinners," the preacher said, his voice wavering. "But hear me, brothers and sisters, Jesus loves each and every one of us. He died on the cross, so that—"

"They're gonna take you away in a straitjacket, buddy," Teresa yelled, then noticed me standing at the stairwell. "Patrick, you're our sergeant at arms. Make this idiot shut up, will you?"

"Jesus died on the cross, so that our babies and their babies should not perish from—"

"Shut the fuck up, you idiot," Teresa screamed. "Patrick, dammit, do something."

"Don't sound like he's hurtin' anything to me," I said. "Why don't you let 'im go for a while. Maybe he'll burn out."

"He's been going for two hours already, and we're sick of it. If you don't do something, we're going to kill him."

"That's right," the twins chimed, "he's nuts," and the surly crowd of partials behind them moaned in unison.

I approached the preacher then and touched his arm. He damn near skinned himself.

"Hey, it's all right," I said. "I just want to talk to you for a minute."

"Do you work here?"

The guy was trying to climb my left leg like a ladder.

"For crissakes, take it easy, will you. C'mon over here a minute."

I stopped to unlock my door. The preacher jogged in place, beside me.

"What's the matter with you?" I said. "You fucked up on somethin'?"

"No, but I smoke cigarettes."

"What's your name?"

"Bernie."

"I'm Patrick. I'm a student here too."

When my hand poked his belly, he went in about six directions at once.

"Christ," I said, "come in here, will you? Here, sit down."

I pulled a chair out and slapped the seat. Bernie moved onto it.

"Now hold still, will you?"

"Sure. Can I move in here with you?"

"No, no. I've already got a roommate."

"Where is he?"

"Look," I said. "You've gotta knock that goddamn preachin' off. It don't do any good to preach if people ain't interested, right?"

"I didn't know that."

"Well take my word for it then. Just calm down a little bit, take it easy and everything'll be all right."

"I'd like to move in here with you, Patrick."

"Can't do that, man. They've got rules here, and you have to do what they say, or the cops'll come and kill your ass."

"Okay, can I smoke?"

I pulled the wastebasket out for an ashtray.

"So what's with all the preachin' anyway?" I said. "Where the hell'd you pick that up?"

"My mom makes me go to church. I'm a Baptist."

"You do anything else?"

"I smoke and watch television."

"You like goin' to church?"

"My mom says I'm bad, so I have to. She says going to church will save me."

"Well you don't seem all that bad to me. You gotta lay off that preachin', though, 'n' you'll make more friends. We ain't got any churches here, and nobody's seen god in over fifteen years. We think the Mafia got 'im."

"I've never seen him either," Bernie said, "but I had a friend at Arm-

133

strong that did. He sniffed glue and passed out and said he saw god and the world and heaven and everything."

"They don't go for glue around here, either. A little tobacco maybe and a beer once in a while, but that's about it."

"Can I have a beer?"

"Sorry, we're fresh out, but one of these days we'll take a hike down to the bar and have a couple. How's that sound?"

"Can we go now?"

"It's almost dinnertime now."

I put him out then, and said I'd come by his room in a while to show him the cafeteria.

"I like you, Patrick. You're my friend."

"You just say that because you don't know me well enough," I said, "and remember, keep that preachin' down, huh?"

Half an hour later, Bernie was still standing there, outside my door, veiled in smoke.

"Hi Patrick."

Cigarette butts mashed under my boots as I closed and locked the door. Bernie pranced beside me, like a shorthair out of its kennel.

"For crissakes," I said. "Get back a couple steps, will you? You ever take any reds?"

"Nope. I don't even know what they are."

"Well it might be something to think about."

Bernie could talk, smoke, and eat all at the same time. The guy was one giant loose nerve, blind from birth, retrolental fibroplasia, couldn't write braille but could read it, twenty-four years old, never finished public school but spent two months at Armstrong, another blink school in Sacramento, hated his stepdad, and at his mother's wedding some months earlier, he drank a bottle of champagne and puked all over her reception.

After dinner, I headed out the snakewalk for a chew. Bernie tagged along like a horsefly, and at the bench I stuffed my lip and handed the can to him.

"Go ahead," I said. "Try some."

"What is it, marijuana?"

"Nope, just plain old tobacco, comes from back east. The Indians pick it and bite it into little pieces with their teeth, then all the young maidens get naked and roll in it to soften it up. That's what gives it the flavor. Go ahead. Stick some in your lip there, in front of your bottom teeth. You won't get any lung cancer from this stuff. Might rot your face off though."

"My uncle died of cancer," Bernie said, "but I didn't like him anyway."

Bernie swallowed his first attempt and got to hacking a bit, then asked for another.

134

"Will this make me drunk, Patrick?"

"Nah. You might get a little jag off it, but that's about all."

"What's a jag?"

Seconds later, he stopped vibrating and began swaying, back and forth, side to side. He leaned forward to spit, but nothing hit the pavement, then a hand went up to wipe at his chin.

"What's a matter," I said, "you sick?"

"Uh uh."

"Well, that's what a jag feels like. It won't last long though, two, three days maybe."

"I really like this stuff, Patrick."

"Well you ain't too bad off then, are you?"

"Shoot no. I remember everything too. Can I have some more?"

I showed Bernie back to the dorm that evening, told him I had to use the can, then walked down to the Indian, looking for Cole, and had a couple of beers with Rena. She was really in love with the guy, worried too, said she had tried everything in her powers of persuasion that first night they went out, but Cole couldn't get it up. I told her not to worry about it, blinkdom took some getting used to. Back in my new room, with the window open, I heard a collision on the avenue, a beauty, three or four cars at least. Sound carried different on that southern exposure, cramped, buffered by buildings. Within minutes, traffic backed up for blocks, wheezing. Horns blasted their traffic-jam invectives. Donald Duck eyes searched for an escape. Hood ornaments became gunsights and fifty-caliber machine guns hidden behind headlamps surfaced, triggers ready, there on the steering wheels under frustrated fingers, time passing them by, moving on without them and that same asshole up there in the Olds-mobile, cutting in—that's it, just a little bit more . . . NOW, let 'er rip. That'd damn sure teach the bastard.

I hit the joint again and held it, feeling the slow smoke blend into my skull, curling about the hot spot. Cool drug cells coaxed hot, white ones toward the darker recesses of my worm's cavity, arms about their shoulders, leading them with lies away from the shooting eye, the hot one. How many times had it instructed, telling the finger to squeeze, that shooting eye attached to the shooting quadrant of the brain, the killing quadrant—that's it, that's it, eeeasy now, bring 'er down, little more, eeeasy, hold it . . . NOW. Right through the goddamn neck. Not even a wiggle, except for the wife and kids somewhere, sitting at the dinner table maybe, faces averted, looking down at their plates instead of the empty chair at the other end of the table—some poor bastards you never knew, never would, never cared, unless you'd smelled them, and listened to them grunt in the dark, and held them, while the warm blood pumped out between your fingers, so fast and strong, like it could never end, and then that great surge of strength when they knew, when their eyes bulged with this new knowledge, and as the blood slowed, you could watch them leave. The eyes changed—windows without faces, and part of you always went with them a ways before stopping, turning back. Yours still pumped. You could feel it, and you knew that was the only difference between you and your dead brothers—out of gas.

At 3:00 A.M. I swallowed four aspirin, smoked another joint—no sleep, no traffic on the avenue. They must have wiped each other out.

By 5:30, I had withdrawn my name from the ranks of functioning personalities. I didn't need to hear Bernie's feet outside my door either, or the hand trying the lock.

"Patrick? Are you awake?"

Both barrels swung in unison, trained on the door handle. When it rattled again, I squeezed.

Bernie was still there at 6:00, when I got up to shower, and at 6:30, when I finally opened the door.

"Do you have any of my cigarettes left?"

"Nope. Threw 'em all away."

We'd done some trading the night before, my chew for his smokes. I'd pitched them into a garbage can downstairs.

"Can I have 'em back? I used up all my chew."

I had a full can in my top drawer and split it with him. We ate breakfast, and leaving the cafeteria, Bernie stuffed his lip full. I dropped him off at Weeds's room. That would teach her, I thought.

On mobility that afternoon, Clappe directed me south, toward Marin Avenue. The brisk whisk of his thick thighs followed some yards behind, that goddamn clipboard slapping. The sidewalk narrowed in front of East Bay Chevrolet, and as I stepped up onto the curb, a woman herded her kids out of my path, crowding them against the building.

"Shush," she said. "I don't want to hear a peep out of you either."

"But, mommy, why's that man—"

"Shush I said."

One little nose worked calmly through a wad of snot. I smiled, looking down at the big eyes looking up.

"Hello," I said.

Mummy had just released them to the real world again when Clappe arrived. He stopped. Somebody's car had draped itself across the sidewalk in front of me, at the service entrance, motor idling. I waited, bending to

136

wave at the window. Air wrenches clattered inside the garage. The smell of new tires and cleaning solvents drifted out to mingle with that of exhaust. To hell with it, I thought, hung a U-turn, and headed back. Clappe, still busy impressing the lady, fell silent until I had passed, like I didn't know the fat bastard was there.

Clappe had soured my saliva earlier that morning in the woodshop. The "good ol' boys" usually took their morning coffee there, in the office of Mel Sohrer, the assistant shop instructor. Another body entered some minutes later, carrying a familiar smell. I didn't recognize it, or Sly, until I heard him in the office, all of them giggling and farting like schoolboys talking pussy, Sly bragging about his latest dip. Clappe had his face right in the middle of it, like he was eating the real thing. When they left, I recognized that scent—Camille's cologne.

Clappe caught up to me in the middle of the next block.

"Going the wrong way, aren't you, Pat?"

"I just ain't up to it today," I said.

"How 'bout a beer then? You up to that?"

My eyes were closed behind the glasses.

"Somebody might say something if we head back in this early."

Two drafts and a medicinal brandy later, my eyes started to open. I sipped a third, one ear slightly cocked to Clappe's monologue. He even talked fat. I could see white powder squirt from the creases in his doughboy body every time he moved.

"So what's new, Pat? Anything interesting going on in the dorm?"

"Nothin' that I know about."

His laugh was fat too, tight, the same laugh slobbering in Mel's office earlier.

"Hey, c'mon. Everybody knows about the cute little fox you had up there last Saturday. How was that? Pretty good stuff?"

"She darned some socks for me."

"Yeah, umm hmm. I hear you. She darned some socks. Couple of holes probably, huh?"

I ignored him.

"Gee, you've got Geri and Camille up there now too, huh? Have you got anything going there?"

"Anything like what?"

"C'mon Pat. Seems like that would be awful tempting."

"That's against the rules. They don't want the inmates getting amorously involved. It fucks with their heads."

That's what his laugh was, obsession, the little kid looking at dirty pictures. I drained my glass, picked up my cane from the floor, and walked out. Clappe hustled up beside me, his polyester sheaths falling in step.

"You know," he said, "if something's bothering you, Pat, we ought to talk about it. It's not good to hold things in."

His hand found my shoulder then.

"I am experienced in this sort of thing, you know. Everything's confidential too."

"What'd you say to that woman in front of the Chevy dealer earlier?"

"Nothing really. She was just asking me about the school."

Sure, I thought, big time.

"What've you got rappin' against your leg there?"

The sound stopped.

"This? Just a clipboard. Something to keep my hand busy while I'm walking."

"You don't write in it? You just carry it around?"

"No. Not exactly. I make a note in it once in a while."

"What kind of notes?"

"Why?"

"Just curious."

"It's uhh, it's my personal journal."

"What do you write in there about blinks?"

"I don't write anything in particular about the blind."

"I think you oughta leave it behind next time we go out, all right?"

"No. I don't know that it is all right. Why should you have a say in what I do, or what I carry with me? I'm the instructor. You're just here on a lesson."

I wanted to smack that plum and watch his flour fly, like sweat off a boxer.

"Look," I said. "I've got a hard enough time getting people to think I'm human without you flashing that goddamn clipboard around like I'm an experiment and you're my goddamn keeper. Does that make any sense?"

"It might to you," he said, "but it's still none of your business what I do."

"All right. Bring it next time and let me hear that sonofabitch slapping against your leg and we'll see what happens. And while you're at it, why don't you get your legs fixed."

Cole roared, naturally, when I related the day's events later that evening. He was pacing slowly across the room and back. Said he had just stopped in to see why I missed dinner. Crow, I thought. I could smell it. I could taste it too, that difference, the sober skull and the altered. My blink brother, the diabetic total, pacing.

"And besides that," I said, "it just ain't right, period. It's a goddamn institution, just like a nuthouse, or anyplace else. They ain't supposed to be fuckin' the inmates, 'specially when they're supposed to be working."

"I don't recall hearin' any of the gals complainin'."

"Don't make any difference, and the rest of the bastards are creepin' around takin' notes on us."

"Why do you even let it bother you?"

"Cause I'm bent goddamnit."

"That ain't no excuse. Fact is, that oughta help. If I didn't know better, I'd think you were jealous."

"Christ."

"Yip. That's all it is. You're just afraid somebody's gettin' more'n you. That motherfreckle might really be draggin' a woman pleaser too. You never know."

He roared then, and grabbed my foot where it hung off the end of the bed.

"Tell me the truth now," he said, shaking my foot. "Ain't that it? You're afraid he's draggin' it through that little dancin' partner of yours."

Somebody entered the can from the other side. We listened to the stall door close, then a moan and rush of diarrhea. We both cracked up.

"That's more like it," Cole said. "C'mon, git up. What say we go find us a little toddy for the body."

"That don't work anymore either," I said.

"You are really gettin' to be a pain in the ass, you know that? What the hell's buggin' you, the eye?"

"I just ain't in the mood. That's all."

"Except when you're plowin' a little ground of your own. Ain't nobody screwin' your brains up but you, and one of these days you'll say fuck it and just laugh your ass off, 'cause you'll be an old man, and you wasted all those years."

"Yeah, maybe, except I ain't laughin' now."

"Well we damn sure gotta do somethin' to sweeten your disposition. You just ain't that much fun to be around anymore."

"I ain't overly joyed with it myself, you know."

Cole paced again in silence—his thinking mode.

"Look," he said, "it's very simple. There's an old Indian saying that you always keep one foot in the river."

"How do you say it in Indian?"

"Beats the hell outa me. My mother knew. She's the one taught it to me, but shootdang, that's a long way in reverse."

"A goddamn war whoop."

"Seems to work as good as anything else."

139

"So what about you," I said, "there ain't nothin' twistin' your skull out of shape?"

"Never happen."

"I had a couple beers with Rena last night. She loves you, you know."

"Well I'll tell you, ol' buddy. As far as I'm concerned, it works just fine, if that's what you're referrin' to. It still pisses good, and don't get in the way."

"What about Rena?"

"Got a goddamn tongue, don't I? You do hear me talkin', don't you?"

"Right. To hell with it. I wasn't tryin' to piss you off. Wasn't even gonna mention it."

"You ain't gotta feel sorry for me either."

"I ain't feelin' sorry for you."

"Good."

"So what about the river?"

"It's very simple. The nature of the thing is motion, the whole of every-thing, the universe and whatever the hell you got on the other side of that. The first thing you have to do, though, is shitcan all your ideas of present time. That's just some bullshit the white man made up so he could invent the stock market, and what you have to understand now is that everything is constantly moving, never stops. So in essence, what you're doing by keepin' your foot in the river is just stayin' in touch with that end of things. Spiritual, see?"

"This ain't another walk in the woods, is it?"

"That's it too, harmony. It's bein' part of it, everything's part of it, even some bent-up old bastard like you."

I laughed. Cole moved over to Lance's bed and parked.

"Your body might be stuck in one place," he said, "but your mind has to move. That part of it anyway. You've got your other foot on the bank takin' care of whatever's at hand at that particular moment, but the other side has to be open to whatever the motion brings you. It's always movin' too, through the knowns and unknowns alike. You dam that up inside your body and you ain't no different 'n the rest of 'em. You got both feet on the bank, like your buddy Sly there, doin' 'em all and the easy ones twice."

"All right, so I've got one foot in the river. How do I know it's there?"

"'Cause everything'll stop buggin' you, especially people. They're the easiest to figure."

"Then I'll be happy."

"Happy ain't part of it. There ain't no such thing as happiness. You'll laugh a lot. You'll laugh when you know somethin', when you recognize that somethin' inside the motion. You'll sleep good. Your beer will taste a hell of a lot better too. You'll feel it when you're there."

"It's liable to take me a while."

"No worse 'n teachin' a chicken how to fetch."

"You know something," I said. "I didn't think about it till now, but with you out of the picture, that just means more color for me, don't it."

"If that's the way you want to look at it. Seems to me your buddy Sly's the one takin' up all the slack."

"Piss on 'em."

"If I was back in action I'd just spoil 'em anyway. Bring a little tear to their eye."

I laughed again.

"How's the water?" Cole said.

"My foot's gettin' cold."

FOURTEEN

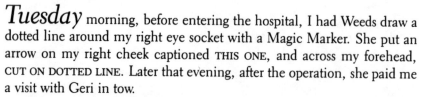

Tuesday morning, before entering the hospital, I had Weeds draw a dotted line around my right eye socket with a Magic Marker. She put an arrow on my right cheek captioned THIS ONE, and across my forehead, CUT ON DOTTED LINE. Later that evening, after the operation, she paid me a visit with Geri in tow.

"You seem very subdued," she said. "Maybe you should do this more often. It might keep you off the streets."

"I'm just waiting for my bath," I said.

"I should've known."

Geri moved up beside the bed, found my arm, and patted it tenderly.

"I'm going to make you a chocolate cake," she said, "with frosting and everything. It'll look just like the one on the package. I can keep it in the dorm refrigerator until you get back."

"Sounds like a lot of unnecessary work," I said. "How'd you like to bathe me instead?"

"You have my permission to smack him," Weeds said.

"I know how to handle bad boys," Geri said.

"So what did they think of the artwork?" Weeds said. "Did you get any laughs?"

"Sure. Everybody got a kick out of it except the ironworker that removed it. I think they called her Marge the Barge."

"I told you it would be hard to get off."

"She started with an SOS pad. When I told her she didn't sweat much for a fat girl, she switched to a wire brush."

"Good for her. You deserved it."

"Thanks. So what else is new back at dear old Blink U? Anything interesting going on? Any modern miracles or multiple births?"

"Stephie got mugged on the snakewalk," Geri said, "for a whole dollar and forty-six cents."

"Christ. Is she all right?"

"She's got a pretty good shiner and a split lip," Weeds said. "I guess the little fart put up a pretty good fight. Her assailant knocked her down three times before she let go of her purse."

"I don't suppose they caught anybody."

"She thinks it was a black gal."

"Then the mugger apologized," Geri said, "and gave her everything back except her coin purse."

"Brother. Leave for a couple of days and the joint starts fallin' apart."

Weeds gave me a comforting pat on top of the head.

"Yes, but don't you worry about it. We'll manage until you get back."

"A bath would sure make me feel better."

"I think it's probably time for your next shot," Weeds said. "I'll see if I can't get it administered where it's needed."

Weeds brought Cole in the following evening. The doc was there, changing my bandage. When he finished, he and Weeds took a stroll.

"Did you get to keep the eye?" Cole said.

"I asked about it. The doc said they use 'em for research. They freeze 'em then slice 'em real thin and check 'em out under the microscope."

"Would've made a nice keychain. You could put it in plastic."

"I don't miss it, I'll tell you that. It's strange too. After a while, I started thinking that headache was only in my mind, and now that it's gone, I don't know if I ever had one or not."

"How's the chow?"

"The drugs are better. Why don't you climb on in here and I'll buzz for the needle lady. All you've got to do is drop your shorts and stick your cheeks out."

"That's all right. I don't mind standin'."

"C'mon, I'll share. Get in. I'll hide in the can."

Cole got in bed and tucked the sheet up around his neck. I hit the call button and locked myself in the bathroom. It might have worked too, except Weeds and the doc slid back in about the same time the needle arrived.

"The bed ain't bad," Cole said. "It's kinda nice not slidin' around on a piss cover."

Aside from a little soreness, my skull felt great—cool, quiet, the gladiators gone, the crowd gone, just the night and the empty coliseum. They'd cut the dosage down on my Demerol, leaving just enough to revive old memories and scatter them along my ragged shore like jetsam.

Harold Adcock occupied the rack next to me, a college professor in for a bowel section. He and his wife talked quietly on the opposite side of the curtain. She read some poetry, and just before noon Thursday, the nurses prepped him and wheeled him off. They brought him back about four with part of his asshole missing. When Adcock came to, the nurses tried to force some broth and Jell-O into him, then finally took the tray away.

"How you feelin'?" I said through the curtain.

He didn't respond. I could hear him breathing, lying there, clearing his throat occasionally—cancer I guess. A couple of hours later I tried him again.

"If you're attempting to engage me in conversation," he said, "I'm afraid you're going to be sadly disappointed."

I was ready to move, anything but just lie there, so I called Weeds and told her they had released me. My last touch of Demerol went in about 7:30. I dressed, checked out the balance in my wobbly legs, and when Weeds arrived at 8:00, I was sitting on the bed, cane in hand.

Geri and Weeds ferried meal trays from the cafeteria to my bedridden bones. I spent the rest of my first week back wandering through my future, sentimental with ideas of a blink commune. Through my open window, I could hear the others between classes in the courtyard below, or in the hallway, laughing at simple things.

I asked the doc about transplants. He told me about tests they had done on chimpanzees, ten at a time, same age, same diet, trying to control as many variables as possible. In the first attempt, only one operation was successful. Another patient went completely insane. Some developed paralysis, much like a stroke victim. Others had digestive problems. The second group had no insanity, or success, and the complications of bodily functions differed from those of the first group.

"I'm in no hurry anyway," I told him.

The first annual C.I.B. blink fertility festival was slated for Tuesday morning, one week after my operation, with a field trip to Lake Merritt, downtown Oakland. Those inclined were to be on the curb at 8:00 A.M. The rest had the day off to do as they pleased. Cole procured another jug of Crow Monday night and brought it to my bedside, forcing that dancing bird down my throat.

"Jesus," I said. "It's amazing how something can be so bad and good at the same time."

"Be nice now," he said. "The old bird's manic-depressive."

I told Cole about my ideas for a blink commune, fish ponds, gardens, interconnecting walkways everywhere, self-sufficiency. Beyond the door, blinks, mostly congenitals, coursed the hallway expressing their excitement over the coming field trip.

"That's what your commune's going to sound like," Cole said.

He laughed, not his usual roar, but something more confined to his thinking mode, something that took another bite of Crow to dissolve.

"Where the hell would you even start?" he said.

"Your place."

He roared.

And Tuesday afternoon our festive field trippers returned, some of the more impressible still in tears, something about seagulls and baby ducks and a little yellow foot sticking out of the former's formidable beak, still wiggling on its way down the gullet. Weeds had apparently translated the incident for them in detail.

"Someday I'll learn to keep my mouth shut," she said and barricaded herself inside her homeroom.

Geri tried to elevate the mood, offering those inclined a piece of her chocolate cake, the one she had made for me and saved in the dorm refrigerator.

"You don't mind, do you?" she said. "I'll save you the biggest piece."

Dead Crow still smoldered in my own guts and chocolate cake was almost the furthest thing from thought.

"It's fine," I said. "It's for a good cause."

I dressed and presented myself downstairs to show my appreciation and donate my share of the cake. Blinks had lined up outside the coffee room, morose from their venture into the real world, the little yellow foot and the marauding gull. As I neared, ravenlike croaks silenced that end of the hall and one small body stormed through the crowd, screaming for revenge. The cake was apparently as dead as the duckling, huge pieces of its body torn away.

I retreated to Cole's room, where I could still hear her curses. Down the hall at my door, Bernie banged away, calling my name. Geri shouted at him to shut up. Teresa nudged him in our direction. He came at a trot.

"Must be important," Cole said, and Bernie hit the doorway, breathing hard.

"I can't find my chew, Patrick."

"You didn't have any, did you?"

"I think so. Maybe I gave it to you."

"C'mon in," Cole said. "I'll fix you up. C'mon, sit down here. You can spit in the wastebasket."

Bernie took a bite out of the can, leaning over to spit.

"You like that stuff, huh?" Cole said.

"He likes it better 'n glue," I said, "don't you, Bernie?"

"Umm hmm."

"Bernie used to go to Armstrong," I said. "It's another blind school up in Sacramento. You lived there, didn't you?"

"For two weeks."

"They used to get loaded on glue and see god."

"I never saw 'im," Bernie said. "My friend Ronny did. He said you'd see god and if you died it wouldn't matter because you'd already be there and you could see."

Geri, still venting, pounded on doors, working her way toward Cole's.

"Who's in here?" she demanded, rapping hard on the open door.

"I'm in here," Bernie said.

Geri stomped, uttered something guttural, and coughed.

"You're lucky you were with us," she said, "or you'd be a prime suspect, Bernie."

She stomped away, mauling words, then down the hall farther, "Carter, you creep. I know you're here someplace."

"How do you sniff glue?" Cole said.

"You put it in a bag, then put your head in and breathe real hard," Bernie said.

"That's what you guys did for excitement, huh?"

"One little kid didn't, and when Ronny didn't wake up, he ran down and told on us."

"Maybe ol' Ronny's still with god then, huh?"

"I don't know. They took him in an ambulance with the siren going, Waaaaaaaaaaa, like that, and my mom came and got me the next day."

"She thought you was keepin' bad company, huh? She oughta see you now."

"They told her to come and get me 'cause I was bad."

"You don't seem all that bad to me," Cole said.

"It's because of what happened before that, too, at my music lesson."

"Oh really?" I said. "What kind of music do you play?"

"Let the boy finish his story, will you," Cole said.

"I took guitar lessons and this other blind girl was taking them with me and we were doing arpeggios one day 'n' she started telling me about the boy and the girl. She's older. Her name's Annette, and she asked me if I'd ever kissed a girl. She said she'd kissed lots of boys and if I wanted, I could kiss her."

"Goddamn," Cole said. "This is startin' to get good. So you got her right there on the treble clef, huh? You're gonna make your buddy Patrick here jealous."

"I let her kiss me and she went Ummmmm, like she could taste it. She said I was a pretty good kisser, so I tried to kiss her again, and kinda ripped her dress. She's the one that did it. She kept trying to get away, and it was only her sleeve anyway. She said, 'you ripped my dress,' and she screamed

146

and the teacher came in, then her mother called the police and said I tried to rape her, and she's the one that wanted to kiss in the first place."

"Goddamn," Cole said. "A story like that'd make a body thirsty, wouldn't it?"

"What happened? What'd the cops do?" I said.

"Nothing. I just had to stay home until I went to Armstrong."

"What d' ya say?" Cole said. "You ready? Or are you just gonna sit around and let 'em make a criminal out of the boy here?"

"I'd sure like to have a beer," Bernie said.

Bernie drank beer like he did everything else. We sat at the bar in the bowling alley lounge.

"Can I have another one?" he said. "My mom's going to send me twenty-five dollars on the first. I'll give it to you when it comes."

"Don't you get S.S.I.?"

"My mom takes it, but she's going to send me twenty-five—"

"Yeah, I know. You just told me."

"Must be the Baptist in 'er," Cole said.

"I'll buy 'im one," a regular on Bernie's left said.

His new buddy bought him five or six in all. Bernie would guzzle them down, belch, and talk about anything the guy wanted. I finally dragged him off the stool and had to damn near carry him back.

"You're just pissed," Cole said, "'cause the guy wasn't buying you any."

"I'm supposed to be keepin' an eye on 'im," I said.

We got him upstairs and found his key. Cole had him propped against the wall.

"Patrick's my friend, 'n' Cole's my friend, 'n' Lou's my friend."

"That's right," I said, opened his door, and gave him a little push inside. About six steps down the hall, his door opened again.

"You think we can have some more beers tomorrow?"

"Next week," I said. "Once a week is plenty."

Lance staggered in a little after midnight, crocked to the gills himself. I played dead. He shuffled over, squatted on the end of his bed and sat there, breathing heavily in my direction.

"I know you ain't asleep," he said.

About a minute later he said it again. I wondered if I sounded that bad when I got gassed up.

"I ain't gonna let you sleep," he said, "till you hear what happened. . . . You better say somethin', man. I'll turn my stereo on."

"Make it short then," I said. "I need my beauty sleep."

147

"I'm in love."

"Glad to hear it. See you in the morning."

"Hey, it's no shit, man. We just killed a gallon of wine in Max's room, me and Max and Camille. I kissed 'er goodnight too, 'n' got some more titty. She's got some nice ones, man."

"Well I'm happy for you," I said. "Goodnight."

"I really love that motherfucker, man."

"Well maybe you'll get a little in your dreams then."

I turned to the wall and wrapped the pillow about my head. Lance took a leak, the splatter of his urine echoing back into the room, then he pulled his guitar case out from under his bed—pring pring twang.

"I'm gonna write that motherfucker a song, man. I ain't shittin' either. I really love 'er."

Lance plucked away at that damn guitar. I pulled the pillow tighter, and after about ten minutes, he petered out—sitting there snoozing, the song muddled in his lap. His silence was very short-winded though.

"She don't like me though, man."

"For crissakes," I said. "Will you shut the fuck up."

"Fuck you, man. I'm bummed out. I love that motherfucker and I know she don't love me. Nobody loves a blind guy."

"You're a trip," I said. "I wish I had a tape recorder going. You'd love yourself in the morning."

"Hey, fuck you, man. That's how it is. Chicks don't like blind guys."

"Look," I said. "I'll discuss anything you want in the morning. How's that?"

"Why should you, man? You don't give a fuck about me either. Nobody does."

I wrapped the pillow again. Lance plucked at his guitar another few minutes, then lay back snoring.

The next morning I got up and showered. When I returned to the room, a humble snicker greeted me.

"How's the head there, lover boy? Get a little in your dreams?"

"Was I drunk?"

"Yeah, a little maybe. You still want to talk about it?"

"About what?"

At 10:30 that night, a cop brought Bernie home. He had been at the bowling alley, mooching drinks, trying to anyway. I heard the siren blow down the block and that familiar idle make the U-turn and park at the curb. Blinks crawled the halls like cockroaches, wondering what the hell was happening. Connie, the night counselor, was already outside talking to the cop, so I dressed and went down.

"I was just looking for my friend Lou," Bernie said. "I thought he might buy me some more beers."

The cop said Bernie had been inside, asking patrons to buy him beer. The bartender asked him to leave a couple of times, so Bernie left and stood outside the door, asking everyone that walked by. An older woman, some bloated Christian, got the ass and phoned in a complaint.

"It was cool," Bernie said. "I got to sit up front and work the siren."

Laughter broke through every open window. Connie was too busy taking notes.

"It makes it look bad for everyone," she said.

"What the hell do you care" I said. "You ain't a blink."

"They'll think all blind people beg."

"It wasn't all that bad," the cop said. "I'm not even sure he knows what's going on."

"That's right," I said. "He ain't been around much. He's got a mother that kept him in a closet all his life."

"He's like a little kid," the cop said.

"Thanks for letting him blow the siren," I said. "There ain't many of you guys that would do that."

I could sense his smile, there in the lights of the blind school, Connie scratching away with her pencil, Bernie beside me, chewing on the end of his cane.

"I'd let him ride around with me if I could. I'd catch hell though."

Bernie stood there, shifting feet, Connie on my left, scribbling away.

"It's really no big deal," the cop said. "I'm not going to fill out a report on it. They should've just called over here. You guys seem to handle things okay."

"I'll let 'im know what's going on," I said.

Bernie followed me back upstairs, obedient, expectant. Hell, I didn't know what I was going to say to him until we got to my room and he asked for some chew. I handed it over, wondering if the effort was worth it.

"You understand," I began, "that by being blind, you have certain advantages over sighted people. Isn't that right?"

"Umm hmm."

"I mean in the sense that you . . ."

I trailed off, the worm hammering its head against the skull, the old film scattered about, useless. Christ, I'd forgotten that Bernie was congenital, that he had never even seen daylight. I'd started to say something about both sides, knowing them, having participated.

"So we have to be a little more cool than regulars," I said, "'cause we know what's going on. Right?"

"Right, Patrick."

"Some regulars have absolutely no idea what's going on, especially where blinks are concerned. Right?"

"Right, Patrick."

"And you never know when you're going to run into one that's a little short on powder. Most of the time you can tell. They'll have a big mouth. Did that gal have a big mouth?"

"She sure did."

"Well see there, you were just a little unlucky. They can't help it though. They're born that way. In another twenty years, they'll be fixing people like that so they can't have kids. But until then, we've got to watch out for them. Right?"

"Right, Patrick."

"I mean watch it close too, real close, 'cause if you don't, you know what happens, don't you?"

"Yep."

"What?"

"I don't get any more beers."

"Oh Christ no. Nothing's that bad."

FIFTEEN

Reno died on a Saturday morning. Teresa woke up next to him and headed west, running. The first one woke me. The second one bounced me out of bed, standing there with a piss hard-on. It was no dead-duckling scream. More like something out of *Psycho*, or somebody with a doberman attached to her ass.

I had seen Reno just the night before. He, Teresa, and the rest of the entourage were headed for the bowling alley, thinking they'd find Geri and me there, but the two of us had slipped out earlier, across the avenue to Petar's to be alone. Geri and I had been sniffing the air around each other all week. Teresa planned the bowling alley affair, a secret supposedly, a celebration of our coming together. Willy, the lovesick twin, had a seizure, locked himself in his wardrobe, and wouldn't talk to anybody. While that melodrama unfolded, Geri and I took the opportunity to sneak out and across the avenue to Petar's.

Geri drank her usual rum and Coke. We had the small table against the back wall, where Weeds and I had parked. I drank one shot of brandy, then stuck to beer, listening to Geri's autobiography, seeing us there, the candle centered on the table, one of those green Shell station giveaway vases with the bumps—romantic eyeball bullshit, just like television. She would have been better off with the twins, I thought, either of them, or both. They were all energetic, all R.L.F.'s. I moved the candle, thinking I'd douse it.

"Don't put it out," she said. "It's very romantic. This is my first date in a long time."

She had been working on her graduate degree in international relations at San Francisco State College and was taking a break to attend C.I.B. Before that she had studied in Montreal, before that, Italy, before that she had graduated from Stonebridge at the top of her class, her mugshot in *Who's Who*. She'd lived in convents in both Italy and Montreal, and had a guide dog, Chelsey, kenneled in San Francisco.

"Why here?" I said.

"Because I've spent my whole life in academics. I want to learn some practical things, to cook and sew and shop. I love to shop, don't you?"

"About as much as ingrown toenails."

"I love the produce section."

"They've got a fan in there, you know, with a ripe peach in front of it, blowing all that good smell at you."

"They do not. That's how things smell naturally."

She'd worked six months at the Italian Embassy in Montreal as a translator, this shortcake who dropped her canes down storm drains and rode a bicycle like other kids. When her family was stationed for a while in Fort Sheridan, a neighbor had started a petition to keep her off her bicycle after an accident, the neighbor's fault. Geri won in court and the city put up a sign on her street: CAUTION: BLIND CHILD PLAYING.

"Sometimes it will take me an hour just to go down one aisle," she said, "there's so many things to look at."

Hit by cars twice besides the bicycle thing, broke her nose twice on light poles running across streets. Six kids in her family, seven homes, seven different Army bases.

"It's a lot different there than here," she said. "My goodness, you wouldn't catch me dead riding my bike here. We don't have sidewalks and big trees grow along the sides about fifty feet apart. You're good on mobility. You know how your facial vision works. Just imagine using it all your life, how good you'd be."

"So now you want to be domestic, huh?"

"I want to do everything. I signed up for woodshop, you know. It's not just for you boys. I might have to fix my chair someday, or something like that."

After the second drink, we had our feet touching under the table. I knew we would wind up in bed. My alternatives had established themselves, I thought, the commune or the egg carton, and the commune was just a dream. The egg carton was practical, right out of the Adipose manual. I could see Geri and me pulling a goddamn shopping cart along the sidewalks of Flatfield, hundred degrees in the shade, a couple of little kids with miniature backpacks and horn-rimmed shades bouncing along behind us, their short canes flailing in open air. She could have been sighted too. Just a little too much oxygen. The same went for Bernie and all the other R.L.F.'s—a bit premature and a little too much oxygen. Erase that, they would be regulars on the street.

Alcohol can make everything practical, even the egg carton. I'd get guide dogs for the kids, puppy guide dogs, toddling along with their tails sticking up over their backs. Geri sipped at her fourth rum and Coke. The same combination had got her eighty-sixed from the convent in Montreal.

"The mother superior caught me," she said. "My room was so tiny, just barely big enough for my trunk, my bed and desk and me, nothing else. I'd open my window and sit there on my trunk listening to the city, drinking my rum and Cokes. I drank a lot too, but not like you guys. My goodness. It doesn't take me that much to get drunk."

I ordered another round.

"You ever have a boyfriend?" I said.

"Sure, lots of them. I dated a lot in high school. Most of them were creeps though. All they wanted to do was feel me up. I knew what I was doing though, believe me. I had two years of karate lessons and boy, I'd let them have it right in the kisser. They knew enough to leave me alone after that."

"Nothing serious then, huh?"

"I had a crush on our football captain. He was good friends with my brother, Paul. I went out for cheerleader that year, so I could be close to him. It was never serious though, not on his part anyway. He took me out once to be nice and that was it. He's married now and has a child."

"Cheerleader, huh. You make it?"

"No. It was sort of political."

"What were your school colors?"

"Green and gold."

"Do you think of things as having color?"

"Sure. I've got all my clothes labeled. I love beige and blue. I've got on blue jeans and a beige sweater right now."

"You can sense color, then."

"Of course. Reds are hot, blues are calm and cool, greens are peaceful, like nature, yellows and orange and things like that are exciting. Reds are exciting too, but deeper. The lighter colors don't get you in as much trouble. I don't care for black that much, but I like browns, especially in summer, and plaids in the fall."

On our way back, we held hands, step for step along the sidewalks. I caned, she carried hers. We would probably take the goddamn Greyhound on vacation, I thought, back to Italy first trip, meet the family. I'd grow calm and old, blue, and we would take that goddamn bus every year, somewhere. I'd die on it someday and Geri would go through my things, my top drawer, everything I had kept since I was a kid, all those objects of fancy, her short, quick fingers lifting, examining them like the entrails of my life.

At the avenue, hand in hand, two blinks in love, I could see the eyes in cars following us as we crossed.

"You want to hit the bowling alley for a drink?" I said.

"It might be fun, and I wouldn't mind really, but I wish we could dance by ourselves, without going there."

The kids could ride in the shopping cart, I thought, in that kid seat, their little legs sticking out like stalks of celery in tennis shoes, the neighbors smiling, waving as we passed. I'd wave back once in a while, just in case, and hold up my manual.

Somebody had a movie going in the TV room. The dialogue was almost inaudible, then the background music would flare. We could hear it from where we parked on the concrete bench just outside the dorm entrance, Geri on my lap, face to face, her legs about my waist, kissing passionately. The worm, true to form, lumped up obviously between us.

"I've got nothing to do with that," I said. "He works on his own."

"He certainly seems to work all right," she said shyly.

My hands moved under the sweater, caressing the bare skin of her back. As she began to move gradually on the hard-on, grinding a little, my hands moved up front, lifting the bra free, cupping her breasts, small, firm, well rounded, her nipples excited.

"I hope you don't think I'm like all those other creeps," I said.

She kissed me long and hard on the mouth. It seemed inevitable, the two of us pulling that goddamn shopping cart down the sidewalks, but not unpleasant. We kissed, our chins wet and lips sore.

"You don't think I'm too easy, do you?" I said.

A small fist rose to my cheek, chucking me a little.

"Don't forget," she said. "I'm still pretty tough."

"You sure you want to get into this, huh? . . . What about your education?"

She laid her cheek against my shoulder. My hand moved across her back, caressing.

"You want to have kids?" I said.

"I'd love to have children."

"Have you ever made love?"

"Once in college. It didn't go very well."

"I don't suppose you're on the pill then."

"I want to learn about that too," she said.

We began to sway, back and forth, just holding.

"We've got lots of time," I said.

"I want to, really. I'm just a little nervous. You won't be mad at me if I don't do good, will you?"

I laughed and she sat up, pulling back some. I put my hand to her face, she to mine, looking.

"I love your body," I said. "Want to check mine out?"

"I couldn't right here. You never know who's watching."

"You ever looked at a guy's body?"

"Just in biology, a plastic model. It didn't impress me that much."

"I'll get some rubbers," I said, "maybe some foam too."

"I don't even know about those things," she said. "I'm sorry."

We held each other, swaying gently for some minutes, like two young trees, their limbs beginning to overlap, the world beginning to shrink small and simple about us.

Upstairs, she jumped, wrapping her legs about me. I pressed her to the wall.

"I'm not afraid either," she said, "just nervous."

"We could right now," I said. "We'd have to be careful though. When was your last period?"

"God," she said. "I want to, but I'd die if Camille came in and caught us."

"Lance is leaving for the weekend. I'll get some rubbers."

Sleep didn't make a direct hit until just before birdsong, just enough to leave the skull vacant, the worm less than enamored with Teresa's morning dirge. Cole knocked about the same time I reached for the door. I had pulled on my jeans and a T-shirt.

"You're shittin' me," I said.

"Go look for yourself," he said. "I'm gonna make a phone call."

Down the hall, Geri's voice comforted a sobbing Teresa, and as I started toward them, Teresa came at a run, crashing into me, her arms tight about my neck, face buried, her body solid under the housecoat.

"Reno's dead, Reno's dead."

Christ, I thought, what a way to start a Saturday. Geri joined our circle then, smooth under her pajamas—one arm for her, one for Teresa. When Cole returned from the phone booth, Geri took Teresa downstairs for coffee. He and I adjourned to my room.

"Where is he," I said, "in bed?"

"What's left of 'im."

Cole moved to the window, laughing, trying to contain it.

"You're sick," I said, and began to laugh too. The whole damn morning had a purple tint to it.

"Goddammit," I said. "Will you knock it off."

"She screwed 'im to death," he said.

Blinks pulsed through the halls like ghosts, whispering, door to door. I closed mine, my hand cupped to my mouth. I could see Reno, lying there, X's in his eyes, with Teresa on top, her back arched, just cranking away, eyes closed, face to the stars.

Cole flopped onto Lance's bed and sighed, coughing.

"Goddamn," he said. "I'm sorry, man. I just ain't used to wakin' up like that. But I ain't shittin' you one bit. He called it too. He's been tellin' me all damn week she was goin' to screw 'im to death some day."

"Jesus," I said, "and she was snoozin' next to 'im like that."

"Well I can understand why she'd be tired."

"You're sure he's dead, huh?'"

"That's funny," Cole said. "The cops asked me the same thing, 'n' like I told them, most of 'im is, near as I can tell."

A siren wailed out on the avenue.

"You mean he might not be dead?"

"Hell yes he's dead. You think I'd be sittin' here laughin' if he wasn't already dead? He's got a boner, that's all, 'n' I ain't no goddamn pervert either, so keep your filthy thoughts to yourself. It just happened to be the first thing I touched when I checked 'im out."

I started laughing then.

"Well it's natural, ain't it?" Cole said. "I mean your hand hits somethin' like that, you're gonna check it out to see what the hell it is."

The siren wailed through a quick U-turn, then moaned to a halt at the curb in front of the school.

"I ain't shittin' you ol' buddy, I'm still in shock. I was sawin' them off pretty good when she let go with that first squawk, 'n' you know how you wake up sometimes and don't know where the hell you are? Well that was it. I'm standin' there in the middle of the floor, every hair on my body wigglin'. Teresa's got me in a bear hug, shakin' like crazy, naked as a goddamn rock herself, 'n' she ain't said anything yet, of course, so I ain't got the faintest goddamn idea what's happenin' 'n' about that time she rears back and lets go with another squawk, grabs her kimono, and out the door she goes."

Booted feet hurried the gurney toward the dorm, wheels rattling.

"So I reached over to see what the hell the story was with Reno, and that was it, first thing my hand hit. I admit, I didn't know what the hell it was till I took a better look. It's been so long since I had one myself."

"You check his pulse?"

"Not there."

The paramedics emerged from the stairwell. Somebody shouted, directing them down the hall, and they rattled by.

"I tell you, ol' buddy," Cole said. "You'd have to of been there to appreciate it. And all the time she was workin' on 'im last night, he was layin' there tellin' me about his ex-wife 'n' how she filed for divorce after his stroke. He said she claimed mental hardship, and as near as he could figure, that referred to his pecker, and the fact that it only got hard on the one side. He said it curved to the right and she was left-handed."

I opened the door. Blinks had hit the hall like a spring hatch, and a moment later the gurney wheeled out of Cole's room, the wheels quiet, those booted feet hurrying it along. One voice talked code into a portable radio, and as he passed my door, he stopped.

"Patrick. What the hell are you doing here?"

"I live here. Who the hell's that?"

"Bill Estes. You know this guy here?"

Bill Estes, I thought. I could see him, Brookings Fire Department, the heavy, brown mustache, black uniform, white hat. We had gone to school together, hunted, fished.

"How's the family doin'," I said.

"Great. You know this guy?"

"Yeah. I hear he's goin' out like a sailboat with a smile."

"Sail on, brother," Cole yelled behind me. "Keep 'er nose to the wind."

"Jesus," Estes said. "I'll see you, huh? We've got to get him out of here. Give me a call, or somethin', we'll get together."

Teresa followed the gurney down, sobbing.

"Goddamn," Cole said. "This calls for special treatment. I'll be back in a minute."

From the window, I heard the doors close, and Teresa's bare feet trotted back toward the dorm. Geri moved up against me as the siren departed. I slid my hands inside her top.

"And how are you doin'," I said.

"I didn't sleep very well last night."

"What's a matter, gas?"

"Stop that. You know very well it wasn't gas, and this is no time to be joking."

One hand worked her breasts. The other slipped into her bottoms.

"I want you bad," I said. "Right now. You think I'm perverted?"

"I do too," she said. "I think we both need it. I'm sorry I couldn't last night. You're not mad, are you?"

"Not at all. I could just close the door though."

"I would," she said, "believe me. If it wasn't for this."

I removed my hands, straightening her jammies.

"It's all right," I said. "It is kind of a strange day anyway. We've got lots of time."

"Tonight," she said. "I'll have to tell Camille though. I don't want her to get upset if I'm not there. She might say something."

"I can wait," I said. "We've got lots of time."

"I don't want to wait any longer either," she said. "It's like a dream, isn't it?"

We met Teresa in the hall. She put her arms about my neck again, sobbing.

"Oh Patrick," she said, "my sergeant at arms Patrick. That sonofabitch Reno. He's dead, Patrick. He's dead. Now where in the hell am I going to get a good screw?"

The worm opened its mouth, but refrained from divulging its thoughts.

"You, Patrick?" she said, looking at me, her body still pressed tight. "No, not you Patrick. You're already taken, you sonofabitch, and Cole can't get it up and there's nobody else here worth screwing."

She tossed her head back and ripped off a good laugh, a little manic, I thought. Geri and I helped her down the hall to Cole's room. She fluctuated, sobbing and laughing, mostly laughing. Cole flew the Crow by her a couple times and she settled onto Reno's bed, crying quietly in Geri's arms.

Bernie made his appearance at the door, wanting to know if Reno was still there, said he'd never seen a dead person before.

"They already got him down at the morgue, guttin 'im out," I said.

"You didn't miss anything anyway," Cole said. "It ain't no different 'n feelin' the sidewalk in the mornin' before the sun hits it."

That afternoon I hiked across the avenue to Ball's Drugs. Bernie tagged along for some chew. An energetic young nymph provided customer service, leading the way to a case of beer, quart of Crow, and the chew.

"Will there be anything else?" she said.

"I need some rubbers," I said.

"Oh. Well I think I'll drop you off at the pharmacy and let them take care of that."

Another sweet voice behind the pharmacy counter filled that order. Bernie stood beside me, swaying, gnawing on the end of his cane.

"Something durable, if you've got it," I said, "something we can wash out and use over."

"Will one dozen be enough?"

"That oughta get us through today."

"Sounds like fun," she said. "You guys must be having a party."

"One of the guys in the dorm died last night, so we're taking advantage of the situation."

"Do you have a color preference?"

158

"Sure, bright red, if you've got it."

Outside, Bernie all but came apart at the perforations.

"Calm down for crissakes," I said. "Don't you know what rubbers are for?"

"I think so."

"You know what sperm is?"

"Yes, that's jiz."

"Well I just got these in case I meet some nice lady. We wouldn't want to get her pregnant, would we?"

"Who's going to get pregnant?"

"Nobody. Here's your chew. Occupy yourself with that."

"You told that lady we're having a party?"

"I lied. You gotta keep those regulars thinking, right?"

Death had a strange effect on blinks. Three different people asked if I had heard about Reno before Bernie and I hit the stairwell.

"That's just a vicious rumor," I told them. "We just saw Reno down at the bowling alley ten minutes ago."

A number of wakes fondled Reno in memory that night. The creeps had cookies and punch in the TV room. The partials got together on the west end, touched feet or some goddamn thing. Geri and Camille put on a little private number for Teresa, girls only, so we threw our own graduation party in Cole's room, Max and Bernie included, classical music playing.

"Cheesus," Max said. "Do we have to listen to that all night?"

"It ain't any stranger 'n anything else that goes on around here," Cole said. "Just listen for a while. You'll hear the secrets of the universe."

Bernie got real quiet about nine. Something in his combination of chew and beer had him sitting on the floor, making green sounds. He went quietly to his room a few minutes later. I walked him down, and on the way back, knocked at Geri's.

"Patrick!" Teresa shouted from inside the room. "Somebody bring my sergeant at arms in here."

Geri stepped into the hall with me, closing the door.

"I can't believe that woman," she said. "She should have been bombed hours ago. I couldn't drink that much in a year."

"Bring my sergeant at arms in here," Teresa yelled. "Patrick? Goddammit he's dead, that sonofabitch Reno. How am I supposed to sleep tonight?"

Geri gave me a hug.

"Are you boys behaving yourselves down there?"

"Doin' just fine."

"We've got lots of time, don't we?"

"You bet," I said. "We're in no hurry."

Cole had the Crow flying when I returned from my visit with Geri. He and Max were still arguing over the radio station.

"That's Horowitz," Cole said. "Now don't that embarrass you?"

I took a bite at the Crow, offering a toast.

"To Reno," I said. "That's what you call going off half cocked."

"Oh cheesus," Max said.

"The boy was beautiful, wasn't he?" Cole said.

We observed a few minutes of silence and Crow, raising the bottle to whatever spirits might have been present. Max passed, then broke the silence, clearing his throat.

"I think I'm about ready for the hay, you guys," he said. "You know? I mean cheesus. Him bein' a buddy and all. Y' know what I mean?"

"You oughta go down and help Teresa out," I said. "She says she needs a little worm or she won't get to sleep."

"Not me buddy. I'd be afraid to touch that."

Time dissolved for a while after Max left. Cole donned his headphones. I got off on some tangent with the Indians on Brookings Hill, watching that first sail like I'd been born two hundred years too late. I thought Cole fell asleep, until the Crow nudged my kneecap. Four beers were left.

"What the hell you thinkin' about?" I said to Cole.

"Rocks."

"What kind of rocks?"

"Big ones and little ones."

"How many times you been in love?"

"Never. Don't even know what it means. It's just another funny word, like rocks. Some people look at a big one and think it's beautiful. They find a small one in their garden and give it the toss. . . . Why? You in love with that little gal?"

"A little further than like, anyway," I said.

"How many times you done that?"

"Oh Christ. I dunno. I tried to figure it out one night and stopped when I hit forty. No one-nighters either. These were all substantial affairs, at least two or three nights."

"That ought to tell you somethin' right there."

"Yeah, but it ain't no fun thinkin' you're screwed up."

"You're all right. Everybody's all right, just in a hurry."

The Crow came by again.

"Make some bubbles in that," he said. "It's full of vitamins."

"So what about you? Not even once, huh?" I said.

"I remember one. I remember thinkin' if I had one wish, I'd have wished she was born ugly."

"Jesus, nice guy."

"Nope. You're missin' it. She was beautiful. I thought she was beautiful anyway. She looked like a dark Janet Leigh. Her mother was Karok too. Her old man was a tall, skinny Irishman. She wanted to get knocked up and have a baby, 'n' I had my head someplace else at the time."

"You ever see 'er again?"

"More 'n I wanted to. She married some merchant seaman. They had a place in town. Whenever he was gone, she'd stay fucked up, whorin' around, still pretty. It was amazin' she could stay pretty so long. Never had any kids either. I don't think she could have any. . . . But anyway, in deer season the bars would always be full of flatlanders, 'n' you could always find her out in the parking lot with two or three of 'em on 'er. They'd dump 'er off with 'er clothes somewhere. Sometimes they wouldn't even bother to pitch 'er clothes out, 'n' the bartender there at the Buckhorn was always tellin' the story how her old man came home one time, found a strange pickup parked in his driveway and commenced to shootin' arrows through the bedroom window. . . . The last time I saw 'er, her face was all puffed up with alcohol. She tried a smile, 'n' I could see 'er eyes tryin' to work up some old memories that'd never really been there to begin with. I don't think we were ever in love."

I reached down for another beer and popped it.

"You ready," I said.

Cole didn't answer. I sipped at the beer, giving him some space. He was still breathing when I finished it.

"You awake?"

I finished off the last two beers and tiptoed out, down the hall to my door, cracking up because I was tiptoeing.

"You dumb sonofabitch," I said under my breath, and somebody's shoes squeaked on the linoleum at the stairwell. Goddamn perverted eyeball of a night counselor, I thought, then smiled and waved.

"Goodnight Connie," I said. "Don't let your bugs bite."

Whoever the hell it was sneaked downstairs.

"Asshole," I said.

My room had that hollow, empty feeling, lifeless. I took a leak, then came back, opened the window, sat on the bed, no traffic, nothing, just the damp fog moving by with all those secrets hidden inside. My genius searched its crevices for antidotes, no beer left, then it hit me. The god-damn lightbulb flashed on, and in stocking feet, I tiptoed on down an-other four doors, just a light knock, I thought, see if she's still awake. Oh

Christ, it was just hilarious, one hand over my mouth, the other raised to knock, then I froze, thinking I heard something inside. She can't sleep either, I thought, putting my ear to the jamb, my brains dropping into my sack with a splash.

Once my heart quieted, I could hear it clearly, the sounds of exaggerated lovemaking, Sly talking his shit, groaning with each stroke. It was suddenly difficult to swallow, my goddamn hand still poised there in midair like an extension of my ignorant skull.

Disinfectant crept up through the stairwell as I walked back to my room.

SIXTEEN

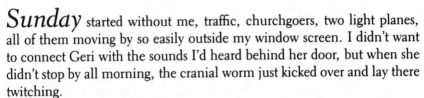

Sunday started without me, traffic, churchgoers, two light planes, all of them moving by so easily outside my window screen. I didn't want to connect Geri with the sounds I'd heard behind her door, but when she didn't stop by all morning, the cranial worm just kicked over and lay there twitching.

I tried out some breakfast about 11:30, cornflakes and a couple of pints of cold milk. I no sooner got my carcass spread on the bed again when someone shouted my name from the stairwell.

"Patrick, telephone."

Christ I was sick, too sick to vomit even, and Elaine's big-toothed, cheery voice jumped out of the receiver onto my face.

"Yes," I said, "something is wrong. You. You're the last goddamn thing I wanted to hear today."

"Sounds like you've got a hangover. What did you do, have another party?"

"Yeah, a beauty too. One of the guys died, so we threw him a graduation party. I still haven't found my clothes."

She laughed.

"You mind if I hang up now?" I said.

"The reason I called is because I've been talking with some people and they think I should get an attorney. They say I'm getting screwed in this do-it-yourself thing."

"As long as they're being so helpful, why don't you let 'em pay your goddamn bills too?"

"Did somebody really die?"

"Either that, or he's been dead all along and just came to life."

"If someone did die, I'm sorry. I guess it wasn't a good time to call. I just don't want to get screwed."

"All right. Well when you get your mind made up, let me know, huh?"

The rest of the day dragged by on my bed, radio on, door and window open, waiting. Everyone seemed constipated, moving around in that purple tint, especially the partials.

Shortly after six I forced myself down to the cafeteria again—two bologna sandwiches, two pints of milk, then gave myself a good push back toward bed. As I exited the stairwell, I stopped, Geri's door in front of me. What the hell, I thought, and knocked. Her pajama feet came scuffing across the floor to answer.

"Hi," I said.

She smelled like she had just crawled out of the blankets.

"What's the matter, shortcake," I said, "you tired?"

"I'm very tired."

"Well I just thought I'd say hi. I'll stop by sometime when you're not so tired."

"What are you mad about?" she said.

I had already taken a couple steps.

"I'm mad," I said, turning, "because I tiptoed down here last night like a goddamn idiot, a goddamn, amorous idiot, thinking I might find my short sweetie on the other side of this door waiting for me. So I sneak an ear to the crack and hear a goddamn Egyptian orgy going on inside."

"You thought that was me?"

"I didn't say that. I don't really know what I thought."

"If you didn't think it was me, then why are you mad?"

"One of the participants came in loud and clear," I said, "and that bastard ain't gettin' paid to be doin' that."

"Apparently he is."

"Yeah, well piss on it anyway. You have fun listening?"

"You should have knocked. All of you would've had a good surprise."

She told me then about spending the night downstairs in the coffee room, wrapped up in her comforter, listening to the refrigerator go on and off. She hadn't even been in her room when I came tiptoeing.

"I left," she said, "because they were disgusting. They're both gross. He was bombed. You could smell it all over the room. It's Camille's fault too, and believe me, I'm going to have a talk with her, and I don't know what you heard, but I hope that isn't your idea of lovemaking."

I would have to start using my brain for something besides a sponge, I thought, walking back to my room. The worm was definitely showing signs of wear.

Lance showed up first thing Monday morning with friends. I was sitting on the bed, fingering braille to occupy my worm, and that hormone kept walking around, heh heh heh, heh heh heh. Every goddamn thirty seconds, heh heh heh, that irritating goddamn snicker.

"What the fuck's the matter with you?" I said. "You been sniffing gas?"

"Heh heh heh. I got crabs again. Six of my buddies 'n' me gangbanged this chick in the back of Helmet-Head's pickup."

"Why didn't you just say so."

"I dunno."

"You got some Raid, or something to spray 'em with?"

"I got some shampoo from the county clinic."

"Well thanks for telling me. I'll use the hall can for a while."

"What about them guys next door? You think I should tell 'em?"

Carter and Lonny Charles shared the can with us.

"That's up to you. Use your imagination."

About a minute later—heh heh heh, heh heh heh.

"Now what?" I said. "Was it somebody we know?"

"Just some old girlfriend, some red freak. We fucked the shit out of 'er, man. Heh heh heh."

"And you guys thought you were the ones dishin' it out."

Administration pulled me out of my braille class later that morning to serve as tour guide for a prospective student, another newly blinded adult, and her parents. The administration preferred totals for tours, if they had one that could find his way around. Geri and the twins usually did the promoting.

I met Lauren and her folks in the lobby, provided a short, flowery introduction, then proceeded room to room. Lauren seemed to have lockjaw.

"How did you lose your sight?" her mother asked.

"In an accident," I said, "a boating accident."

"Lauren was in a riding accident last year. She was off gallivanting on our new Morgan and she rode it onto the highway and got hit by a red M.G. How long did we have that mare, dear? A month? Two months? Anyway the horse shied, or something. She's hardly spoken to anyone since. Her doctor thinks this school might be good for her, to be around her kind of people."

After lunch, I showed them back to the lobby.

"I wish I had my things and could stay right now," Lauren said.

Her father shook my hand, the other on my shoulder, squeezing. Her mother hugged me and cried.

Stan rewarded my efforts that afternoon with two bus tokens and a slip of paper, a brailled address, 1035 Shattuck Avenue, Berkeley. Weeds had told me about the solo mobility runs, excursions into the outer world for those blinks capable of making a round trip. I always figured it would be a beer run, hide for a while in some smoke hole and walk back smiling.

"Find it and get this signed," he said. "Take your time. You've got all afternoon. It's printed out on the other side if you need help."

I hit the avenue, found the bus stop in front of the carwash, caught a bus to University Avenue, then transferred east. I got off just before Shattuck, into a tangle of hyperenergy, bodies, motorbikes, little cars with four speeds. Through the middle of this sound pollution, the buses bullied, spewing diesel fog. I crossed to the east side in a crowd, then turned south. In that first block, I questioned three people on the address, but Berkeley had no time for blinks with addresses.

Each block took me farther away from that trap of sound, and at the next light, waiting, another body stopped beside me.

"Can you tell me what block we're in here?" I said. "Can you see an address?"

The light changed, the guy ran, and about halfway across he yelled back.

"That's the twenty-five hundred block."

I waved. That fucking Stan, I thought. Fourteen goddamn blocks. Take your time, you've got all afternoon.

Six or seven blocks later, I lost count. The traffic and sound had thinned enough to let me drift, the worm humping that question over and over—"we have lots of time, don't we?" I ran my left hand along a building front, found the door, opened it and leaned inside. A body several feet in front of me sucked ten yards of air.

"Sorry to bother you," I said. "Can you tell me what the address is here?"

Two women whispered in Chinese. I smiled and backed out.

At the next corner, I stopped another body and presented the address card.

"Are you familiar with this place?" I said.

"Oh sure. The Yellow Cafe. They've got great sprouts there. You'll love it."

He handed the card back and split.

A door opened on the next block and a black couple stepped out onto the sidewalk some distance in front of me. They stood there talking, so I approached and showed my card.

"I'm trying to find this address," I said.

"What're all these bumps?" the guy said.

"I'm sorry," I said. "That's the braille side. Turn it over."

"You can really read this shit here?"

"It's a lot easier when you're drunk," I said.

The woman laughed, a good, chesty, full-bodied laugh, a gospel singer in the background.

166

"Boy, I guess," the guy said. "This don't look like shit to me. Look at this honey. Ain't this a bitch? And this man here says he can read that. I don't know how you do it, brutha. Must be that fifth sense or sum'pin."

"I bet this one here's a seven," the woman said. "See right here?"

She took my hand and rubbed it on the card.

"Is that one a seven right there?"

"That's a period," I said.

"Well, I tried anyway."

The guy turned the card over then and read the address.

"Oh, yeah," he said, "that's jus' up the street a ways," he said, then turned the card to examine the braille again.

"Honey," his wife said. "Will you show this man where he's goin' so we can do some of the same."

The guy got behind me, turning my shoulders to face me directly south, then strung his arm along the side of my head, pointing.

"Right down there, jus' this side of the car dealer. The yellow one. See it? About the middle of the block there. Right where that bus is passin' now."

"The middle of the next block?" I said.

"Yeah, you got it."

"Morris," his wife growled. "You done seen the man's stick, didn't you? Now if he could see somethin' yella, you think he'd be axin' you? You playin' the fool again, Morris."

I left the two of them standing there arguing, crossed the street, and halfway down the next block smelled burgers on the grill. My nose missed the door the first pass, but caught it coming back, up three steps, tight inside, close walls, tables, lots of bodies, noise, and a waiter in my face wanting to seat me—an Arab I thought. I asked him what was on the menu—burgers, swiss burgers, mushroom burgers, onion burgers, cheddar and sprout burgers. The guy kept trying to drag me off by the arm.

"That's all right," I said. "I just need you to sign this card."

He looked at it, then handed it back.

"I'm sorry, I do not understand."

"You gotta sign your name on it," I said, "or the cops are gonna come and kill my ass."

He left abruptly, and a minute later the manager approached me. I explained. He laughed and signed it.

At the first corner, I hung a right, satiated for the moment with Shattuckism. One block farther east on a parallel street, the noise level dropped considerably. Birds frolicked in the many trees, no buses, no exhaust, no whirlpools of sound. Shattuck leaked through at each corner like a hole in the fence, but in between, residential Berkeley played a

167

much softer tune—kids in backyards, squeals of delight, swing sets creaking, dogs barking at me through gates.

In the fourth block, Led Zeppelin pumped out of a second-story window. I slowed, holding it with my left ear: In a tree by the brook there's a songbird who sings sometimes all of our thoughts are misgiven—We have lots of time, don't we? I could see Geri in childbirth, me holding her hand, sounds of pain, the grip of her hand, the antiseptic state of the delivery room, everything waiting for that one sound. We could spend Sundays in bed, that small, naked sound lying between us, suckling, taking my place at its mother's breasts. I would pull that goddamn shopping cart right through the middle of Flatfield's egg carton, past half the goddamn air force captains and light colonels in the world, with their wives and kids and potted shrubs and roll-out sod lawns and privacy fences and barbecues . . . Christ, we have lots of time, don't we?

The song some houses back had attached a tendril to my ear, and in front of me some thirty feet, voices occupied the sidewalk, three of them, two men and a woman. I made a move to the right, found the curb strip, Zeppelin still trailing from the left ear like gut, my skull playing its own primal drum, and on the very next step, right on the "Stairway to Heaven," my right foot settled down into a large pile of something soft, and stopped. Instinct labeled the mass immediately, but my skull had to sort other reasonable possibilities—not ice cream, not alive, not overly resistant, not vegetable. The fumes pried at my nostrils then, pushing the worm through a moment of insanity. The right foot raised completely on its own and kicked, slinging great chunks of the substance loose. Two more kicks followed. I vaguely remembered the voices then, the other bodies occupying the sidewalk, and heard the sound of that shit splattering through them like flak.

"Jesus Christ, man," a male falsetto rang, "what are you doing?"

My boot jerked through another kick before I could control it, snapping one last chunk free. My cane found the curb strip again, and crabwalking, I dragged that right boot through the grass.

"My god," the woman yelled, "it's in my hair."

She coughed, then gagged.

"What the hell'd you do that for?" her companion shouted.

"Looks like we're all in it together," I said.

"Why the hell'd you do that?"

"Sorry man. Just didn't see you. It's that simple."

"Asshole," the other guy muttered.

"It was probably your dog anyway," I said, and dragged my foot off toward University.

Back at Shattuck, I waited with the crowd to cross. As they surged forward on the light, I gave them some space, then followed. I faintly heard the car. I heard the warning shout from the far side too, but in that sound pool, I couldn't be sure. About the same time I stopped, a front tire smashed the toe of my right boot. My cane landed some distance down the street, clattering to the pavement. A couple of bodies hurried to my side, touching me lightly, directing me across.

"You all right?"

"Fine," I said.

"It was one of them goddamn ragheads," the voice on the curb yelled.

Led Zeppelin trickled out my left ear in broken phrases. I smiled.

"Fine," I said. "I'm fine."

When my cane returned to my hand I moved on, west.

"Goddamn ragheads," the guy said. "They pull that shit all the time around here. I swear I'm gonna start packing a forty-four mag and the next time one of 'em pulls that shit, I'll bust 'im right through the fucking beehive as he goes by and I'll bet'cha nothin' comes out the other side. It's that shit they eat, all that funny shit, drive like maniacs and do whatever the hell they . . ."

Two or three blocks west of that nerve center, a bus stopped ahead of me, then pulled away again. I found the bench, caught the next one in line, and transferred north at San Gabriel. I took a seat behind the driver, parallel with the aisle.

"I'd appreciate it," I said, "if you could give me a holler when we reach the Brookings Plaza."

"You got it, babe. I've packed a few of you guys in my time. I'll take good care of you."

Three school kids got on at the next stop and parked across from me, sliding their lunch pails under the seat. I reclined, my head against the backrest, the bus and motion vibrating my eyelids closed. Just before the next stop, a spit wad hit me in the forehead. As we pulled back into traffic, one popped me on the cheek, another hit my chest and a couple close misses found the window behind my head. The kids, unable to contain their glee, started butt-fucking each other. Without opening my eyes or lifting my head, I slid my cane across the aisle, found a leg and gave the shinbone a good whack. Two of them continued laughing.

The driver broke my trance some minutes farther down the road, informing me that he had missed my stop.

"I'm gonna let you off right here in front of Violet's Chinese Food, babe. You're only a couple blocks outa your way."

More like six blocks, I thought.

"You know where you are?" the driver said. "Sorry babe."

"I need the walk anyway," I said.

A spit wad hit me in the ear as I started down the steps.

Geri spent every night that week in the coffee room, then nutted up when I got homicidal over it and told me to mind my own business, she'd take care of her own. So I did. Christ, the worm and I were on a mental luge, one icy turn after another, and at the end, the cosmos waited. I would leave the edge doing about ninety someday, me and about half a million empty beer cans. We would shoot off into black space to become our own little galaxy, tumbling through an eternal night of nothing but old film.

Friday evening, the phone rang again, with my name on it—Cole, half gassed, down at the Indian. He'd been living there all week.

"Tania's leaving for Seattle. She'd like to see you," he said.

I could hear Tania laughing in the background.

"Tell 'im we're partying tonight," she shouted. "Tell 'im my ovaries are screaming again."

The worm fell mute, sorting snapshots of our last encounter.

"Can you handle it?" Cole said, "or is that gonna interfere with the rest of your life?"

Geri was just around the corner and across the hall, the little blind girl who would have her babies in the dark and get shopping-cart calluses between Greyhounds.

"It's a full moon," Cole said. "You got a natural excuse."

"Tell 'im we'll pick 'im up in ten minutes," Tania shouted.

"You hear that?" Cole said.

"I'll be at the snakewalk bench," I said.

They brought a twelve-pack with them, and for the first hour we just cruised, nowhere in particular, Tania and me squeezed into the back seat of Rena's Volkswagen bug. Tania didn't say much about Washington, just that she was leaving in a few days, something about her ex-old man and some overdue notes. I could see Interstate 5 all the way up through Oregon, across the top of Portland, the Columbia River, into Vancouver, thick and green and dark under that perpetual rain cloud, the taverns full, the lack of vitamin D in every face, February 1969, a fresh-killed bear cub on 5, just north of Vancouver, very black, very red.

We wound up at Ducci's that night, live music, country rock, Rena's suggestion.

"They're good," she said. "I saw them down at the Longbranch last month. The bass player's been in a couple times."

Three guitars and a drummer fed high-decibel sound drugs to the robotized crowd of regulars in Ducci's. I knew the bartender, Boyd, an old

170

drinking buddy, fisherman, hunter. He asked a couple to move, clearing four stools at the end of the bar for us. I had to shout, leaning across, to make the introductions. He returned with a pitcher of margaritas and tapped me twice on the back of my left hand—no charge.

"You mean to tell me this big sonofabitch can't see either?" he asked in reference to Cole.

Cole roared. Tania and Rena laughed.

"I guess the girls are gonna have to tell him what a good-looking son-ofagun I am then, huh?"

I could see Boyd's face across our last campfire, Babette Peak, clean-shaven, terminally gray, his glasses reflecting, and at the edge of that fire-light, a ghost-white muslin deerbag hanging from the meatpole.

"You bastard," Boyd said, taking my hands. "I oughta kill you for doing this. You know that, don't you? Where the hell you been?"

"Workin'," I said. "I've got a job as night watchman."

He leaned closer then.

"You know," he said, "the thought just struck me. You guys don't have any idea what these young ladies look like."

"We have to look with our hands," I said.

"I was afraid of that," Boyd said.

The purple tint of change, another sunset, had stayed with me. I could feel it on my skin, in my hair. Tania's blossom seemed a deep burgundy. We danced a few times, neither of us saying much, then sat close, legs touching. Boyd made sure the pitcher of margaritas never saw bottom, and at one point Tania put her hand to the back of my neck and drew our mouths together.

"Can we keep it happy tonight?" she said.

"You want me to laugh more?"

She and Rena hit the can some minutes later and in their absence, a body moved up behind me, one hand on my shoulder.

"You old sonofabitch."

I turned to face him.

"It's Tony, man?"

Tony Perona's voice suspended from the song, that phony, slick head of his jerking, the hand squeezing.

"I cried, man," he said, "when I heard about it. You can ask Boyd. I cried like a baby, man."

He swung his ass onto Tania's stool just as she and Rena returned, and sat there waiting for an introduction.

"Patrick and me go back a long way, don't we, buddy," talking to me, his eyes on Tania, about as far as it would take to knock him on his ass, I thought. The last time I'd seen him was on the floor.

171

"I know I've seen you somewhere before," he said to Tania. "T. M. maybe."

The band, back from a break, twanged a key note, then jumped into "Tulsa Time."

"You mind if I ask your girl to dance?" Tony said.

"Ask her for crissakes. She's the one that has to dance with you."

"C'mon," he said, standing, "just one. I gotta warm up for the main event."

With the floor packed already, they weren't more than six feet behind me, at the edge of the carpet. I didn't mean to listen. I just didn't have anything better to do. T. M., Christ, I thought, that endless pathetic rap of the loser. "Wouldn't you rather be with a whole man?" he said, and the words just seemed to peel themselves free from the crowd and settle in my mouth like so many dirty dog hairs. Then Tania was back on her stool, scooted up close.

"He's your friend?" she said, filling our glasses.

I didn't answer.

"Your friend's an asshole," she said.

"He's a harmless asshole," I said. "He was born that way."

We left an hour later. A breeze off the bay's mudflats met us in the parking lot, my arm about Tania, the door closing behind us, sealing that sound inside Ducci's, the building bulging with whole men and whole women, like maggots in a mouse skin.

We headed for the Pablo Club out at the bottom of Tank Farm Hill. The Pablo was just as loud as Ducci's, but nearly empty. We sat at the bar and Tania worked my fly open, stroking the wart, while she sipped a beer. I could see her small hand and fingers wrapped about my penis, almost the same color, her burgundy seeping into my purple.

We danced a couple more times then left shortly before two. Back in Rena's apartment, she and Cole took the bedroom, the door closed. Tania and I lay on the carpet with a blanket in front of an aquarium, the purr of its filter vacuuming the silence. We worked quietly, conscious of our candle, the last nub of wax, resting between acts without words. The room grew hot, then cool, then hot, hair in sweat. I wanted everything inside her, my entire body tubular, hung like dogs in the constriction of tissue, siamesed at the genitals forever with constant, clockwork orgasms so the mind could be freed to search its other sides.

Tania eventually slept, her head on my arm, her face close. As we cooled, I pulled the blanket up around her shoulders, and lay there for the next hour listening to her breathe, until birdsong outside the window played louder than the fish tank.

Rena made coffee at six. We all drank a cup, then she drove Cole and me back to the snakewalk. The tapping of our canes seemed so foreign to the dew and dawn—one day, then another, I thought, then another and the next and someday, the last, somewhere.

"You know that little gal was cryin' when we left, don't you?" Cole said.

"Some regulars get that way around blinks," I said. "It has something to do with being whole people."

His laugh broke into the surrounding boughs, not exactly crazy and wild, but with enough on it to hold up against morning. I could see Tania bent over the washbasin, her face hidden between her hands, the black braids tied behind her neck, out of the way.

SEVENTEEN

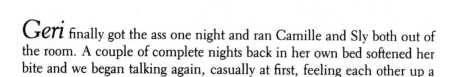

Geri finally got the ass one night and ran Camille and Sly both out of the room. A couple of complete nights back in her own bed softened her bite and we began talking again, casually at first, feeling each other up a bit, listening to the rush of blood engorging our genitalia.

Saturday evening, sitting at my table in the cafeteria, I heard Geri enter alone, whistling. I had just finished an hour of iron and had two plump dagwoods on the tray in front of me.

"Look pretty cute in those shorts," I said as she passed.

She brought her tray around and sat beside me.

"You live around here?" I said.

"You look pretty cute in the dark," she said, "and it's none of your business where I live. I already know about boys like you."

Lance was off again on one of his weekend crab hunts, leaving that side of the room vacant and the other open to suggestion. The idea just seemed to blossom out of nowhere, so I set my sandwich down and leaned toward her.

"Wanta go up and fool around a little when you get done? Check out the difference?"

She sipped her coffee, then lowered her cup slowly, setting it quietly onto her tray. No response.

"Just thought I'd ask."

I finished my sandwiches in silence, wiped my mouth, and started to get up, when she spoke, her voice emerging small, nervous.

"I'd like to shower first," she said.

We kept the window open all night, July breathing in across our naked bodies. Christ, she was amazing, cracking her nuts two or three times to each of my own, like they had been multiplying in there for years and had finally broken down the barrier. She cried after the first one. I had her on top, working down, moving slow. We'd just found a little rhythm when she began to vibrate and lunged into it, grabbing a couple handholds in my ribs, and after, she lay there on top of me, breathing hard.

"I've just never felt anything like that before," she said. "You're not mad at me are you, for crying?"

Weeds apparently noticed the color in her cheeks the following Monday and rushed her down to the county clinic for birth control pills. Geri and I both crossed our fingers and agreed to thirty days of abstinence for the chemicals to take effect.

Every morning her door would swing open at 5:45 and the tracks of her padded jammies would come at a trot for a morning hug.

"All those years," she would say, "and I never even knew what I was missing." When the quarantine period ended, Weeds invited us to her home for the weekend. She and her husband, Paul, had built a beautiful five-level structure in the country near Pleasanton. Paul worked for Standard Oil, top floor, and traveled a lot overseas. "We see just enough of each other," Weeds said.

She parked Geri and me upstairs that night, in one of her creations, a room with french doors, french windows, a beautiful but short antique brass bed, flannel sheets with a ruffled border, and duck-down pillows. The can next door had an old-fashioned footed tub, with bubble baths, oils, the whole bit.

Geri enjoyed looking at my body in bed. She was especially fond of the wart and testicles, examining them at length, at short too, flipping the flaccid little devil about, toylike. That night at Weeds's, she went down on me for the first time, holding the shaft, licking the glans like an ice cream cone.

"Gwenda told me to do this. She said you'd like it."

Her little tongue flicked about my brains like an anteater, then returned to the cone routine, almost sad it was so innocent.

"Am I doing it right?" she said, poking her head out of the covers.

"I don't know," I said. "Nobody's ever done that to me before. But it feels great."

Dear Weeds, I thought, already marking our calendar for us. She had taken me to Danz and Sons in San Francisco earlier in the week to score the new eyeball. They made a casting, filling my socket with liquid rubber, then fit me with a temporary for the rest of the afternoon. Weeds and I ate lunch in a small, aromatic deli, some place she'd hung out as a hippie chick. After lunch we cruised some craft shops, old friends, all gals, lots of incense burning. She would introduce me as her friend. I could feel the other eyes checking me out.

"Not bad," one set said. She had a long, bony hand, very thin, very cold. She and Weeds both laughed, old snapshots I thought, mutual memories maybe, of bare asses and paisley pillows from those extinct nights in the Haight.

I bought a handmade tomato there, a pincushion filled with spices. Weeds had handed it to me. "You should buy this," she'd said. "For another friend."

At 3:00, Danz fitted the new eye. Weeds had picked the color, my blue she said. At 4:00 we were crossing the lower deck of the Bay Bridge, headed back, the scented guts of that tomato drifting out of a small sack beside me. I wished I had thought of buying it myself.

"I want to know more about your divorce," Weeds said. "Specifically whether it's in progress or not."

"It's in progress," I said. "I've already signed the papers. I'm just waiting on Elaine."

"You should get those papers finished, so certain people can relax. You've got a good thing there with Geri. You don't want to mess it up."

So I lay there in Weeds's antique bed, the fancy flannel sheets thrown back, Geri snuggled in beside me, sleeping, her arm draped across my chest. We had the french windows open wide onto a pleasant country night, still except for crickets. On the sill of the open window, one knee cocked up in just enough moonlight to illuminate the question on his brow, sat my slick-haired buddy. I knew what he was thinking. He was wrong too. I had made my choice. Concession had brought the shopping cart closer. So close, I could smell the changing season. I could hear clothes dryers running in garages with blue jeans and a pair of sneakers thumping around inside, and all through the streets the elms shedding their year's color. The crisp rustle of that falling skin scattered across yards and pavement, waiting for the bamboo rake and predawn moan of the street sweeper with its rotary steel whiskers.

Geri started having severe headaches within a few days of our stay with Weeds—migraines they thought. They were sporadic at first, but in the days that followed their numbers increased, as did the opinions of specialists. They were all very quick to diagnose the pill as a prime suspect. One suggested diet as another contributing factor. Another suggested a combination of things, diet, the pill, stress, life changes, sex, love, guilt due to Geri's Catholic background. The cure was easy, become a vegetarian nun.

Geri just shook her head.

"No way," she said. "I'll stop taking the pill, and I can change my diet, but you're crazy if you think I'm giving up anything else. I'll live with it."

She fainted the following day in cooking class, and Weeds hustled me in from woodshop to carry her into a small room adjacent to the sewing class where they kept a day bed. I heard a couple of bodies make a hasty retreat out the opposite door as Weeds turned her key, and I stood there, Geri in my arms, while Weeds wiped the cum from the sheet.

"Fucking assholes," she said. I never did find out who it was, somebody on the staff.

Geri seemed to stabilize after that interlude. The doc returned her walking papers, so I took her across the avenue to Petar's for dinner, in memory of our first date. We had a booth to ourselves, another candle, a cold Bud in my hand and a rum and Coke with a straw for Geri. Our feet touched under the table. The dinner house sounded a hell of a lot like the cafeteria that night, packed, silverware and plates, people gabbing in high octaves, children squealing through full mouths. The kids loved to watch us. One concerned mother at a nearby table had already checked her brood: "Stop that. Open your eyes and eat properly."

I excused myself to use the can and on my way back, near the register, a woman stopped me, touching my arm lightly as I passed. She was sucking on a mint.

"I hope you'll forgive me for asking this," she said. "I saw you sitting there with your little friend, and I know this may sound stupid, but how do you eat?"

My head tossed garishly, a smile ripping out the lower portion of my face, showing my eagerness to please this curious regular.

"There's nothing to it," I said. "I just tie a string here to my front tooth, then stretch it down to the back of my plate and hold it there with my left hand. It's easy to tell when you've got something on your fork, by the weight, then you just find the string and slide that baby up into your mouth."

"Ooooh yes," she said. "That makes sense. You have no idea how long that's been bothering me."

"It's in the *Adipose People's Guide to Life*," I said. "They've got a diagram and everything."

"Ooooh yes. I'll look for that next time I'm in the bookstore."

I related the incident to Geri back at the table. She cracked up and as her laugh faded, I thought I could hear her losing power. She sipped her drink and continued relating a story about her guide dog, Chelsey, how they'd run in the park together in San Francisco. We'd been talking about the dog prior to my nature call.

"It was terrible of me," she said. "They spend a year and lots and lots of money training those dogs not to run. It took me one week to teach her bad habits. She loved it too. We both love to run. We go to that park and just run forever, even in harness."

I sensed it spread about her and begin tightening. When she suddenly went still, I set my beer down and slipped out, around to her side, just in

177

time to catch her as she toppled. I sat there, holding her in my arms, limp as a goddamn dead puppy, every regular in the place gawking. They quit chewing and banging their goddamn silverware, one table after another turning to see what the hell everyone else was looking at. It got so quiet, I could hear the goddamn candle burning.

Then the waitress and the manager arrived.

"She's all right," I said. "It happens all the time on rum and Coke."

Geri's longest trip, prior to that, had been seventy seconds. I forced a smile, those seconds plodding by, the manager standing beside me with his goddamn nerves hanging out, talking paramedics, ambulance, laws about serving blinks liquor. I kept smiling, rocking Geri in my arms, touching her hair and face, wondering if she'd remain so.

She made her entrance just like her exits, fast. Pop, she was up again, ready to roller skate. The manager, with his nerves still showing, wanted us out, leaning over the table to whisper.

"You're disturbing my business," he said. "She needs professional help."

I could understand. It's hard enough for regulars to eat and watch blinks at the same time, without the act going limp on them.

Convalescence came about as natural to Geri as peckers to pumpkins. She had plenty of company though, evenings. Teresa helped a lot. Weeds usually stayed too. The three of them would stretch material out on Geri's bed, pinning patterns on, with special braille tags for indentations or special cuts.

Outside this enclave, blinkdom rocked on. The administration found room for two more blinks. Theo, a gay total, had been a prominent designer in San Francisco until three drunk high-school Nazis cracked his melon open one night with a length of pipe. Mary was another partial, young, lovely, diabetic. Sly hit her trail like a hound dog.

Camille and Sly, following the shortcake's wrath, had moved their affair to the back of Sly's van in the parking lot. The candle finally burned together and Camille woke up half the fossils early one morning reading Sly his rights in the middle of the street. I had an ear present, smiling. She had no sooner cut him off than Clappe asked her out to dinner three nights in a row. She said they ate at Charlie Brown's, a nice restaurant nestled into the Emeryville mudflats, lobster all three nights. Clappe kept trying to put the make on her in the car. She would toy with him, she said, give him a light lip on the mouth, just enough to twist his cellulite into imaginative spasms, then tell him to drive her back to the school. A distinct air of venom spread about her as she related each incident.

That same week, Sally Andrews ran off with the dishwasher, a young guy, twenty-two, left his job and everything. Teresa seemed to be the only one genuinely pissed. Had she known the boy was into screwing blinks, she said, she'd have sent him a personal invitation.

Teresa packed her whereabouts pretty tight after Reno's funeral. I would see her once in a while in the cafeteria, or Geri's room, but she stayed to her room a lot, reading. It was across the hall from Geri's, and when I'd leave nights, standing there in the empty hall, I could hear the hum of a vibrator behind Teresa's door, smell that slight hint of hair burning.

Lance continued his weekend workouts with the same red freak, and after snickering himself into a tight circle at the end of his bed one Monday morning, informed me of their love pact. He had given her two hundred dollars the day before to find an apartment, set up housekeeping, and become a saint. She was supposed to pick him up Friday after school to start the rest of their lives together.

"She's a good lady," he said. "We had a long talk about things. I respect 'er, man. She don't care about me bein' blind and I don't care what she's done, or what people say about 'er."

He sat on the curb until midnight Friday waiting for her, loaded, crying. I spent the rest of the night talking him out of suicide.

Carter hadn't gone far either. I would hear him leave, ghosting out at 1:00, 2:00 A.M. maybe. The next day he'd be in the hall peddling appliances and personal items, mostly jewelry, from a suitcase, said he'd picked them up at garage sales. Geri bought a set of electric curlers. When people got suspicious and stopped buying, he fell to begging. Hamburger money, he said, his breath reeking.

"Gimme a dollah, man. They ain't feedin' me enough."

And when that didn't work, he resorted to stiff-arm tactics, slamming people against the wall, a fist up under their nose. Max told me about it. The school didn't do shit.

One evening, as I returned Geri's tray to the cafeteria, I heard classical guitar melting out through the auditorium door. I stopped, just outside, nailed for the moment by the power, the great gusts of talent blowing by free, like sprays of multicolored pigeons, absorbing sunlight over city parks. I realized I'd never done anything that well in my entire life.

"That's Bernie," Theresa said, passing.

Christ, I thought, Bernie. I could see him in there, bent over the guitar, his long white mane streaming wet against a black satin tuxedo, the veins of his neck and temples protruding like a lathered thoroughbred and the froth of that classical magic flecking his lips, slinging with each jerk of his head. My old buddy Bernie.

I listened for a moment more, then walked away so I didn't have to meet him coming out.

Mother Night nailed me later, dragging me into another well-lighted auditorium. From the podium, megaphone in hand, I vowed to a crowd of smirking regulars that I would be as happy as humanly possible for the rest of my life. Portions of the audience began spilling into the aisles, fits of laughter convulsing their frames into pink, fetal shapes, after which they would explode, blossoming into bouquets of expanding color, spores to the new world.

"What about all that other shit?" some guy yelled from the back row. He kicked a sack over and empty beer cans came rolling forward, clinkety clink from tier to tier. Slick stood against the back wall, watching from the shadows, and when I awoke, it was as if someone had just left the room.

The following morning, I informed Weeds and Geri of my intentions. The worm had finally found its apple tree, I told them, in furthering its education. I could take a proficiency exam for a high school diploma easily enough, and Solano Community College was only twenty miles from Flatfield. I could hitchhike if nothing else. But state edict required I.Q. tests of any blinks wishing to further their education. It wasn't enough to have the bug, I had to prove myself mentally capable first, through an afternoon of testing in Solano County, heir to my future genius.

Weeds took me the following week. Air-conditioned, Adipose desk types presented most of it orally. Weeds took dictation on the essay questions. I blew them away, kept it clean too.

This urge to educate the worm had its reasons, one of which was a time factor. I didn't have to look at the end of the road and wonder which way to go. Weeds agreed, driving back from the testing. And there were other implications she thought I should consider as well.

"Two years at a community college will give you that much more time to adjust," she said, "and decide what you're going to do in the way of vocational activities."

"I'm gonna start a woodshop in my garage," I said, "call it Wood'n'-Things. I'll make toys for kids."

"That's nice," she said, "but you might want to think about transferring to a four-year school when you finish at Solano. Geri's no hick, you know. She'll get tired of talking about wooden things or fishing trips. You have to respond to her needs too, you know."

That voice from my dream, the one in the back row, echoed inside my skull.

"But besides that," Weeds said, "it's worth it. That's a free education and you're stupid if you don't take advantage of it. Rehab will cover just about all your expenses, your tuition and readers. They'll give you all your equipment on loan, which is just the same as owning it. They don't usually ask for it back until you die."

At the top of the stairs, back in the dorm, I turned left, away from Geri's room, something I hadn't done in a month and a half. Something about having it all laid out like that seemed unnatural.

My knock went unanswered at Cole's door. I knew he'd be at the snakewalk. I could sense him out there, sitting in the fog. They come like that sometimes, the insights, with such purity that you almost remember what that thing was you lost as a child.

At the bench, I stuck a chew in, working it down inside my lip, the worm trying to work words down into my mouth.

"Fuck ya," I said. "I ain't gonna say anything. I didn't forget you, either. I fell and hit my head real hard and I've been incognito for the last month."

Cole laughed a little. It was him laughing, too, not the Crow.

"You ain't gotta say anything," he said. "You ain't the first guy to get his head stuck up a vagina. You should never get incognito with your friends though."

I turned to look at him.

"That's right," I said, "I'm guilty."

"Hey. I already told you, you don't have to say anything. There's no need. It'd be different if it mattered."

If it mattered, I thought. If any of it ever mattered. If any of it made a goddamn difference.

Cole spit, then swung the backhand against my shoulder.

"'Course it matters," he said. "I'm happy for you guys, both of you. I mean that too, 'n' you ain't got to feel guilty about nothin' either, 'cause if you remember correctly, I was sittin' here when you met me. This is what I do best, alone."

"You still seein' Rena?"

"I was down there last Friday and closed the joint up with her."

"I took an I.Q. test today," I said, "so I can go to college."

"Think that'll do it for you, huh?"

"We're gonna live in the egg carton with our smart brains and take vacations on the Greyhound, the whole damn family, kids and all, grandma too, might even take the goddamn pope along."

I knew he was grinning.

"That's right," I said. "They checked my fuckin' skull out today to see if I could handle it."

"They find anything?"

"An old bone-handled pocket knife with a busted blade, half a dozen sinkers, and a couple skin mags I hid up there when I was a kid."

"That was it?"

"That was enough, I guess. They told me I could study medicine, metaphysics, anything I wanted, long as I left them the skin mags."

"You'll make it," he said. "I knew why you quit comin' around. Just don't forget what I said about the river, though. Huh? Think of it in bigger chunks too. Think of it in moons, 'stead of suns. They'll all tell you one day at a time, but it's bullshit."

"I oughta be happy, you know? I mean that's what you're supposed to do, isn't it? Settle down and raise your family?"

Cole and I had talked about it more than once, the rest of our lives, like an avenue of signs. The near future, the days just ahead, seemed bright, distinct, or if not bright, at least legible. Distance obscured design accordingly, but hints of color ahead always seemed familiar, some recognizable enough to anticipate.

"I ain't quite sure about the in-betweens," Cole said, "but I know the last thing I'll ever do, and that's going to be a hike up Eagle Peak. I got an old friend up there waitin' for me, an old scrub cedar tree growin' out of a crack in the rocks, 'bout a quarter mile above timberline. Shouldn't even be there."

And while he talked, I could see the boy again. I could smell the creosote of oak railroad ties near the Sante Fe yards in Bay City, and feel the weight of slag in my hand before pitching it at the sides of passing boxcars.

". . . all by its lonesome," Cole said, "all bent up by wind and storms into its own shape of survival. . . ."

And when the trains had passed, he would lay his cheek against the warm steel and watch the caboose disappear around that last bend, knowing it was still moving, wondering where in the hell it went.

". . . Whenever somethin' got a little sideways in the head, I'd take the hike, major things, you know, and by sundown I'd usually remember how foolish it was to let anything bother me.

"I decided to jump that freight one day. I didn't know squat about how to do it either, standing there beside the tracks, hands stuffed into my jacket pockets, kicking rocks around, waiting. It must have been doing forty when it passed, so I walked back, thinking I had seen those same damned cars before anyway. All they did was go in circles.

"So I promised myself years ago that's where I'd die. I will too. When I feel the time gettin' close I'll use what's left to get back and make it up the hill. The buzzards'll take care of the rest. . . . I might carve some totem poles in between."

Traffic sneaked by us, fog drugged.

"It wasn't like this around here when I was a kid," I said. "The fog used to hang up on the Gate. We'd have summer all the way through September."

"I'm gonna be takin' a little vacation here in a couple weeks," Cole said. "There's a woman I have to talk to, somethin' I can't do by letter."

"You love 'er?"

"She loves me, and has for the last three or four years, I guess."

"What about you?"

"I told you before, I never knew enough about it."

"How do you know she loves you then?"

"By the way she talked mostly. You can tell a lot by the way a woman talks. Some just move their mouth outa habit. Their brain's off in another section of the county. Guys do it too. It ain't just peculiar to women. But when a woman's in love with you, she means every word. You'll feel that connection, if somebody cares about you enough."

"What's her name?" I said.

"Niesha."

"This ain't that same Indian gal, is it? The one you wished was born ugly?"

"No. This is an altogether different person."

"Sounds Indian."

"She's been married once already, got a couple kids."

"Is that why?"

"Had nothin' to do with it. At the time, I just knew I wouldn't be any good for her. It's easy to be selfish, you know, 'n' keep 'em tailin' along 'cause the thought of somebody else in bed with 'em scalds your balance. It don't do either of you any good though, so I split up with 'er over a year ago, then when I got sick, she was there again, moved in, took care of me. I didn't even speak to her for the first eleven days."

"I thought I was hardheaded."

"I remember layin' with 'er, feelin' the connection of each word she made. They'd break off in one fine point when her lips touched. It's a physical thing too, you know. I'd feel it in my body, like her hands were on me, but all the while it was just her mind, her soul tryin' to touch mine. It was beautiful."

"You didn't even fool around?"

"Didn't need to, I guess, or I didn't anyway. She's a very physical woman too, very sensual, very quiet 'n' to herself sometimes, but she could damn sure let me know when she was touchin'. You might not think so, but I knew she loved me. Her soul was sayin', this is love, this is how a man and woman love in their minds, and I couldn't return it.

183

Not in the same way. So, I'm gonna take a little time off, now that I can, 'n' try to explain it to her. I think it might mean somethin' to 'er."

"What if she's with somebody else now?"

"Don't matter. She ain't anyway. I just got a letter from 'er last week. Gwenda read it to me. So the least I can do is let 'er know. I owe 'er that much."

Cole stood then and stretched. I knew he wouldn't come back if he left. We would take our different roads.

"It's a damn nice feelin' too," he said. "I think I'm gonna hit the hay and dream about it."

I stopped off at Geri's room for a nightcap. She was busy gabbing with Camille about an upcoming Neil Diamond concert at the Oakland Coliseum. I stood there near her bed, thinking about what Cole had just said, the closeness, the connection, feeling it. Christ, I got chills just thinking about it, wondering if she and I would ever have that, being that close, and yet it seemed to be the finest thing two people could ever have.

We chartered a Greyhound the following weekend, a gambling run to South Shore, Lake Tahoe, blinks and staff together. Geri and I snuggled into a rear seat and slept most of the way. At Harrah's Casino, Geri took off nickel-hunting with Weeds. Max, Bernie, Lance, and I found a keno bar and stayed there all day, lots of free drink chips, lots of Chivas Regal, lots of Heineken. Change girls and cocktail waitresses took turns towing us to the can and back. I figured the route after the first trip, but had a hell of a lot more fun on an elbow. They got a kick out of it too, especially with Bernie, until the boy faded and security guards carried him back to the bus. One cocktail waitress asked if I would be around when she finished her shift and I stood at the urinal, draining my wart, thinking about it. I was gassed. The worm had his horns on. She was sighted, new ground to plow. I laughed it off, but not completely.

Geri found me sitting at a blackjack table, just before the bus left, and climbed onto the stool beside me, broke. I had been winning all day, big too, in blink terms, almost five hundred clams, so I gave her twenty. She lost it in four hands, so I handed her another and attempted to explain my winning strategy.

"I'm no idiot," she said. "I know how to play cards."

She lost that one too, but kept quiet. I didn't offer another, so she left. It was maybe fifteen minutes later when I flopped down beside her on the bus, half gassed, teasing her about being a bad loser. What the hell. I had a good jag on. I was smiling.

"I definitely do not need your advice on anything," she said.

"Well goddamn," I said. "I definitely do not hear your lips touching me in a compassionate point."

"What's that supposed to mean?"

"It means I haven't heard our souls make contact yet."

"You're drunk."

"You're right. You think we'll ever really know what it's all about?"

"I don't know that I care to."

"Piss on you then."

She swatted me open-handed right across the face, pretty good one too, so naturally I laughed.

"I think we're making progress," I said. "You've finally touched me."

"You won't talk to me that way," she said.

By the time I stopped laughing, she had moved up front with her buddy Weeds. Clappe sat across from me, snickering. I remembered a liquor store's whereabouts from my previous life, dug out a couple twenties, and held them out.

"Why don't you make your fat self useful," I said. "Go up there and get the driver to stop. There's a liquor store up here on the left. If you need some help, just holler."

I listened to him waddle up the aisle. The bus slowed, stopped, and ten minutes later Clappe returned, successful, a case of Coors talls, two quarts of vodka, two of mix, cups, ice, and a case of Cokes. Clappe mixed drinks and served them up the aisle. I think he had a vodka IV going in his own arm. Bernie was snoring, laid out on the rear seat. Lance was behind me, soaking up the half-quarts.

Somewhere north of Sacramento, Clappe and I started arguing, something about his damn clipboard. That's what it started with anyway. I could find any number of things to argue about, putting the make on Camille, snickering at Geri and me, his goddamn patchouli oil. It didn't matter as long as we had something to drink. The worm had his gloves on. We were both gassed. Lance was still sitting behind me and he was gassed too.

At the school, everybody got off and left, except Lance, Clappe, and myself.

We were still arguing about something, Lance cheering me on, telling me to kick Clappe's ass, the three of us laughing and Clappe sucking at that vodka tit.

"You guys can finish your conversation outside," the driver shouted.

"Hit 'im, Patrick," Lance blurted, well slurred. "Hit that sighted sonofabitch. Hit Clappe too."

The two of us laughed, heads back, just gone. I wanted to lie down on the seat and just laugh my goddamn teeth out, thinking about the waitress, thinking how goddamn sick I was, how we all wanted our sight. Lance sounded like his sand was running out, then Clappe was gone, the vodka was gone, everything was gone but us and the driver.

"I'll clean it up," he said, standing beside me.

"Where'd the fat guy go?" I said.

"If you two don't want to take a trip to Oakland, you better get it in gear," the driver said.

"Hit that prick, Patrick," Lance said.

We cracked up again, swaying down the aisle, down the steps into cold air. I turned, looking back at Lance, still swaying at the top of the steps.

"You gonna make it all right?" I said.

"Kiss my ass, Patrick. What d'ya think I am, crippled?"

He started laughing then. His body folded, flopped down the steps like a sack of guts and bones and splattered out onto the sidewalk at my feet. His head came last, with a dull thunk against the curb. The driver closed the door and punched it, leaving us in a warm cloud of diesel fumes. Lance could have been dead. I didn't know. I had never given mouth to mouth either and as the night moved over us, I could feel the last of our laughter, that touch left in the cheeks, begin to fade with the high. I had Lance's head tipped back a bit, ready to administer the lip, when I heard the bus stop and the driver's feet come running back.

"Is that dude okay?" the driver shouted, then he was beside us, breathing hard. Lance coughed, then tried to laugh.

"I'm fine, you ugly prick," Lance said. "I was just waiting to see if this asshole would really kiss me."

The driver took off with his bus. Lance and I laughed, me on the curb, him on his back, nothing else in the entire world at that moment except us—two blinks laughing in front of a goddamn blind school in the dark, the night cold against our cheeks and hands.

"Where's that goddamn Clappe?" Lance said.

It made no difference what we said, or who said it. The laughter tried to heat the air around us. We could hear it growing weak though.

"I'm gonna kick his ass myself . . . tomorrow," Lance said. "They treat us like shit, man."

He tried to get up then, but started vomiting. I moved his head so it went in the gutter. When he stopped contracting, I picked him up and got him over my shoulder, just like they did in the goddamn cowboy movies, my cane in my left hand, awkward as hell. I felt his hot urine run down my chest and soak in under my belt. He tried to laugh again, patting my back with his hand.

"Sorry buddy," he said weakly. "I took some ludes." The hand patted, then dropped loosely. He was out when I flopped him down on his bed.

Clappe confronted me the next day just before my mobility lesson. We shook hands and laughed. Geri and I didn't fare as well, though, both of us holding our own again, until two days later, when she collapsed in the hall after lunch. Blinks gathered about her in a circle, making little chirping noises. I picked her up and carried her back to her room, then sat there on her bed, holding her, rocking, tears in my eyes, rubbing her back and rocking.

"We'll make it," I kept saying, my face turned away from the door. The bodies there, the eyes.

"We'll make it," I whispered.

When she came to, she cried. Everybody vacated the room and doorway and left us for the moment. I think it was the closest we ever got.

EIGHTEEN

Geri had been confined to bed again, heavy antibiotics this time. Her doctor suggested the possibility of some new virus as the cause. I took it personally.

So I'm walking about the plaza one evening, thinking if I had to spend the rest of my life around regulars, I ought to get used to them. The plan entailed moving through shoppers with the least amount of contact, short caning, excusing myself for being alive. The real trick was lateral motion, like a healthy cell dodging its way through cancer. My halo had already grown to the size of a small orange rind, gentleness flooding my face. A little kid thought so anyway. He waddled out from a bench as I passed, grabbed my cane and started tugging, like a pup with a sock.

"Isn't that cute?" a woman said from the bench.

"Yes it is," another said. "Nice body too."

I smiled, yanked my cane free from the little clutchers, and moved on.

Just outside the south entrance to Emerson's, in heavy traffic, a body presented itself in my path. I smiled, dodged right, and tried to make myself disappear. He did the same. When I moved left, the same again, the guy maybe two feet in front of me, his breath oddly forced, frustrated. When I stepped back, motioning for him to pass, a finger started poking me in the chest. Christ, my lips curled, my halo clattered to the pavement. I thought about going for the throat, then remembered, bringing my hands to ease atop my cane. The finger returned, tapping again on the back of my hand.

Christ, I thought, some goddamn retarded regular wants to shake hands, so I tossed my head in recognition and reached out. He put something in my hand—a goddamn keychain with a little trinket and a card attached.

I nodded again, my face red. How the hell was I supposed to know he was mute. Forty-seven cents was all the change I had in my pocket. I pulled it out and counted it in front of him, a quarter, two dimes, and two pennies. Fuck 'im, I thought. I had a five in my wallet, but my halo wasn't that big.

So I shrugged my shoulders to show my embarrassment over being poor, and extended the change. He swiped it out of my palm in one quick stroke, snatched the keychain from my fingers, and split. The worm fell back in complete awe, momentarily dazed. Then I howled. Just letting it boil, face up, mouth wide, eyes closed. Shoppers stumbled, grabbed their kids, bit their lips in fear, and scattered like I was contagious.

Weeds understood. My needs were very simple, very concise. She knew how to sign. Just one more of her many talents—a state requirement for working with cappers.

"All I want to know is how to say, Fuck you up your ass, you sighted bastard."

She taught me the alphabet in two days. It was something I could do in bed at night, she said, then invited me to her home for the weekend to do some garden work, some manual labor, subjective R and R. I knew her design had more to do with keeping me out of the dorm, away from Geri.

I enjoyed it too, for the most part. I cut brush with a hacksaw, chopped roots, ran the roto-tiller, got into the earth a little. Weeds raked rocks, kept a small burn pile going, and brought me a cold beer every hour or so. Her husband, Paul, hid in his study all day, business I supposed. I didn't see him until dinner. Weeds fried the chicken. I made the salad, and after dinner, she set a bottle of brandy on the table, Hennesey cognac. Paul declined and faded back behind his door. At times, our conversation appeared serious, shopping carts, Geri, the egg carton, common fences, Greyhounds, sex. Weeds was interested in Geri's orgasms, whether I satisfied her or not.

Outside, a thunderhead worked its rump along the foothills, distant at first. We went out onto the deck to listen. I thought I could feel the lightning, and as it drew near, the rain dumped hard, the roof and deck loud with its wash. Weeds went inside and returned with the brandy, and the two of us stood at the rail, wind and water mauling us gently. The brandy traced my arteries. The worm soaked everything up. We didn't speak the whole time, maybe fifteen minutes, then the show moved on, rolling off the far side, northeast, toward Mt. Diablo.

"C'mon," Weeds said. "I've got a big box of faggots on the hearth. I'll get some paper and start a fire. We can sit there and dry out."

The fire smoked, a down draft pushing it back into the house. Weeds threw a few fucks at it, something about the goddamn chimney never working right. I downed my glass of brandy and opted for bed. Weeds brought me a dry towel from a hall closet.

I had the covers pulled back, sitting on the side of the bed, just my unders on, toweling my head, when I heard Weeds coming up the stairs again. I lowered the towel, spreading it across my lap, as she entered, flicked the light switch, and laughed.

"Cute legs," she said. "They could use some sun, though. You can finish drying your hair too. I've seen guys in their underwear before."

I hesitated at first, then raised the towel.

"I brought you an extra blanket," she said. "In case it gets cold."

I dropped the towel to my lap again, facing her. She stood beside the bed, both of us silent for some seconds, then she laid the blanket across the foot board.

"It's there, if you need it," she said, then walked out, closing the door quietly behind her. The worm just lowered its face into its hand, twitching, blood lights flashing.

Morning came too soon, the hangover too strong. I stood at the open window, no traffic, just the birds and the cool fragrance of damp earth as the sun stroked it. A long way off, somebody's tractor took advantage of that soft ground.

Weeds was up, tinkering in the kitchen. The smell of coffee had already arrived. As I descended the stairs, I could sense the distance, the cold awkward air hanging about the floor.

"You want some help?" I said.

"Nooo. I think I've got it all under control here. I set a cup of coffee on the table for you. Why don't you just sit and practice your sign language while I whip us up some breakfast."

"What's a matter," I said, "you got a hangover?"

"I don't let them bother me," she said. "There's too much to do usually. I'll drive you back after we eat. The ground's too wet to really do any more, and I've got some other things I should take care of in town."

I arrived at school to find Geri's back turned. Teresa and Camille had a toaster oven set up on a chair next to her bed. They had been making cookies all morning for a party. The twins were leaving. The woman I loved rolled dough into small balls and placed them on a cookie tin, pretending to have a good time. I stood at the end of her bed, ignored. Teresa followed me out into the hall.

"You know what it is," she said. "These things just . . . and she's taking all the medication too. She'll get over it though. She's just a tiny bit jealous about her sweetie, you know, spending the night with another woman."

Cole, of course, found the whole thing amusing, so we pointed the afternoon toward Ducci's, mostly for the therapeutics of the hike. Besides that, the Indian didn't serve Bloody Marys.

Boyd happened to be tending bar at Ducci's. Half a dozen guys sat there involved in a game of liar's dice, Boyd included, mixing drinks between calls. Bloody Marys had always reminded me of a self-contained meal— carrot stick, celery stick, all that vitamin C. I could feel my body growing healthier with each sip.

"I want you two blind bastards to know I've been in the doghouse ever since I saw you the last time," Boyd said.

We waited. Dice cups banged down in gestures of strength and superstition, forming their own constricted aura of intense concentration.

"That's right," Boyd said. "The old lady's got me down on her shit list in capital letters and it's all your fault. I was walking around the house with my eyes closed and my friggin' hands out in front of me, like this, and I'll bet I didn't get ten feet before I knocked over a set of glass swans my mother-in-law got us for a wedding present."

"Four sixes to you, Boyd," a voice on the end called.

"I was just trying to get some idea of what you guys go through, you know?"

"Four sixes to you," the voice said again.

"Four sixes, huh? I wish I had four nuts. I always hated those goddamn swans anyway."

"Four sixes, Boyd."

"Six sixes," Boyd said. "And you know, I never knew there was a damn blind school up there. Made me feel bad for about thirty seconds. I'd like to come up and see it some day if I could. Is that possible?"

"Let us know when you're comin'," I said. "We'll make sure everybody's got their clothes on."

"You can leave them off the girls if you want."

"We usually do," I said. "Makes it easier to tell who you're bumping into."

"Yeah, I'll bet," he said. "I know damn well you bastards have got something going up there."

"Seven sixes," the next voice in line said.

"You guys should've seen the two nurses that brought these bastards in the other night," Boyd said. "Made my prostate ache just thinking about it."

By early evening, we were all grinning like pigs under an outhouse. Boyd's shift ended and he joined Cole and me at a table. He wanted to know about eye transplants. I told him about the dead monkeys and the crazy ones.

"I know I'm not telling you anything you don't already know," he said, "but I felt bad as hell after seeing you guys. I've got these damn things here in my head and never really took a good look at them before. You never think about them being gone, you know, and then you've got all your hunting and fishing, all the things I enjoy. Even if it's just getting away, you know? And then you, you bastard. I figured I could probably double whatever I felt. That was your life, you know? Nope, don't say anything. Just let me finish here. I haven't got a decent night's sleep since I saw you. The old lady thinks I'm going nuts. Little does she know, huh? I woke her up about three the other morning and told her I'd made up my mind, that I was going to give you one of my eyes."

The ghost of something small, a dove maybe, settled lightly down in the center of our table. The three of us stared at it, quiet. I didn't doubt Boyd's sincerity. It must have been the vitamins had us all a little extra emotional.

"Yeaaaah," Boyd sighed, "and you know what she said? She said, 'You're fucked up Boyd Lynch.' But it didn't matter. I'd already made my decision. . . . And you ain't getting the right one either. Not the shootin' eye. I don't give a good goddamn what your doctor says."

A laugh shook loose that burning sensation behind the bridge of my nose. Another body, in the meantime, parked its uninvited ass across the table from me.

"Looks like a party," Tony Perona said. "What the hell you guys so quiet about? You got some kinda dope deal goin' down here?"

He sprayed us all with that phony laugh, then slapped Cole on the shoulder.

"I just told this bastard I'd give him one of my eyeballs," Boyd said, "and he tells me he doesn't want it. Can you believe that? Says they can't do transplants 'cause they turn you into dead monkeys, or some goddamn thing."

"You're shittin' me," Tony said.

"And I want you to know, you bastard, it wouldn't be that easy giving up the left one either. That's the one all the girls like. They say it twinkles when I think nasty things."

The ghost, whatever it was, disappeared, replaced by Tony's bad breath.

"That's no shit either," Tony said. "I've seen it, with the girls I mean. I ain't seen it twinkle at me yet."

"Yessir," Boyd said. "I had it all figured out. I was going to get me one of those fancy plastic jobs with a naked woman in the iris, you know? Remember those pens you used to get? You'd tip 'em upside down and the gal's clothes fell off? I figured I could get something along those lines, where I could blink and do the same thing. Maybe a black gal, huh? What d' ya think?"

"It'd look like a goat's eye, unless you were up close," I said.

Tony fairly bellowed with that one, then shouted to the bar for a round of drinks. I could write a letter, I thought, see if I couldn't get him enrolled with the next set of test monkeys.

"Nothing for me," Boyd said. "I gotta get going. I wasn't kidding you guys about the old lady. She's hot as hell about those swans."

He started for the door, then walked back, wrapping an arm about my neck, squeezing.

"And that was no line I was feeding you either," he said. "I want you to know that. And I'm still going to call my own doctor and ask him about these specialists."

Then at the door, he turned again.

"Actually, Patrick, I'm very relieved. The offer still goes though. If they can't do it now, maybe next year. We got some more huntin' trips comin' up. And I'm gonna come up to that school and see you guys too. I might want to take some night courses."

After Boyd left, I hit the can, drained the lizard, and poked about in some old film. When I came out, Cole and Tony had joined the dice game at the bar. I declined the offer, content with digging a hermitage for my cranial worm.

Cole didn't say much through the games. He didn't lose much either and I sat for the next couple of hours sipping cold beer from an iced mug. Each beer had a large Italian olive submerged on a wooden stick. More vitamins. Cole slipped me a Crow occasionally from his winnings.

Boyd's offer had left some strangeness behind too, transplants, changing an eye like you'd change the headlight in a car. I could see ten monkeys strapped to parallel gurneys, lined along a gray wall a few feet apart. Wild-eyed regulars in white smocks paraded about with raised scalpels, dangling fresh orbs from their fingertips like fat mice.

The dice game ended abruptly with a sore loser. Cole was next to him in rotation and called the guy's hand five times in a row, caught him dirty each time, so the guy made an ass of himself and then moved to the other end of the bar. Cole slid the last of his winnings in front of me.

"Be my guest," he said. "I'm already about as black as I can get."

"You're a lucky bastard," I said.

"Ain't luck."

"What is it then?"

"I dunno, but it ain't luck. These guys are just easy to read, I guess."

I could hear the whiner at the other end, commiserating with Tony. "I know that guy can see something," he said, referring to Cole. "He ain't shittin' me. Either that, or he's feelin' the spots. I got an uncle that's blind and he feels the spots. He cheats too. They got a way, you know."

Cole chuckled.

"You hear that fucker down there?" I said.

"Don't let it bother you."

"The fuckin' creep. What the hell difference would it make if you could feel them? They're lookin' at the goddamn things."

"Don't let it bother you."

But I did let it bother me. The cellophane world shrunk uncomfortably tight about me again, like a gas, an exhaust of burned brain cells that choked you with your own hands. Then you smell it, the fear, the sickness, the insignificance, whatever, like you could forget the damned thing anyway. It's always there. You can cover it up and move around it until somebody drags it out in front of you and kicks it, then the past pops out and spins away, like a yoyo, then back again, away and back, the kid, everything, away then back to black and drunk and sitting in a goddamn bar.

Cole sensed it. He was sitting there going through some film too, both of us sipping beer, suspended by the nuts for the moment, over that black hole of our weakness.

"You're right," I said. "Fuck 'em. I'm gonna get smart brains and you're gonna carve totem poles."

"You'd like the cabin," he said. "We got a sign above the door. You can't help but see it everytime you walk out. My mother put it there. It says, 'I watch my sun rise and my shadow grows small. As it sets, I'll grow tall again.'"

Geri came to mind, kids, the egg carton. I could run a thought like that through my skull and evaluate it, test its strength in a simple color graph, black to white and the shades in between. Geri and family had a very white color, but I had darker thoughts about my own head. Maybe I just wanted that family thing because I'd never had it, because the Adipose manual pushed it. What happens when the sides collapse and the wind blows through and you see it's just as empty as the last thing in line.

"We ain't got no power," Cole said. "We got a good well and a nice outhouse though. You can sit there 'n' the mornin' sun comes through and warms your kneecaps while you're thinkin', 'n' down the hill a bit, just past the trees, you can hear the river, just a cool, quiet hush. . . ."

Jesus, I thought, a cool, quiet hush. The sense of it eased into my skull, cool, quiet.

"You've got your mockingbirds too. There's always a couple of 'em around goin' through their list. . . ."

194

Just a cool, quiet hush, I thought, and nothing could get inside to fuck it up.

"You know them damn mockingbirds even imitate squirrels? Digger squirrels especially, *cheeta cheeta.*"

The regulars had another dice game going at the other end of the bar. The night crowd was filtering in too, the cocktail sector, a different tone to the revolutions. Somebody fed the jukebox, the big bass drum vibrating the air, regulars vibrating my skull.

Cole was still painting pictures of poverty, the empty run-down shacks surrounded by rusting gutted cars, and barefoot buck-toothed kids, and those little tumbling feeder streams where you could always catch your mess of trout if you wanted to crawl through the brush—five, six inchers, just throw 'em in whole, fry 'em up crisp like french fries, head and all. I didn't know what the hell time it was. I knew it was Tony though. You could hang your hat on his goddamn breath. I was that close to the river, too, almost hearing the hush, when his hand landed on my shoulder, splitting the trance and filling the air around me with voices again.

"You know," I said turning sideways on my stool. "Somebody should've left you at the drive-in inside a goddamn rubber."

He laughed, the hand squeezing.

"Same old Pat," he said. "You ain't ever gonna change, are you?"

I hadn't been aware of the body behind him.

"This other guy here's my buddy too," Tony said. "This is Cole. Fellas, I'd like you to meet Shirley."

I smiled for the lady's sake. Her thighs rubbed as she stepped up to take my hand—slim hand, big hips, I thought, then docked her another five points for knowing Tony.

"Shirley and me have been havin' a heart to heart down at the other end," Tony said. "She wanted to meet you."

I turned back to the bar, preferring the company of my beer. Tony's hand still worked my shoulder.

"I was tellin' her about you guys and how you're probably the two strongest people I've ever known in my life."

The hand raised, then fell again.

"I ain't shittin' you, Pat. The way you guys get around, walk all the way down here usin' your sticks and make it back. You know I couldn't do it, man."

That end of the bar grew quiet, listening. Tony had the stage. He knew it too.

"So anyway, the more Shirley and I got talkin' about it, the more I got thinkin' how there's a lot of people goin' through life with just one eye, and ever since I seen you in here that first day, Pat, I've been thinkin' about it. I'm serious too, so I want you to listen close to what I'm sayin'. I want you to have one of my eyes, man, and that's comin' from the bottom of my heart. We can lay side by side in that operatin' room . . . one from me, to you."

Doors began to slam closed inside my head. All I wanted at that moment was to be away from regulars, forever.

"I want you to have it, Pat. You don't have to say anything right now either. I know how you must feel, but I want you to have it, man, and if I had another I could spare, it would be yours, Cole. But I know ol' Pat here. I've known him for a long time. I know how much his sight meant to him and I'd like to see 'im get another chance at it. It'd be doin' me a great honor too, if he could see the world again through one of my eyes."

I raised my glass, filled my mouth with beer, turned slowly, and spit it in Tony's face. He stumbled back, gasping. Shirley and the rest of the audience sucked air. I swiveled around to the bar again, drained my glass, and sat there looking straight ahead. Tony headed for the other end, mumbling, wiping at his face.

"Jesus," he said, "what can I say. I mean you make somebody an offer like that and this is what you get? The guy must be more disturbed 'n I thought he was."

"Nice shot," Cole said. "I wondered what was takin' you so long."

I didn't say anything.

"You all right?" Cole said.

"Fine," I said.

I called to the bartender then for a refill.

"Get Tony and his girl there a drink too," I said, "whatever they're drinkin'."

"I'm not serving you any more," the bartender said.

"Why not?"

"I don't need to give you an explanation. I'm just not serving you guys any more. And that's it."

"For crissakes," I said. "You don't even know what the hell was goin' on here. None of you guys do, and it's nothin' to get all pushed outa shape over."

"You're eighty-sixed," the bartender said, "and the sooner you get out of here, the better off you'll be."

I lowered my face, wanting the quiet hush of that river so goddamn bad. Cole sat there beside me, motionless, waiting.

"Fuck it," I said. "If I'm getting eighty-sixed, I'll at least have a good reason for it."

I stood and winged my empty mug into the wall of glass behind the bar.

The high, tinsel sound of shattering was followed by more air-sucking. Stools toppled as regulars vacated the immediate vicinity.

"I'm gonna call the cops," the bartender shouted from the other end.

I laughed. The phone was on our end. My hand swept the bar in front of me then, found an ashtray, and flung it. Bottles shattered. I reached in front of Cole, grabbed his half-full mug and sent that in the direction of the bartender's voice. More glass splattered, all that good booze.

"Call the fuckin' cops," I said, then moved around Cole, pitching ashtrays, bottles, glasses, anything I found on the bar. The regulars, crowded at the far end like sheep in a corral, began heading for the door. My last pitch didn't break much, so I picked up a bar stool, thought about it, then set it down and went back for my cane. Cole hadn't moved.

"Sorry about your beer," I said. "I hate to waste it like that."

"Anything for a good cause," he said. "You done?"

"Just leavin'," I said.

"Right behind you," Cole said.

The worst part of fucking up like that is the next day. I had a hangover hot enough to remove paint and paranoia whipping me like a suck-egg dog. Geri wasn't in much better shape. I told her about Ducci's, omitting a few of the details, just in case the cops did arrive.

"God I'm sick," she kept saying.

She had entertained the grapes the night before at their party. They had made cookies all day, ferrying them downstairs to the dorm refrigerator. Thieves had licked them up as fast as they could make them. So Geri got drunk.

I talked with Teresa at breakfast. She said Geri and the twins got to crying about something, all three of them drunk, sobbing their blink hearts out, until Geri flashed. The twins weren't far behind. Geri puked for an hour, hugging the commode. The twins textured the hall.

I brought her up some chicken soup for lunch and some crackers.

"God I'm sick," she said.

A phone call to Boyd later that afternoon settled the suspense.

"Jesus," he said. "What'd that asshole say to wind you up like that?"

"Nothing really," I said. "I just wasn't in the mood for 'im."

"Well if it makes you feel any better, they're still talking about it. You scared the shit out of 'em, m' boy, not to mention a grand or so in glass and booze."

My asshole dropped to the cold linoleum like a raw egg.

"What about the cops?" I said.

"Don't worry about it. Tommy asked me if I knew where you lived. I told 'im I didn't know. I didn't say anything about the school. He won't press it anyway, so you can stop sweating. There is a note on the register though, in bold print, that says we're not to serve you or any of your buddies."

"That ain't right," I said, "I mean about the other guys. That pisses me off."

"Well I wish you'd just kicked the shit out of Tony and left it at that. Everybody's treating the prick like he's some goddamn hero."

I could see that bastard eating it up.

"Gotta go, man," Boyd said. "There's a cop down at the end wants to talk to me. . . . Hey, just shittin' you, man. Give my best to the girls, huh?"

Everything seemed foreign that day, like the chemical change was outside my head. Even the snakewalk had a hostile, withdrawn air about it as I tapped on the bench with Cole.

"It's done," Cole said. "If you can salvage somethin' out of it for future reference, go ahead, but you soak it up like it's the end of the world. You gotta get that foot back in the river, ol' buddy."

"Just wasn't the right way to handle it," I said.

"It was impressive. I imagine you gave 'em somethin' to talk about anyway."

"I ain't gonna blame it on the booze either. I shoulda just knocked that asshole out the first time I saw 'im."

"Whatever. You got a strange way of doin' things sometimes, but I gotta admit, you get 'em done."

"How long you think it'll be 'fore they serve us again?"

I tried to laugh with him. My cheeks raised some, letting a little daylight in, and off the port side, I could hear Carter, Lonny Charles, and a third, unfamiliar, voice coming down the snakewalk. None of them used canes until they got close to the avenue, where people could see them.

"Watch this," Cole said.

He took a quarter from his pocket and tossed it out onto the pavement, eight, ten feet in front of us. The trio neared, canes beginning to tap. Carter barely lost stride, stooping to pick the quarter up. Cole chuckled.

"What the hell was that all about?" I said.

"Nothin' much. I just like to make sure the world didn't change overnight."

198

NINETEEN

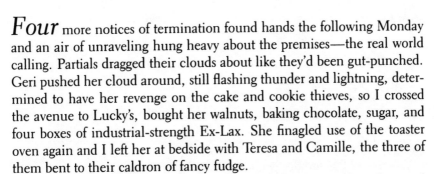

Four more notices of termination found hands the following Monday and an air of unraveling hung heavy about the premises—the real world calling. Partials dragged their clouds about like they'd been gut-punched. Geri pushed her cloud around, still flashing thunder and lightning, determined to have her revenge on the cake and cookie thieves, so I crossed the avenue to Lucky's, bought her walnuts, baking chocolate, sugar, and four boxes of industrial-strength Ex-Lax. She finagled use of the toaster oven again and I left her at bedside with Teresa and Camille, the three of them bent to their caldron of fancy fudge.

Bernie hit on me the same night at the snakewalk bench. I'd invited him out for a chew with a little brotherly love in mind, intending to prep him, steer him away from the presiding disillusion over leaving that clammy atmosphere. We parked, stuck a chew in.

"You know what I wish, Patrick?"

"Jesus, that's a rough one," I said. "Probably that you were a car or something."

"Nope. I wish we could have some beers right now."

"You don't always have to drink to have a good time, you know? Sometimes it's kinda nice to just sit and bullshit. Don't you think? Your brains work better. You can discuss your subject matter more intelligently, and you can talk about anything you want, as long as you've got a good buddy. Right?"

Bernie fidgeted, picking at the bench.

"That's why a lot of people drink," I said. "It's hard for 'em to be honest about the things that are goin' on inside their skull. You ever feel that way?"

"Yep."

"We oughta talk about it then. What're you gonna do when you leave here?"

"Oh, I guess I'll probably take the bus back to my mom's."

"Oh Christ," I said. "I didn't mean anything that exciting. I was thinking more along the lines of going back to school. You could do it, you know. You like cars. You could take some courses in auto mechanics. You might even wind up working on race cars. That wouldn't be bad, huh?"

"Boy, that would be neat."

"Well what the hell then. You got 'er made. Rehab will help you through school, you know. Couple years from now, you might be building race cars. You might not drive 'em very far, but you could sure as hell build 'em and keep 'em running, huh?"

Bernie scooted over close, almost touching my leg.

"What's up?" I said. "You need more chew?"

"Nope."

The worm saw it coming then, flushed alternately with pain and embarrassment over being caught with its pants down. My slick-haired buddy, in his usual pose against the nearest light standard, just turned away, hiding his face. Bernie tried to scoot closer, vibrating a little, his face pointed at me.

"You know what my friend Ron and me used to do at Armstrong?"

I had to lean forward then, my elbows across my knees. Christ, I thought, hating my narrow, goddamn skull.

"Was this before or after you guys sniffed glue?" I said.

"Before."

"I give," I said. "What did you and your buddy Ron do at Armstrong?"

His mouth was damn near on my ear. I could see regulars driving by, pointing, laughing.

"We used to play hotdog," he said.

I coughed to keep from laughing, then sat back to put a little air between us. His head followed, like it was attached to my goddamn ear.

"I don't think I know much about playing hotdog," I said.

The little kid inside him vibrated with its special secret.

"All you do is get on your bed and take your pants off and grab each other's hotdog," he whispered. "That's pretty funny, isn't it?"

He perked there beside me like a goddamn ground squirrel on a fence post, waiting for my response. I had none.

"You want to go up to my room and play hotdog, Patrick?"

The laugh yanked itself free, jumping from my mouth. Bernie shrunk back, offended.

"Hey, I'm sorry, man," I said. "I wasn't laughin' at you, Bernie. I'm just laughing at myself for having a soft skull."

He scooted away a couple of feet, rigid, so I gave him a light backhand across the shoulder.

"We're buddies, right?" I said. "You can say anything you want to me. Okay?"

"Okay, Patrick."

"I didn't mean to hurt your feelings. I'm just not familiar with your hotdog thing. I'm used to fooling around with girls, you know? You ever been with a girl?"

"Just that one that says I raped her."

"You never dipped your wart then, huh?"

"What's that?"

"That's having sexual intercourse with a woman."

"You mean fuck 'em?" he said, turning toward me.

"Yeah, that's the general idea. It ain't quite like workin' on a car, but everybody's gotta start someplace, so you can learn what the hell you're doin'. There's a lot to it. Takes lots of practice. Christ, I've probably done it three or four times now and I still don't know what I'm doing."

"I just kissed that one girl," he said.

Bernie had relaxed again somewhat, his feet swinging, scuffing at the pavement.

"So what do you think?" I said. "Would you like to make love to a woman?"

"You mean really fuck 'er?"

"You bet. There's usually a little more to it than that, but you're poking in the right direction. Christ, who knows, you might even want to talk to 'er."

Bernie's feet stopped moving under the bench.

"Can I touch her tits too?"

"You bet. You can do it all. We'll even find you one with big tits if you want. It'll be the best class you ever took, huh?"

"Who is it?" he said. "Somebody here?"

"No no no. It'll be somebody special. Somebody that can handle herself and teach you what to do. I'll sneak 'er in the upstairs door. She'll show you how to be a good lover, so when you get a girlfriend someday, you won't scare the hell out of 'er."

"Tonight?"

"Not tonight. It's gonna take a little while. I gotta find the right girl for you. You wouldn't want just anybody, would you?"

Boyd answered at home when I called later that evening and explained the Bernie situation in an appeal to his sense of philanthropic tangents.

"Think about it," I said. "Think what you'd be doing for your fellow man. It might be the only chance he ever gets."

Silence disguised his mental process, then some seconds later, "I just thought about it. I've got Sunday off. I'll pick you up about noon."

"I'll be here."

• • •

201

Geri's depression bled on into Wednesday. The fudge, two plates wrapped in foil, were still in the dorm refrigerator, untouched. Then Thursday morning, on my way downstairs, a commotion of sorts funneled up from the first floor. Alan the hype, one of the more recently arrived partials, had himself stuck in the phone booth, sobbing, screaming, in general just losing it. Teresa and a few of the other diabetics had formed a half circle about the booth, offering encouragement.

"You have to pull it in," somebody shouted as I exited the stairwell. "Pull the handle in, toward you."

"He's overreacting a bit, isn't he?" I said.

"God, I don't know," Teresa said. "I mean he's always been weird, but he was just standing here a minute ago, and the next he's screaming something about an ambulance and dying. I think he flipped."

The booth continued its small-life drama, jerking like a cocoon in some frantic insect ritual.

"Pull it in," somebody shouted again.

A thin fist finally shattered one of the glass door panes, making his fit more audible. In that same instant something else inside the booth became equally noticeable, moving his audience en masse toward the front doors and fresh air.

While the nurse administered a sedative, I checked the refrigerator—both plates clean as an elk's bugle. The nurse had called an ambulance, and with the head count rising rapidly, fearing some viral epidemic, she notified a county doctor. Clappe's wife had called in. She had taken him to Brookside Hospital early that morning, and Lou Abrams, the business instructor, was also M.I.A.

With the sudden, viral scare, Weeds had rushed right to Geri's room, and found our private celebration in progress. I smiled, shrugging my shoulders. Geri, finding it difficult to contain herself, bounced on her bed, mitts clapping. It refreshed me to see her like that, capable of doing bodily harm.

"Four boxes?" Weeds said. "My god, that could kill somebody."

"I'll bet it keeps them out of the refrigerator," Geri said.

At the time, the casualty count was six—Carter, Damond, and another new student, the pants pisser, included. The latter was found in the wood-shop can, moaning, just his feet and jeans visible under the stall door. The seventh victim was Rusty's roommate, the used-car salesman. He went to his knees in Weeds's class later that morning, sweating, whipped out a rosary, and got with the Hail Mary's. Weeds had to leave the room to keep from laughing.

Geri's bounce had a false bottom in it though. Just before noon she dropped again. It seemed that every time she got excited, the lights went out.

"If you knew she was gonna have those headaches forever," Cole said, "would it make any difference?"

My slick-haired buddy was leaning against the wall beside the door, watching me, the toothpick at ease, his eyes very quiet, very blue.

"I can't answer that," I said. "The worm's a little thin at the moment."

Elaine called that night, my voice from the past—half gassed.

"Did I catch you at a good time?" she said. "Nobody else died or anything?"

A male voice in the background laughed with her.

"You got company," I said, "or is that just the radio?"

"What? Oh, that," she laughed. "Yes, that's the radio."

The radio laughed again too.

"The reason I called," she said, "is I've changed my mind. I'll take the new car and the bank account, and you can have your old truck and the house. There's no equity in it anyway, and besides that, I can't afford the payments."

I didn't say anything.

"Aren't you happy?"

"Did you send the papers in?"

"I had them notarized at the bank this morning and mailed them. In six months you'll be a free man."

I could see her standing at the phone beside the back door, still in her bank attire, dark polyester, and the guy behind her at the table, one leg crossed, his right elbow propped, two glasses and a corked half-gallon wine jug—Almaden Chablis. Him checking her ass out, remembering how he came the night before, how good it felt, the new sock, driving my new car too, probably, spending my bank account. Fuck it, I thought.

"I'm sorry for everything," I said. "I hope things work out for you. I hope you find someone to love you."

"I hope you find someone to love you too," she said.

"I think I already have."

Her mood split like a ripe melon, letting the real Elaine dribble out.

"Oh really," she sneered. "Who?"

"You met her," I said, "that day you were here. Geri."

"You mean the blind girl?"

That macaw laugh of hers burned through the receiver, the radio behind her at the table laughing too, without even knowing why.

"Oh that's all right," Elaine said. "That doesn't bother me."

I didn't say goodbye, just hung up and stood there in the hall for a moment. To my right, one of the partials had his door open, a portable TV blaring the news.

Friday, the dorm got ripped off, the second floor anyway. Everybody was in class except Carter. He wasn't around. Radios, tape decks, jewelry, some cash. Geri lost her stereo. They took some underwear too, women's. No investigation, no cops, nothing besides a list of the stolen articles and a lecture from Stan about keeping doors locked. Mine had been locked. But somebody had gotten sloppy—Lance. They got in through the bathroom from Carter's side.

Cole was the only one to salvage a laugh. Whoever hit his room had swiped a half jug of Crow he kept on top of his dresser.

"I keep the good stuff behind my mattress," he said. "They been hittin' that one every time they mop, so I been mixin' it for 'em, two parts Crow, one part piss. They don't seem to mind."

The atmosphere, already so darkly laden, presented the proper opportunity for some extended partying. Camille, her termination notice nearby, christened the festivities with a gallon of Burgundy, lining her own dark cloud. Lance recognized the weather and joined her, the two of them hand in hand making bubbles in the wine jug. By evening, regulars on the avenue were privileged to spectate a pilgrimage of happy faces caning their way back from the liquor store to the shrine of the altered. Teresa bought a blender and cranked out margaritas. All of blinkdom seemed to respond. Partials hugged totals, raw emotions flowing. This was no hall dance either. It was premeditated abuse, hard drinking and housecleaning.

Geri joined too. What the hell. I offered my opinion, concerned about her immediate health and obvious appetite. She told me to keep it, so I spent the evening in Cole's room, sober.

Lance stopped by every half hour or so to fill us in on his latest move with Camille. No question about it. He would be in her pants before dawn.

About eleven I walked down to Geri's room, idiocy propelling me. She was standing on her bed, margarita in hand, singing along with Paul McCartney's "Michelle," in French. I walked back. Geri arrived a moment later, margarita still in hand. I stepped out into the hall with her.

"Teresa said you came by," she said, swaying, arms about my waist, spilling her drink down the back of my jeans. I tried to sway with her, my teeth tight, then a small hand moved around front, working at my fly.

"What's a matter?" she said, looking up. "You don't wanna hmm hmm hmm?"

"For crissakes," I said, "pinch it or something, will you? We're not doing anything. Not tonight anyway."

"You don't love me anymore?"

"Of course I love you. More than ever."

"You've got a funny way of showing it."

She was already moving then, toward her room, her voice rising. "Who's got the blender?"

She passed out just before midnight. Everybody passed out just before midnight except Camille and Lance. Cole had designated an area between the beds as river. We each had a foot in, chewing, listening to the dark clouds carrying on. Then Lance was back with his final report.

"We're gonna move in together," he said.

"Who is?"

"Me and Camille. I just asked 'er, man. She's gonna get an apartment and when I get done here, I'm gonna move in with 'er. I told 'er I've been secretly in love with 'er all this time."

"Some secret," I said.

"Hey. I got my finger wet too, man," he said, moving up in front of me. "Here. Check it out."

"Save it," I said, pushing his hand away.

"No shit, man. I been workin' on that all night. I'm gonna eat it too. Here. C'mon, take a whiff. That's some good pussy, man."

I heard the first one about half an hour later. Lance was in our room, throwing empty beer bottles through the open door, against the hall wall. Teresa wasn't too far behind.

"Patrick? You better get him," she shouted. "That'll bring Connie up for sure."

Four more bottles smashed against the wall before I got there. The fifth one was full, prompting more immediate action on my part. I ducked, covered my face, and caught him just as his arm went back. He wheezed, trying to hook the bottle at my head. When I relaxed the bear hug, he spit in my face and tried the bottle hand again. Connie stood in the open doorway.

"I'll have to report this," she said. "Which one of you is responsible? Or was it both of you?"

"Fuck you," Lance screamed. "Report the motherfucker, then get one of your niggers up here to clean it up."

I squeezed again. Connie padded off. Lance went limp and began to cry, so I dropped him on his bed.

"Fuck 'er," he said. "Fuck 'em all."

"You done?" I said.

He tried to laugh, his three-note snicker.

It was hard enough just being young, I thought.

"I need a beer, man," he said.

I found the carton, four left, and handed him one. He snickered again.

"You fucker," he said. "I never knew you were that big. Your arms must be as long as my legs."

I stopped by Geri's on my way to breakfast the next morning. The shortcake was still in her jammies.

"How are your horns this morning?" I said.

"I beg your pardon. I don't have any horns and never did. Cows have horns, and cars, but I don't."

Boyd found me in Cole's room Sunday. Teresa showed him the way. I could hear them carrying on as they came down the hall. Out on the freeway, I noticed my old films seemed faded, taking on a texture of fatigue like old photographs do, just the eyes remaining clear, suspended, captured.

"That Teresa's a frisky morsel," Boyd said.

The race track, Golden Gate Fields, the white fence lined with pines, some fillies maybe, morning exercises.

"She's no child," I said.

"What does she do, work there?"

"She's a patient," I said. "Just like the rest of us."

"C'mon. That babe ain't blind. She looked me right in the eye and I know what she was sayin'."

The mast orchard in Berkeley Marina, frontage road mudflats, winter, burning driftwood, blacks, whites, poles propped, hands in pockets, watching, waiting, unemployment checks, fish stories.

"I'll fix you up," I said. "If you want, we could double date some night."

"Nobody's takin' care of that?"

"Just P. G. and E. at the moment."

"What? She's doin' the meter reader?"

"She's doin' a vibrator."

"All right. She'd love my tongue then, wouldn't she."

Bay Bridge, Nimitz Interchange, West Oakland, Seventh Street, razor slashing, "see yo guts, boy"—dark.

"So what's going on with these girls today?" I said. "You know 'em pretty good?"

"Yeah. They stop by for a drink once in a while. You'll like 'em. They ain't your run-of-the-mill whores."

"Did you explain the situation to 'em?"

"That's your business. I don't even know who this Bernie character is.

You know, you guys got more lights on in that school. I walked in and I'll bet you every light in the place was burning."

Fifteenth Street turnoff, East Fourteenth, Lake Merritt like a hole in that colorless city where the other side of the world leaked through, lots of lake, lots of lawn, lots of kids, lots of ducks. Sundays, small sails pop to the surface chasing the breeze like paper in a parking lot.

"These gals are high class. They might cut me off if I set 'em up with something in red and blue socks. You know?"

The Follies, Broadway, tattoo parlors, winos and postprime prostitutes with good legs, tired faces. Stairs, footworn rug, second-floor mattress, smell of cigarette butts, no curtain.

"Hey. Don't get pissed off. I mean the guy's got to be halfway normal, you know? Now how the hell do you want to do this?" Boyd said. "You want to hang onto my shirt?"

"Just go," I said. "I'll follow your feet."

Wrought iron bordered the sidewalk. At the gate, Boyd pushed a call button and an attractive voice answered back over the intercom. An elevator took us up three flights and I followed Boyd down a carpeted hall. A different voice answered the door, very soft, with an accent—Barbados, she said. Incense and a slight touch of cigarette smoke caught my nostrils as we entered, and to my right somewhere, Herbie Mann blew soft and smooth, watching me. I smiled, nodding, like I knew.

And leaving, I took that slender hand again, long nails. I could see her, six years old, maybe seven, skinny, big brown eyes, barefoot, Barbados. I'd see her again the following Sunday. All set, I thought—for Bernie.

"I wish you had your eyes back for just a minute so you could see that, Pat. You'll probably never see anything prettier with or without clothes."

"What the hell took you so long?"

"I'm not shittin' you either. It's every bit as good as it looks."

"I think it's beer time," I said.

Oakland ignored me while Boyd went into the liquor store—traffic, pedestrians, concrete, wood, and the parking meters so you didn't stay any longer than what you paid for. Then Boyd was driving again, a cold beer open in my hand.

"I oughta call your wife and tell her," I said.

"She's the one that gave me the money and told me to get lost."

"You're sure they're reliable, huh?"

"You didn't have to give 'em a deposit, you know."

"I didn't think I'd have to pay for both of 'em either."

"I can understand it. I mean your version sounds like a piece of cake, but like she said, they got to look out for each other."

"I just wanted 'em to know I was serious. It'll mean a lot to 'im. Might even change the rest of his life."

"Might cure his blindness, too," Boyd said.

"At least he'll know how to act with a girl, if he ever gets one."

"Every boy deserves his first piece of ass. I won't argue that. But a hundred bucks? Whew. Your heart's a hell of a lot bigger 'n mine."

"It'll be worth it."

We shot off the Nimitz onto Eastshore, two hundred feet from the bay, with its almost-salt, almost-sand smells—no more clam beds or clean blue water. The kid and the old man used to go out to the gate with porpoises racing alongside—the black and white ones. The same kid walked the beach along that Bay City side, dragging a herring net and five-gallon bucket, the sand strewn with rubbers that floated up from raw sewage and washed ashore. I thought they came from the yachts and pleasure boats, the fancy jobs. I had seen the women before, the bright suits and sails covering the bay, like money to the wind—Sausalito, Belvedere, Tiburon. They would be out there on warm days, at the rail, smiling. We would be coming back in, the fish boxes full, me aft cleaning fish, tossing guts over the side to the waiting, hovering gulls. That was all they did, I thought, that and stand in the wind with their hair flying and toenails painted. Red.

TWENTY

Our A.W.O.L. dishwasher returned on a Tuesday, three days after my business trip to Oakland with Boyd. He and Sally had shacked up in Los Angeles with some of her friends, until she woke up one morning to a totally black world and immediately went spastic. The next morning she woke up in the L.A. County nuthouse. Our young, impressionable dishwasher found Jesus somewhere in the same time frame. Weeds said that was the only reason he got his job back.

Geri's new roommate moved in the same day. Lauren, the newly blinded cowgirl I'd given a tour to, the one who did it with a quarterhorse and a sports car. While she unpacked her things, Geri and I entertained some quiet thoughts about living together.

"My grandmother will just die," she said.

"Let 'er die," I said.

She started to protest, but pushed familial loyalty aside as I went down on her, then squirmed like an addict in a poppy patch, both hands in my hair assisting. Across the room, Lauren busied herself with instant coffee on her new hot plate.

"What're you guys doing?" she said, turning toward us.

I damn near laughed, in it, but Geri's grip had tightened, threatening to separate my hair from my scalp. Since she was apparently unable to speak at the moment, I said, "I'm giving her a little rubdown. It helps her sleep."

Lauren stirred her coffee, the spoon moving slowly about the cup, distracted. What the hell, I thought, and finished, keeping it as quiet as possible. Geri went rigid, bit her lip, fired off a quick volley, and melted.

Sally's story didn't do a hell of a lot for local morale, especially for the partials. Half of them refused to sleep that night.

"You know what they need," Cole said, "is a fishing trip, all of 'em. Ain't nothin' like a good fishin' trip to straighten out a body's perspective."

I could see the entire student body spread out along the beach, campfires burning, hooks and sinkers whistling by in the dark.

209

"We need a boat to do it right though," Cole said.

The worm made a sudden channel change, back to the numb, sluggish sensation of shock as my body crawled onto the overturned boat, my tongue searching the blood-warm hole where my front teeth and upper lip used to be. Shock wraps you up in her wool sweater and slips you a mickey.

"What's a matter," Cole said. "Does that bother you?"

"You're serious, huh?"

"Damn right. I heard on the news this morning, some guy caught a 280-pound sturgeon out there somewhere. I'd give what's left of both nuts to have that on the end of my stringer."

"Can you imagine one of these guys tyin' into something like that," I said. "We'd all be on TV, all spiffed up lookin' pretty."

"It's done then," he said. "I'll leave the rest to you."

The idea caught like gasoline, with the staff anyway. We had a lot of yes hands that didn't mind getting paid to chaperone a fishing trip. Hooking bucks out of the recreation fund presented no problem either. The school was allotted five hundred a month, and had to spend it or send it back.

Convincing enough blinks to fill a party boat was another story. I started at dinner that evening, getting their attention with a coffee cup as a gavel.

"We have a fishing trip planned on a party boat," I said. "Fishing for giant sturgeon and striped bass. I need a list of names, those of you that are interested."

As their well-oiled wheels whirred through contemplation, ten, fifteen seconds, then the assembly line started again, fork to mouth. I banged the cup.

"This is serious business," I said. "We're not talking gas chambers, god-dammit, we're talking fun, a party boat, catching fish—seagulls, bell buoys clanging, porpoises leaping playfully alongside, and a two- or three-hundred-pound sturgeon smoking the drag on your fishing reel. How many of you guys have ever gone fishing, or been on a boat for that matter."

"I caught a bluegill once," Theo said. "I was a mere child at the time. I gave it a name and kept it in my toilet, until my father discovered it and pulled the handle on the poor creature."

"What'd you name it?" Teresa yelled.

"Bigfoot," Theo said.

"So how many are going?" I said. "We're talking big boats too, maybe even a little salt spray over the bow."

"A seagull pooped on my sandwich once," Rusty said.

Christ, I thought. Who the hell wanted to work with blinks anyway. Nobody piped for the next ten minutes, either, all of them so goddamn glued to their corners. Then Theo called out, "I might as well go. There might be a sailor on that party boat."

"C'mon, you guys," I said. "We need a full boat or nobody goes."

Eighteen blinks finally came to their senses, but only two were partials, Lonny Charles and Teresa.

"This'll be our Mediterranean cruise," Lonny Charles said. "We'll pretend it's the love boat."

Jack O'Brien ran a forty-six footer out of Crockett, or had for years anyway, when he was conscious. I started my search in the phone booth, with a handful of change and the information operator. No Jack O'Brien listed. I tried the Crockett Marina next, and the salty old gal on the other end happened to know Jack, or had. She said his ex-wife had rolled him up in a sheet one night, sewed it closed, and beat the sea breeze out of him with an iron skillet. He lay there, bound like that, for a day and a half, cotton-mouthed, bruised, contused, and confused, and evidently short-circuited before somebody finally found him. This gal also happened to know the guy who bought O'Brien's boat and had my call transferred from the baitshop to the bar.

"There's about twenty-five of us," I said. He wanted five hundred for the day, three fifty for half a day. We had four something in the rec fund.

"We'll try it for half a day," I said, "for sturgeon, right? That's poles and bait and everything included? Sounds good. How 'bout beer? Yeah, I'll bet you do. How come you're not fishing today?"

He marked us down for Friday morning, 7:00 A.M. We had to get our deposit in by Thursday afternoon to secure the boat. I didn't say anything about blinkdom, then got to thinking maybe he should know. I didn't want him to freak and jump overboard when he saw us coming down the pier.

"One more thing," I said. "Most of us have poor eyesight, but it's nothing to get excited over. No no, it's more than just glasses. We're what you call visually impaired. Yeah. That's right. Some people call it that. There's no problem though. You ain't gonna have to change diapers or anything. I can't answer for our chaperones of course, they're regulars, sighted folk. You might have to take care of them. No no. We're all grown people, all adults. Sons and daughters of congressmen, corporate executives, blue-collar workers, and assorted illegitimate claims. We've got insurance too. Yes, yes that's right. Nope, no wheelchairs. Most of 'em have never even been on a boat. Fifteen of us have never even been fishing. Just think what that'll do for your heart. . . . Fine," I said. "Thanks."

He had to call me back. Something about the boat, motor problems. Should've kept my goddamn mouth shut, I thought, then called information again, asking the operator to check for another charter service.

"I'm sorry," I said. "I don't know the name. I was hoping you'd let your fingers do a little walking for me. Yes yes, I know that, and believe me, if I could, I would, but I can't, so that's why I'm talking to you. No, there isn't even a book here. Some attorney or real estate agent took it home, and I've got eighteen angry blinks standing outside the booth here in the sun, waiting, with their lunch sacks in their hands. Yes, that's right, fishing boats. Why don't you look under Moby Dick, or better yet, look under your skirt. I'm gonna tell 'em what you said too. You just pissed off a lot of people, lady. They'll probably put a curse on you, a perpetual yeast infection or something."

Doctor Cole's office was open down the hall. He prescribed two drams of Crow, administered orally.

"Fuckin' regulars," I said. "You can never find a good one when you need 'em."

"You should've told them it was an experiment for the space program," Cole said, "that the C.I.A. was involved."

"I'll get my own boat again someday," I said. "Paint it black, with some big, white buck teeth in front and a set of giant shades painted across the wheelhouse glass. We'll be river pirates. I'll load it up with blinks and stand them around the rail up front, with their canes out like cat's whiskers. We'll cruise the river, raiding all the little fishing villages at night. All we need is a compass and a depth finder, use a weighted line like Mark Twain did. We'll mount a whaling cannon on the bow and stock enough beer to buy off half the goddamned judicial system and all the cops."

Fifteen minutes later, the skipper called back.

"That's beautiful," I said. "You don't know how much I appreciate this, pal. I could kiss you. . . . No, not usually. Just a figure of speech, you know? Yeah, you bet, 7:00 A.M., the *Happy Hooker*, Crockett Marina. We'll be there. I'll have one of our flunkies run that deposit out."

Clappe dropped the deposit off on his way home Thursday. He and Weeds would chaperone. Sly and Mel Sohrer, the assistant woodshop instructor, somehow got their faces included as well.

Thursday night, dormside, would have warmed the heart of the most impotent of whoremongers. Excited blinks padded the linoleum, goosier than a first-grade nature hike, shark stories, intimate, long-harbored fears, and some plain old good-natured irrational fantasies. Cole and I stocked our survival packs, case of beer, jug of Crow, pint of blackberry brandy, some snacks too, jerky and peanuts, and all the while, that hallway clamor.

"That's the way this joint oughta sound," Cole said. "Listen to 'em out there. They ain't drinkin' either. Kinda scary, ain't it?"

"I know," I said. "I might just wind up working with them someday."

"That's very admirable. What makes you think they'd let you near 'em?"

"I'll see to it that every blink in the country, no, in the world," I said, "gets to go fishing at least once. And the ones that survive that can go camping next. I've already got a couple places mapped out in my skull. That canyon I told you about is one. It's perfect. You can set up camp beside the creek, catch a few trout, get a good campfire going, tell some beer stories, bring a couple dancing girls along maybe."

"Who's gonna get you there and back?"

"We'll rent a regular to do the driving. There's plenty of 'em around. We can tie 'em to a shade tree with a dish of food and water till we're ready to leave."

The cafeteria opened the next morning at 5:30 for coffee and sweet rolls. Weeds was there bright and early, playing mother to all those bright blink faces in their eight layers of clothing. You'd have thought we were headed for Antarctica. Clappe, Mel, and Sly had their balls nailed to their shoulders, standing in the street beside the vans, bigtime fish talk, one-upping each other.

At the marina, wired blinks piled out of warm vans into thick fog, lunch sacks in hand. Foghorns moaned at each other in the distance like bull sealions. Two young female fish cops helped us board. In the mooring across from us, another diesel, loaded with regulars, idled, laughter rising occasionally. We listened to them leave, their sound soon swallowed by that fog.

Cole and I had a bench in the stern, Geri seated between us. The smell of diesel, salt, and fish slime soaked into deck planking threaded strong, thin memories through my day. Some good, some like a bad acid trip, where it seemed my only recall was mistakes.

An hour passed, plodding through anxious blinks scattered along both rails, turning their banter into tooth-chattering complaints. When the shivers hit Geri, I took my denim jacket with its blanket liner and wrapped it about her, just the top of her head sticking out.

Our skipper finally showed up at 8:30, smelling like he'd used his shirt to wash out a fishbox. Sly, Clappe, and Mel greeted him as he climbed on board.

"All right," Sly said. "I understand you know where all the big ones are hiding today."

He ignored Sly and moved to the aft line, beside Cole, casting off, his breath plastered on the fog for the moment like wallpaper.

"You smell that?" Cole said.

"Definitely critical," I said. "Smells like somebody just jump-started him with about four fingers of your Crow."

"You sure he ain't one of your buddies, huh?"

"Just remember to get your boots and jacket off and swim into the waves," I said.

Geri's head popped out of her wrappings like a turtle.

"You stop that," she said. "It's not funny."

We made about two knots, east, up the Carquinez Strait, diesel exhaust billowing over the stern, warm to the face and hands. I measured our pace by the foghorns. As one faded, the next in line became faintly audible over the drum of our engine. I remembered the sea, flat under fog, barely swelling and that thick silence when you would shut down to change fuel tanks, adrift, with just the skin of the boat between you and it. I had always known, even as a kid, that I would find out how cold it was someday. I expected it. You'd listen to the starter motor crank, knowing so clearly in that moment how crucial the sound of combustion was to your existence.

"You ever seen the Farallons?" I said.

"Not lately," Cole said.

"They look like they're from another planet. The middle and north islands are just rocks sticking out, mountaintops, but the south is creepy, maybe a half mile wide, kind of a chamois brown in places, but most of it, the cliffs and slope, are an off-white with thousands of years of bird shit. We hit a great white out there one day. Come cruisin' over the top of a swell in the fog and nailed that baby just behind the pectoral, 'bout a twenty-footer. It's like hitting a log.

"The boat bounced. I was in back, rigging baits, and he come thrashing out, maybe ten feet off the stern, his saucer-sized eyeball checking me out, mouth open, water streaming off his teeth, blood all over. You could see three deep gashes in his side, where the prop got 'im, and all I could think about was how two of me would fit so easy, side by side in that mouth."

"That's just about enough of that too," Geri said.

The sun broke through just east of the Benicia Bridge. Our anchor chain rattled out on the flats, off the Mothball Fleet, the skipper cut the engine and we swung in line with a strong outgoing tide. Clappe, Mel, and Sly hit the water first, talking their bullshit, biggest fish, most fish, first fish, a buck on each. Weeds helped the two aides rig leaders. Cole and I baited hooks from a coffee can with a couple pounds of lively grass shrimp in the bottom. They'd go off like springs when you touched them.

"Go ahead," I told Bernie. "Stick your hand in there and grab a couple."

Geri moved up front with Weeds. Everybody else had a line in when Cole and I turned to our own, 10:30 A.M., beer time.

"Who said you have to catch fish to have fun?" Cole said.

We barely had our tops popped before lines started tangling. Clappe and Sly were first to reel in a bird's nest, their accusations further snarling the knotted tackle, and from the opposite side, Bernie yelled, "I got 'im, I got 'im."

"You've probably got somebody else," an aide said.

"No. I got 'im. He tried to jerk my pole out of my hand."

Bernie cranked like a speed freak, then his sinker slammed into the hull and the aide pulled his leader and fish up over the rail and onto the deck, flippity flopping.

Behind Bernie, a wooden structure about five foot high covered the exhaust stack. Bernie dropped his pole and climbed it, the aide in hysterics.

"It isn't a shark," she said. "It's a flounder."

"How big are his teeth?"

"They don't have teeth. It's only about a foot long. See? Give me your hand."

"You hold him for me," Bernie said, climbing down.

Rusty came next, catching one up front, another flounder, then Geri yelled, then Cole, and Bernie again, his shoes banging against the side of that stack cover as he climbed, his catch break-dancing on the deck.

Clappe made the next catch. He baited up, gave it a big heave ho, and hooked Sly right in the cheek of his ass. Sly got to bucking and squealing, and when the argument over who should have been watching where ended, the skipper took him inside, pushed the barb through, cut it off and pulled the shank free. Cole and I toasted that one.

At noon, when the anchor winch started dragging chain, we had twelve flounder and one small striper in the fishbox.

"It's about time," Sly said. "This is bullshit. We ain't catchin' no sturgeon here."

Those three had been out of the water more than in, tangled up, cussing each other, not a fish between them.

"I guess that's it," one of the aides said. "He says it's going to take us an hour to get back in and that's half a day. He says he's not responsible for the fog this morning."

"We ought to mutiny," I said. "Which way to the wheelhouse?"

She laughed.

"He's got it locked," she said. "He looks terrible. I think he's sick."

Most of the blinks moved forward to the bow, sticking their faces in the light wind. Cole and I held down the rear, soaking up sun and beer. Somewhere off Benicia the motor cut, the anchor chain rattled out fast into deep water, grabbed, and swung us about with the current, blinks cheering. Sly, Clappe, and Mel went for their poles. The starter motor cranked, stopped, cranked again, then the skipper was out, lifting the deck lid over the engine compartment.

"We ain't fishin'," he said. "So don't get in a hurry."

"You got a problem there?" Sly said.

"You don't hear it runnin', do you?"

"I'm in charge of maintenance at the Orientation Center," Sly added, "and if I don't mind saying so, I'm pretty good at trouble-shooting."

"I'll bet," the skipper said.

"If you could give me some idea of what's been acting up lately, we can take it from there," Sly said.

The skipper went forward, cranked it over again. Nothing, except his muffled cursing from the wheelhouse.

"Sounds like it might be the carburetor," Sly said.

"It's diesel," the skipper said. "It don't have a goddamn carburetor."

Cole passed me the Crow.

"I think we've got enough to last all day," he said, "long as we don't share."

The skipper stood behind us, looking down into the hold, scratching.

"You got fuel?" I said.

"Should be good," he said. "I told my deckhand to fill it last night."

He scratched a while longer, then got his reading stick, unscrewed the cap to his fuel tank and dropped it in. A hollow, empty *thunk* answered back. He dropped it again, then a third time and began beating his fist against the gunwale, a tangy strain of invective forcing out between his teeth.

"Here you go," Cole said. "Make some bubbles in this. It'll clear your head."

"Sweet Jesus," the skipper said, "a life preserver."

He took a couple good pulls at the Crow then handed it back.

"I do appreciate your kindness," he said. "I've got to go up front for just a second to use the radio. Make sure you don't drop that overboard while I'm gone, huh?"

The absent-minded deckhand ferried two jeep cans of diesel out. And an hour later, back in the marina, our two aides made their rounds saying goodbye, providing hugs. The one Cole held started crying.

"Don't take it so hard," he said. "It ain't like you're never gonna see us again."

"I'm sorry," she said. "I don't know why I'm crying. Jill and I made fun of it last night, thinking today would be so boring. We were just stupid. We didn't know anything about blind people."

"We have to thank you all for that," Jill said. "You're beautiful, all of you."

"Goddamn," Cole said. "You're making me blush."

The skipper bought a six-pack in the baitshop and took Cole and me aside.

"Next time," he said, "we'll catch the tide right and spend all day out there. I'll charge you the same price."

"You're really gonna keep all that money for an hour's fishing?" I said.

He sucked at his beer, scratching, then belched.

"I suppose you're right. I got all fucked up last night on your deposit. That's why I was late. And I gotta admit, it wasn't dull. Somebody kept climbing the wall of my cabin and waking me up."

He pulled his wallet out and thumbed through it.

"Here," he said. "Take this before I change my mind, and don't you dare tell anybody. I'll lose my reputation."

"I'll take that," Clappe said.

"That's a hundred and twenty bucks there," the skipper said. "I'm givin' it back to the blind kids. They can get a sandwich, or a couple drinks on it, huh?"

"I'll see it gets back into the recreation fund," Clappe said.

"I'll bet," the skipper said, turning back to us. "You take those three assholes with you everywhere you go?"

"Somebody's got to drive," Cole said.

"Let me know when you want to go again, and I'll come pick you up, all of you. I'll bring a movie camera too. That was all right out there today."

"If you'd like to drop by the school," Clappe said, "I'd be glad to give you the tour and show you the students at work. It's quite the setup we've got there."

"Jesus," the skipper said. "I'll see you guys, huh? I think I just heard a cocktail crow."

Saturday moved by like a herd of cattle, grazing. I lay in bed until eleven, rehearsing the Adipose oath—raise your right hand, touch the Bible and solemnly swear to be a law-abiding consumer, malleable to the media and almighty advertising. To observe the common alias, Occupant, with full understanding that any use whatsoever of the imagination is punishable by ostracism.

Saturday afternoon, I searched for Bernie to prep him for his Sunday night biology lesson. His new roommate said he'd left earlier with some-one named Carter. My guts tightened, anticipating Bernie and beer, hear-ing him tell Carter about my promise. Sure, and that asshole Carter trying to horn in on a piece of Bernie's pie.

I called Rena next. She said she would cash a check for Bernie's big event. I almost reconsidered, too. That hundred-dollar bite for his sexual education made me awful thirsty. Cole took the edge off that when I returned to the Crow's nest.

"That's the sadness of living on your imagination," Cole said. "Your pocketbook always runs out first."

"You can't consider them both in the same hand," I said.

"Sure you can," he said, "if you can cover your expenses. We'll take some pictures. Call 'em graduation exercises, and sell a couple copies to his mother."

Sunday morning was strolling by without me when the knock resounded faintly through my room. It seemed to come from a dream, but I couldn't remember dreaming. I vaguely remembered drinking dinner with Cole—Saturday night, last night. Alcoholism, I thought, dehydration, reality. Then the hand knocked again. I stood with some difficulty, going through the motions of blinking, a piss hard-on sticking up like a pot handle—Geri, I thought. It must be, and that sweetheart spasm of orgasm trickled through my prostate.

"Patrick? You in there?"

Christ. It was Weeds. I couldn't even remember what day it was then. Everything was misfiled, except pain and lust, and neither of them seemed in any hurry to leave.

"Patrick? Open up."

She was whispering.

"Just a minute," I said, got my shorts and jeans on, then pulled a T-shirt over my head and left it out to hide my frantic wart.

"Dammit Patrick. Do you have someone in there with you?"

"Just a goddamn minute, will you?"

When I opened the door, she jammed by, turned at the desk, and stopped, facing me.

"Were you out with Bernie last night?"

I shook my head, dizziness forcing me to sit.

"You didn't see him at all last night?"

I raised my hand and signed, Nope.

"Knock that shit off," she said. "I want the truth too. You guys didn't go out and hit the bars and get in a fight someplace?"

My head tried to shake, my hard-on throbbing cruelly. Weeds paced to the bathroom door and back.

"Connie's got him downstairs in her office. She calls me at five-thirty in the fucking morning because she caught him sneaking out the front door with his suitcase packed. Why, in Christ's name, does it always have to be me? I have my own life, and a loving husband waiting in bed. Every time one of you goddamn blinks stumbles and falls, Mother Gwenda has to come running."

She paced to the bathroom door again.

"He's fucked up, Patrick. I mean the boy has gone bye-bye. I know. I've seen this before in the Haight. You know when they've lost it. You can see it in their eyes and face, but more than that, you feel it. There's no music, Patrick."

I groaned, my head between my hands, my stomach on the move.

"I haven't seen him since Friday," I said.

"Connie heard him come in about one with somebody. She thought it was you. She said Bernie was laughing like he was drunk."

Weeds paced again.

"He's got deep, bloody gouges on both sides of his neck, and I don't even want to begin to think where they came from, Patrick."

I puked, hand to mouth, the other out front leading the way into the can where I emptied my guts into the sink, convulsions squirting sweat from my pores, leaning there quivering in a trail of bile and body fluids.

"C'mon, goddammit, you don't have time for that," Weeds said. "I need your help. He won't talk to anybody. I don't even know if he can talk."

I cupped water to my face and neck, then drank some and heaved again.

"All right," Weeds said, "I'm going, but I'll expect you downstairs in two minutes. Get it together."

I found two warm beers in a sack on my dresser, gagged down half of one, let it bounce a couple of times, then finished it, brushed the bugs off my teeth and damn near broke my neck going downstairs. The hall was empty, no blinks, nothing. Then I heard Weeds outside.

"Oh, look who's here," she said. "It's your friend Patrick. I was just telling Bernie what a nice packing job he did here, Patrick. Looks a lot like lettuce sticking out of a sandwich. I thought I taught you better than that, Bernie."

She grabbed my arm and yanked me over in front of him.

"It seems that Bernie was going somewhere without saying goodbye to anyone. I knew you'd want to see him before he left, so I think I'll go over to my office and make some coffee and let you two have your little chat. You can meet me there in about ten minutes. How's that sound?"

Weeds's feet trotted across to the administration building. The door closed, no traffic, no airplanes, just the faint sound of my nerves vibrating.

"C'mon," I said. "Let's move to the bench here. I need a seat."

Bernie didn't respond, so I took his arm and dragged him over, the suitcase slapping against his leg.

"What happened last night?" I said. "Did somebody fuck you up last night? Was it Carter? Say something, goddammit. Did he make you do something you didn't want to do?"

My guts bounced again, sweat oozing. I took a few deep breaths. Bernie got up and started for the street.

"Look," I said, stopping him. "I don't know what the hell's going on, but I can tell you, I'd much rather be back in bed right now. I'd like it to be tomorrow too. But as long as we're here, there's something we have to deal with, and that means you're gonna start by telling me who fucked you up and we'll figure out what we're going to do about it. . . . You're my buddy, Bernie. It makes me very sick to my stomach to think things like I'm thinking right now. So you're gonna help me out. Right?"

Bernie moved for the street again. I had a painful desire to slap him.

"All right," I said. "Look, we've gotta get this out of the way, 'cause we've got business tonight. Remember? I got that girl for you. She's gonna be here at ten o'clock, so we gotta get you in shape, man. Can't have you runnin' around on your first date lookin' like a zombie. What the hell's she gonna think, she sees you like this? She's beautiful too, man. I mean a knockout. Great personality, and the biggest, most luscious set of tits you ever slid your hands across. She showed 'em to me, and I told 'er those are exactly what Bernie's lookin' for, and now she can hardly wait to meet you."

"I want to go home," he said, and started for the street.

"Well at least you're talkin' anyway," I said. "But I'm sorry. You can't go home. We got too many things to take care of first. So let's start with what happened last night."

"I want to go home."

"All right, if that's what you want, we'll get you home, but first, I want to know, so I can take care of it for you. That's what buddies are for, you know?"

He tugged, trying to get loose, his body in slow motion.

"Goddammit," I yelled. "If I'm gonna kill that sonofabitch, Bernie, it would damn sure help to know why. Can you understand that?"

I took him by both arms then, facing me.

"Look," I said. "I'm sorry, but I'm serious too. I'm not gonna let 'im get away with it, and I guarantee you, he'll never touch you again. Is that what he told you? Did he tell you if you said anything he'd fuck you up again? All you gotta do is nod, man. You ain't got to say a word, just nod."

I put my hand to his head. He pulled away.

"All right. Let's get a cup of coffee, then we'll try it again."

In Weeds's office, I held him while she cleaned his neck with cotton and alcohol. Pain didn't seem to bother him. He just kept trying to walk out.

"You should've at least changed your T-shirt, Bernie," Weeds said. "This one's all soaked with blood. You can't feel that, huh? That doesn't sting? Jesus, Patrick. These things go all the way up into his hair. Have you ever felt Carter's fingernails? Well, take my word for it then."

"I want to go home," Bernie said.

"I'm going to make a couple phone calls," Weeds said. "I want you to take Bernie outside and wait for me."

He moved fine, as long as we headed toward the avenue. When we got to the snakewalk, I had to make him sit, that damn suitcase welded to his fist. A few cars sneaked by out on the avenue. In the tree overhead, a bird warbled his ass off, looking for bird pussy. Every time I let go of Bernie's arm, he tried to get up.

Weeds finally came out of the building, her footsteps neither light nor quick. I couldn't feel the sun.

"Well well, how's it going, fellas?" she said. "Anything new?"

"Nothing new here," I said.

"Well I made my phone calls, and Stan says if Bernie wants to go home, then we should take him to the bus depot and send him home, and that he will gladly reimburse me tomorrow for the cost of a ticket."

"That's it?"

"Of course not. He also made it quite clear that I'm not to call anyone else except Bernie's mother to let her know he's on his way home. So, let's take Bernie over, put him in my car, and drive him to the bus depot. The sooner we're done, the sooner we can get back to whatever the hell we were doing before this began."

Weeds bought him a soda and sandwich at the Oakland depot and wrapped them in a paper bag. We waited an hour for the bus. He never said a word.

I didn't notice my body shaking until Weeds dropped me off and I walked toward the dorm. Just the hangover, I told myself. Nothing to worry about.

A radio played through an upstairs window. Jazz. The halls were quiet, disinfected. The shaking would stop, I thought, as soon as my muscles flexed. I almost stopped in the stairwell to limber up, knee bends, but I was there already, my hand knocking at Carter's door. Not loud. There was no hurry. Just move quick, go with the door when it opened. Move quick, get your hold, take 'im down, and go from there. There's no need to shake. He's going to open it any second now. I'll hear his feet coming. Move with it, as it opens. Did I hear feet?

I knocked again, louder. Should've exercised, I thought, limbered up, shook this goddamn tightness in my chest. Then my hand pounded.

"You sonofabitch," I yelled, my mouth to the door, sweat pouring.

"He's not there," Weeds said.

She stood no more than three feet from me. I hadn't heard her walk up.

"I saw him walking out the snakewalk with a grip as we were leaving with Bernie."

I had to move then, toward my door. The second beer, I thought, still there, my throat so tight, so dry, and my heart, Jesus.

"It's not worth it," Weeds said. "Nobody's worth that. They'd put you in prison, you know."

Geri came into my room, touching my arm. I was sitting on the bed.

"What's going on here?" she said. "What sort of secrets are you people telling?"

Carter didn't come back that day. I knocked on his door several times, ate dinner, had a couple shots with Cole, and at nine headed out the snake-walk, alone, with forty bucks in my wallet. That would cover their gas and time and whatever. I figured they'd understand. If they didn't, there was nothing they could do. I wanted them to know though.

I chewed. Traffic seemed preoccupied. I tried counting the seconds in each light sequence for a while. A land breeze kept the night air fairly warm. It was pleasant, actually, and time had run down one of those queer alleys where you never know if it's a minute or an hour. When I checked my watch it showed 11:00 P.M., the avenue vacant, everybody off somewhere, doing their thing.

I waited until 11:30, then headed for the dorm. Mother Night stepped out from the shadows, taking my arm as we walked, her fragrance just a hush, a touch to the lips for silence.

TWENTY-ONE

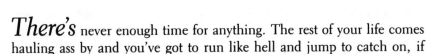

There's never enough time for anything. The rest of your life comes hauling ass by and you've got to run like hell and jump to catch on, if you're going anywhere.

Elaine apparently heard the whistle. She called one night to inform me that she had found the perfect apartment, had already signed a rental contract, and that it would please her immensely if I could return home by October first, to take possession of my material wealth. "I don't want to be responsible for your things," she said, "so I'm just letting you know."

Christ. So I'm just letting you know, I thought, in mid September. The worm had already been programmed for its debut at the end of six months, in mid November.

Geri got her own notice of termination the next day—two weeks. Makes you wonder sometimes who the hell is dealing. We were ready though. Geri would move back to her apartment in San Francisco, get settled, catch a bus the following weekend, meet me in Flatfield, and house-sit for me. I would return to C.I.B. for a week or so to finish up my typing lessons, some shorthand braille, and a woodshop project, a table that wasn't half finished. We were both pushed, but excited. Her headaches had adiosed. Our future was rising bright again, warm.

I called Elaine back that evening to tell her that I would be there Friday night, the twenty-eighth of September. We could go through the inventory list, I would take the keys, and we could forget we ever knew each other.

Stan advanced my mobility lessons, four hours each day, rapid transit, underground stations, the bay tube. Christ, it gave me the creeps being under water like that, sober.

Geri had it in fast forward too, packing, finishing projects. What little time we scraped aside for each other was spent touching, hands mostly. I had already enrolled in the community college. Geri would finish her studies in San Francisco, another six months, then move to Flatfield.

Living together twisted her Catholic roots a bit, but we figured time would handle that.

My route that week, on mobility lessons to the rapid transit station, led me past a convenience store, a hangout for convenience types, I guess. I'd hear all sorts of amusing things.

"Hey you guys, look. I'm blind," an intelligent male suggested one day.

"Knock it off, you dumb fuck. It ain't funny," a husky female entry added. For the next two days she made her presence known to me as I approached. "Hi," she'd shout, or, "Hey, how's it going today?" I'd wave. Then the following afternoon this tons-of-fun came sliding up behind me, her thighs rubbing the sheen from what may have been black polyester. It's funny, instinct I guess, but you're suddenly aware it's your body that fits another's design. The worm took notice and turned to watch the advancing hormones. She eventually made up her mind and hoofed up alongside. I turned and smiled, nodding.

"Beautiful day, isn't it," she said, impressing the hell out of me with her clever approach. A sultry curve had been added to the husky voice—good head, I thought.

"Not too bad," I said.

"Where are you going?"

"Nowhere in particular," I said. "I'm just practicing being a regular."

"You're a good-looking guy."

"Thanks," I said. "I bet you say that to all the blind guys."

She didn't quite know why, but she laughed anyway.

"I'll bet you're a good lover too," she said.

Right to the issue, anyway. I liked her for that. The prospects of rubbing bellies wasn't missed either. It struck its usual, sensual note, the wart on its knees, pleading. I had to laugh.

"Are you laughing at me?" she said.

"Not at all, just the idea. Us blind guys don't get much, you know. There ain't that many blind women around."

"I'll bet you're a *real* good lover."

"Does that mean you'd like to try it out?"

"You look like you could use some," she said.

"Ooooh, I see. Now it's me that needs it and you're going to do me a big favor by being charitable."

"What do you mean by that?"

"It was your design, wasn't it? You figured since I was blind, I wouldn't see how fat you were, so you'd suggest a little swat and smell session, and I wouldn't know any different until the clothes came off, and by then it would be too late, 'cause you'd prove you could get it up and take care of it."

224

"Just who the fuck do you think you are, buddy?"

"You're the one with the proposition, aren't you?"

"You can fuck off and die waiting for it, for all I care," she said, and blended back into the sounds of traffic.

I returned that afternoon from my jaunt in the Adipose world to find my future partner in warpaint. She had asked Lou Abrams if he would show her the revised procedure for division on the abacus.

"That wasn't asking much, was it?" she said. "I explained that I was leaving, that I knew he was busy. I was very nice too, and that's difficult when you hate somebody's guts. But I was. I can't believe how nice I was to that pipsqueak, and you know what he said? I still can't believe my ears heard this. He said, " 'Why should I. You'll all wind up in a kitchen anyway.' "

I left her in Lauren's care, a cup of coffee in her hand, and headed for the gym. My skull needed a break from the pace, then back upstairs in the shower, the wart got a little out of hand, fantasies I guess, and a little extra soaping. I heard another body enter the bathroom, whistling. A janitor, I thought, then thinking he might get the wrong idea if I stepped out with a hard-on, I waited a bit, then turned the water off. It was Carter. I hadn't heard the bastard since Bernie left.

The tightness returned to my chest. My hand shook slightly as I turned the water back on, standing there another minute until he had gone out and closed his door behind him, then I dried off and sat in my room, dislocated. Not long after that, his hall door closed, and he passed mine, still whistling.

Weeds told me the next day he was gone for good. Someone had told him that his eligibility for S.S.I. benefits dated back to the onset of his phony blindness. He had filed a claim, and waited, and won. They had paid him off, retroactive, even for his time in the can. Fifteen hundred and forty-three bucks, she said.

"You know," Cole said. "You're really a case. The guy's gone. It's over and done. I don't know why you always have to get your head so screwed up with things. Some you have to, don't get me wrong, but a lot of it is only worth forgetting. If you don't, it'll just eat at you and in the end, you'll wind up doin' nothin' about it anyway."

"I'd 've done it Sunday," I said. "If he'd been there, I'd 've done it."

"What makes you think so?"

"'Cause it was different Sunday. I didn't have a chance to think about it, like I did today."

"So what stopped you today?"

"I don't know. Just chicken, I guess."

"You wouldn't 've done it Sunday either," he said.

"How the hell do you know?"

"Because they've been watchin' you. You might've tried to do it, but you wouldn't 've finished. It wasn't just Gwenda either. I heard Zeke Potter talkin' with one of the janitors just this mornin', down in the laundry room, about you and Carter, how they all been keepin' an eye on you. When you gonna learn, ol' buddy? You know what goes on around here."

"They watch everybody but the right ones," I said.

"Boy, I'll say. I even found a peephole in my shorts last week. . . . See there? Now don't that feel better? Open up a bit. Keep that foot in the water. You done right for the boy too. Your ideas were all good, your intentions in the right place, but you still lost the case."

Cole had the Crow handy, and took a pull. I passed.

"That's good," he said. "I'm quittin' after this one's gone."

"Every time I quit, I feel worse instead of better."

"Exactly," he said. "I was lyin' about quittin'. I got another hid under the bed."

"What the hell," I said. "I guess he got educated anyway."

Cole left that next weekend. Weeds drove him to the bus depot Saturday morning. I gave him a hug and a paper sack with a jug of Crow and a rubber dogturd stashed inside.

"Just a little snack," I said. "Case you get hungry."

"Thanks," he said. "I can read the label through the bag. I got one just like it in my suitcase. Oughta be a quick trip home."

There'd been no going-away party, no graduation exercises the night before—just the two of us. I had been pissed at him all week for staying drunk.

"I'll slide outa this processing plant like I slid in," he said. "Like I told you before, you take care of yourself 'n' don't worry 'bout me."

"I'll be there," I said. "Soon as I get finished here and situated with everything else, I'll hop that grey dog."

"Spring'd be a good time," he said, "or next fall. The fishin's better in the fall."

"Give me the damn jug, will you," I said. "I'm not gonna sit here and watch you get happy all by yourself. Not on the last damn night. I'm glad you're leavin' too, you know that? You're a bad influence."

"I'm lucky to be alive after followin' your ass around. I got you figured out too," he said. "After you left the other night, it come to me, like a goddamn vision."

"Straight from St. Crow, huh?"

"This ain't no Aesops fable, either. This is the straight scranny. Right from the river, ol' buddy. I was floatin' a hole this one particular day, couple years ago, October, clear, crisp, the water so damn blue you could paint with it. Everything was out that day. Every leaf and rock and bush and tree, everything bein' its individual self, watchin' me and the river go at it, then Boom. I hit this fish. Forty pounds or better the way it was strippin' line. Hell, when I got 'er in, she weighed sixteen pounds. She just fought like she was four times 'er size, and it was fun at first. I was gettin' my kicks out of it, talkin' to 'er. You know how it is, and then half an hour later she's still goin'. I'd already decided to release 'er. If she wanted to live that bad, I wasn't gonna be the one to stop her. So I started givin' 'er some—What? Here goddammit. If you'd brought your own, you wouldn't have to interrupt a good story."

I swallowed Crow. The damn stuff seemed to taste different every time.

"So anyway, I started givin' 'er some slack, seein' if she'd shake off, and hell, she just stripped more, up the hole, then down, then through the riffle below into the next hole, still strippin' line, me talkin' to 'er the whole way, tellin' 'er to take it easy, that I'm gonna release 'er for doin' so well, all them good genes. But it never happened. Took me over an hour to get 'er in, and when I did get backed into some slack water, she come up to the net dead. She just couldn't quit fightin', see? Just kept on till she burst her goddamn heart, and I set there holdin' 'er, talkin' to 'er, tryin' to explain what I thought the difference was."

The difference ain't ever any further than the worm, I thought.

"I quit fishin' for a while after that," Cole said. "Bothered me for weeks. What the hell is it that makes one particular thing want to live more 'n another? You know? They're just a little crazier. Somethin' that's in 'em from the getgo. They don't know no different, 'n' they can't do no different."

"That fish probably got a good look at your mug and freaked out," I said.

"That's possible, and that thing with Carter. Wantin' to kill 'im and all. There was nothin' wrong with that either."

"I ain't forgot it."

"When my mother died, I went through somethin' similar, 'cept it was my father and brother I had my sights on. I was seventeen at the time. They couldn't even wait till she was buried to put the cabin up for sale, talkin' all their shit, what they was gonna do with the money, 'cept my mother'd already transferred title in my name. The cabin was hers to begin with. It'd come down through the family. I just got real numb feelin', you know? Like there was nothin' else in the world that mattered at the moment, and I had to do it 'cause nobody else would. I didn't though. It ain't 'cause you're chicken either. It's nothin' but your brain workin' again."

"Your own brother and father, huh?"

I could feel him drift then. Something in him just clear as hell moved out into the room a ways, then gathered back in around him, like the aura of a streetlight in the rain.

"I think I'm gonna ask Geri to marry me," I said. "Get busy, quit screwin' around, start doin' somethin' right for a—"

"My old man thought my mother was ugly," Cole said. "Least ways, that's what he was always tellin' 'er. She was smarter 'n him 'n' it pissed him off 'cause he knew it, so he'd tell 'er shit like how he was just waitin' for 'er to die so he could get 'im a new bride, a young woman. He and my brother, both of 'em, just alike. Neither of 'em ever knew what beauty was, and never will."

"What is it, then?"

"It's nothin'. 'Cause there's no such thing as ugly. Nature ain't got anything that's ugly. She ain't got nothin' that's wrong, either. Beauty's just a word that man made up, 'cause he got tired of always comin' in second. You, though, are the only exception, Patrick. You are definitely an ugly blink, and the next time you come down to my room, bring somethin' to drink, will you?"

"I'm going to ask Geri to marry me," I said again.

"I heard you the first time."

Cole and I stood beside the bus, neither of us knowing how to break it. The bus driver waited beside his open door, clearing his throat.

"That's nice, fellas," he said, "but you'll have to save some of it for next time. We've got a lot of highway in front of us and people waiting."

"I'll be there," I said to Cole, our hands together. "I'll come up before I start school."

"There ain't no hurry. Get yourself good and edufuckingcated. It'll help, and take care of the smoothbore. It's gonna take 'er a while to know you."

"Maybe we'll both come up."

"I'll be there. Don't forget your river, huh?"

Weeds helped him find a seat, and as she and I headed across the parking lot, I heard Cole roar. I could see the other passengers cringe, clutching their valuables.

"Sounds like he found the dogturd," I said.

The day seemed tired for some reason, lazy, its colors blending instead of standing out. Like it had grown tired of starting over. That's California though. It'll spoil you, make you lazy.

"Would you like to stop somewhere?" Weeds said. "I know it's early, but I'll buy if you're interested."

"I'll make it up there, too," I said.

"You like the guy, don't you."

"I never had many friends," I said, "but that's one of 'em there."

"Where does Geri fit into that?"

"She's there too. We're gonna get married."

"Oh really. Have you told her about this?"

"Not yet."

"Did you already buy a ring?"

"I figured I'd use a poptop."

"I think this definitely warrants a stop, then. A good belt won't hurt you after losing a friend. I don't think your sweetie will miss us for a while. Do you?"

That was 11:00. By 1:00, we had hit half a dozen jewelry stores and as many bars, refills in between tray after tray of rings. Christ. You'd think it would be easy. Nothing fancy, just plain, simple, the color beginning to fade again into lazy disillusion.

"C'mon," Weeds said. "One more. Finish your beer and we'll try the plaza. If we don't find it there, I'll take you to San Francisco Tuesday. I know we'll find one there."

And there it was, one store away. Just a thin gold band with a double knot, a friendship ring they called it. The pomp and flutter of romance radiated from my skull.

Weeds took us home for the weekend as part of the plan. Geri had the ass a bit with us for coming in happy, so we stopped at Safeway, bought the fixings for a feast, got a bottle of rum, some Cokes, and sat Geri down in the shade of a mulberry on Weeds's deck. After the third rum and Coke, she softened appreciably, and scooted over next to me.

"Hi," she said.

"Oh, hi there," I said. "I remember you. The bowling alley. Wasn't that it? We had a couple dances together?"

"Hasn't a lot happened since then," she said.

"Yeah. It's almost sickening sometimes."

"You should see the face on that munchkin," Weeds said. "Makes me want to reach over and pinch her cheek."

"I know," Geri said. "I get drunk too easy."

"There's always better things to do. Right, Pat?"

"Geez," I said, grinning. "I don't know. You mean better than cold beer?"

"There's a fresh box of bubble bath next to the tub," she said. "I know. I just opened it."

"That don't sound too bad," I said. "I can probably reach my beer from the tub."

"Hah. Aren't you a silly boy?" Geri said.

"Oh no, it's a great idea," Weeds said, "and by the time you're done, I'll have dinner ready. I'll put the potatoes in now, and when you come down, you'll be all fresh and ready to eat."

"You mean together?" Geri said.

"Sure," I said. "It saves water."

"I haven't finished my drink yet."

She brought her drink upstairs to the tub. We had bubbles piled up to our necks, the ring behind me on top of the toilet, wrapped up in a shoe-box, ribbon and all. I lay back, warm, sweating a bit in that fragrant heat. Geri had her foot in my crotch, examining its occupants with her toes.

"My goodness," she said. "You're getting excited. What are you excited about?"

"Oh, I don't know," I said. "Starting over, I guess, and doing it right this time."

"And you're looking forward to me coming up to your house?"

"That's the whole thing."

"And you're not just saying that? Even if I get these headaches forever, and can't work?"

I reached behind me for the package and handed it to her across the suds.

"Here," I said. "This is a little something for your headaches. That's what took us so long today."

"What is it?"

"Well, take it. Open it up and you'll see."

"I won't. You're playing a trick on me. I can tell when you laugh like that."

"C'mon. It ain't gonna hurt you."

"It's probably another of your sick jokes, like that rubber dogdoo."

"It's a present for crissakes. See? Feel the box."

She felt it, then took it, opened it, and began pulling the wads of news-paper out, slinging them onto the floor.

"You really get into it, don't you," I said.

"I love presents. You should've seen me at Christmas time. My family hated me. I'd rip everything open, even if it wasn't mine."

She kept tossing paper, looking.

"There's nothing in here," she said. "I should've known. . . . Oh, wait a minute. What's this?"

Her toes stopped moving in my crotch.

"Did you find it?" I said.

"Umm hmm."

"It's called a friendship ring. I thought that after we try things out for a year, we could get something better. You could pick it out, and I'll get down on one knee and offer you my hand."

She didn't move or speak. I thought I'd been premature. I hadn't even considered a no.

"You don't like it?"

"I'm just busy crying, if you don't mind."

She slid across on top of me then, like a seal. Everything came together in the right places. We lost a few bubbles over the side, but what the hell, I loved her.

Weeds had the dinner set, the wine poured. Geri sat beside me, her hand on my thigh.

"My my," Weeds said. "Aren't we both a little pink in the cheeks?"

"Isn't life wonderful?" Geri cooed.

"Oh, I was wondering," Weeds said. "I didn't think a bath and a ring would do all that."

"Now we're a team," I said. "When we start our own school, we're gonna give C.I.B. some competition."

"Oh really," Weeds said. "And where's all this going to take place?"

"Up in the mountains, with Cole. We'll teach blinks how to survive in the woods, so they can handle the city when they're done. We'll have our own resident baby sitters."

"I can't have my babies in the woods," Geri said. "What if something happened?"

"It ain't exactly wilderness," I said. "You won't be that far from civilization."

Her hand started patting my leg.

"He's just kidding," she said. "Besides, your house sounds just perfect for us. I can walk to the store to shop, and if I buy something too big to carry, I can call a cab. You've got all those nice neighbors too, if we need to ask anybody for help."

Her hand moved up, scratching at my fly.

"We'll have everything we need right there," she said. "That's why people moved into the cities, so they could have those things. We'll find a doctor that's close, so I can go by myself. I mean we have to look at this thing sensibly."

"She's certainly right," Weeds said.

Geri's hand had stopped patting. It sat there a second, then slipped away.

"Look," she said. "If you're serious about this, I'm not saying no to anything, but we have to finish what we're doing now first. You'll finish college. That's four years right there, and heaven only knows what we'll be thinking in four years."

"That's right, big boy," Weeds said. "You're looking out for somebody besides yourself now."

"You're such a dreamer," Geri said. "This is for real. We have to be practical. There's nothing wrong with dreaming either, don't get me wrong, but the world is full of dreamers. You'll see. Believe me."

Her hand returned, patting again.

"I have my dreams too," she said, "but I think they're a lot more solid than yours. . . . Don't get mad now. Is he getting mad, Gwenda? . . . I'm telling you the truth," she said, the hand patting in rhythm with her words. "You always want to change things. Don't you remember me telling you? You can't be angry either. You have to accept things as they are, then your life becomes a lot easier. Besides that, if we're stuck out in the woods, heaven only knows what could happen. I might get attacked and eaten by a wild animal."

"Cheers," I said, raising my wineglass. "I ain't gonna argue. The idea ain't bad, though."

"It's a good idea," Geri said. "It just isn't practical."

I smiled, my face tired, like after a long day with company, when the booze wears thinner than the conversation, and you start thinking how good the bed will feel.

"That calls for a brandy," I said. "A toast to the new, practical me."

"You'll like it," Geri said. "You'll see. Everything works out when two people love each other."

TWENTY-TWO

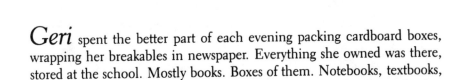

Geri spent the better part of each evening packing cardboard boxes, wrapping her breakables in newspaper. Everything she owned was there, stored at the school. Mostly books. Boxes of them. Notebooks, textbooks, all in braille. The worm got a little sentimental seeing the shortcake, her goddamn life packed up like that—Italy, Montreal, San Francisco, C.I.B., alone.

Lauren and I carried most of the conversation. The woman seemed to genuinely enjoy being blind, addicted to the hiss and burp of the coffee machine on her side of the room.

"I'll admit it," she said. "I like it. For the first time in my life, I actually have people caring about me."

I could see her on the Morgan mare, the astonished faces in automobiles whipping by.

"Did you aim for that car?" I said.

"Patrick!" Geri shouted.

"It's okay," Lauren said. "I'm not really sure what I did. I was unconscious for thirty days, and I still have partial amnesia. The police report said I was on drugs. But I just don't remember."

Geri got her goodnight kiss about eleven. Lauren knew what was going on. Every time I went down on Geri, she would move around to her coffee pot, occupying herself, the spoon stirring slowly, stopping at times. That night, Geri started vibrating a little more than usual. Squeals of delight snuck out. The spoon stopped.

"Is something wrong?" Lauren said.

Geri tightened her grip in my hair.

"Is she getting another massage?" Lauren said.

"She's fine," I said. "Aren't you, babe?"

"I'm fine," Geri gasped, her voice a little perforated. Lauren's spoon began to move again, slow, methodical. I felt like a thief doing that in front of her, taking advantage of her dark side.

Weeds liked her too. She was obviously the next child, the protégée, with Geri and me leaving.

On Wednesday, Stan dropped me off way the hell out in the Berkeley sticks for a test of my mobility skills. He laughed and drove away, but not far.

"You can ask anybody you want for directions," he said. "If you can find anyone. I'll see you back at the school. You might make it by dinnertime."

"Get the hell outa here," I said. "If I find a bar, I won't be back."

I stood there a moment, checked the wind and sun, then walked. It was a circular block. I knew it when I passed the same house twice without hitting a corner, sprinklers going, a big knot in the sidewalk where a tree root had raised it, and the same damned miniature whatever yapping at me. I crossed the street, found a corner, and hung a left, keeping the breeze on my left cheek.

Stan had parked and waited. That was usual procedure, drive a ways, park, and watch. When I heard the Dodge start and cruise by, I waved at him. He laughed and kept going. It took me two and a half hours to walk back.

The following day, he let me out somewhere above the Rose Gardens. I had mapped our course from the school, rights, lefts. Stan kept a conversation going, trying to crack my concentration.

"You're good, Pat," he said. "You're uncanny, in fact. I've never had this much trouble losing a student."

To screw me up even further, he drove the same block half a dozen times in different directions.

"You're on your own today, Pat," he said. "This is no piece of cake, either. I'll tell them to keep your dinner warm."

The sky was overcast, nothing obvious. I stood there on the sidewalk for maybe ten minutes, straining to home in like a goddamn pigeon—no sun, no wind, just instinctual hints. When I finally made a choice, the first street I turned on started uphill. It had been a long time since I questioned myself and felt that faint edge of fear.

The hill crested, and started down. I smiled, sensing pressures, the bay beyond, the hills behind me, air currents. When I hit a main artery, I stuck my thumb out. The third car by stopped, a Jehovah's Witness. I nodded and smiled all the way back to the school, right up to the curb in front.

"You bet," I told the guy. "I'll give you a call in a couple weeks, soon as I get settled here. Yeah. I'm looking forward to it too. You bet. Thanks again. Give my best to the boss, huh?"

A voice hailed me in front of the administration building as I tapped toward the dorm. Sarah, a new recruit, another total. She had only been there two days.

"Can you tell me where the dorm is?" she said. "I'm lost."

"They close it on Thursdays," I said. "Didn't they tell you?"

Dear Sarah was a wall crawler, her slothlike progress confused by my bullshit, a mosaic of question marks spinning about her.

"C'mon," I said. "I'm just kiddin'. It's over this way. Grab an elbow."

The Dodge pulled up across the street and parked. Stan got out and headed toward us. I'd beaten him back.

"Shortcut," I said. "I found Jesus and flew in."

Friday morning found Geri, Lauren, Weeds, and me in San Francisco, with Geri's gear in the back of a borrowed pickup. Our first stop was the kennel, to bail out Geri's guide dog, Chelsey. I couldn't tell which of them jumped the highest. They liked each other.

Two hours later, we had packed all her boxes upstairs into her new lodging, and pointed our faces toward the Wharf, for lunch. Geri put Chelsey to work. I followed, caning, the mile or so. Weeds and Lauren drove and met us there, standing in the sea breeze, an organ grinder cranking away. His monkey took me for an easy mark and dug a searching mitt into my left front pocket. I thought it was Geri, and reached down casually, unconcerned, to find this goddamn skinny, hairy thing with an arm attached. My nerves went in several directions, much to the morbid glee of some nearby regulars. The poor monkey needed mouth to mouth, too.

"I'm just not used to finding other hands in my pockets," I said. "What if I had a hole in there?"

"Don't be gross," Geri said.

We ate fried clams and squid at the snackstand, sitting on a bench in the sun, a portion of the fishing fleet within earshot, rattling in their moorings, creaking like a waiting team in harness. Overhead, gulls and terns taunted us for being landbound.

Weeds and Lauren dropped me off at the Oakland Greyhound depot that evening, and an hour and a half later, suitcase in hand, I was back in the egg carton, prepared for my rendezvous with Elaine.

Downtown Flatfield smelled the same, night or day, thanks to the onion factory a couple of blocks from the bus station. It was 11:00 P.M. when I stepped down and started walking, the streets quiet, different. A sleeping town is like a child, innocent, vulnerable. The avenue, the bigger city at the end of the snakewalk, had a hardness to it, a survival factor. These slumbering, tree-lined streets of Flatfield seemed to give off an air of security. I sensed it more with each block I walked, like a stray cat—cautious but wanting. My two-mile hike home passed too quickly.

The last mile was all new construction, the road widened with new asphalt, sidewalks with wheelchair ramps. Peach and plum orchards had thrived there before. Each year it spread that much farther, the orchards scalped, the lines staked, slabs poured, the common fences, fire hydrants, cable TV, and the green ceramic frog families in the corner of each lawn for the neighborhood dogs to piss on.

Mixed thoughts lingered where Elaine was concerned. Another good-bye, one last night in the house together, maybe even one final *funichingilario*. But when I turned the last corner, she was gone already. I sensed it, and as I turned up the empty driveway and onto the familiar walkway to the porch, I felt cheated. She had lied to me, hauled ass before I got there.

A sheet of paper, a note, had been rolled up and tucked into the front door handle, but no keys. I laughed, went through the side gate and started removing screens. The fourth window, a bathroom, was slightly open. I pulled myself up and in.

The house smelled like Elaine. It also smelled as if it hadn't been cleaned well, dusty, but the rest was definitely Elaine, the powder, that hint of cologne, the same goddamn soap she always used. All of it combined, followed from room to room like a ghost that had been waiting for me.

I didn't bother with an inventory check that night. The silverware tray was still in the top kitchen drawer. Just an empty refrigerator, running. That seemed strange for some reason. An empty refrigerator, running. So I opened every window in the house, got my backpack from the suitcase, and hiked back into town to a convenience store for the essentials of the coming morning, beer, bread, bacon, eggs, and a jar of Taster's Choice. On my return, I entered through the front door. That made it more like a home. It smelled better too, and after putting the few groceries away, I popped a beer and stood in the kitchen, listening to the refrigerator run.

Geri would be there in two days, and it would be ours then, the house with no lights, the missing tooth in that particular jawbone. She would be a novelty, Geri, a blink woman to get that neighborhood jaw working, stirring the soft, fat strands of Adipose minds. I reached for the wall phone, thinking of her, alone in her San Francisco apartment, the little beaver snuggled in her jammies. I was surprised to find a dial tone.

That first night in the house, I slept on the carpet. Elaine had taken the bed. In the morning, I showered, fried up a couple of bacon and egg sandwiches, drank two cups of the instant, took a deep breath, and made my rounds of the house to see what was left.

Elaine's ghost followed me from room to room, pointing things out, hair clips, the toothpaste cap in the bathroom sink, the tub and shower

236

that needed sandblasting, all the plants gone. She had taken what was hers, and some of mine, things I accumulated long before I met her, including picture albums. She couldn't take the smell though. It lingered strongest in the bedroom, around the dresser. The right top drawer contained two pair of unders, shot, their elastic stretched. I raised them to my nose, an almost fragrant hint of perfume, cheap stuff, taking me back to the first time.

Outside, the backyard waited for me, three feet high with natural flora, wild oats, star thistle, tarweed. The front wasn't a hell of a lot better. Both had been in lawn when I left. A neighbor's boy had kept them clean, trimmed, watered. My personal little piece of suburbia. That in itself helped, seeing the difference. I had to change that picture in my sight memory, the tired, overgrown, brown reminder. But it was mine, a steppingstone.

Elaine had left two of everything in the towel, washcloth, sheet, and silverware categories, and one blanket. I brought in an old double box-spring and mattress from overhead in the garage, cleaned it up, and made it. A shaky dinette I had used in the garage for car parts became my kitchen table. I brought that and its two ragged chairs in and sat down, trying it out. It wasn't bad, and after a couple beers, I liked it even more.

The washer and dryer were still there, and still worked. Shock at this moved me back to the fridge for another beer. Then, back in the garage, I ran my hands along the workbench. The toolbox was there, my jigsaw and drill motor. Hand tools were scattered around where somebody had used them. The other male, I thought, the radio. And at the very end of the bench, on a stack of old newspapers, sat the dog's dish. My hands moved over it quickly, at first, then returned, slowly tracing the circle, hefting it, testing the weight, the old film clicking back frame by frame, the liver and white Springer and master hunting together, his color so vivid against the dark fields, and darker memories. I set the dish back down and blubbered like an idiot.

Christ. I couldn't remember the last time I had stuffed my sinuses up like that. The dog was fine too. I had placed an ad in the paper and given him to an older, level-headed retired fella that loved to hunt. Buck, I thought, ol' Bucky boy. When I came home from the hospital he had gone nuts, licking at my bandages. He'd spend his days lying quietly outside the screen door, waiting for me. Weeks later, when the bandages were off, his tongue would always find the eyes first, trying to heal them.

I had called his new owner once, just to check. He had chained him up to keep him from running away, said he found him twice on the side of the freeway, headed north toward Flatfield, on his way home, like everything would be just the same again someday. The dumb sonofabitch would sit there and wag and wait because he didn't know any better. He never wanted much either. Just me.

Tom Baylor, my neighbor to the east, walked over at five o'clock. I was out front pulling weeds. I didn't know him well, but liked him. He was a captain in the air force and hated it, no gold braid around his pecker. He had my keys.

"I left the note," he said, "and didn't think about it until this morning. Elaine brought them over Tuesday night, and said she didn't know when you'd get here."

He followed me into the house, watching.

"Grab a chair," I said. "Does your wife let you drink beer yet?"

He laughed, so I popped him a can and brought it to the table.

"Are you all finished at your school?"

"Just about," I said. "I'm going back down in a week to take care of a few things."

"I bet you learned a lot. I mean . . ."

He hesitated, trying to decipher his own meaning.

"I mean they must teach you blind things, don't they?"

"Among other things," I said.

"Elaine says you have a blind girlfriend."

"She'll be here tomorrow. You can meet 'er."

"Sherry and I were talking about it last night. It's nice you could find somebody that's your own kind."

"You bet. Geri's a real cute black girl."

He jerked off a single, quick laugh, watching. I kept a straight face.

"You're kidding. . . . You're not kidding? Oh boy."

"Hey, you fall in love, that's it, man. We hit it off for a couple months before anybody even told me."

He tried the laugh again, hesitant.

"No shit," I said. "We were walking down the street one day, and some woman tugged at my arm and whispered it in my ear, but by then it was too late."

The laugh came this time, controlled. He looked like JFK, the eyes a little pinched, the hairdo.

"C'mon," he said. "You're pulling my leg. You would've smelled her, or something, wouldn't you? I mean everybody says they've got a different smell."

"Geri don't. She's a sweetie. She's got some choppers on 'er, you know, them big buck teeth. I damn near lost a lip the first time we made out, but they make a damn good bottle opener."

Sherry, Tom's wife, called thirty seconds after the laughter started. Probably had a window open. She'd always been a nerve about Tom and me getting together. I found his beer on the table where he'd left it, a couple sips gone, and drank it.

Salvation presented itself at my door that evening, another neighbor, a real two-fisted hand-pumper with the local Lion's Club. I had never met the guy.

"I didn't know if you were home, or not," he said, "when I didn't see any lights on, but I thought I'd knock anyway. The wife said she saw you earlier, and I just wanted to let you know we're available, if you ever need anything. Our organization sponsors a lot of dogs, you know."

I thanked him, explaining I didn't need a dog, my mobility was fine with the cane.

"Well, we'd like to make a place for you in the organization, if you're interested. We need people like you. I mean you're a good-looking guy, you handle yourself well. We could make a good speaker out of you. That's what it takes, you know? Somebody that can appeal to the community. Gets you into that area between the needy and the working public."

"I don't think so," I said.

"I know you'd like it. If you want, I could pick you up and introduce you at our next meeting. A lot of our members are what you might call the backbone of the community."

"I've four more years of school to finish," I said. "It keeps me busy."

"Why that's even better. An educated man. What're you studying?"

"Nuclear physics."

"Well you got one on me there. I don't know much about the medical field, but we'd like to hear about it."

"I'll give you a call when I'm done," I said. "How's that?"

The guy, Crawford, Coughford, whatever the hell his name was, must've snacked on garlic. I fanned the door a couple times after he left, and listened to his feet, followed them off my driveway and across the street into the court. Some kids were playing up there.

Geri arrived Sunday evening. I walked down to the depot and we took a cab back. A couple days of airing had the house almost neutral. Chelsey sat pretty in the entry hall, waiting for her harness to be removed. I got the dog dish from the garage and took her out back, gave her some fresh water, then returned to her two-legged buddy.

"You seem awfully quiet," Geri said. "Are you okay?"

"Couldn't be better," I said. "I just had some funny idea you'd smell the other woman when you came in."

"You had me worried," she said. "I thought you and Elaine had a bad argument or something. I even had a weird dream last night, where the two of you got back together and left me out on the porch."

"I shot 'er," I said. "She's out in the garage covered up with newspapers. The whole thing started over the television, can you believe it?"

Geri had her arms about me, her face to my chest.

"Chelsey likes it too," she said. "I can hear her out there, running. She thinks she's a hunting dog."

After a quick tour, explaining the general layout, I set her bags in by the dresser and joined Chelsey outside while Geri unpacked a few things and checked out the can. Chelsey came romping from the overgrowth to lay a little tongue on me. I sat there, scratching her ears, and inside, through the open bathroom window, Geri was whistling some sweet god-damn Carpenters song.

"It's a light yellow," I told her when she came out later, "with a cedar shake roof. This deck here goes all the way across the back of the house. There's another slider off the master bedroom at that end. We've got a small concrete patio out front, with a rail around it, where we can sit and watch the neighbors."

We rose early the next morning, pink-cheeked—bacon, eggs, toast, and coffee at opposite ends of the table, then a more in-depth tour of the farm.

"All the walls inside are painted white," I said, "except this one here in the center and the one behind the couch."

"Ooooo, I like these shelves," she said, "and what's this here? What kind of wood is this?"

"Blue pine."

"See, if I'd taken woodshop, I'd probably know that."

"At the end of this wall is a fireplace. It's got a nice mantel up here for the clock, when we get one. Then you've got a big window here to the left, and two more on the corner down here, by the back slider."

"What's this hanging here? It's a macrame, that's what it is."

"I had a plant there," I said. "I guess she didn't care for the ropework. Either that or it's broken."

"This is nice. You probably get a lot of sun through these windows. I can sit here and read."

I left Geri to look on her own and went back out front to my weeds, scooting along on my keister, trying to distinguish petunias from the healthy conglomeration around them. Two bodies just happened to be passing on the sidewalk when Geri screamed. They hit the brakes. I smiled apologetically, jumped up, and cracked my melon against the corner of the garage hurrying inside. She had found one of the deer heads on the living room wall. I'd forgotten them.

240

"My god," she said. "I almost had a heart attack right here on the spot. You should've told me. I kept noticing it there, watching me, every time I came through this room, and when I finally reached up to look, it was all hairy and my god, I'm not kidding you. I thought it was something that Elaine left, something terrible. Feel my heart. See how it's beating? Stop that, nasty. You know that's not my heart. It's not funny, either."

I brought a kitchen chair for her to stand on. She checked out each of the mounted heads, their ears and antlers. On the walls of another bedroom, I showed her the pheasant and ducks—mallard, pintail, and a pair of wood ducks. Geri had never seen wildlife, especially anything with antlers.

"Why would you want to stuff them and put them on your walls?"

"I was young," I said. "And at the time, they were trophies, the deer anyway. They're symbols of prowess, a form of bragging. You do it to make others jealous, but I didn't know it then. Now, they're good reminders."

"I'll always feel like they're watching me."

Geri and Chelsey followed me to the grocery store that afternoon. I described the route as we went, only one big intersection, the four-way stop by the store—no lights. Geri wanted to shop on her own, so I held Chelsey's harness and followed her down the aisles.

In the produce section, an old acquaintance hailed me, Frank Paulson. Elaine worked with his wife, Janet. We had partied a bit together, gone fishing a few times. Frank liked to drink. I could tell he was a little nervous, his eyes moving from me, to Geri, to the dog, and finally he said, "Far out, man. It's a small world sometimes, isn't it? The old lady sends me down for a loaf of bread so she can feed the brats a sandwich, and I just happened to be looking in this direction, and hey man, you crossed the end of the aisle with the dog here, and I said, Nah. It can't be, man. So I snuck down the next aisle, to get a better look, and hey. I just stood there, man. Fuck, I didn't know what to say. It's been a while, you know? I didn't know where your head was, or what was happening. You know? I bet I stood there and watched you guys for ten minutes. These store nerds probably think I'm some kind of pervert."

By the time the introduction was over and the hand shaking finished, I had accepted an invitation to a barbecue the following Friday. Two other couples would be there. I had met them before, bank people, Elaine's friends.

Geri baked a chicken for dinner that night. We split a bottle of Blue Nun, the tension obvious, incubating.

"I'm not mad," she said.

"I wasn't that crazy about the idea either," I said, "except I thought it would be good for us. You'd probably like 'em. They ain't bad people, and you're going to be here by yourself for a while. You might want to call someone, or go shopping, or just get together and bullshit. Hell, I don't know. I guess I was wrong."

"I wasn't worried about not liking them."

"T' hell with it then. I'll just call 'im and tell 'im we can't make it. I never did care much for that crap anyway."

"No you won't. I'm sorry I even brought it up now. I just thought it would be nice to have the time to ourselves, but we'll have lots of time."

"Bullshit. I'll just call 'im."

She was up then, standing beside me, fist to my cheek.

"You're not that big, you know," she said. "I think you're forgetting I'm still pretty tough."

"I just figured," I said, "if we're going to live in this damned egg carton, we might as well get used to it, and I know they're Elaine's friends, or ex-friends, but they were my friends too. You'll like Janet. DeeDee ain't bad either. Karen's kind of a bitch, used to be anyway, always tellin' her husband what to do, but she ain't bad. What the hell, we might even enjoy ourselves."

"I'm glad you did," she said. "I was just being selfish, and I was just a tiny bit nervous, because they're Elaine's friends. It's good for us though. We'll show them, won't we. It's going to be fun."

One block north of the house, country prevailed. The housing tracts ended and old orchards followed the creek out through Pleasant Valley. Fall nights still held that breath of summer, and each evening after dinner, we would walk, Chelsey in harness, into that first orchard of aged walnut trees. A small irrigation ditch flowed off the main creek through the trees. Geri would release Chelsey from her harness, and we would listen to her run, out of hearing, then back, splashing through the shallow water, hell bent just for running.

We made love in every conceivable corner of time that week. I did yardwork. Geri rearranged the kitchen, stocking the pantry with goods we backpacked in each day, and in the orchard, in the evenings while Chelsey ran, we talked about kids.

Nobody came by to bug us. They watched though, especially on our store runs. It's easy enough to understand how the sighted mind hits a wall. They'd get used to us.

Karen and her husband, Dennis, picked us up Friday afternoon. They lived the closest. Geri put Chelsey in harness on the front porch and I could hear that bitch tongue of Karen's already slashing in the car.

"The dog too? A goddamn, smelly dog in my new car?"

We were all a little stiff on the ride to Frank's, Chelsey on the floor at Geri's feet. Dennis, embarrassed I guess, tried anyway.

"Sure," I said. "It's nice to be back."

"We're only a couple blocks away," he said. "You guys need anything, don't hesitate to call."

"Thanks anyway," I said. "We'll do fine. That's what they teach you at the blind school, how to get by on your own, hit the toilet, find the grocery store, stay out of the streets, all your basic survival techniques."

Geri kept shut. Karen kept gawking back over the seat to make sure Chelsey wasn't fouling her Chevrolet.

We walked into Frank's house with Bob Seger pounding away on the living room wall. DeeDee and her husband, Ron, were already there. Hands and names made their exchange quickly and Janet wore a fast path from the blender to the dining room table with pitchers of margaritas. We put them away as fast as she could mix them. Geri had Chelsey under the table at her feet, and Karen had to corner the other two women in the kitchen, first thing, to voice her disapproval. Janet laughed.

The booze did its job. Good sauce bridges ignorance, or welds it. I hadn't indulged all week, and as the tequila loosened my joints, the air warmed, and curiosity spawned a question and answer session on C.I.B., educational material for the regulars.

"Actually," I said, "I'm bullshitting. The place was a nuthouse, complete with parasites, hypes, and perverts. They got a black janitor that makes his rounds every night, room to room, poking the blind girls, tellin' them all how much he loves them, twisting their brains."

"Faaaar out," Frank said. "Fuckin' niggers. They're everywhere."

"We went to concerts," Geri said, "and on field trips to Lake Tahoe, and had parties. It was fun."

"And we had another black guy in the room next to me," I said, "some loser junkie with one eye, that just stayed drunk. He never did attend classes and anytime they looked at him crooked, he'd scream N.A.A.C.P. and they'd back off."

"You're making it sound worse than it was," Geri said.

"Not to mention the thieves," I said, "and when we weren't having race riots, we were all busy getting drunk."

"Right on," Frank said.

When I returned from my first piss stop, the other guys had moved outside to get the coals going.

"You too," Janet said. "You get your butt out of here. Frank's got everything you guys need out there in the ice chest. And I want to keep this door closed. There's a hole in the screen and the flies come in."

"And it's girl talk time," DeeDee said from the kitchen.

Geri was the only one sitting at the table.

Frank handed me a beer and showed me to a patio chair.

"Just relax man, take it easy. This is old times. Right? We got it under control."

A couple kids next door clambered up the fence to look over.

"Where's little Frank?" one of them chirped.

"Beat it, you brats," Frank said. "Go play with your sister or something."

Across the back fence, bodies banged off a diving board into a pool, spots of laughter rising. Frank, Dennis, and Ron stood near me on the deck, talking jobs, bosses, taxes. A couple of sparrows rat-packed another in the upper branches of a tree to my left. Frank handed me a bottle.

"This ain't Crow, is it?" I said.

"Hell no it ain't Crow. That's V.O., man. We go first class around here."

I sniffed it anyway, then took a pull.

"You know, man," Frank said. "I was thinkin' that you could probably still go huntin'. Have you thought about that? I mean your hearing must be unreal by now, and if you had somebody to tell you what was there, you could shoot at the sound. What d' ya think?"

"There's already enough idiots out there doin' that, and they can see."

"You must miss it though, man."

"Sure you miss it. You miss bein' there more than anything, but it just don't fit anymore, so you look for somethin' else to compensate."

"Fuck, man, what else is there? You know? I'd go fuckin' crazy if I couldn't get outa here once in a while."

"You just gotta learn how to take the trips in your skull," I said.

"Hey, right, and never come back. I know how that works."

I liked the guys. It wasn't a matter of wanting to join, either. It was knowing I couldn't join. The black talk inside had been part of it, trying to tell them what they wanted to hear, right from the Adipose manual.

When I used the can again a few minutes later, Geri was still at the table, alone.

"We should've stayed home," I said.

"Nonsense," she said. "I've been listening to you boys out there. You're having fun, and you ought to be ashamed of yourselves for some of that language I'm hearing."

Her hand patted my forearm. She was a good little actress, a little gassed.

"I'm having fun too," she said. "I'm going in the kitchen with them in just a minute. It's just a little headache. You know? If I sit here for a few more minutes it'll go. The drinks are really good, aren't they. I think they help."

Janet opened the kitchen door and stuck her head out.

"Are you back again? You act like she's going to run off or something. Really. We're almost done in here, then we're all going to come out. I want to relax too, you know. So get your bootie back outside there. We'll take good care of your sweetie."

"Once you get her going," I said, "you'll have a hard time shutting her off. I'm not kidding you either. This shortcake's done some funny stuff. She hopped a plane to Rome to study for a year, and didn't even have a place to stay when she got there."

"You're kidding me," Janet said. "You've been to Italy?"

Then DeeDee stuck her face out.

"Who's been to Italy? Geri's been to Italy?"

"And from there," Geri said, "Montreal. I studied there for a year too. I've been in Portugal, and Spain, and Germany, and most of the Mediterranean countries."

"She was an interpreter at the Italian Embassy in Montreal for six months," I said.

"You're kidding?"

Geri had the floor when I left, priming up her rum and Coke incident in the Canadian convent. And outside, the guys were still talking jobs and asshole bosses and cars.

"I moved your chair over here," Frank said, "to get you out of the smoke. Just a little farther. There you go. Here, try some more of this. I know you ain't changed that much. How 'bout another beer to go with it?"

"Might as well bring two," I said. "Saves another trip."

"So you're all done down there at that school now, huh?"

"Just about."

"That's a trip, man, that black dude fuckin' all the chicks. We were just talkin' about that. The dude could even rape 'em and get away with it, huh? They couldn't squeal on 'im."

Frank had my chair positioned under the kitchen window. A Stones album carried from the living room, out through the screen.

"I'd like to kill that fuckin' nigger," Frank said.

Killing switched the talk to hunting, opening day of deer season, big bucks, the one so and so got, some guy on the job and the new guns, tight groups on the target range, hand loads. Inside, somebody laughed at the dining room table. I could see Geri, perked, primed for her audience. Then Karen and DeeDee were behind me in the kitchen, fixing more drinks.

"Didn't you look at her eyes yet?" Karen said. "God, they give me the creeps. I don't think I'm going to be able to eat my dinner. And I swear, if it was my house, that dog would be outside. I'd tell her too. I wouldn't have some stinking dog on my carpet."

"I can't smell it," DeeDee said.

"Well it stinks. All dogs stink. Who invited them anyway?"

"We didn't," DeeDee said.

"I swear," Karen said. "If I have to look at her eyes all night, I'm going to scream. She should at least wear dark glasses, like he does."

I waited for them to leave, then scooted my chair forward, away from the window to a point where all sounds seemed to converge, but nothing clear.

"Hey Pat. What the fuck's the matter with you, man? You sick?"

"Just gas," I said, digging a Rolaid from my pocket.

"You ever hunt up around Loyalton?" Dennis said.

"Yeah, I've been there," I said, and squashed my empty beer can.

"My boss shot a big four-pointer up there last year, somewhere around Babett Peak."

"That's nice country," I said. "You can see the lights of Reno on top."

"You sure you're okay?" Frank said.

"Just a quart low," I said. "A couple more drinks, I'll be fine."

I made another can run shortly after that and found Geri under a small, dark cloud, the others in the kitchen with the door closed.

"You're the best-looking gal here," I said. "You know that?"

Her hand moved slowly over to touch my arm.

"How's the headache?"

"It's just a little one, really. It'll probably get better after we eat. I think I had too many drinks."

"Are these girls keeping you occupied?"

"We had a nice talk," she said. "I like them."

Through dinner, I ate like a regular, a little show for the benefit of eye-balls, cutting my steak, laying the knife down, forking it, chewing that goddamn hunk of fat like I enjoyed it. Geri sat on the end, to my left. Karen on her left, across from me, with her phony face on, asking Geri about her travels like she was truly interested. Frank poured wine for everyone, except Dennis and myself. We had the bottle of V.O. between us.

Karen had her grape leg full by the time dinner was over, flashing that big goddamn smile of hers at Geri, the shortcake believing every inch of it, numb to the gills herself.

When the V.O. tap dried, Frank brought another from the kitchen.

"You're right," I said. "That stuff ain't bad at all."

246

"You guys are cleanin' me out," Frank said.

Dennis had grown quiet, across from me, but he could still pour without spilling. His loving wife, Karen, seeing the new jug uncorked, took a few seconds away from Geri's ear to plant a gentle suggestion in her husband's. She whispered a lot like Elaine, like a cat with its ass on fire.

"That's enough, Dennis," she said. "And I mean it."

Ron and I cracked up. When Dennis set his glass down, Ron reached over and filled it.

"I mean it," Karen said. "That Is Enough."

Dennis laughed with us on that one, and on the next.

"What the hell's going on in here?" Frank said, returning from the can.

"Dennis can't have any more," Karen said, "and I don't want any of you offering, either. I have things for him to do around the house tomorrow and I'm not going to baby him on the couch all damn day, like I always do."

"This sucks," Ron said. "Why don't you tell your old lady to shut her big, fucking mouth once in a while. It's the same goddamn thing every time we get together."

I reached across, found Dennis's glass, and filled it. He drank it down.

"You bastard," Karen spat across to me. She and Geri were the only ones not laughing.

"Geri told us you guys are getting married," Karen said. "I feel sorry for her already."

"Is that right," I said. "Well I'll tell you what, sweet cheeks, if she turns out anything like you, there won't be a marriage."

"You bastard."

Geri's hand moved onto my arm, patting.

"Karen's probably right," she said. "Maybe you shouldn't have any more either. You know how you get sometimes."

"I don't believe my fucking ears," I said.

Karen leaned across toward me, her teeth bared.

"I do," she said. "And I really feel sorry for Geri. There's a few things she should know about you. Did you tell her you were a murderer? Did you tell her you were driving a boat and killed two other men?"

"Fuck you in your ass, cunt."

She straightened abruptly, indignant feathers fluffing about her.

"Are you just going to sit there and let him talk to me that way, Dennis?"

Geri decided to blubber, and Karen, leaning into it again, said, "Now look what you've done, you bastard. You made her cry." Then turning, "Don't let him bother you, Geri. They're all alike. They're all bastards."

Dennis found a rope dangling in front of his face and pulled his brain out of the V.O. far enough to take a look around.

247

"Hey. She's right, Pat. She's my wife and I love 'er, 'n' you can't talk to 'er like that."

"Fuck it," Ron said. "See you all later. I'm not going to sit and listen to this again."

Frank got up and followed Ron and DeeDee to the door. Janet cleared dishes and carried them into the kitchen. Karen had an arm around Geri, comforting her.

"My wife's right, Pat, 'n' I love 'er. You shouldn't've said what you said. I have to defend her honor."

Dennis slid his chair back from the table and stood.

"Sit down," I said. "There's no sense gettin' crazy over it. I'll apologize to your ignorant, fucking wife, if that's what you want."

Dennis started around the table for me.

"I gotta fight you, Pat. She's my wife 'n' I love 'er."

I rose and met him just behind Geri's chair. His first shot glanced off the top of my head as I ducked, covering. The next one caught me in the shoulder, and as I moved in, a third landed on my right temple before I could catch hold of him.

"What the fuck is going on over there?" Frank shouted.

I got Dennis in a bear hug and tried to squeeze him unconscious, the two of us bouncing off the wall and furniture, Geri blubbering, Chelsey howling from under the table, Karen shrieking like a parrot.

Frank hurried over to intervene. Janet hustled Geri, Chelsey, and Karen outside into the front yard. We had knocked a big planter over beside the couch and broken it. Dennis took advantage of the cease-fire to pour himself another quick shot.

"We're gonna have to finish it, Pat," he said, and gagged another down.

"You can finish it by yourself," I said.

"We're leaving now, Dennis," Karen shouted from the porch. "We're taking Geri with us."

"We've gotta finish it, Pat," Dennis said.

"Jesus Christ," Frank said. "Look at my fucking wall. One of you guys is going to have to paint that. I just painted the sonofabitch a month ago."

"I'll take a cab home," I said. "You mind if I stay a little longer?"

"Oh, man, I don't know. Maybe you oughta go too, Pat. You know? My old lady's standing over there shooting darts at me."

I got my stick and started for the can. Frank stopped me.

"Hey, fuck it man. You ain't got to go with 'em. I'll give you a ride home."

"No sweat," I said. "Just tell 'em to wait, will you. I gotta take a leak and I'll be right out. Geri can't get in the house, anyway, without me."

In the car, I had the back window down, the air friendly to my face. I

248

reached across for Geri's hand a couple times. She kept jerking it away. Karen kept her mouth shut, driving. Dennis was fine too, for a ways, then his jaw had to drop.

"We really do have to finish it, Pat. I love my wife. I have to defend her honor."

I reached over to Geri again. She jerked away, hostile. Chelsey raised her head and licked my hand. I cracked up.

"Fuck all of you," I said. "You're all a pain in the ass."

"We're gonna have to fight, Pat. It's gotta be finished."

Karen slowed, then stopped for a light. Traffic crossed in front of us. Just another two miles, I thought, and reached across, setting my hand on Geri's leg. She damn near broke it with her fucking karate chop.

"I love my wife, Pat. You can't—"

I reached up, across the front seat, grabbed Dennis by the back of his hair, and slung my left into the middle of his head.

"All right," I said, swinging again, "let's stop the bullshit and do it, then."

I had my head down, swinging as best I could, the top of my body draped over the seat. He punched across the top of my head and shoulders, glancing blows. I just kept that left hooking. Karen screamed. Geri screamed. The goddamn dog screamed, and I kept swinging.

"That's what you wanted, ain't it?" I said. "You want to finish the son-ofabitch, we're finishing it."

Karen brought both her hands around the front of my face, digging her nails in. The goddamn car was a madhouse, me twisting, trying to get her hands off, Geri and the dog harmonizing. When her fingers found my eye sockets, I let go of Dennis's hair, turned a bit, and poked a quick right over my shoulder, catching Karen right between the horns. She slumped to the floor, under the steering wheel, cars honking behind us.

"No more, no more. Please, no more," Karen screamed.

Dennis was still throwing, trying to connect with my skull, so I popped him again, then grabbed his head with both hands and started smacking it against the doorjamb.

"Stop it, stop it," somebody screamed, the dog and Geri, both with their heads tipped back to the moon.

"Get out, Dennis," I said. "We'll take it to the sidewalk. I ain't the only crazy bastard in this car. You wanted it. Now's your chance."

"Yes yes, get out," Karen bellowed from the floorboard.

I stepped out, cane in hand. Horns honked. Nobody moved in the car.

"C'mon, Geri, we'll walk," I said.

Some guy shouted about five cars back.

"C'mon," I said. "One of you get out."

249

"You're crazy," Geri shouted, still hysterical. "I'm not staying with you."

"I'm sorry, Pat," Karen said, suddenly sweet. "I didn't mean to scratch your face. Just close the door and I'll pull over to the curb. Please? Just shut it?"

I gave the door a shove. Karen hit the gas, burning rubber, her head out the window.

"You bastard," she screamed back at me. "You crazy bastard."

I walked, a chew in, oblivious to time and pain. When a car approached, I would break from my trance long enough to hear it pass, then close again. I finished the chew on my porch. Cole would laugh his ass off over this one, I thought.

Time fractures, everything fractures. One thought chased another, then the guilt began to seep through, fogging my skull, the worm thin, surrendered. My whole goddamn life tasted of failure. I'd just washed it liberally with alcohol to keep the inflammation down.

When I checked my watch, it was almost midnight. My joints ached as I walked, then the house, warm, touching my face and hands, like it welcomed me. I called Dennis. He was in bed, but Karen informed me that Geri had called a friend, somebody named Gwenda, and they had left over an hour ago.

Morning came, regardless, quiet, unimpressed. I showered, ate aspirin, then sat out back with a cup of coffee, getting used to my new freedom. She would do much better without me, I decided, the little creepy-eyed blind girl.

I indulged in a tomato beer while my bacon and eggs cooked, and drank another while it cooled on the counter. Through the kitchen window, the sound of weeds growing seemed pleasant enough. There were always a million things to do. Too many to slow down, sit around and sweat for nothing. Got to keep those trees moving by.

In the middle of doing dishes, I heard a car pull up in the driveway. I recognized its sound. Weeds stomped in like a kicked hen, followed by Lauren and Geri. Lauren watched me finish the dishes while Weeds and Geri collected her things and packed them out.

Lauren accepted a cup of coffee. We didn't say much. She kept telling me everything would be okay. I wanted to tell her it was already okay, then Weeds was standing beside Lauren, breathing sharp blasts through her nostrils.

"Well, Mr. Maniac. I guess you really showed them, didn't you."

I didn't even turn. Then the short body moved up next to me. I dried my hands and reached out for a hug. She caught my hand and placed something in it—that fucking ring. Then she turned and walked out the door with Weeds on her heels.

"You could've done better than that," I shouted. "How fucking clichéd can you get."

Lauren administered the hug, big, strong, easygoing.

"She loves you," she said. "I don't know what happened last night, but it's okay. People don't understand me either."

"I'll make it," I said, then walked her almost to the car, smiled, and waved bye-bye, listening to the tires slow and turn the corner without stopping. A very singular breeze, a gentle touch and gone.

What the hell, I thought. Welcome back, Mr. Todd.

TWENTY-THREE

The rain came light, just enough to tease, a little foreplay, and while I stood there in front of the snakewalk bench, earth smells began popping out from their hiding places, an earth orgasm.

I had waited until Tuesday to catch the Greyhound back to Oakland. Local transit dropped me off in front of the plaza. Tom Baylor, my neighbor, had agreed to watch the house for me. As I approached the snakewalk, I could sense the residue left by another body. It's funny how the skull projects another's presence like that, so all-inclusive. The fucker, I thought, laughing, our first meeting so vivid. I would see him too, just a matter of weeks, and reattach that presence to its sound.

In the dorm, it was obvious I had a new roommate, the door unlocked, the room full of cigar smoke. My braille books and radio had been tossed onto my bed and in their place on the writing desk I found a hot plate and coffee machine. My wardrobe was open. Somebody had gone through the drawers. I guess the underwear I'd left didn't meet their standards. Most of it was see-through, anyway.

Defense lines had positioned themselves across the front of my skull, ready, expecting some form of attack, but nobody said a word, nobody asked, nothing was offered. I hit the woodshop, and as the familiar grain of my project warmed to my hands, the stiff joints of anticipation eased. I liked the project, a coffee table. I could already see it in my house in front of the couch. It was made of redwood, heart wood, doweled together. The legs I had fashioned from elk antlers, the long, brow tines arching up, embedded in the wood. The bottom shelf, also redwood, was secured to the main beam of each antler at either side. Magazines would occupy that space, stacked neatly for the benefit of any regulars that might stop by. It would look like something out of *Ladies' Home Journal*.

Part of me, a very small part, felt sure Geri and I would see each other again and talk. The greater portion of my worm knew better, and had already moved on.

A body entered the shop and stopped beside my table, watching. I paid

252

little attention, my hands absorbed with the wood, the left feeling, the right following with its 120-grit sandpaper.

"What do you think?" I said. "Don't look too bad, does it?"

"It's very nice," Weeds said.

My asshole dropped a foot or so before the lines tightened and drew it back into place. I'd expected to see her eventually. I'd expected fire too, some sort of confrontation, but her voice seemed calm, almost sad. I looked at her, waiting, neither of us offering until the silence grew uncomfortable.

"I'm sorry I interrupted you," she said, then turned and walked out.

Goddamn, I thought. Adrenaline goosed disillusion through a split-second fantasy, thinking something sensible had been salvaged, before the worm shook it off.

Orville, my new roommate, introduced himself from his bed when I returned from lunch. Cigar smoke hung heavy about the spit and sputter of his goddamn coffee machine.

"Got to have my coffee," he said. "I ain't about to drink that stuff they serve down in the cafeteria. No tellin' what goes on around here. I mean you got your blacks and all workin' in there, and that little girl that serves your lunch up don't look that clean to me. She don't even wear a hair net."

Orville slurped coffee and sighed. I offered something positive, appropriate for a tour guide, a veteran.

"It might be," he said, "but if I had my druthers, I wouldn't be here at all. I didn't want to come in the first place. I didn't want a woman counselor, either. You can't talk to 'em, and I told 'er that. I bet if I told 'er once, I told 'er a thousand times, I just don't need it. I had all the schoolin' I want, Pat. Graduated class of forty-one, Fresno High. What I need now is a maid, someone that can keep her mouth shut, and one of them TV units, where you got all your whatchamadiggers in one little box, your sound and your channel selector."

I thought it was just me, the shell I'd formed, the halls, the students, so unfamiliar, the voices.

"No sir," Orville said. "I never asked for any of it. Another four years I'd be retired from the railroad. You know that? No, I guess you wouldn't know that, would you. Four years, Patrick. Don't seem like much, does it? And then this. I probably picked the damn stuff up in some bathroom. You know? Lucky that's all I got."

I lay down with the window open, thinking how fast the week would pass, how easy it is to do anything when you can see the finish line.

"Women," Orville snorted. "Shi-hoooot, boy, I'll tell you. You ever been married, Pat? That's good. You're a smart boy, 'long as you stay that way. And I'll tell you another thing. If they'd put a bounty on that pelt two hundred years ago, we'd be a lot better off right now."

Max was still around. He had a new nerve for a roommate, some Jesus freak with bugs, scratching constantly, grunting his disdain over our presence, so we moved our conversation into the stairwell.

"Cheesus, I know," Max said. "Ain't that somethin'? And it's only been a week or two. Teresa and Lance both left Friday, and I gave Momma a call last night. She and the kids are gettin' things ready for me to come home."

"You're goin' back home, huh?"

"Yeah. Cheesus, Pat. I got no business doin' anything else. You know that. So what about you and Geri? When's the big day?"

Christ, I didn't know what to say.

"I already asked Gwenda," he said. "She ain't lettin' nothin' out. You guys aren't gonna forget your old buddies, are you?"

"We split up for a while," I said.

"C'mon?"

"We just need a little time to figure some things out. It's a little different outside than it is here."

"C'mon, cheesus. I never seen two people as much in love as you guys. You know? You ain't gonna put one like that across on ol' Maxie."

Orville's jaw sucked at that caffeine nonstop, rattling on well past midnight with his life history, whether I cared or not, conducting Southern Pacific freights through the San Joaquin Valley. He was the guy in the caboose, until his glaucoma set in.

"Yessir, Pat. I'll bet you every kid in that whole damn valley's thrown at least one rock at me."

On and on, I thought, just like a goddamn train. His worm must have soaked in that sound so long it didn't know any better.

After breakfast, I hit Weeds's class early, thinking I'd catch her alone, get down to some peace and understanding, good will toward animals. But two canes arrived first, new students, a guy and a gal. The guy bumped my chair and moved left. The gal stopped, felt my neck, shoulders, hair.

"I was sitting here the other day," she said.

"That's nice," I said.

"I thought we were supposed to keep the same seats?"

"Why would you want to do that?"

"I guess so we don't get mixed up."

"That's right," I said. "We might forget who we are, huh?"

"No. I mean I sat here last time, and I just expected I'd sit in the same chair again today, and now that you're here, I don't know where to sit."

I conceded, moved to my right, and introduced myself.

"I heard about you the first day I was here," the gal said. "Somebody said that you and a girl from the school here are getting married."

The barbecue scene flashed through—the unsaid, the irrevocable.

"Stan says you have the weight-lifting record," the guy said.

And I smiled. There wasn't much else I could do.

"Do a lot of people get married here?" the gal said.

"You'll go through a lot of things here," I said, "lots of feelings, and the only thing you can count on is that it's all gonna change."

"I've only been here a week," the gal said.

"Well, you've got a long way to go then, and while you're at it, you'll learn a lot about yourself. That's what you're here for. You've got to keep your rear in gear though, do as much as you can, and don't be afraid to try something new, especially with your mobility. And you'll taste your fears, too. Everybody's a little shaky at first, and this joint will get real comfortable and secure. It'll become your nest and you won't want to leave it, so you've got to keep moving, always keep it in mind that you're leaving, and each day is one day closer, and if anything bothers you too much, you can bring it in here to Gwenda. She'll help you, as long as she can see you're working on it yourself."

The two of them sat there, looking at me.

"What you do," I said, "is tell yourself, every morning soon as you get up, that the only reason you're here is to get your brain straight, and there ain't nobody here gonna do it for you. You've got to do it yourself. Use that cane. Get out there and take hikes in the evening, make yourself do it."

Weeds stood in the doorway. I sensed her then, and turned.

"Don't let me interrupt," she said. "That's a good introduction, and you guys should listen to it, because if anybody knows about being screwed up in the head, Patrick does."

Her tongue had a definite edge, a flip-flop from the woodshop. She moved around the table to her hot plate and coffee, the morning fix.

"Yessiree, folks, that was some real good advice," she said. "Maybe if we're nice, he'll tell us some more and we'll see just how much he really did learn."

"What say we knock off the bullshit," I said. "If you want to be pissed off, that's fine. I'll leave. If you want to talk about it, I can do that too, but I'm not about to take your crap, or anybody else's, and I'm not your general, run-of-the-mill, unfeeling maniac, either, Weeds dear."

255

"There's no need to get defensive," she said. "I don't think I heard anybody blame you for anything."

"You could've fooled me."

"I didn't think anybody could fool Patrick Todd."

"Fine," I said. "You can finish this conversation by yourself. I would appreciate it, though, if you'd do me one little favor, and get into that file of yours and get me Cole's phone number. I like talking with people who are a little more congenial."

Weeds stood there on her side, looking. I looked back, that space suddenly open again.

"Jim, I want you and Stacy to take the rest of the morning off," Weeds said. "I'd like to talk with Patrick alone."

"Where should we go?" Stacy said.

"Try your room, if nothing else."

"You guys don't have to leave," I said. "Just get me that number and I'll get outa here."

"C'mon, you two," Weeds said, "up you go. I'll bring some cookies next time and make it up to you. Thank you, thank you, umm hmm. You can always practice your mobility, you know. Never know when it might come in handy. Might keep you off the wall there, right, Stacy?"

She closed the door and returned to her side of the table. I lowered my lines, thinking the connection had warmed again.

"Look," I said. "I apologize for getting loud, but I just ain't ready for this. You know? I'm just not in the right sort of mood to even begin with it, so I'd appreciate it if you'd pull that number and I'll be on my way."

"I could do that," she said. "I could get you the number, but I don't think you'll be able to get through to him."

"Well at least your voice is changing anyway. That's an improvement, and if you're interested, I'm not overly happy with my part in recent events, but it's already done and gone. I don't have the room in my skull to hang myself again, and I'm sorry too, but you weren't there. I don't think you know the whole story, so be a good buddy and get me the number, will you?"

"I'm sorry too," she said, "and you can believe me, the number isn't going to do you any good."

"Well why don't you let me be the judge of that. I won't know till I try, will I."

"He's dead, Patrick. He died last week."

Jesus. You talk about the film breaking. I tried to laugh, my right hand moving to my face for no particular reason. It had been a while, I guess, since I took a good look at it. Everything behind it had scattered, and at the moment, I didn't feel much like working with it. The bridge of my nose started burning too, so I rubbed it, and laughed again, face down.

"The letter came last Wednesday," Weeds said. "It's addressed to you, but they read it. Stan read it anyway, then gave it to me to do the honors, so I had it with me yesterday when I came in the woodshop. I thought I'd be able to do it then. . . . You piss me off, Patrick. You know that? You really do."

"They're just ideas anyway," I said. "Just like the names on the trees."

"What?"

The trail was easy up through that canyon. I'd walked it so many times, with its deer tracks, the triangular stick tracks of the grouse, the pad marks of that sow bear and her two cubs, the earth soft and moist, dark, and from the rimrock above, I could just lean into it, just spread my arms and lift. That's how the eagles do it, just lean, and the sun takes you in harness. The control is in your hands, tilting your palms, your fingers like pinions, spread, the sun taking you, pulling you higher. I could see the cottontail below dart from under his sage patch across open ground, running, soft feet, soft earth, and that damn little cotton swab on his ass, dancing—

"Do you want me to read it?" Weeds said.

I nodded. I couldn't feel my legs on that trail, or see them either if I looked down, but I could see empty gallon wine jugs and rusted olive oil tins in the Basque sheep camps, the coyotes watching, waiting for their chance at a lamb. The eagles watched, waiting for the coyote pups, drawing their names in great, sweeping letters across the bottom of clouds, and in the creeks, the rocks wore smooth, but you didn't notice it like you did the footprints, or the names on tree trunks. That one beside the trail— KILLED BUCK 1906. I could feel his knife in my hand, the sun on the back of my neck, the blade cutting through the gray, hard outer bark into the pale yellow lining, just before wood.

"Are you listening to me?" Weeds said.

I nodded. Twenty feet from me, beside the creek, a large aspen, maybe eighteen inches across the butt, had been felled by a beaver only to lodge itself at an angle in the fork of another tree. I could see the beaver, black in the shadows, on his hind legs, the mouth working, the yellowed teeth gnawing, until it cracked, then leaned, waiting for the resounding crash, black round eyes waiting, the mouth still open waiting, all that work, all those days, the jaw tilted slightly to the side, the blunt gray tongue pushing chips to pile at his webbed feet, the musky smell of his efforts drifting.

"If you're not listening, I'm not going to read this. I don't find a lot of pleasure in this sort of thing."

I nodded, noticing another aspen to the left of that one lost by the beaver, its wide flank clean, unused.

" ' . . . I can't paint what made it special, or why Cole was special, but I'll remember his song. It plays for me now, at the oddest times. . . .' "

I raised my knife, waiting, Weeds's voice distant, and that of the woman Cole loved, in her words.

" 'I heard it this morning in the trees, as I walked a gravel road, then it seemed to change, coming up from the river. As I write this, I'm sitting on the porch of his cabin, listening. I'm not afraid to let go. What is never owned cannot be lost. . . .' "

I moved the knife closer, the tip of the blade poised, then waited, the aspen quiet, the stream quiet.

" 'He laughed a lot about your idea, a commune for the blind. He laughed a lot whenever he spoke of you. Two nights ago, I watched him sitting here, his back to the porch, telling me about a salmon he once caught. . . .' "

I knew that bastard would never make it up the mountain to his cedar tree. It was a good story, a good idea, but nobody ever does that crap. Talk about it, and float on it, soar off on it like it's actually holding you, like it's something outside of your own skull, or the bottom of an overturned boat in the wind.

" 'A light snow was falling, the year's first, just enough to soften the angles and hide the struggle. I left him sitting here that night. He asked me to leave. He had his whiskey bottle, and when I found him the next morning, he hadn't moved. His hands rested in his lap. A light mantle of snow capped his knees, shoulders and hat. He slept well.' "

I moved the knife blade into the bark and carved the words: GONE FISH-ING. DON'T KNOW WHEN I'LL BE BACK. and then below it, C. SAUNDERS.

"You knew he was sick," Weeds said. "You had to. He hadn't taken insulin in god knows how long. He told the nurse he was doing his own, but you could tell. You could see his color changing. He should've been on dialysis a year ago, and to tell you the truth, I don't know how he lasted as long as he did. The booze should've done it long ago. . . . Where are you going?"

"On mobility. I've got to move."

"Don't go out and get all screwed up. Your luck hasn't been that good lately."

"I'll meet you at five," I said, "across the street at Petar's. We can finish our talk."

"You could probably use it."

"That's sweet of you," I said. "You gonna be there?"

"Maybe."

258

I extended my hand. She shook it. Down the hall a braille writer poked away. Lou Abrams's voice, explaining the basics of the abacus, seemed surprisingly energetic. Outside, I headed for the snakewalk, insulated, moving at a good clip. I nodded to other pedestrians on the avenue.

"Hello, hello, nice day, isn't it?"

Just cooking right along, buildings on my right, traffic on the left.

"Howdy, howdy, how's it hangin'?"

Plastic banners flapped over used car lots. A traffic cop on a three wheeler marked tires, putt pop putt, and some cool breeze blew by in a Chevy, stereo blasting.

I stayed two steps ahead of it all, my slick-haired buddy following at a safe distance, until University Avenue loomed ahead. I slowed, then stopped, listening, wanting no part of that whirlpool. A check of my vital signs showed water temp and amp gauge fine, just the oil pressure a little low. I could feel it then, catching up, so I crossed the avenue and headed back, past a used car dealer, checked slacks and pink shirt, telling some sucker about the supreme sacrifice.

"Howdy howdy, how's it hangin'?"

They both clammed, watching me pass, like I'd lost a prop. And by the time my cane found the Buckhorn's dutch door, I was ready. The Horn was the perfect place, thumping jukebox, septic fumes. The urinals were filled with ice cubes to keep the smell down.

"Shot a beer and a bottle of Christian Brothers," I said, squatting on the nearest stool. The bartender laughed.

"How 'bout a shot and a Bud, then," I said.

Several other voices farther down the bar stopped to watch. I raised the shot glass, sniffed it.

"To an old friend," I said, toasting. "He's on the river somewhere, watching the rocks wear smooth."

I asked for another and received it, then raised the glass in toast again.

"This one's to beautiful, naked Indian women, and to a short, beautiful blind woman who never saw horns."

Christ, getting a rise out of them was like coaxing farts out of dead seagulls. I kept my toasts to myself after that, sipping beer. The body felt pretty good, damned good actually, ready.

A chopper pulled up out front, idling, backing up to the curb, an old panhead I thought, then the boots slopped in, keys jingling on a belt loop, one stool to my left.

"Curs," he said.

I thought about stealing his bike, moving fast through tall trees, passing between cars and bugs and piss stops, so drunk I'd have to keep moving to stay upright.

"You're empty, man," the biker said. "You wanna shake for one?"

"You talkin' to me?" I said.

"You're the only one sittin' there, ain't you?"

Saw the shades, I thought, figured I was into drugs.

"Sure," I said. "How 'bout liars?"

He agreed. The bartender brought the cups, and we both slammed them down with finesse, covering our dice.

"Pair a sixes," the biker called.

"Three sixes," I said.

"Is that right? Got some sixes, huh?"

He called four, I called him up and won, then beat him again the second hand.

"Fuuuuck," he said.

The bartender was chuckling. I chuckled, the biker grunted. Another body entered shortly after that, then called back from the end of the bar.

"What's happenin', Jimbo?"

The biker grunted a salute.

"You want a little revenge there, Jimbo?" I said. "Same game?"

He grunted. I won.

"You're about a lucky fuck," Jimbo said.

"Just ain't your day, man."

"How the fuck would you know?"

"You ain't bein' positive," I said. "You gotta be positive, man, especially when you're lyin'."

"Suck my cock."

"What's a matter Jimbo?" I said. "Somethin' buggin' you today?"

"Yeah, you."

"Gotta stay positive, man. Keeps you healthy. You sound like you've been drinkin' piss or somethin'. I tell you what. I'll shake you again for a shot a Crow. That'll clean you out."

Jimbo breathed through his nose, a rumble building inside his bronchials.

"Just being friendly," I said.

"Well maybe I don't feel like bein' friendly."

I finished that beer and found the full one. My slick-haired buddy leaned against the wall, just inside the door, watching, a pensive tilt to his toothpick.

"It's a good day for learning, Jimbo," I said, "even if it's just dice games."

"Hey, fuck you, man. If I say it sucks, then it sucks."

I turned to face him, grinning.

"You're about an ignorant bastard, you know that, Jimbo?"

His quick mind flashed back through the ten cubic centimeters of his available memory, and his light went on. A half-bellow, half-grunt bubbled out, as he grabbed the edge of the bar and lifted. Wood cracked, the countertop raising. I watched, beer in hand.

"Hey!" the bartender shouted. "What the hell do you think you're—"

Jimbo heaved into it, one final grunt. I think he shit too, then let go, exhausted.

"Gee," I said. "That was very impressive. Cheers."

The first one caught me on the left temple, my glasses flying. I ignored the rush of tight air through that ear, turned, and grinned.

"Is that all the harder you can hit?" I said.

Jimbo bellowed and let fly. That one caught me just a bit higher. I stood up to meet him then, still strong, but when his third one caught me on the same side, I realized I couldn't hear anything except the dull bass thumping from the jukebox. I shook my head, taking a couple steps forward, covering, no facial vision, no idea where he stood.

"The guy's blind," the bartender yelled.

"I don't give a fuck what he is," Jimbo said.

I turned toward the voice, his foot slamming into my thigh, inches from my nuts, and it was me that bellowed that time.

"You sonofabitch," I said, and crouched like I was about to spring. My elbow bumped a bar stool. It was over my head, that fast, through half its arc, then stopped. I couldn't hear. The bar stool was still in the air, my arms extended. I just couldn't hear and I knew damn well if I swung, I'd hit the wrong thing, somebody else, so I set the stool back down and sat on it.

"That's it, Jimbo," I said. "No more punching bag."

"The guy's blind," the bartender said.

"You hit me again, Jimbo," I said, "and I'm gonna kill you. We're even. Sit down and I'll buy you a beer."

Jimbo moved to the far end. The bartender handed me a fresh beer and the frames to my glasses. I straightened them and put them on—no lenses.

The worm was out, flat on his back, X's in his eyes, colder than frog pussy, and the soft, puffy area on the left side of my head, where all that wisdom had just entered, had my gyro misaligned. My body kept turning left, so I compensated, steered a bit to the right, and tapped on down the avenue.

I don't remember how many bars I hit, just that they were all the same. I would sit through a couple beers, feel it catching up again, and leave. My slick-haired buddy found a convenient pole each time and waited. When I'd pass, he'd just smile and shake his head.

Traffic flanked me on one side, thirst on the other, back into familiar territory, and later that afternoon, old habits slowed me at the snakewalk. I bumped the bench with my cane. Nothing, just that flimsy, youthful ache of returning to a favorite spot and finding it gone.

So I continued north, to the Indian, thinking I'd catch Rena, buy her a beer, tell her, but Rena was elsewhere. Some fried minus sign hobbled the racks behind the bar. Took me ten minutes to get a beer, so I offered to buy her one. She accepted, decided she liked me then, and wanted to talk. Her old man had the two kids, two little girls, five and three, a joint-custody deal she said, but he'd left the state with them. I nodded, smiling, raising my eyebrows occasionally.

More bodies entered. The jukebox seemed to play the same damn song over and over. Kenny Rogers. I hated Kenny Rogers, and beyond the wall, the sound of traffic grew to an audible groan, 4:30, quitting time. I had some reservations about meeting Weeds, but downed the beer anyway, and made a trip to the can. Somebody followed me in. No big deal. The skull had enough litter floating around at the time, but as my three-minute piss continued, I became more aware of that body standing behind me. Queer, I thought. What the hell. Maybe he got his kicks watching peckers piss.

I shook it off, zipped up, and started for the door. The guy snickered.

"Tough guy, huh?"

"You talkin' to me?" I said.

"Yeah. You think you're a tough guy, don't you?"

"What gives you that idea?"

"I was in The Buckhorn earlier, when Jimbo kicked the shit out of you."

"Wasn't much of a fight, was it."

The asshole snickered again. I could see him, T-shirt, sleeves rolled up, skinny arms.

"What's so fucking funny?" I said.

"Not much. I just thought you might want to try me out, since you're such a tough guy."

"You mean fuck you, or fight you? You're the one standin' there watchin' me piss. What do you do, get your kicks in bathrooms?"

"Tough guy," he snickered again.

"So you want to throw a few hands, huh?" I said. "You watched me get the shit knocked out of me and figured it looked like fun. Is that it?"

"You're bigger 'n me."

"Well it shouldn't take too long then, should it."

The light switch was on the wall, just inside the door, and reaching over, I found the trim, followed it down, and hit the switch.

"Hey! What the fuck are you doin'?"

"Just makin' it even," I said, and stomped my feet like I was heading for him. He bounced off a wall, then slammed into the stall door.

"Hey, I was just shittin' you, man," he squeaked. "I was just givin' you a bad time. That's all."

"We all open our mouths at the wrong time once in a while, don't we," I said.

"Boy, you're damn sure right about that. I ain't shittin', man. It was just a joke."

I switched his eyes back on as I went out the door.

"See you, man," he said.

I bought a couple beers to go, put them in my back pockets, and adjourned to the snakewalk. The bench had lost its appeal, so I crossed the lawn to the fence, one foot on the lower rail, toasting my waterfall. Weeds spotted me on her way out.

"What's wrong with your head?"

"If I knew, I'd fix it," I said.

"I mean the lump. You've been fighting. Jesus. I swear."

She lifted the hair on that side.

"You'll never learn, will you."

"Bullshit," I said. "I just did."

She touched the swollen portion again, poking gently.

"Jesus," she said again.

I pulled my head away from her hand, my back still to her.

"You want a beer?" I said.

"No thanks. I prefer a table and chair, and different lighting."

"That's good," I said. "It's my last one."

"We might as well talk here," she said. "Where would you like to start?"

"Let's start with dreams," I said.

"Dream on. I can hardly wait."

"There ain't no fairy tales, no storybook couples."

"I'm listening."

I drained the can, crunched it, and stuck it in my back pocket.

"That's enough," I said.

"No it isn't," she said. "There's a hell of a lot more. There's a person here at this school, who will go unnamed, who's been ridiculed recently for her involvement with students. That person's been accused of favoritism, and that same person also said why the hell not. She was tired of pants pissers and niggers going through her purse, and putting their hands on her ass and other body parts. That person even forgot about the paychecks, because she thought she saw a speck of sanity, a place where she could be helpful. That person does know a few things. She's been around. . . . She's been around and maybe she's seen the error in her ways, but there's still a lot of good rubber left, and that person knows how to bounce, and she's already started to bounce out of this place. It took a while, but that person has definitely learned a few things."

"You ain't sore about a certain short blind woman, are you?"

"Sure. I'm upset. I'd be lying if I said I wasn't. I just hope there're some better brains because of it."

"It's all just sex anyway," I said.

She didn't respond, so I turned.

"Ain't it?"

"It's part of the education," she said.

I could see her face, the mouth tight, the nose slim, good nostrils, the eyes not large, but wildly blue, the ears small, attractive, tight to her head.

"You still want a brandy?" I said.

"I think I'll take a raincheck. I promised Paul I'd be home for dinner tonight."

"Fine with me," I said. "I'd just as soon stay here and listen to my waterfall anyway."

"What?"

"That's my waterfall over there. I know it may not sound like much, but there's plenty there to listen to. That's the sound of reality. It's all in the motion."

"You want to know what your reality really is?" she said. "It's a dirty, nasty mudhole. There's a crusted old culvert there that comes under the street and out through a crude slab of concrete, and the water trickles off a scummy, diseased-looking tongue of moss, and it doesn't go anywhere. It just sits there, soaking into the muck, with the hundreds of beer cans and gin bottles that are sticking out of it. The whole damn creek here is nothing but a garbage can. Everywhere I look right now, it's beer cans and bottles and shitty weeds and muck. The only thing growing there is shit. That's your reality, big boy. Now what do you think of it?"

I laughed.

"All depends on how you look at it."

TWENTY-FOUR

Risk never bothered me. You couldn't live outside the Adipose manual without knowing the taste of it. The trans-bay tube bothered me though. That wasn't risk. That was cruising underwater, in something man-made, with some guy I'd never met driving. A woman two seats in front of me apparently had the same idea.

"Oh God," she said. "I knew this would happen. . . . Oh Goooood?"

"Here, change seats with me," another woman said. "Sometimes sitting backwards is what does it."

My own skin felt a hell of a lot better after the Embarcadero station escalator brought me back up to sea level. The ticket agent, a black guy in a glass booth, directed me toward the mob waiting for the local transit—bodies, colognes, all kinds of fabrics rubbing together, and all those shoes, hurrying across laid brick.

My bus traveled Market as far as Van Ness, along the edge of something old and stagnant, sweet wines, a pool of blood for a pillow, that smell of piss just south of the financial district. You don't need to see that section of San Francisco to know it's there. Maybe I would move in, get a small apartment there, over a grocery store, with a bar next door. I could lie there with the window open, listening to that array of human ideas, all of it scabbed over dark earth, sealed to keep the underground from seeping out uninvited.

At Van Ness I transferred north, then jogged west on Lombard toward the Golden Gate Bridge. I could see the Presidio wall, the entire area dark with trees, Letterman Hospital, Palace of Fine Arts. I could smell the change too, where the city ended and the sea breathed hard. I'd passed under that bridge so many times, looking up, that the thought of walking across it seemed trivial, Adipose at best, nothing to tighten the scrote sack.

"You can come back down Columbus," Stan had said, "and have lunch at Fisherman's Wharf. Go ahead, take the whole day. Walk around. Take the city in. I know I'm still somewhat in awe every time I go there."

"Don't bullshit me, Stan."

"Do it for the other students, then," he said. "They need a model."

I laughed.

"Bring me back a crab, too, will you? If they're fresh. And a loaf of french bread?"

"If I make it back."

"Go on, get out of here," he said.

I was already on the snakewalk when he shouted from the administration building.

"And don't forget my crab."

"You should've said something a couple months ago," I shouted back. "I could've got you a whole handful for free."

At the edge of the city, that familiar breath waited for me, raw, so goddamn powerful, and I could see the people again, moving, crossing streets in light-manipulated herds, fingers with rings swinging at their sides, the shine of patent leather, smiling faces with a line around the edge where the makeup ended. Bank vaults and high-risers, climate-controlled sex behind glass, a blowjob fifty-five stories up.

The bus stopped just east of the Golden Gate toll plaza, and as I stepped down into the wind, I was that much closer to the scars of youth.

"Where you headed, boss?" the driver said.

I turned slowly, a very sober look on my face, and pointed.

"Out there," I said.

"There ain't no buses runnin' that way, boss. That's the bridge."

"I know," I said, straight-faced, fucking with him. What the hell. A blink can't walk out on a bridge without blowing skirts up.

He followed me off, and called to someone. Traffic, even in the wind, provided a good fence ahead of me. No toll in that direction, I thought, straight through, too windy for fog, but its properties were still there, stretched thin and cold.

Planter boxes obstructed my path for a ways, then it opened again. I could tell when I had the bridge under me. There's just the slightest change, a loss of balance.

"Do you need some help?" a black voice asked.

"No thanks," I said. "Got 'er made, man."

A woman's voice conversed with him then, in low tones, then the two of them followed me a ways before they approached again.

"Where you headed, pal?" the black guy said.

I pointed and kept walking. They followed, maybe twenty feet behind, the man's footsteps and the woman's, lighter, more distinct, three steps to his two, and below me, California draining its tanks into the Pacific septic system.

The bridge motion, that lateral sway, increased the farther I went, traffic and wind combining on my left. Spot groups of pedestrians moved by, excited voices lost to the wind, some foreign, that *zzzt zzzt* of their cameras as they spun the film into frames, and underneath, the thousands of gallons of red lead paint.

That's what you see at dawn, on your way out, the preservatives and painting scaffolds. A body would look so small coming off the side—birdshit, fish food. I could understand the attraction though, the rawness of the setting, the wind, the clear, crisp taste of insignificance. But I never saw one drop. The bridge never held my attention that long, either. I would lower my face back to frozen herring and brass harness, wondering if a speck like that, falling, would still have a mind.

It always looked different on the way back in, especially on a bad day, after long hours of seasickness, those twin spires hours away. The old man would drink his dago red, content. I would look up every once in a while to see if I could notice a marked difference in our travel, the bridge a growing speck in the distance.

On a good day, ideas of swimming that far came easy enough, the mystery quiet, its dark depths comfortably distant, its surface hypnotic.

I couldn't remember the width of that damn span, three, four miles, so I walked what seemed to be halfway, and stopped. The sway dissolved my balance, equilibrium did a somersault, and I dropped to one knee, the pavement cool, the rail maybe ten feet in front of me. The feet behind me stopped too, watching. I smiled, crossed myself just for effect, and got with the rhythm of the bridge.

That goddamn Cole, I thought, out there with the old men. They knew. Waiting was a hell of a lot harder. I stood then and moved toward the rail. To my right, footsteps hurried toward me, convinced, no doubt, that I intended to fly.

"Hey, pal, whoa it up there. You know where you're going?"

He had his hand on my arm, good grip.

"Sure," I said. "I've known it for some time now. It just took a while to get my ass in gear."

"You sure you're all right?" the woman said.

"I never had any complaints, but I'm always better with a couple drinks in me. You guys wouldn't happen to have a flask handy, would you?"

"He's all right," the woman said.

"Yes, I'm fine," I said.

"I'm sure you are," the guy said, "but I'd feel a hell of a lot better if you'd walk the rest of the way across with us. To tell you the truth, I don't want you messing up my day."

"What are you guys, bridge cops?"

"We're security officers with the Golden Gate Bridge Authority. A young woman stopped her car out here three weeks ago and jumped, and whenever one does it, it seems to attract others, so they keep us out here for a while. I'm sure you can understand."

"I just wanted to spit and see if I could hear it hit," I said.

"Okay, okay, whatever, but right now I want you to walk with us."

"I'll take her arm, then," I said.

She was short, a little nervous as a sighted guide—had a chubby arm inside her down jacket.

"I'm afraid of heights anyway," I said.

That afternoon, Max and I sponsored our own graduation party at the snakewalk bench. We had a twelve-pack in a sack on the ground between us and one in hand. To our left, a cane approached along the snakewalk. We could hear Stan too. Max put his beer in the bag. Whoever the hell it was moved slow. I finished mine before they got there.

"Hey, how'd it go today, Pat?" Stan said.

"Very inspiring. I don't think I'll ever forget it."

"This is Mary, one of our new students, Pat. She's making her first trip out to the avenue today. Isn't that right, Mary?"

"Umm hmm."

"Pat and Max here are both finishing students, Mary. Pat just got back from a trip to San Francisco. He left this morning, walked across the Golden Gate Bridge and back, and took public transportation the whole way."

"Really?" Mary said. "Is he a total?"

"What's in the bag there, Pat? Don't tell me you remembered my order?"

"All right, I won't tell you."

"Pat's been with us for five months, Mary, and I know a trip to San Francisco on your own sounds difficult right now, but in five or six months you'll probably be ready to do the same thing yourself."

"I don't know about that," Mary said.

We listened to Mary scratch her way toward the intersection. Max retrieved his beer. Traffic bled by, as usual. Six months seemed much longer—skull time, I guess, and the wind. I'd seen something else from the bridge that morning. I'd looked down and seen the kid aft, rigging baits, the old man standing, controlling, his face in the wind—bonds, trust, transparencies. Confidence was always the greatest risk.

"Cheesus," Max said. "I've lived there all my life, and never walked across it. Ain't that somethin'?"

268

I could hear Weeds then, faintly, other voices too—on the lawn, I thought. They weren't moving.

"You hear that over there, Max?"

"I don't hear nothin'."

Stan and Mary returned some minutes later, scratching toward us.

"What the hell's going on over there?" I said. "A little wilderness hike?"

"That's Gwenda," Stan said. "She's got a work crew in there cleaning the creek up. She said it was giving the school a black eye. Ha ha. Get it?"

"I'll be damned," Max said.

"I guess some of the guys have been littering over there. You two wouldn't know anything about that, would you?"

"Not me, boss. Max might know somethin'."

"Cheesus. I don't know nothin' about it."

"Yeah, I think she's got Carter and Alan and Lonny Charles over there. Carter's going to another school now. Did you know that, Pat?"

"Good place for 'im," I said.

Somebody, Carter I thought, rattled the air with a blast of profanity. The others laughed.

"He's in a business school in Sacramento," Stan said. "They teach you how to operate your own business, then set you up with a snack stand in one of the state buildings."

"What's he doin' here?"

"We had his counselor bring him down this morning. Gwenda made the appointment."

Even that seemed a long way off, my hand knocking, his room empty.

"Great gal, that Gwenda," Stan said. "I'm going to hate to see her leave. You knew about that, didn't you, Pat? After the first of the year, Gwenda won't be with us any longer."

When Stan and Mary faded out of scratch distance, we popped another beer.

"Cheesus," Max said, "ain't that somethin'? Carter's goin' into business. Hmmph. He deserves a break though, I guess. You know? It'd be tough, wouldn't it? Cheesus."

We moved our party a little closer, under a shade tree. On the other side of the fence, feet sucked through the muck.

"Life ain't nothin' but a shit sandwich," Carter spouted, "and all I ever get is the shit, no bread."

"Don't worry your little mind about that," Weeds said. "We've got plenty of bags too. When you get one full, bring it up here and take another. I'll worry about what we're going to do with them once they're full."

"What about them two muthafuckas over there?" Carter said. "Git their ass down here. They're probably the ones what done it. Look at 'em. They got a beer right now. The same kind I'm pickin' up."

"You just worry about your sack there, Cyclops," I said.

Max snoozed early that night. The halls were quiet, new blinks behind their doors, a fresh touch of wax and disinfectant waiting. I walked to the liquor store, bought a pint of Crow, and sat on the snakewalk bench for a while, then came back to my room. Orville didn't drink. He should have. Ten minutes of his jaw had my worm in fits, so I sat in the hall awhile, then walked the four doors down to Lauren's room. I'd promised myself I wouldn't do that.

Lauren had her coffee cup glued to her hand. I sat on Geri's bed, sweeping that time alley. Lauren, that easygoing, comfortable blink, didn't say peep about it either. I liked her for that.

"To well-waxed floors and their bearing on the universe," I said, and tinked my bottle against her cup.

We toasted anything that came to mind, sitting across from each other. No actual conversation, just the toasts, and silence in between. Appropriate subjects too, accidents, modern technology, taxes, rehab counselors, Mother Night, everything but sex and roommates. Lauren sat there on the bed, her dark little pie folded neatly in her lap. I started to tell her about Cole, then stopped.

"Never mind," I said. "T'hell with it. They're all the same anyway. One story's no different 'n another."

Just the ideas remained, I thought, looking down from the bridge again, at the kid's worm, squirming in the kid's skull. Lauren had her own wheels in soft sand, quiet.

"One more day," I said, "I'm gone. I got my table all packed up and ready to go on U.P.S. Two more meals at the trough, five minutes to pack my bag. . . . Feels kinda good, really. I guess I'll go drink another beer or two and listen to Orville's train song."

"Don't go," she said.

"Nah, I've got to go," I said, and stood up.

Lauren stood in front of me. We wrapped our arms and hugged.

"It's okay," she said. "Everything's okay."

"It's not okay," I said, "but it's there."

When I let go, she clung, her hips warm against me, inviting, her breasts cushioned to my chest. She started quivering then, just a little, asking.

"Don't go," she said.

Back in my room, I still had the Crow. Orville was stretched out on his bed, imitating a garbage disposal.

So goddamn soft, I thought, all of us, California anyway. Mild climate, distinct seasons, no bears chasing your ass around the cave. The only things you had to watch out for were the goddamn parasites, attorneys, realtors. The shortcake had been right, too, about changing things.

Christ, I just shook my head, like it had something loose inside—all the fighting, all the twisting . . . out of ignorance, or laziness. The sickness is the fear, the weakness, the mind so easy with complaints, so empty with solutions. I hated to think that Stan's goddamn bridge walk was anything but fluff. I felt it though, in the wind, the wild raw energy always within reach, and me, infancy reaching out, my mouth open. That's what the kid lost. He got a little flimsy with the imagination, a little too human, and lost his eyes on the inside.

A cart wheeled quietly by out in the hall. Sly, I thought, slopping a little disinfectant around.

"They're keepin' it safe for you out there, Orville," I said, took a swig, shook the bottle, a little less than half I thought, took another swig, and hit the can. Orville had his brogans parked in the middle of the floor. I kicked them back under his bed, took my leak, and lay on top of the covers with the window open for another hour. I'd find it, I thought, the peace. The worm would heal and grow. Geri and I would never get back together. I knew it then. I had a long way to go, with no finish lines.

Orville's adenoids had a way of vibrating that would make a mute's teeth tight. He didn't respond when I called his name a couple times, so I got up, pulled one of his shoes from under the bed, took the sock, rolled it up, and tucked it gently into his mouth. He didn't miss a lick.

TWENTY-FIVE

Weeds called late one night, half gassed. I hadn't heard her voice in over two months. I hadn't heard from anyone.

"I just thought I'd let you know that Miss Lauren Kay Delmer was asked to leave C.I.B. today, by yours truly. It may have taken me a while, but I finally caught her, red-handed. Noooobody can be that smooth. Nobody. Not Lauren Kay Delmer, or Patrick Todd, or Geri Sicone. Nobody. . . . You there?"

"I thought you guys were tight," I said.

"Sure we were tight. I mean the woman practically lived with Paul and me for the last two months. How the hell do you think I feel? When you find out that somebody that close is trying to put one over on you, hey hey, let me tell you baby, it hurts. Believe me. And I'll tell you, what hurts more is when you first suspect. She was just too smooth, Patrick. You remember? Did you ever hear her knock anything over? I made her admit it too. She claims she was blind when she came for the tour, but started getting it back a month or so before she was accepted, and by the time she got there, she was almost twenty-twenty. That's sick, Patrick. I don't care how much I liked her. She's a sick person. I told her that too. I gave her four hours to get her things together, and I watched that bus door close behind her. Didn't tell Stan, didn't tell anybody, just packed her butt off to play her sick game somewhere else. But anyway, the reason I called is I just thought you'd like to know that."

She laughed then, cracked one on. I held the phone away from my ear.

"Ooooh Patrick. The reason I called is because it's sooo funny. It really is. Think about it. Think back a ways to you and Geri."

I waited through another burst of bent laughter.

"You still there?"

"I'm here," I said.

"You remember, don't you? Geri Sicone? That short, sweet person you were so madly in love with? Well she was a friend of mine too, you know, and girls will talk, and believe me big boy, girl talk can be just as crude and fleshy as boy talk, sometimes, and she did tell me a few things. You know? And the little fart hasn't called, or written, or anything since I took her back to San Francisco. Bless her heart. But anyway, there were some personal items going on between you two in that room with Lauren present. You remember? They weren't as private as you thought they were and that's funny, Patrick. Think about it. I knew you'd enjoy it."

Laughter spewed from the phone as I hung up, and stood there, ten minutes maybe. Not pissed, but strangely sad.

It rained all night, then blew like hell and cleared, leaving everything damp and tired, heads down, waiting for momma sun to come and stroke their genitals and pinch a little color into the cheeks of their ass. I was halfway to the liquor store when I realized it was Sunday, accounting for the inactivity. I'd argued with myself all through breakfast about how goddamn healthy I was, how I deserved a break, a vacation from structure, how good and cold a beer would feel going down. I knew the worm's procedure though—fifty or eighty beers later it would revert, wanting to hide in some dark, moist vaginal experience, never anything more, never anything less. Failure positioned its hard clay mask in front of me.

I'd been clean too, sober, since that last night at C.I.B. A month further down the sidewalk I would be taking courses at Solano Community College. I'd have a mile and a half walk to the bus stop downtown, but from there it was only twenty minutes to get to the Solano campus. The campus was a blink's dream, set up like a wagon wheel, with a small courtyard as the central hub. Concrete walkways like spokes led off through lawn to the different departments, good edges to follow, plenty of bodies, doors banging.

I'd been practicing mobility there, learning the place. The campus had an Enabling Center, something new, a trial agency just for cappers. They provided readers, transportation, elbows. A lot of Vietnam vets were enrolled. I was their only blink.

I was ready too, with my catalogs from the Library of Congress and books on tape. The only thing I could remember reading in my sighted past, besides magazines, was a book called *Fur, Fin, and Feathers*. I think I read it three or four times in elementary school. My name was the only one on the card. So I ordered enough books to keep the mailman busy. Somebody suggested I should read James Joyce, another crazy Irishman. I slept through most of *Ulysses* twice, on tape, and didn't remember anything except the smell of piss cooking out of a kidney.

My most stirring discovery was an *Introduction to Philosophy*. The first damn story in it was about a Greek, a guy named Thales. He thought everything in the world, dirt, rocks, people, everything, had originated from water. Thales was all right. You could tell he spent some time getting altered, and it went on through fifteen or twenty more guys, each with a different angle. Not a goddamn American in the bunch, but it was beautiful. The worm gleaned long overdue vitamins from those pages, knowing it wasn't the only crazy sonofabitch in the world. They'd been around forever.

The woodshop evolved too. Sears extended me a little credit for a table saw, drill press, router, and wood lathe, and after a few trips to the local lumberyard on foot, the guy started delivering. Chopping blocks were the first items off the assembly line. I made three of them, just getting used to the machinery. Wood, Jesus. The worm could wander forever through wood, as long as the power was off.

The money end of matters kept me out of the real world—state disability payments, union benefits. The paper was never more than three days late. I just pushed it through, never saw the figures. Abacus beads defined my limits—the silent paper was signed and mailed by silent names.

I sat down one night and figured how much I'd saved that month in cash and brain cells by not drinking. Then I walked for three hours, through early morning, along unfamiliar streets. The walks grew frequent as long as it was halfway clear. I would go late, when the streets rested. Every dog in three square miles knew me. Calm nights were best. No cane. I carried it with me, of course, but the worm had found detail, like the difference in the sound of each footfall as I neared a curb. The map, the sounds, the intricacies of facial vision, the worm in motion, occupied, tentacles trailing.

The dogs would stick their noses under the gates, whining, as I passed. I'd lie, tell them I would open all the gates some night, and we'd run.

The clerk at the liquor store smelled like he kept a skin mag under the counter. He fetched my bottle of Crow and twelve-pack, his distant, skeptical eye checking me out, waiting at his counter, smiling, shades on, nine o'clock on a Sunday morning.

"It's a little early, isn't it?" he said.

"Your time, maybe."

He cleared his throat, like he might do the same in similar circumstances.

Outside, the sun, four days short of its U-turn, bent a few rays in my direction. Sparrows offered sincere thanks from their perch in bordering shrubbery. Two blocks north, a sun spot between trees slowed me. I removed my pack and sat on the curb with the intention of popping that first beer, consummating my affair with weakness.

"Do it, goddammit," the worm said. "Placate the bastard. Numb it and start over, humble, until it catches up again. You know how."

274

An occasional car passed, sucking what was left of the night's moisture from the asphalt. Me, curbed, with a straight face and shallow memory, hearing Weeds laugh, seeing Lauren, cup in hand, watching. Jesus, there was a lonely woman. Cole would have laughed his ass off over that one. I could hear the bastard.

If I'd stayed any longer, I would have popped that beer, but I stood, strapped the pack on, and noticed my slick-haired buddy leaning against the next light standard, legs crossed, fingering that toothpick in his mouth—no smiles, no eyebrows, just watching.

In the next block, a clothes dryer droned away in one garage. A car idled in a driveway, exhaust hanging close to the ground. Across the street, in the park, a rubber-shod body chased a tennis ball to the wall and back—*pap pomp pap pomp,* and in the playground, a few kids checked out the possibilities of wet sand.

"Stop it, you big nigger, I'm gonna tell," a very young, female voice threatened. Another, a male, laughed back.

I picked up a tail in that same block, a kid I thought, two steps to my one, hurrying to keep the pace. When I stopped at the next corner, it stopped, ten feet back. When I crossed, it crossed, keeping pace, my imagination playing with any number of prospective forms—a juvenile Jesus freak, or some horned-up dwarf.

The little feet stayed with me for three blocks, and at the next corner I stopped, waiting, providing my end of the game. They stopped, waited a few seconds, then came up beside me.

"Are you looking for money?" she said.

I smiled down at her, five, maybe six years old. They'd probably throw my ass in jail just for talking to her.

"You mean this?" I said, presenting my cane.

"Umm hmm."

"Nope. I was just killin' ants."

She looked around, then lifted each foot.

"I don't see any ants."

"I must've got 'em all then, huh."

"Umm hmm."

She burned rubber in the direction of the park. I held onto that sound, her sneakers, until a car passed and erased it.

Back in the house, it was just me again, and one fly wearing his mind out against the goddamn windowpane. I set the party goods on the kitchen table and cracked the Crow. It smelled the same. I capped it without indulging and stood there for some minutes, then put it in the backpack along with the half-case of beer, strapped it on, and locked the door behind me. The plan was simple enough, motion again, thinking I'd hit the road out through Pleasant Valley, hitchhike. Anything was better than the house, alone.

Around that first bend, my plan modified. Not because the orchard retained the tracks of two blinks and one dog. The worm just refused to participate in any more blue idiocy.

The earth gave a bit underfoot, not quite muddy, but requiring care, a ginger step. I hit the irrigation ditch and followed it a hundred feet or so, to where it passed within a yard of a thick-trunked walnut.

With my back to the tree, the party pack beside me, I sat facing the small stream. Time, winged like the osprey, negotiated the orchard's alleys every few minutes, reconnoitering its wayward blink. An hour or more must have passed, I was only aware of the wings when they came close. And when the tears finally rolled down my cheeks, I laughed. You could call it laughing. Such a goddamn, simple thing, too, accepting weakness, accepting the fact that I was human enough to want human things, and know so fucking clearly the pain of your demands. The simple mind, so stubbornly demanding recognition.

I craved, so bitterly at times, the freedom of sight, repressing it in the same instance, but none the less craving it, because it's human to feel that way, and human to learn from your mistakes, and just as human to keep making them.

I rolled up my jeans then, removed the boots and socks, scooched forward, and stuck both feet into the water—about ten inches deep, a soft layer of silt on the bottom, filling the gaps between my toes. Christ, it was perfect.

"You're a fucker, Cole Saunders," I said. "I know you're watching, too, just like I knew you'd never make it to your goddamn cedar tree. It was a good story, though, and I love you for it.

"Even at the expense of being labeled queer," I said, "I loved you dearly, you bastard, and I never loved a woman the same way. I couldn't. It's just not the same."

It felt good to laugh. The water felt good too, moving around my legs, and in its light current, silt accumulated against the side of my left foot. Enough that it worked a thin layer across the top, then filtered down to pile against the right. I couldn't love them the same, I thought. I was never complete, the worm lacked that ability. Maybe it wasn't even humanly possible, or maybe it was just male, to be incomplete. And Geri, and Elaine, all the other faces, maybe even Weeds too. It could be so damn good to have it all with a woman.

"And I miss you, you fucker," I said. "I don't need you, but I miss you because I'm weak sometimes."

I stood then, arm raised, fist clenched. It started, even before I got my head tilted back, the vibrations forming in my throat, the mouth open, forgiving, the sound strong, rising up through the branches, and as my lungs emptied, I could hear the water again and wiggled my toes.

"Goddamn, boy, not bad," I said, taking my seat again. "Clean and ready and the eyes wide open."

I took the Crow from my pack, uncapped it, and started pouring it into the water.

"Here's to you, brother," I said. "You deserve it."

A short nip, just for the occasion, found my own throat.

"Thank you," I said. "Don't mind if I do. Might as well have a little fun along the way, enjoy things for a change."

Across the creek, propped at length against a tree, my slick-haired buddy smiled back.

"No shit," I said. "It's a long ways off, but I can see the light, bub."

Voices, out on the road, turned my ear for a moment, hikers, or bicycles, I thought, and laughed. Sorry, private party, folks.

After the first car arrived, its sound so unmistakably familiar, I quit counting the voices. Then a second unit arrived, door open, radio squawking, and a woman's voice.

"His wife left him, I know that," she said. "Two months ago, or was it three? Betty? How long ago did his wife leave? Was it three months ago? He just comes and goes. Nobody really knows anything about him."

Two of the boys in blue had started out through the orchard toward me, one cursing his luck.

"I just polished these goddamn boots last night."

My slick-haired buddy removed his toothpick, eyed it, then flicked it into the stream.

"Don't worry about me," I said. "There ain't nothin' wrong with bein' a little out of the ordinary."

I turned my ear to the foot traffic a second, and when I looked back, ol' Slick had wandered off along the stream, face to the sky. He looked back just long enough to salute, and disappeared.

With the blue closing in, I simulated a trance, mouth slightly open, face lax. They stopped a few feet away, watching. I still had the empty Crow bottle between my legs.

"Hello there, how's it going today?"

I held the expression, my head tipped slightly back. One cleared his throat and knelt beside me.

"What'cha up to, fella, havin' a little party?"

He waved a hand in front of my face. Number-two cop came around the tree and stood on my left.

"I'm Sergeant Thorton, Flatfield P.D.," the hand waver said. "That's

Officer Powell on your left there. We'd like to ask you a few questions, if you don't mind."

Not even a twitch.

"I don't think he can hear you," Powell said. "She didn't say anything about him being deaf too, did she?"

"You got here first," Thorton said. "Did any of 'em give you a name?"

"Negatory."

"Christ," Thorton said. "Let's get him up on his feet. See if you can get his arm there."

Powell leaned over, one hand under my tricep, the other making a move on the Crow. When I grabbed for it, his nerves went. A little push got him started backwards. Just enough to remove his hands. He did the rest of the dance on his own, landing on his cheeks.

"Jesus H.," Powell said. "You think it's funny, you grab 'im. I ain't gonna mess with 'im. They're strong as bulls, you know. No tellin' what he's gonna do. He damn near put me in the water, right then."

"You shouldn't've tried to take his bottle," Thorton said.

"You get 'im up then. You're the one with all the answers."

Thorton knelt again, tapping my shoulder with one finger.

"Hey, buddy, can you hear me?"

"I've seen the poor bastard downtown a couple times," Powell said. "You can tell he ain't all there."

Thorton's finger continued tapping, so I turned my head just a bit and raised my eyebrows, like I was aware.

"Can you hear me?" he said.

I tipped my head back, turning it slowly from side to side, like I was looking for vibrations. Then I signed him.

"What the hell's that?" Thorton said.

"I think it's sign language."

"What's he saying?"

"How the hell would I know," Powell said. "I ain't no goddamn mor-phidite."

I really blabbed up a storm, too, telling them all sorts of things they could do with themselves and each other.

"Go back there and see if anyone knows his full name, then run it through and see if we've got anything on 'im."

"Through the goddamn mud again?" Powell said. "Jesus."

We had a record crowd going out on the road. Several more cars had stopped. Kids on bikes cruised, shouting to each other. Thorton stood beside me, waiting.

"The stupid fucker," he said to himself. "Just get his name, goddammit, and . . . Christ. I should've gone myself."

Then he shouted.

"You got anything yet?"

"Somebody's going back to see if his neighbor's home," Powell yelled back. "You want me to call the paramedics?"

"Kee-ryst," Thorton said, then motioned with his arm. Powell hustled back.

"We don't need the goddamn paramedics to do our job," Thorton said. "Let's get 'im up and take 'im in. Get on the other side there and grab his arm."

Powell grabbed. I yanked free. Thorton chuckled.

"You're going to pay my cleaning bill if I wind up rolling in the mud with this ape," Powell said.

"C'mon. Just get down there, and wait for me this time. I'll count three."

"Why don't I just give him a little love tap behind the ear," Powell said.

"Right. With half the goddamn city out there watching."

I moved my head again, the side to side vibration thing, let go of the Crow, and made motions like I was writing, pencil in my right hand, my left, the pad.

"Now what?" Powell said.

"Run back and get your clipboard and a pencil," Thorton said, "and see if they've got a name yet."

When the clipboard returned, I placed it against my knees, and wrote, clear and straight.

"I tell you," Powell said. "We oughta just call the paramedics, let them give 'im a goddamn sedative, and be done with it . . . What did he write there?"

Thorton had the clipboard, standing.

"It says, I'VE GOT BOTH FEET IN THE RIVER."

"Oh Jesus," Powell said, then laughed, turning his back to the road. "Now what are we gonna do with 'im?"

279